The Final Analysis

Also by Keith McCarthy

A Feast of Carrion
The Silent Sleep of the Dying

The Final Analysis

Keith McCarthy

Constable • London

Constable & Robinson Ltd
3 The Lanchesters
162 Fulham Palace Road
London W6 9ER
www.constablerobinson.com

First published in the UK by Constable,
an imprint of Constable & Robinson Ltd 2005

A copy of the British Library Cataloguing in
Publication Data is available from the British Library

ISBN 1-84529-059-3

Printed and bound in the EU

To my parents

Prologue

The letter dropped on to the coconut mat that proffered welcome, a promise not sustained by the house's single occupant. It lay there unnoticed until the evening when, tired and bad-tempered as ever, Dr Wilson Milroy picked it up and took it to his study.

He didn't open it at once because he did not recognize its significance, but when he did and when he read its contents, an unaccustomed smile grew wide on his sour face.

'We can't ignore this.'

Charles Hunter was Clinical Governance Lead and was paid to say things like that. Geoffrey Bence-Jones, though, had other considerations as Medical Director. His next comment – 'Of course not, Charles' – was designed merely to hold the line while he thought through implications. He was examining the letter again when he went on. 'It's anonymous, though.' They were in Bence-Jones' clinical office (he merited one office as Medical Director and one as a consultant neurologist), Hunter seeing him in between cases. Bence-Jones was used to Hunter becoming excited by situations such as this and he invariably had to adopt calming tactics.

'That doesn't matter. According to our whistle-blowing policy, the informant doesn't have to identify himself or herself.'

'No.' A mistake, in the Medical Director's opinion, giving a green light to every malcontent and troublemaker in the Trust. 'I think, though, that we are entitled to take it into account when we are making decisions about what actions we should take.'

Hunter said nothing in direct reply but Bence-Jones knew that

1

he wasn't in full agreement with this. Instead he pointed out, 'It's not as if we haven't got supporting evidence.' He indicated the file on the desk in front of Bence-Jones. 'We've had a steady stream of Adverse Clinical Incidents involving Dr Ludwig, most of them indicating failing performance.'

Bence-Jones sighed. 'It's not as simple as that, Charles. Histopathology's changed out of all recognition in the last few years. Their workload has risen exponentially.'

Hunter would have been surprised by this defence of another speciality had he not known of the Medical Director's marriage to a histopathologist. Bence-Jones took off his glasses, his eyes at once reduced to weak, watery, lifeless things. He sucked one of the earpieces. Hunter pointed out, 'Isn't that true of the whole of medicine?'

Bence-Jones' sigh was admission that it was.

'What do you want to do?'

He was due in the Outpatients' Department, indeed, he was overdue and those waiting there were probably becoming impatient. 'Well, we obviously can't ignore it, but I'd rather not rush in with hobnailed boots; there's been enough trouble in that department recently.' Hunter said nothing to this. Eventually Bence-Jones put his glasses back on, signalling a decision had been made. 'I'll have a word with Alison von Guerke informally. Perhaps she can persuade Trevor Ludwig to take early retirement. He's over sixty, for God's sake; it's not as if he isn't close.'

'I'll have to log the letter, start the processes. We have to be seen to be going through the motions.'

'Of course, of course.' The Medical Director stood up. 'If Ludwig proves obstinate, then he'll have to face the consequences. Fair enough?'

Hunter would have preferred stronger action sooner, but he knew that Bence-Jones was primarily a doctor and therefore going to look after his own. He acquiesced without further argument.

The man's fingers were fine and delicate, the nails neat and the skin unblemished. It was with practised ease that they tied the bow tie and then straightened it in the mirror. Sitting behind him on the edge of the bed, the other's eyes were obsessive in their hungry appreciation.

The man turned, his chin lifted slightly in readiness for admiration and appreciation, and asked, 'Do I look all right?' His companion rose from the bed, unembarrassed by nakedness. 'Fine,' was the judgement. 'Except, maybe . . .' The tie was straightened almost imperceptibly. 'There.'

A moment of awkwardness blossomed between them. 'I wish you didn't have to go.'

The man smiled tolerantly. 'So do I, but . . .' The unfinished sentence served for explanation and the other understood, then turned away, the movement one of sadness. The man reached out to touch smooth chestnut skin. 'I'll be back before midnight. It's just one of those tedious academic things that professors have to do.'

A sad, slow nod that caused the man to step forward, put hands on shoulders and embrace the other. The kiss that followed was long and deep and passionate. When at last it finished and they separated again, they were both slightly breathless.

The man moved quickly away and picked up his coat. As he left the bedroom he turned back and said quietly, 'I love you.'

Amr Shaheen said, 'And I love you.' When Adam Piringer had gone, he lay on the bed and smiled a lover's smile.

Part One

At eight thirty-eight on a cold spring evening, Mrs Jenny Muir left her place of work – a large and anonymous office block that rested in one of the less salubrious parts of the city like an ugly spaceship landed amidst a decaying civilization's entrails – and headed for home. She had a headache and she felt sick. The headaches were becoming more frequent and of greater severity, the sickness following on like a demon's lapdog. This was the third time in a month that she had left her cleaning job early, and she knew that her dismissal would shortly follow if it occurred too much more. Yet this attack was the worst yet, the pain starting behind her eyes, spreading in a tightly sprung band around her skull, and then seeping down into her face and even her neck. This time, in addition to the intense nausea that filled her stomach and forced bile into the back of her mouth, she was also having trouble seeing, her vision clouded by hazes and ink-spots. At least today she had managed to hang on for most of her allotted time, being forced to find the supervisor only thirty minutes early. Not that her work had been of the highest standard during the evening; shoddy was her opinion, for she was a conscientious woman, hating the slapdash attitude that pervaded most of the world around her, embodied in her husband and son.

It was a short walk to the bus stop, a long wait thereafter. She stood with her eyes closed, battling the desire that had been forced upon her to vomit. Thus she didn't pay much attention to her companion in the vandalized shelter; alas for Jenny Muir, this lack of interest was not reciprocated.

At last the bus came, surrounded by a stench of diesel fumes that made her certain that she would soon be forced to display

5

her stomach contents for all to see. It was nearly empty and brightly lit, the illumination hurting her eyes as if sharp needles were being inserted through her upper eyelids.

She paid her money to the driver, although the details of the process never pierced her misery. She made her way to the back of the bus and sat down, her hands clutching the cold tubular steel of the seat in front. As they moved off, the jerking movement made her clench her teeth and hold her breath. The noises of the engine and the groaning of the substructure assaulted her.

Dave will want me to cook.

This was the only coherent thought she seemed able to contain. It recurred endlessly as the bus tried its best to break her by means of its screams and roars, its jagged movements from side to side, its sudden accelerations and stops.

Surely he'll understand this time.

He hadn't been pleased when before she had gone straight to bed, ignoring his indignant questions concerning his immediate nutritional future. Her pleas for clemency had been met with a slammed door and twenty-four hours of sulkiness.

No, he probably wouldn't understand.

Not that he was a bad man. Too soft with Tom, and inclined to laziness, but she could have done a lot worse . . .

Her past was not a land that she liked to visit much, and certainly not in Dave's company. She had never told her husband how she had supplemented her meagre shop assistant's income in those younger days when she had been attractive and less inclined to bouts of conscience.

She found herself these days almost hysterical with the realization of what might have happened to her; in her naivety she had not considered the dangers and costs of prostitution, only the rewards. Now she appreciated how closely she had flirted with venereal disease, casual brutality and things much, much darker than thirty minutes of loveless lovemaking and twenty-five pounds left on the bedside table. If a pimp had caught her, she knew that probably she would by now be dependent on drugs, effectively a slave.

It had been the business with the Pendreds that had made her realize how dangerous her life was. Martin had been a regular customer; quiet to the point of strangeness but nonetheless harmless, she thought. Paid up when asked and no funny

6

business. At least none until the end, when he had come to her and asked in his halting, almost foreign tongue that she should help him, that the police wanted to put him in prison and only she could help . . .

The bus took a sharp turn to the right as it swung into Carmine Street, not far from her stop. Its front seemed to swing around in front of her like the arm of a giant centrifuge. The movement was bad enough but the suddenness with which the brakes were jammed on – so that she was thrown both forward and to her left – meant that she almost bumped her head on the back of the seat in front. The agony took another twist downwards.

God, I hope Dr Ackermann's right.

Could it really be just migraine? How could this agony be something that thousands of people put up with as part of their daily lives?

And she wasn't entirely sure that Dr Ackermann had absolute confidence in her own diagnosis. Why had the doctor arranged for her to see a specialist, Dr Bence-Jones, at the hospital? Did that mean Dr Ackermann wasn't sure what was wrong with her?

Her stop arrived. She got up unsteadily, her vision now so painful that she had to see the world through near-closed eyes. Her head was throbbing as if it were actually pulsing to the slow beat of the pain, expanding and contracting like some sort of giant puffball. She almost had to feel her way to the doors. They opened before she got there, another passenger having pressed the button. As he alighted, his mobile phone began to shrill, a painfully sharp razor in her head. She stepped down carefully from the bus, into the dark street. It was starting to rain, the cold wetness on her bare head bringing a minimal relief.

She only had three streets to go now. Streets she had walked ten thousand times before, in day, in night, rain and snow, happiness and sadness. She knew them so well that she was no long aware of her journeys along them; the time that passed was outside her conscious experience.

The middle road was the darkest, for it had few houses (and those were set well back) and so less street lighting, but it no longer appeared to her to be in any way sinister or frightening, as once it had done. There had been a time when, as a child, she had consistently refused to walk down that street, even in daylight. But not now.

Her head was beginning to ease off; the feeling of sickness, too, had retreated slightly. Thus encouraged, she began to walk a little faster, her head turning up so that she was looking less to the ground, more to the pavement ahead. She was halfway along the road now, the lights of the better-lit street ahead beginning to cast faint shadows.

She didn't see the shape hidden by the darkness of an elder bush as she hurried past. She didn't hear it move quickly up behind her. She didn't know that she was about to die.

When the hand came over her right shoulder, she had only a moment to react, first in a purely non-cortical, instinctive way, immediately thereafter with real, intense, sentient fear. By the time she had begun to struggle, the hand was over her mouth, clamping the screams within. She thought in a deep, unregarded part of her mind that there was an odd odour of *sweetness*, but it was little more than a stillborn thing, pathetic and mewling for only a moment before it died, killed by a blade.

The blade in question sliced neatly from just above the medial end of her right clavicle to its partner on the opposite side. It went very deep very easily, transecting in its passage the lower end of the thyroid cartilage, the anterior wall of the trachea and both external carotid arteries. These details were lost on Jenny Muir, as was the fact that the incision was curiously low in comparison with the standard technique for cutting a throat.

Nevertheless, despite this lamentable ignorance of the mechanics of her death, she played her part and played it well. She felt the pain of the slice only briefly, just as the experience of blood pulsating from her severed arteries (with some of it inevitably succumbing to gravity and trickling down her trachea into her lungs) was relatively short-lived.

Indeed, thereafter, Jenny Muir herself was relatively short-lived.

She dropped to her knees, thence to the cold wet pavement, her eyes and mouth open, her life closed.

The night was cooling, the darkness around deep. There was occasional sound from passing cars, accompanied by a sweeping brilliance of light, this latter swamping the soft illumination of the small lamp that hung from a branch of the conifer above the body.

The blade began its first journey, clean and bright, at the left shoulder tip, ending at a point on the right exactly symmetrical to the starting position. Then it was withdrawn and replaced at the midpoint of the cut. From there it travelled down in what would be its longest, smoothest stroke, first along the sternum, then launching itself over the soft curve of the abdomen, a soft and bottomless sea; the voyage was ended by reaching the shallow shelf of the pubis.

The T inscribed, the entry made, the real work could begin and, before long, the coils of intestine, restrained by translucent membrane, lay revealed and the liver, light brown and lavishly smooth, seeped down from beneath the remaining ribs on the right.

Back to the chest then. For several minutes thereafter, the blade was worked parallel to the skin, peeling it away from the ribs of the chest. The flesh was still warm, the blood still ready to flow and escape as soon as it was liberated. Eventually enough of the skin and subcutis were separated to allow the whole of the chest and abdomen to be exposed and framed by large flaps of flesh.

Two arcing lines were cut through the ribs with a tenon saw, lines that almost met at the neck and that splayed out to the sides above the abdomen. The knife was then used to cut any remaining sinews as the central part of the chest wall was lifted clear and pulled away from the central chest organs with the soft sound of tearing.

In the warm radiance of the lamplight, the vivid colours were hushed into dark reds and browns. The nocturnal scents of damp and decay were as yet undisturbed.

The blade, again flat, was now used to work on the neck. The skin of the throat was still firmly attached and needed to be separated as near the lower jaw as possible. Several more minutes, each as precious as a dying man's breaths, were used to achieve success before there was enough leeway to allow the knife sufficient freedom to push right up through the floor of the mouth, then to saw around the inside of the mandible, thus freeing the tongue and allowing it to be pulled down.

The noise of approaching footsteps on the roadside of the hedge, previously unappreciated, made a sudden pause. Immediately the lamp was switched off, the pose was as still as possible, the breath was held as the heart's beat became painfully strong.

Nearer and nearer came the steps, a faint echo ringing from nowhere and everywhere. They were those of a man – heavy and regular but nonetheless rapid, as if this particular pedestrian could sense evil being done somewhere nearby. At their closest, the steps were no more than a metre away. Then, having reached their loudest, there came a moment when time was arrested, when the chances of the intruder stopping were exactly balanced by those of him continuing, before they passed without stopping, without even faltering, and soon were fading into distance.

Two more minutes passed, though, before the lamp was switched on and the work recommenced, now with even greater alacrity. The tongue was grasped anew and tugged upwards as the major vessels of the arms were incised. Then it was pulled down towards the feet, a hard and steady force that separated aorta from backbone, bringing with it the heart and lungs, rising up out of the chest with surprising ease. The first characteristic sound – a burst of harsh, intense white noise – sounded loud and intrusive.

A shift of position, for now attention was to be paid to the pelvis. Gloved fingers worked their way beneath the pubis, over the bladder, down towards the vagina. Soft, slurping noises, slow and languorous, whispered into the night's hush.

This blunt dissection achieved, a hand then delved deep into the left side of the pelvis, squeezing bowel away from the side wall to create a space and allow the blade deep into its secure interior. On each side the major vessels to the legs were cut. Lastly, the blade was inserted under the pubis in the midline, cutting through first the urethra, then the vagina, then, with a tugging motion to pull the freed organs out of the depths and create more space, the rectum; this last hidden in the darkest recess of the body cavity.

A faecal smell was liberated at last, the first evidence of imperfection found only in these final acts.

With a quiet grunt of exertion, the tongue having again been grasped, the whole connected organ mass came out, by now dripping slowly and thickly with clotted and drying blood, as well as faeces. Surprisingly heavy – it could only just be held by one hand – it dangled uncertainly and hesitantly before being dumped into an open plastic sack.

And then there was another intrusive sound. The sound of a

nearby front door opening; when it was shut, the sound was quiet and hesitant, as if someone were afraid of waking the neighbours. Footsteps sounded upon the gravel of the path not three metres from the slaughter.

But again the footsteps failed to stop and reached a maximum before receding and again the thump of the heart went unheard by all but one.

Attention now could be paid to the head.

'Enjoying it?'

Beverley smiled and sighed. 'Oh, yes.'

He smiled in return. 'Good.'

Her life had changed since Peter Anderson had come into her life. In retrospect her previous existence had been empty, and her shock now was based as much in the comparison with her present circumstances as in her incomprehension that she could have lived such a lonely, ultimately worthless life. Had she been in some way mad? Had she been immersed in some sort of overwhelming psychosis, in which she had been deprived of all sense of proportion and perspective? Now she could hardly bring herself to recall specific instances of her behaviour in that former life, a time when she willingly (*enthusiastically, you silly bitch!*) used sexual favours to solve her problems, salve her hurts, achieve her ambition. It had been another life, one that was well ended.

And she had Peter, and Peter alone, to thank for this epiphanic miracle. Peter who was gentle and kind, who was over two metres tall and whose stature was even greater, who had glided into her life at a juncture when she had been so low and so despondent that she had felt paralysed, crushed by failure. It was he who had persuaded her to stay in the police, that she was a worthy human being, that she was something special.

He had come into her life barely ten weeks before. A barrister who had been mugged for his gold watch and slim calfskin wallet, he had initially been solely another victim in her eyes, yet by the end of the first hour in his company, she had fallen in love with his charm, his smile and his confidence. She had found an excuse to see him again, found also that the feelings were mutual. Meetings became dates, dates became highlights of her life. Each occasion had increased her attraction to Peter, lodged

11

upon foundations of gratitude and respect. He had always shown himself to be not only decorous and learned, but genuine and, most importantly, content. It seemed to Beverley that the whole of her life she had been surrounded by malcontents.

Not that he was a saint, not in the traditional sense, at least. He had his faults – he could be irritable, he drove too fast because he thought he was a superb driver but wasn't, and he had a tendency to forget that she did not always want him to decide for her – but these were not faults that she found too daunting; he would change, she felt sure. In any case he was extremely good-looking and quite wonderful in bed, attributes that she would settle for, at least for the time being.

And so here they were, on the summit of a hill, one of the foot-soldiers of the Malverns, enjoying a view that stretched out over miles of Gloucestershire countryside, a view that shimmered in heat and brightness, that implored them to believe again that England was a green and pleasant land.

Behind them the horses, loosely tied to a beech tree, played their part in the tableau. The picnic, now spread around its hamper, was annihilated, detritus everywhere. Only the wine had held its own, but that was now fighting a battle long lost. They lay side by side, the sky above them a brilliant unending blue. In Beverley's nose there was a scent of something that she had not at first recognized, and that only after perhaps an hour she appreciated was nothing more than unpolluted air.

'Beverley?'

'Mmm?'

'I was thinking . . .'

He had a voice that was silky and deep, almost hypnotic. When they lay side by side in bed late at night, he would talk and she would listen but hear only the resonance, sink into the warmth of its comfiness.

She murmured, 'Yes?'

'I have tickets for Barbados . . .'

Somehow she missed it for a second or two. When the meaning met her understanding she jerked her head up, her eyes coming open to see him smiling beneath amused eyes. 'Could you spare the time? Early July, flights and hotel.' He paused for a brief moment then, 'Well, if you don't think it's your kind of thing . . .'

She was shaken from the paralysis of her surprise, first to utter a sharp squeak, then to reach over and thump his shoulder with her fist. 'You dare!'

They both laughed while he explained how he had got them on a whim, how he had been three times before to the resort and that he was sure she would love it. Was there a problem with her getting the leave, he wondered?

She would have to check, but she thought that she could manage things to her advantage. They talked on, laying plans, Beverley barely able to contain her excitement and barely able to believe her luck in meeting such a man.

This is too good to be true. It must be a dream.

Their conversation took the afternoon away in its warm, humid haze. Then, as they finally got up and started to pack the remains of their meal away, she took Peter's arm and, as he looked at her, she put her arms around him and kissed him. It was a long, warm embrace in the course of which she found herself thanking God that she had at last found someone like this, someone who was rescuing her from a self-imposed destruction.

It was just as they finished and were preparing to mount the horses that the call came through on her mobile.

Eisenmenger sat in his new office, trying to generate a positive attitude, failing completely. Every aspect of his situation that came to him depressed him, chasing concepts such as satisfaction, contentment and optimism far over his own personal horizon. True, he was physically healthy – far healthier than he had been a year before – but he now suffered from chronic insomnia, rarely sleeping longer than four hours a night, sometimes not at all. Often his sleep was troubled by his personal demons, rendering it effectively useless.

He was in work, moreover; the first time for twelve months. Paid employment to supplement his dwindling reserves. Yet his surroundings whispered a subtler, less uplifting position. Not that it bothered him that it was only a locum appointment, for he didn't yet feel capable of taking on a permanent position. If he were honest, he wasn't sure if he ever would be. Pathology had become both tedious and exhausting, something that had to be performed perfectly but that was also boring, and he recognized this as a dangerous combination.

And then there was Helena.

He still didn't understand what had happened with Helena, and that hurt. Not that it had been dramatic or explosive. Actually it had been so subtle that he couldn't precisely date the start, but his fancy told him that it was at about the time that she had been recovering from the injuries she had received on Rouna. So subtle that it was to him undefinable, a problem compounded by Helena's refusal either to explain what was wrong, or even to admit that there was a problem.

He hated mysteries, wanted them explained: an obsessive need to deconstruct problems and puzzles. It was why he had chosen pathology – where diagnosis was king – as opposed to other forms of medicine where the purity of problem-solving was sullied by such uncertainties as the unpredictable response to therapy and the unpredictable patient.

Yet despite his best efforts, this particular puzzle would not allow solution. Helena these days became irritated if he said anything, so that the situation, seven months on, remained unresolved, the tension unreleased, the itch still irritating.

Alison von Guerke came in, as ever just beaten into second place by a bust that Eisenmenger had found frightening on first acquaintance. Try as he might to stop them, thoughts of the horror that lay beneath her clothes came to him unbidden whenever he saw her.

'Settling in?'

It was Eisenmenger's opinion that there was generally an inverse correlation between bust size and facial attractiveness, the more famous exceptions only highlighting this relationship. Unfortunately, Alison von Guerke fully conformed. Her mouth was large and slightly crooked, her nose was prominent, her eyes curiously unaccentuated. Perhaps in an attempt to overcome this last, her eyebrows were large and prominent; it was not a happy adjustment.

'Fine,' he lied.

She had already shown him about the large but decrepit department, her pride in what she showed him only underlining the deficiencies present. New NHS funding had not found its way into this particular pocket of entropy. Then she had taken him through the tricky question of remuneration; not the paltry sum provided by the hospital, but the supplementary monies that a jobbing pathologist might expect – coroners' autopsies and private practice fees. These were often a source of a decent increment to the proverbial take-home but, as he had feared, this was not to be. The Department of Histopathology at the Western Royal Infirmary clung to its academic roots despite their decay and near-putrefaction. All such fees went into the 'Research Account'. That Eisenmenger as a fly-by-night locum would never see benefit from this did not weigh heavily as an argument. His only consolation was that he had suspected that such would be the case. He merely nodded in acquiescence.

'Good.' Then, in a conspiratorial style, she added, 'I'd take you to meet Professor Piringer, but he's not around today.'

An absence – the collective noun for professors. It was an old joke but a truthful one.

'You'll get to meet the others in the course of the day, I expect. Do you know any of them from old?'

'I was at medical school with Victoria. Apart from that, I don't think I've met any of the others.'

Dr von Guerke's face fell – perhaps collapsed would be a more accurate, less charitable, term – as she said, 'Oh, that's a pity. It's Victoria that you're locuming for. She's been told to rest.'

'Really?'

'Things got a bit on top of her.'

He recalled the bright, attractive blonde from his student days, remembering how he had wanted her from afar but had never amassed the courage to act on the desire. He found it hard to reconcile this image with the one being presented by Alison von Guerke. She hadn't used the dreaded 's' word, but the hole around which her sentences had been bent had been noticeably 'stress'-shaped.

'Such a shock, too. Did you know that she'd just won the College Medal for Research?'

He had heard the news vaguely, been surprised, too. Victoria had been no shining meteor in the academic pathology firmament. The College Research Medal was generally won by crusted professors in places such as Oxford or Cambridge.

'Oh, yes,' continued von Guerke. 'Some very interesting work on vaccine modification of oncogenic expression in tumour cell lines. The pharmaceutical companies are very interested.'

'Really?' And curiously, this word seemed to open up a small pool of embarrassed silence in which they both waded for a short while before she smiled and left him. He had twenty minutes before he would have to begin the cut-up of that day's larger surgical excision specimens. Twenty minutes in which to contemplate just what he had come to.

Chief Inspector Homer looked around the small and untidy garden with a smile of satisfaction that was, if not broad, perhaps slightly wider than might have been considered appropriate, given the circumstances. Murder scenes were not places to be seen enjoying oneself, and he did not often exercise the particular combination of facial muscles required for smiling, but this was a special occasion.

Vengeance.

He was educated enough to know the difference between vengeance and revenge, and self-righteous enough to think that the latter did not apply. His was a task imbued with nobility, with a sense of God-given justification; it was, in short, about the righting of wrongs done, both to himself, to the community at large and to one particular individual – Melkior Pendred, who had never really been able to defend himself against the forces of ignorance, stupidity and (not to hide behind pusillanimous euphemism) evil, and who most definitely could not now (as he was dead).

Therefore, it fell to him, William Homer, to strike the blows for justice. He had few pleasures in life, but vengeance for wrongs and slights, real or imagined, was one. He had never admitted it, but it was this sort of classic heroic role that he had always envisaged for himself in the police. The Man They Couldn't Gag, The Defender of the –

'Sir?'

The sibilant syllable interrupted his reverie, insinuating its way into his feelings of righteous anger, diluting them and dispersing them. 'What is it?' he demanded with consequent asperity.

'Neumann's found something, sir.'

He was young, Homer noted from afar, young and inexperienced; his uniform enveloping him like the carapace of a wasted cockroach. Certainly he looked nervous, his close-cropped blond hair not able to cover the sheen of worried sweat that had formed on his face and scalp. There was a slight twitch to his left eyelid, the faintest of tremors, while the bright blue of his eyes stared at him in an almost lupine manner.

Probably his first murder, he looked so young.

16

If it is, it'll be one to remember, son.

This thought brought him some sour comfort to leaven the bitterness he felt towards the youth of Police Constable Cooley.

Homer's smile might have graced Dr Guillotine's face after his first successful trial run. 'Where?'

Cooley nodded towards the house. 'Over there. Behind the dustbins, by the shed.'

'He better not have touched anything,' he muttered as he pushed past Cooley. Neumann was a good and experienced copper, though – two adjectives that were not always linked amongst the lower, more primitive levels of the constabulary – and he didn't feel that it was absolutely vital to hurry over to the scene. Scenes-of-Crime would be there and it would be a few minutes yet before he would be required.

He turned back to Cooley. 'Where's the husband?'

'Inside. Clark's with him.'

'What state's he in?'

'Bad, sir.'

Homer nodded briefly. *Who wouldn't be?*

He looked around the garden. It was one of perhaps twenty, all stretching out side by side from the small terraced houses some hundred metres distant, thin strips of land in varying degrees of cultivation and care, each one the vestigium of an estate, the figleaf covering total disenfranchisement from any form of heritage. They were standing at the far end, by a large but essentially crumbling shed. A back alley ran along the bottom, accessible by a gate that clung drunkenly to a rotting post. Homer had nosed around in this alley already. He had expected nothing to come of it, but had been joyously disappointed in this anticipation. Just outside the gate was a small clump of sycamores. Behind it he had come across a patch of grass that had been recently trodden down, the wounded grass littered with cigarettes. Of course it might merely be a group of kids indulging in illicit smoking, but equally it might be an observation post; one from which to lay plans for murder . . .

'Not much of a gardener, was she?'

At his question, Cooley surveyed the Muirs' land, a not so stout Cortez not standing on a peak. He saw grass that needed mowing, flower beds that needed weeding, fences that needed repair, and trees that were so overgrown and diseased they needed euthanasia.

17

Presented with the evidence, PC Cooley, like the good copper that he would one day prove to be, agreed. Homer made a noise that might have been a grunt of satisfaction but might easily have been a acid reflux since he had neglected to take his medication that morning. He said, 'There's a clump of trees in the back alley, just through the gate on the left. Make sure that no one, but no one, goes anywhere near it until SOCO and forensics have been. Understand?'

Cooley wanted to know why he was being asked to guard such an outpost but was not so naive as to ask. He accepted both the task and the accompanying ignorance with stoicism. Homer made his way up the garden, past abandoned toys and neglected weeds.

At the back of the house there was a crowd, a composite of uniformed and un-uniformed; the former tending only to stand, the latter to be doing things. The pathologist, Bloomenthal, was directing Moll, Scenes-of-Crime, as to which photographs he wanted. Moll was a large man who wore a permanent worried frown. He never moaned, despite the fact that his job involved being constantly harassed to take photographs of unspeakable things, and that not infrequently he found himself being pulled simultaneously in perhaps three different directions by imperious commands uttered with threats of castration, demotion or death.

The unspeakable thing in this case was not at all visible to Homer, so many people were clustered around Moll and Bloomenthal. The pathologist stood out not only because of his rather fetching white one-piece, complete with elasticated cuffs and ankles, and matching slip-on overshoes, but also because of his height and his shock of greying hair. Not for nothing was he known as Tin-Tin. There were multiple flashes from Moll's oversized flashgun, each flare accompanied by a muffled cough of white noise.

Homer said in a not particularly low voice to one of the uniformed backs in front of him, 'Where's Dr Jessner?' Not that he was interested in the whereabouts of the police surgeon, but he received the effect he had intended, being given both an answer to his question – 'He's round the front, sir, supervising the removal of the body' – and a passage through to the front of the onlooking throng.

The object of attention was the dustbin. Bloomenthal was

delicately picking out items of domestic rubbish using forceps. Each one was being transferred into a sack held open by a member of the forensics team who was similarly attired. Somehow she wore the white suit with greater dignity than the pathologist did. This odd attention to what the Muirs had so thoughtlessly discarded was merely the prelude, clearing the stage for the main performance. As the final items of detritus were taken out, there was exposed a rounded mass, filling perhaps half the dustbin, wrapped tightly in a grey plastic binbag.

Homer felt excitement beginning to rise within him. In his head was whispered the single word, *Yes!* It was exactly as he had known it would be; the pattern was reforming itself as if ordained by natural law.

Moll took a few more holiday snaps. Bloomenthal looked up at Homer. 'Is this what you were looking for?' His voice held a tint of cynicism, more than a hint of irritation. He might have admired Homer's professional abilities, but that didn't mean he was going to like him. Whether this sentiment impacted on Homer, or whether it was lost in a host of similar attitudes from all those others who worked with him, was not clear.

Homer nodded and Bloomenthal sighed, turning back to the dustbin. He reached in, the posture accentuating his rounded shoulders. He kept his face turned away; it bore a look of world-weary disgust and said quite plainly, *A professional man shouldn't have to do this.*

He had trouble getting a grip but eventually the bag and its contents were lifted out with no little effort on his part. Clearly it was heavy and clearly, from the growing smugness of his expression, Homer expected it to be so.

Bloomenthal put it down on a sheet of clean, green paper that the forensics woman had spread out specially. Once left to its own devices, it spread and settled with ominous deliberation. More pictures were taken, then Bloomenthal began to unwrap the parcel. He found the neck of the bag, opened it wide (his face again turned away, his expression again one of anguished questioning of his place in the universe), and then began to roll the edges of the bag down.

It didn't take long to expose the contents, an event that coincided exactly with the emergence of a smell and the loss of the majority of the audience. The smell was strong, repellent and almost tangible. Homer knew it slightly but few meetings were required for familiarity; Bloomenthal, while not treating it as an old friend, was inured to it. The accompanying sight was bloody and beneath this poorly applied coating of partially clotted red there were various dull hues of green, brown and grey. As Bloomenthal flattened the rolled sides of the bag to the ground, this thing seemed to sit there, resembling vaguely a chimera of a small humanoid and a large slug; it even seemed to slump forward in a demeanour of slumber.

Homer knew exactly what it was and, given the sight before him, the triumph he exuded seemed somewhat distasteful. Only he, it appeared, was unaffected by it; Bloomenthal looked distressed at the state of the world and the state of his blood-spattered clothing, the forensics woman had turned away and was breathing heavily, and the four other police officers who had retired to a safe distance were all standing with either closed eyes, open mouths or both. One hurried away, his hand to his mouth, as Bloomenthal remarked sourly, 'You know what this is, I take it?'

Homer nodded slowly. In fact it was many things – vengeance for him, discomfort for Chief Inspector Cox (now retired), the complete destruction of Beverley Wharton – but he had the sense to remain tacit about all but one. 'It's the internal organs of Mrs Muir.'

If Bloomenthal was surprised by Homer's expert knowledge of anatomy, he didn't show it. He merely nodded and called to Moll, now, quite astonishingly, even more deeply frowned than ever, for more photographs. It was noticeable that the Scenes-of-Crime man held his breath for long periods while he complied with this request.

Bloomenthal said loudly, 'At least the autopsy won't take long. Homicidal bugger's already done most of the hard work.'

Homer turned around to the peripheral audience of the scene. 'What the bloody hell are you lot doing? Stop gawping and get back to searching.'

They began to disperse but Cooley turned back. 'What are we looking for now?'

Homer turned back briefly to Bloomenthal and his organ mass. 'Is it there?' he asked.

Bloomenthal shook his head and Homer said then to Cooley, 'Somewhere round here, son, you'll find Mrs Muir's brain.'

Martin Pendred pushed the chair at a constant speed in a straight line, just as he always did. The occupant of the chair was small and frail, staring straight ahead with a fixity that suggested either intense concentration or extreme vacancy. She had a drip inserted into a thick bandage on her right forearm and bright purpuric spots where the skin of her hands and arms was exposed. A huge bruise in the crook of her left elbow might have suggested over-enthusiastic and under-experienced venepuncture; it suggested nothing at all to Martin.

No form of communication – neither verbal nor non-verbal, sonic, optical nor olfactory – took place between driver and passenger. They might have been pre-programmed and rather simple robots. They might have been completely without sentience, doomed to obey needs and requirements that had nothing to do with either of them.

The impression of roboticism remained even when Martin turned the chair to the left and followed it into X-ray. The patient and chair were deposited into the care of a radiographer, again without any communication that was obvious to the observer. No change in facial expression, no movement of the head, no widening and thinning of the lips. With no sign to the universe in which he made his way, Martin Pendred, having discharged his task, began the return journey to the porters' lodge.

Occasionally the radio on his belt spoke forth in a travesty of the human tongue, words (already mangled by elision of syllables, dropping of consonants and the malicious torture of grammar) were taken by this device and subjected to hideous contortion and degradation so that the unpractised ear could find no point of contact, no place at which to meet and transfer information. Martin ignored every one of these bursts of noise, these messages from the other realm; although he wore a radio, he never used it and it was never used by others to communicate with him.

His arrival at the porters' lodge was unheralded. He sank slowly into a chair and sat there, back straight, face rigid, staring into nothing.

The Deputy Head Porter (the Head Porter had his own office

from which neither he nor evidence of labour emerged with any great frequency) sat at the desk in the corner of the room and looked at Martin with tired tolerance. His face had been likened unflatteringly to an uncooked spotted dick, because his skin suggested pale dough and because he was cursed with a covering of moles, most of which were pigmented to blackness. He had little to do and did it entirely to his own satisfaction. He was, on the whole, pleased with his lot.

But only on the whole, which caused him to contemplate Martin Pendred.

Martin had worked as a porter for three years now, and they had been thirty-six months in which he had exhibited no sign of function much higher than his present attitude. True, he did his job. True, he never complained. True, no one had ever complained about him. Yet the undeniability of these statements belied the reality of working with the emotional, intellectual and spiritual vacuum that was Martin Pendred.

The spirit amongst the portering staff of the hospital was generally good. They considered themselves to be an oppressed and misunderstood group who were blamed unfairly when things went wrong, and never praised for the good work they performed. This sense of injustice bonded them, men and women, resulting in brotherhood (and sisterhood). Although there were rare occasions on which isolated bouts of ill feeling arose between individuals, on the whole there was constant good-natured, if coarse, chatter in the porters' lodge.

The arrival of Martin, who rarely spoke unless directly addressed (even then tending to use only single words), who never laughed, who insisted on placing his large frame in the same chair and staring vacantly at the same point in non-space when he wasn't out performing a chore, had dealt a considerable blow to this atmosphere. And then, as well, Martin came with something of a reputation. The twin brother of Melkior, the man who had taken murder to new extremes. It was only natural that there should be gossip wondering whether they had got the right man, especially in view of the new man's odd behaviour.

Only recently had they learned to ignore him, learned to forget what he had done to Budd.

Not that Budd hadn't deserved some sort of lesson, being quite often loud-mouthed and occasionally downright vicious, but what Martin had done had been way out of order. Everyone

22

had agreed on that. Only the fact that there had been such obvious provocation had saved Martin Pendred from instant dismissal.

Still, no one any more chose to make Martin the subject of jokes or insults, and he could be relied upon to be punctual and, once the information had been impressed into his head, certain to perform any task satisfactorily.

All the same, the Deputy Head Porter thought with something that might have been a suppressed shiver, *he gives me the creeps.*

Martin continued to stare at a landscape unknown to anyone else.

Sergeant Wright looked up into the early afternoon sky and tried to think about anything that didn't involve corpses with their throats slit and their bodily organs distributed around the garden, as if the Easter Bunny had turned psychotic and lost the taste for chocolate. Although he had thus far kept his breakfast and the outside world apart, it had not been without considerable effort, but he hoped now that the departure of Jenny Muir (with her insides in a separate bag) would bring some release; thus far, however, there had been little noticeable improvement.

He heard Homer inside the house directing investigations, his slightly nasal intonation readily recognizable even in the faintness given to it by distance and closed windows. Homer was not an easy boss but not the worst he'd worked with in his seventeen years with the police. He was neither corrupt nor lazy – two attributes that Wright had found common in the higher echelons of the police – and he wasn't stupid either (Wright had noted that intelligence was not mandatory for promotion), but he did possess drive; when Homer thought that something should be done, he did it or at least made sure that someone else did it. It was his height, Wright had long ago decided. Not fantastically below average but definitely enough centimetres beneath the majority of the male population to produce a Napoleon complex; Wright had read about it in one of his wife's magazines. Short men who overcompensated. Some of them became world leaders or dictators, some of them became great womanizers and, presumably (although this had not been made explicit in the article), some of them became police inspectors.

'Wright!'

Homer was standing in the front door of the house looking, as always, annoyed. Wright hurried over. 'Sir?'

'Report, Sergeant, Give me your report.' Homer liked reports. Verbal ones, if fed to him continually and frequently, kept his hunger for information and communication at a reasonable level, but it was only paper and ink that kept his temper at a level safe for human habitation. A constant flow of words was his basic diet, supplemented by Scenes-of-Crime photographs and results from the forensic laboratory; these last were his vitamins and essential trace elements, small in volume but nonetheless necessary for health. Strangely, grammar did not seem to be a prerequisite for Homer's informational well-being; it did not bother him that there was a range of syntactic styles from free-form through to tortured, with only occasional peaks of near-lucidity. Sentences that meant all things to all men went into Homer's head and somehow he extracted sense. Wright assumed that this was because of his single-mindedness; the meaning that he took from these paradigms of perplexity was the one that he wanted. This quality of blinkered certainty meant that he was capable of both brilliant success and catastrophic failure; investigation was a quantum process where either he succeeded because his initial impression was correct, or he crashed to the ground because he couldn't decide which suspect was guilty or because his initial choice of perpetrator proved eventually to be disastrously wrong.

Wright had been with Homer for three years now and was accustomed to his methods; the successes had marginally outweighed the failures and Homer's reputation was slowly rising, a fact that Wright was astute enough to recognize could only do himself good.

'Body's gone, sir,' he said briskly, the tone that he knew Homer liked. 'Husband's next door; Clark's with him. Forensics and SOCO are just finishing up around where the body was.'

'And the little boy?'

'With his grandparents.'

'And house-to-house? Have you organized that?' This was an unfair question. Wright did not possess the authority and Homer knew it; the question was merely an excuse for Homer to express faked exasperation that he, and he alone, had the brains and skill to organize all aspects of the investigation. 'Don't worry, I'll do it,' he said, not quite sighing.

Wright made neither verbal nor non-verbal comment. Homer was already on to another subject. It was almost wistfully that he said, 'And no sign of Mrs Muir's brain?'

Combined with wonder that his superior could manage to make such a grotesque question sound so prosaic, was the return of the feeling that he was shortly going to make a Technicolor statement on the paving stones at his feet. Through contracted throat and imperfectly occluded teeth Wright said only, 'No, sir.'

Homer frowned. 'Where did he put it?' he asked rhetorically, as if they were contemplating a child's hidden toy. 'What did the bastard do with it?'

'Are we absolutely sure that he did actually remove the brain, sir?'

Homer treated this question with a fine display of contempt. Wright noted resignedly and silently that his superior was good at contempt. 'Of course he did, Wright. Read your history. Pendred always eviscerates the bodies, removing the organs from the main cavity, the brain from the head.'

Wright, who read as much history as he did higher dimensional mathematics, but who had most certainly heard of the Pendred case, was at a loss, a habitat in which he often found himself. Ever since the call had come in, he had been perplexed by Homer's attitude. In his years with the small, egotistical but somehow endearing Inspector, he had never seen him quite like this. Normally the thought of a homicide would have induced in Homer an air of detached studiousness, a clinical interest in whatever grisliness confronted him – always tinged, of course, with the correct amount of revulsion – but on this occasion, things had been different from the outset. As soon as he had learned of the state of the body, Homer had emanated an air of what Wright had been forced to describe as satisfaction. This had grown as the day had proceeded and Wright, ignorant of the context and with only the awfulness of what had happened to judge by, had found himself more and more confused. How could anyone, he kept asking himself, enjoy this horror?

'Maybe this time's an exception, sir.'

Homer moved his gaze from the small house and the untidy front garden in which they stood, swinging around to rest incredulous, almost despairing eyes upon Wright. 'Didn't you hear what I said?' he asked irritably. 'Pendred always removes the brain. Puts it somewhere. Like a joke.'

Not for the first time, Wright was wondering whether Homer had finally lost it, wandering off into a sort of lunacy. It was with a tentative tone and not a little trepidation that he pointed out, 'But Pendred's dead, sir.'

Homer managed the near impossible and cranked the contempt up to eleven on the dial. He opened his mouth, his demeanour suggesting that what was coming would undoubtedly have been more caustic than quicklime, but it never came, stemmed by a commotion from the house. Homer's attention was hijacked by the noise. An impossibly callow plain-clothes constable emerged from the front door, breathlessly mixing excitement and distress.

'We've found it, sir,' he reported.

Homer, Wright's insubordinate questioning scrubbed from history, hurried inside. He had clasped his small, delicate hands together in front of him as he went; Wright couldn't be sure, but he thought Homer might have been rubbing them together.

Tossed over his shoulder was the uninterested command, 'Go and get a statement from the husband. And ask him about Pendred.'

Martin Pendred had lived in the same house all of his life. The house was terraced and small, poorly maintained and obscenely snug with its neighbours, amongst whom it crouched in dark and silent muttering. The street was quiet but it was the calm of decay, the tranquillity of despair. These dwellings did not house their residents, they hid them, they swallowed them, only letting them forth in skulking secret.

On one side of Martin was an old man, Wilms, who was fiercely proud of his independence and curiously unaware of his dependencies. Martin and he had lived side by side for all of Martin's forty years, their relationship never having warmed. When Martin had been born – three minutes after his brother, and not breathing for four – Wilms had already been an inhabitant of Battledown Terrace for twenty years. Martin could only remember him as old and alone, as if he were aged and widowed when the world was young and would be aged and widowed when it died.

The Pendreds and Wilms did not get on from the day that they moved in, the Pendred's small twin sons screaming in their pram as they continuously did. Thin walls meant that their peculiar intolerant attitude to the world was shared by their neighbours and, if it was accepted by Mr and Mrs Sharpey and their small family in the house to the right, the same could not be said for Wilms in his castle to the left. When the twin babies became small twin boys, almost identical in appearance and oddness, their screaming lessened; indeed, they became preternaturally quiet, but what they now lacked in amplitude they compensated for with activity. Overactivity. Overactivity of such a frenetic, cease-less, uncompromising kind that it soon led their father and even their mother into shouting, so that it seemed as if making a barrage of noise had become the family tradition.

Not that it made any appreciable difference to the boys. The boys did what the boys wanted to do. A form of intensity of interest came upon them, but it was an interest that would not be denied and that could not be defined by the observer. That they were interested in something, and that the interest was deep, was all that anyone – even their parents – could say. They took to whispering together and, although they appeared to understand what they were saying each to the other, no one else could. No words, merely sounds; no expressions, nor variances in tone. It seemed impossible that any information could be transferred, but it seemed also that it was.

While the twins were playing once in the garden, Martin had kicked the ball over the fence into Wilms' back garden. They had been perhaps four, an age when balls and ballgames are impor-tant, perhaps more important than life itself; there was an inevitability to their silent decision to sneak into the garden through the back gate, an inevitability, too, that they would be caught.

Wilms had been in the Commandos, although the Pendred family did not know it. He might have appeared old and doddery – 'a bloody old bastard' in the opinion of Pendred Senior, a car mechanic with strong views on all subjects – but Wilms had been given training that he found impossible to forget, that his body enacted with considerably less ease but with only slightly less effect.

His grip had been frightening both in its suddenness and in its strength; each boy held by the shoulder with pale, bony fingers like a spider crab's legs. Even small, wiry and struggling small boys could not escape it, no matter how hard they tried. And even in the middle of this, Wilms noted that neither of them said anything: a chilling silence, cooled to liquidity by the glances they threw each other, glances that communicated on a deeper, almost primordial level. It unnerved him.

One of them – he never discovered which – somehow bent his head around to an impossible angle and bit his captor's hand with feral teeth, small and sharp, but Wilms held his grip. Violently shaking the child until it was forced to let go, he then forced it to the ground where he leant on it with his knee, still grasping the other one. Wilms was light but his knee was sharp, a round-headed stick pressed painfully on the sternum.

And still neither said anything, yet still he somehow knew that they were talking to each other.

Wilms brought the child that remained standing close to his face. He didn't know it but it was Martin to whom he snarled from parchment-dry lips and through nut-brown, haphazard teeth, 'Trespassing!'

The sibilance was reptilian, the breath was decayed.

'Trespassing!' he repeated. Martin looked into his eyes. Through his mind ran thoughts that were pertinent but not connected. He saw the yellowing, the clouding, the veins and the small sty, but these were like tracer bullets in darkness, flashing through his mind one after the other, no pattern forming. He continued to stare, continued to remain mute.

'If I ever find you here again . . .'

Wilms didn't finish the threat with words but with a painful increase in his grip. Then he pushed Martin away, the small boy staggering backwards to fall on to the threadbare grass. Wilms turned his gaze upon the boy beneath his knee. He straightened slowly and almost creakily, allowing him some room.

'And as for you.' This was a completed statement. 'I'll remember you. Understand? I'll remember you and if ever you come into my garden again, I'll kill you.' He looked at the bite on his hand, the broken skin bleeding in a neat arc of punctures. 'You did this.' This was pronounced as if Melkior might have forgotten. 'I could kill you, do you know that? I could snap your neck.'

He stared at the small boy and the small boy stared back, the look a curious mix of interest and discomfort, but not as afraid as Wilms expected. After perhaps ten seconds he threw the boy towards his brother. 'Get out!' he ordered.

They glanced at each other, then turned away.

Oddly unsatisfied, Wilms watched them leave.

He had won, hadn't he?

The Ashleafs' garden was spotless and neat and spoke of many hours of labour in the week. Wright wondered what they thought as they looked across the rickety garden fence at the unkempt and wilfully undisciplined acreage of the Muirs. Did they feel contempt? Or was it sorrow? Or, more amazingly, was it understanding?

He rang the bell to the house, noting that here, too, there was a contrast to be made with the neighbours, for this house was newly redecorated and he could see through the windows that the curtains were symmetrical in arrangement, the ornaments were placed *just so*. Wright looked across to the Muirs' house with its air of decay and found an immediate and strong sense of kinship with it; it might not be perfect but at least its degeneration was somehow human, somehow understandable. There was something about the way the Ashleafs lived that faintly revolted Wright. At least he could see parallels with his own life when he saw that the paint on the Muirs' window frames had seen a few summers, and that cobwebs daintily infested the sides of the small porch.

The door was opened by Constable Fisher, a likeable and not unhandsome man with as much chance of rising above his present station as Wright had of becoming mankind's first ambassador on Jupiter. Wright, who had seen a thousand young recruits to the police, didn't mind him; at least he wasn't a thug, or a racist, or a weirdo.

At least he didn't think he was.

The interior was as immaculate as the exterior. As dustless as it was soulless, as symmetrical as it was impersonal. Individually and cumulatively, the ornaments – the photographs of earlier lives and children, the souvenirs of seaside holidays, the unfashionable chinaware – were eloquent of long lives, perhaps happy lives, but the regimentation and sterilization silenced the two men. Wright looked about him and the things that he saw reminded him of his own parents' house and his own childhood, but their display – as if in a museum or a tourist shop – only cheapened the emotion. He wondered why the Ashleafs needed to live in such a straight-line world.

Fisher told him that David Muir was in the front room, but before he could go in, the door at the end of the hall opened and Wright caught his one and only glimpse of the Ashleafs. It was Mr Ashleaf who had opened the door, his thin, almost skeletal hand clutching the wood, his expression a mix of prurient curiosity and suspicion, his eyes grown to bulbous dimensions behind thick, slightly sepia glasses. In the background Mrs Ashleaf sat at a kitchen table, her head twisted round in concentrated scrutiny on a neck that seemed more pleated and knotted than a human neck had any right to be.

Wright smiled and nodded but declined to offer further acknowledgement. He went into the front room.

Helena arrived back from Paris feeling better than she had done for twelve months. Although the trip had been nominally work-related and only four days long, the change – change in every-thing, including routine, food, lifestyle and, inevitably, herself – had brought back to her a sense of life and hope, of optimism as opposed to pessimism.

Why, she had not even thought once of the question that had been tormenting her for the past nine months . . .

And then, of course, with the cruelty that only the universe can muster, her moment of triumph at this realization collapsed under its own achievement.

John.

She felt at once thrust back into her churning mess of doubt and question, the good of the break itself broken, relaxation tightening back into the cords of hurt and suspected disappoint-ment.

John Eisenmenger.

The name had become so charged with meaning and emotion, its very existence within her mind seemed to sear and burn, as if some hex lay within it, some magical power to brand was laced into the letters and phonemes.

She had finished unpacking and had been waiting for some coffee to perc. She now took a mug of it into the bathroom, wanting a shower before an early night. She thought ruefully of the inadequacy of hot water and soap to rub away life's experi-ences, especially its disappointments.

Had he really slept with Beverley Wharton?

She had asked the question so often in the past months that meaning had almost become completely divorced from the sound of the words, so that now it had the quality of gibberish – something heard but not immediately something that evoked thought.

That didn't mean, though, that the question had lost its association of hurt and despair. Simultaneously she suspected it was true and could not believe it. Beverley must have been lying.

Must have been.

She had thought that at long last, after all the years of exile from feelings of warmth and seclusion, from participation in the emotional life of normal humans, she had discovered somewhere safe, a person in whom she could trust. John had seemed different, and that he wasn't had wounded her at several levels.

She had turned on the shower and was now undressing, dropping the clothes into the laundry bin that was already full with garments from her suitcase. Before she got into the shower, she found herself staring into the mirror, again going through her feelings; an endlessly iterated task that she could not complete and so could not abandon.

She had replayed the conversation from nine months before a thousand times in her memory, each time finding new inferences and nuances in Beverley Wharton's words. There had been no direct admission, but the bitch's subtext had been written in block capitals.

Which led Helena first to consider it all a lie, then to wonder . . .

Damn that bitch!

Would she have felt like this had his infidelity – once she had caught herself using the term 'adultery', and this had sparked off a luxuriant side-shoot of speculation about the connotations of such a usage – been with any other than Beverley Wharton? She doubted it; she was convinced that his bedding of anyone else, no matter how alluring, would have caused much less pain, much less scarring.

Not that she would have found it easy to laugh off; her parents had given her a sense of morality that precluded acceptance of others' weakness. If John had shown himself incapable of commitment to her and her alone, there would certainly have been no future. Yet she knew also that there had been no commitment at the time of his crime; she knew with certainty not from her and she suspected not from him either. She could not hope to indict him on such a charge alone.

And she had not had the courage to ask him. That annoyed her, as much as the concept of his betrayal, forcing the pain to fester deep within her, walled off and angry.

She sighed, making a determined and, she thought, successful effort to break the loop of deliberation. Her eyes looked at last at what they were seeing and she rubbed her hand over the skin of her face, feeling the dirt that she knew was there, the grease that fought constantly with her for dominion.

Was she attractive?

Another question that would not die and could not be satisfied. She had never felt able to use the word 'beautiful' about herself, but the years seemed to bring ever more stringent rules about the adjectives that were left to her. 'Pretty' and 'sexy' seemed to be on the way out and she was moving with inexorable decay into the territory of 'pleasing' and 'attractive'. Yet she could find little that was objective as a foundation for these real but ultimately subjective views. Her eyes, when taken alone, seemed to her to be just as darkly brown, just as large and soft, as ever they had been; her cheekbones remained high and the skin over them taut and smooth; her mouth retained a fullness of the lips that she could still find satisfying. And if there were wrinkles, they were still small enough and in such a position that she did not find them too threatening, merely adding detail where perhaps some would not go amiss.

So what was the problem?

Her eyes travelled down her neck to her breasts; not her favourite body part – too small, as an ex-boyfriend had once informed her on being told that he was surplus to requirements – but at least their diminutive nature meant that mother earth had less to hang on to. Her stomach remained flat although she suspected that there was probably a little more fat than there once had been around her hips. She did not need the mirror to view her legs; these had always been her best feature, reliably long and possessing just the right amount of suggestiveness. At the present there was a slight swelling around the ankles, she noticed, but the journey had been long and the weather in Paris warm.

She stepped into the shower, closing her eyes in the hot, moist vapour and, as if this were a sign to switch, at once the questions came again.

Did he sleep with her?

Was his penis so dominant that he couldn't help himself, that it led him to her bed as if it were a lead around his waist? The cow was attractive – Helena wasn't so hung up on her that she couldn't acknowledge that – but not mesmerizingly so. Not so incontestably, hypnotically ravishing that he could be excused, that he had obviously lost the power of conscious decision-making, that he blacked out only to find himself in her arms in post-coital embrace.

So he had known what he was doing and had presumably hoped to have them both. This conclusion recurred like a judicial indictment after the verdict, the sentence – one of execution – to follow. No mitigation to be found, no plea for mercy to be entered.

She rubbed shampoo into her short, thick hair, her fingers kneading her scalp in response to her hot indignation.

The two of them had known and she had been ignorant. The bitch must have loved that; almost as much as she had loved letting her in on the secret. *Oh, by the way. You know John? John with whom you're so obviously falling in love? John, whom you think is different? Well, maybe he isn't as different as you think . . .*

Helena found herself becoming consumed by her resentment, lost in the heat of the water and the heat of her embarrassment. She began to soap her neck vigorously, then her shoulders and then her breasts.

Which was when she felt the lump.

Wright had done this perhaps two hundred times, and it was no different in any important respect to the previous one hundred and ninety-nine occasions. Because of this, because of the reiteration of emotions, thoughts, phrases and circumstances both within him and before him, he had feared that he would find it impossible to connect on an empathetic level with the scenario he was charged with enacting. He had suspected that he would be merely a player in the middle of a long theatrical run, spouting the words, reproducing the gestures, fabricating the feelings.

In the room with him were Amanda Clark, a middle-aged and

33

more than slightly butch police constable, and David Muir, Jenny's widower. Clark sat next to Muir and it became at once obvious that she was profoundly moved, for he noticed that there was the most powerful expression of sorrow he had ever seen on her rather square features. This more than anything shocked him from his embittered, cynical state of weariness into something akin to a virginal viewpoint. If Clark felt something (and she was as used to the tawdriness of homicide as he was), then perhaps it really was possible to reawaken sadness and sympathy. After all, so grotesque and macabre was the way that David Muir had been widowed, that alone merited a response slightly deeper than disgust.

Something dormant stirred in Wright, an understanding of what had just happened; not just the facts but the implications physical, spiritual and intellectual of such an awful act. It was an epiphany for Wright.

David Muir had been crying and the tears had brought with them rawness, so that his eyes now looked diseased, painful. Wright had seen the full gamut of reactions to the loss of a loved one. He had witnessed denial both fragile and indestructible, acceptance both faked and genuine, anger both white hot and icy blue, and shock both incredulous and totally debilitating. He had been in the presence of the most devastated, crushed human beings, and he had been there when such reactions had been faked, when he had known at once that he was talking to a murderer.

In David Muir he saw nothing at first glance to suggest artifice. He saw that Muir, having had the news of his wife's death for some hours now, had reached a low, a dim landscape in which he groped for answers to questions that no man could answer. It wouldn't be the last time, nor probably the worst time, but at least for the time being he had stopped falling, tumbling, panicking.

'Mr Muir?'

He was quite a small man, seemingly delicate, although much of the impression of paleness might have been due to his shock. Wright noticed that his hands were scratched and callused. He was wearing a uniform – grey cloth cut into a sort of tunic bearing badges with the initials *TBC*.

He didn't respond to Wright, his face worked into a scrutiny of thought, his jaw moving slowly and slightly as if his only problem was an obstinate piece of gristle.

'You work for the council, do you, Mr Muir?'

Still nothing. Wright glanced at Clark, his eyebrows raised. She put her hand gently on David Muir's arm. 'Mr Muir? David?'

He responded at last, a small grunt suggesting that he had been jerked back from his reverie. He looked up into the angular, slightly intimidating face of the policewoman, hope fleeting across his face, chased away by realization. Clark gestured with her head and her eyes towards Wright and Muir followed slowly and sadly but obediently.

'I need to ask you about some things, Mr Muir.'

Wright was already framing his first question before Muir nodded, the delay for a moment imparting a curious dislocation to the proceedings.

'When did you first miss your wife?'

No answer. Clark gently shook the arm of a man who was slipping in and out of fearful terror. He jerked at the touch, his head with widened eyes swinging around to look at her hand as if it were a being complete. Only slowly did he look up to her face and thence, at her silent suggestion, back to Wright, who began to wonder if he was going to get anything from his witness.

'Mr Muir, I know you've had a great shock, but I've got to ask you some questions. We want to catch the bas . . . the person who did this, but we're going to have a really hard time unless we find out as much as we can about what happened last night.'

It was a long speech for Wright, but it had an impact. David Muir nodded – slowly at first, then more rapidly – and something that might have been intelligence came into his eyes.

'When did you first miss your wife, Mr Muir?'

He didn't reply immediately, but this time it was because he was trying to concentrate. 'She was due in at about nine forty, I guess. She was due to finish work at nine. It was only a short bus ride.'

'Where did she work?'

'She had a part-time cleaning job. At Ostertag Financial, in the city.' Wright was noting this down in an untidy scrawl that Homer had once likened to the marks made by an ink-sodden, decapitated cockroach.

'And which bus did she get?'

'Uh . . . number forty-two, I think.'

'And which stop did she get off at?'

He waved his hand in the direction behind Wright. 'Pyramid Way.'

A pause while this information was translated into penmanship. 'So you were expecting her at nine forty, nine forty-five . . . but she didn't turn up.'

Muir shook his head and then, when Wright said nothing and merely looked at him, he added, 'At about ten fifteen I rang Ostertag's. When they said that she'd left work early, I *knew* . . .'

Wright had seen it a hundred times before, this prescience. Everyone had precognition when it came to sudden death; wives always guessed, husbands always had certainty, parents were always unerringly convinced. He checked his notebook. 'According to the station, you didn't ring in until eleven twenty-eight.' He raised his eyebrows questioningly. 'What were you doing in that hour, sir?'

Some might have heard other questions in his words: *Is that when you murdered her? Did it take you an hour to cut her up?* David Muir, though, seemed to hear only the surface – a good sign. He said simply, 'Tom woke up. Had a nightmare. He's been having them a lot recently.'

An hour? The question flitted through Wright's mind and he commented, 'Must have been a bad one.'

Muir looked at him with a flat expression on his face, then shrugged. Wright let it pass. 'And then you rang the station.'

'They said that there was nothing they could do.' This might have been accusatory but it wasn't. David Muir wasn't yet into the retribution stage of his grief.

'And then what did you do?'

He looked perplexed. He was pale, Wright noticed, pale and shaking slightly.

'I rang some of her friends. I wondered if she might have met someone and forgotten the time. She liked to gossip.' This last was said with a dying fall.

'But none of them had seen her.'

He shook his head.

'What did you do then?'

'I went out looking for her.'

Wright thought about this. 'But what about Tom? What did you do with him?'

For the first time, Wright caught the whiff of guilt as Muir said, 'I left him in bed.' Wright's lack of apparent sympathy with this led him to say defensively, 'I was becoming desperate by then. No one had seen Jenny and she was nearly two hours late. I had to do something.'

Wright wrote this down while Clark stared at Muir's profile, and Muir looked down at his clasped hands. Wright then asked, 'So where did you look?'

Muir seemed to find this enquiry incomprehensible, as if Wright had used one of the lesser-known dialects of Swahili. 'Where?' he repeated and Wright merely waited. Muir frowned. 'First I went to the bus stop, I think,' he said at last. 'I wanted to go back along the way she had come.'

Wright took his time digesting this. '"Way she had come",' he quoted thoughtfully. 'So you knew that she had made her way from the bus stop, did you?'

Muir's face told the story clear and loud. Suddenly he was very aware of where he was and why, and suddenly Wright favoured that he was rather scared. 'But I didn't mean that!'

Wright looked at him impassively.

'What I meant was that I went back along the route she used to take from the bus stop.'

Wright held his gaze for a moment longer than he knew would be comfortable for Muir. 'And then where did you look?'

'Around.' This was helped along by a shrug.

'Around? Around where? Can you give me some names of streets?'

Muir was suddenly angry, as if fed up with Wright's slightly harrying tone. 'I was worried sick! It was dark and I was starting to panic. I just walked around, looking up and down streets. I can't tell you which ones, but I reckon I walked up and down every road around here.'

Ignoring the rising emotion, Wright asked, 'How long were you out for?'

'About an hour and half. I had to go back because I was getting worried about Tom. Anyway, I began to hope that I might have missed her. I thought that she might be back at home, worrying about me.' He paused, then whispered, 'But she wasn't.'

'And then?'

'I went to bed, but I couldn't sleep. I spent most of the night in the kitchen.'

'And in the morning?' They were approaching the horror and Wright, well aware of this, was watching him closely.

'Tom woke at about seven. I was dreading that. He asked me at once where his mum was.'

It was Clark who asked, 'What did you say?'

'That she had had to go to work.'

Wright steered him back to the business at hand. 'And then what?'

'I got him dressed and made him some breakfast. I was wondering what I was going to do with him. I had to go to work.'

Once again Wright found himself wondering about David Muir. *Go to work? When your wife has gone missing?*

He said, 'You telephoned the station again.'

Muir nodded. 'I couldn't think what else to do. But they just said the same. They'd had nothing reported to them and they couldn't do anything until she'd been missing for twenty-four hours.'

Wright suddenly found that he had nowhere else to go. As gently as he could he asked, 'And you discovered your wife . . . when?'

Muir had been through the entire cycle, was now back to the horror, and it showed in his eyes as he looked at Wright through white windows of despair. 'I had to get the milk in,' he said in a voice that was quiet and husky and almost awed. 'I took the empties out . . .' He was beginning to cry. Clark squeezed his arm. 'I put them down, but one fell over. It rolled down the path and I walked after it . . .' He stopped. He was contorting his face, trying to dam the tears. Wright looked on and a small part of him was wondering if this was an act.

'I saw her foot, under the hedge . . .'

Wright let silence work for a while. Muir was blubbing and Clark was comforting and Wright was wondering.

Muir asked eventually, 'What did he do to her?'

It was a fearful question, asked by a child seeing terrors in the darkness.

And Wright didn't know what to tell him. 'I'm not really certain,' he lied.

For a moment that was both endless and brief, Muir accepted this. He said plaintively, nearly wondrously, 'There was so much blood . . .' When neither of the police officers commented, he whispered, 'I heard someone say that her throat had been cut.'

Wright caught Clark looking at him and he in turn passed his eyes down to his notebook. To cover the gap he asked, 'Don't you and your wife have mobile phones?'

The widower in front of him shook his head. 'Couldn't really see the need.'

'How long have you been married?'

'Three, nearly four years.'

'And Tom is how old?'

'Three.'

Wright noted all these data down assiduously, hiding completely the fact that he had no interest in them whatsoever. To the top of Wright's head, aimed quite accurately at the small bald spot that he had recently developed, Muir asked, 'Why?'

Wright wasn't sure exactly what he meant and it was Clark who said, 'Why what?'

Turning to her, Muir said, 'Why was she killed?' Then, almost as if his brain was running through pathways of conjecture for the first time, he asked, 'She wasn't . . . raped, was she?'

Wright's mind was filled with his views of Jenny Muir's corpse. The clothes had been ripped open at the front and there was so much blood it had been difficult for Wright to make out much at all. He wanted to reassure this small and lost man before him that rape, at least, was an atrocity that he didn't need to worry about, but the last thing Muir needed was false reassurance.

'We won't know the details until the post-mortem,' he said as gently as he could manage. Then, as if to try to smooth over the dissatisfaction of such a response, he asked, 'Tell me, Mr Muir, can you think of anyone – anyone at all – who might have had a grudge against your wife?'

But the question was absurd. Who would have such enmity towards the wife of a council employee, a part-time cleaner, to murder her by such a means?

Wright's next question was posed almost as if he were voicing his thoughts aloud. 'She didn't happen to know Martin Pendred, did she?'

Muir looked up at the name and Wright saw vague recognition that subsided at once. He shook his head. 'Not that I know.'

Although he was actually mistaken, Wright thought that he caught something odd and so pressed the point. 'Are you sure?

She couldn't have known someone of that name before she met you?'

'She didn't have any real boyfriends before me.' He said this proudly, unaware that Clark looked at Wright with raised and unbelieving eyebrows.

Wright asked, 'What did she do before she married you, Mr Muir?'

'She was a temp secretary.'

'Did she ever work at the Western Royal Infirmary as a temp?'

He didn't know and Wright decided that it was worth checking this out, so he asked for her maiden name.

'Paget.'

Wright had started to put this in his notebook before the significance struck. 'Jenny Paget?' he said. He didn't know much of the Pendred case, but that name was notorious.

'That's right.' Muir caught the surprise. 'Why?'

But Wright, his mind full of excitement, merely reassured him with bland words and lies.

The Pendred twins were in their first year at school when their behaviour became not merely a nuisance but an illness. So disruptive were they that the primary school brought in an educational psychologist and Martin and Melkior were diagnosed formally as being autistic, later moving from this to severe Asperger's syndrome, a diagnostic change that said more about sociomedical fashions than it did about the actual condition.

Neither parent ever fully appreciated the significance of this. Although explanations were given, they could not and would not accept that their twin sons were anything other than unusual; the idea that they were *ill*, was beyond anything that they could encompass. After all, it wasn't as if there was an effective treatment, so what did it matter what names were applied to the reasons for Martin and Melkior behaving in the ways that they did?

It did, however, matter that, for whatever the name of the reason, year on year of education produced neither leading out of understanding nor placing in of information. The boys remained introverted to the point of isolation, their reactions unpredictable, their view of the world a secret, their expressions a mirror of blank indifference.

Their scholastic achievements remained notional.

Thus they might have passed like the rest of us into blessed obscurity, had Gary Ormond not happened into their lives.

Cooley was sitting down in the kitchen and Homer might have supposed him to be having an asthmatic attack. Pale, shivering and clearly unable to exist on the amount of oxygen that his breathing could supply, Cooley did not look well; he looked, Homer decided, about to collapse. Bloomenthal leaned over him solicitously, glancing up as Homer came in, but offering no more acknowledgement of the small man's presence.

'Where is it? Where's the brain?' Homer's voice was unmistakably layered with delighted anticipation.

Bloomenthal merely said, 'Out the back, in the shed.' He didn't look directly at Homer, contenting himself with ministering to Cooley.

The interior of the shed was exactly as Homer had imagined it would be save for one anomaly. Amidst the cobwebbed tins of ancient paint, broken toys, empty and damp cardboard boxes, and rusted, silent garden tools, there was a small chest freezer. There was only room in the shed for two people at a time, and an anonymous forensics woman had to make way for Homer. She smelt vaguely of lilac, a fragrance that Homer's mother had favoured.

Inside, Moll was taking the kind of photographs Salvador Dali was never quite mad enough to paint. The freezer was open, the light on and amidst the haze of water vapour that drifted languidly across the everyday packets of foodstuff, there rested a frozen human brain.

Homer, vindicated, smiled over the shoulder of Moll, whose breathing rattled, gurgled and hissed as if his adipose frame hid an ancient geyser that was five years past its last service. So boisterous was this exhibition of sonic plumbing that Homer asked, 'Are you all right?'

Moll, his first name long lost to most of his colleagues (although thankfully not to the Pay Department), smiled weakly. All his facial movements were weak, as if the muscles therein had atrophied. 'Fine, Chief Inspector. Just fine.' The tone was cheerful, for ten thousand scenes of carnage, slaughter, atrocity and massacre had left Moll without the means to be shocked.

Homer returned to the kitchen and to a scene substantially unchanged, Cooley apparently no better. 'What's wrong with him?' he asked of Bloomenthal, who was still bending over the young constable. Bloomenthal was tall and thin and scholarly. He had a goatee beard and an air that suggested omniscience without omnipotence; *I know everything, but I leave it to an idiocracy to act upon my findings.*

'He's having a panic attack.'

Homer swam in a sea of incompetents and was always ready to proclaim so. 'Oh, for God's sake! Tell him to pull himself together!'

Bloomenthal, Cooley and Homer were crowded into the small galley kitchen with no one else present, although various bodies drifted past the back door and the door to the front hall. It wasn't an ideal location for a slanging match, but Bloomenthal had had enough of Homer for the day. 'You might be rubbing your hands with glee for whatever macabre reason, Homer, but the rest of us aren't. The rest of us are having a lot of trouble coping and people like Cooley here are having more trouble than most. He's only been in the job for nine months; he's not used to psychotic loonies and their playful ways. He's just had the unique experience of opening a chest freezer and finding a human brain nestling between the frozen peas and the chicken nuggets. I think he's entitled to feel a bit queasy.'

Homer and Bloomenthal knew each other well, a relationship characterized not just by verbal sticks and stones, all enhanced by barbs of varying sharpness, but also a perverse kind of respect. He merely grunted, a noise that from a pig meant little, from Homer meant that despite everything he could have said, he was going to remain tacit.

Homer looked again at Cooley. 'Queasy is one thing. He looks ready for hospitalization.'

Bloomenthal sighed. He rose from his attention to Cooley and taking the Inspector into the hall he said, 'My dear Homer, you have never been possessed of a caring personality, but this particular day finds you beyond human endurance. Whence comes this intolerability?'

Homer did not habitually confide in others, a tendency that drove Wright to the ends of irritation when it came to working together on an investigation, but today he relented.

'It's identical, isn't it?'

'It is?'

'Absolutely.'

To Bloomenthal, conversing with Homer was like listening to Moses passing on the loftier commandments to the less deserving of the chosen people. 'Explain,' he suggested.

'The Pendred case! You must have noticed! You can't have forgotten!'

Bloomenthal raised his eyes to the ceiling, possibly beyond. 'Only the dementing have forgotten, Homer. Otherwise it's difficult to cast from one's mind the horrors of what Melkior Pendred did. And yes, the points of reference have not escaped me. The throat slit, the body eviscerated, the brain hidden. No one else, though, finds any of this a cause of celebration.'

But Homer was thinking of Beverley Wharton, uncaring of what others might say.

Arnold Cox had mixed and extreme feelings about retirement. Thirteen months into the next phase of his life (he refused to describe it as the last), he still found that the ripples induced by his abrupt change in lifestyle were too destabilizing to allow him to survey either his present or his future with any reassurance. He felt agitated and discomforted to be in such a predicament, to be uncertain of what he was and where he fitted in.

Yet, as he had known he would, he was at the same time relishing the company of Pam, his wife, and he was making what he considered to be a decent enough job for a first timer of both the garden and an allotment (and in all aspects of his life, Arnold Cox was a harsh critic). True, he had attempted to take up golf and failed spectacularly, but that had been a speculative venture, undertaken with a large sum of intrepidness and a consequently small sum of hope.

He kept telling himself that it only needed a change of perspective, but it was easier to say it than to achieve it. Time was required. He was a great believer in patience and method; he had lived his whole professional life by this dictum, and he was damned (perhaps literally) if he didn't live his retired life in the same way.

'Where have you put the car keys?' Her tone was one of tolerant exasperation.

He still found the enormities of domestic life strangely minuscule; another marker stone to be reached and passed. He had them in his trouser pockets and Pam took them with good-natured annoyance.

'Where are you off to?'

She was off to the supermarket; he refused to be drawn into that habit – trailing around the supermarket after the wife. He had seen and been contemptuous of the sight too many times when he had been working. 'I've got to stock up, haven't I? Make sure that you don't starve while I'm away.'

'You're visiting your sister for a few days, not sailing round the world.'

She smiled but made no reply.

He said, 'I thought I'd make a start on the spare bedroom.'

This, of course, found great approval, in the grand tradition of the wives of retired men. Leisure time was not meant to be filled with either leisure or pleasure but with activity; gardening was acceptable but redecorating was the ideal. She left him in the garage with her customary warning not to overdo it and his customary bland reassurance, while he looked through the cardboard box that contained the tools of the decorating trade. 'It's only a bit of angina,' he said to her departing back. Having found buckets, sponges, glass-paper and sugar soap, he decided that he had enough to make a start.

It was as he was filling the bucket with hot water that the telephone rang. It was an old friend from the force; close to retirement but still clinging on with a determination that Cox greatly admired, even as he thought it futile.

The news was not good.

Eisenmenger felt rather like a lot in a livestock sale as he made his entrance into the consultants' meeting that evening. During the course of the day, all his colleagues seemed to have been absent on one errand or another – either teaching or researching or management or audit – so that by the time of the five o'clock monthly get-together of the senior medical staff, he had met no one else. Consequent to this and the fact that he was five minutes late, all heads and all eyes turned to him as he entered. The expressions on the former and around the latter ranged from indifference, through curiosity, to one or two that seemed to Eisenmenger to harbour elements of hostility.

44

Alison von Guerke was the only face he recognized and even hers, for a moment or two, was plastered with irritation at the interruption. Then it cleared and she heaved her mammary glands into the air and clear of the table, much, no doubt, to its relief.

'John! Come in, come in. I'll introduce you.'

And introduced he was, to a disparate group that allowed him little immediate relief from his newness. Amr Shaheen, Wilson Milroy, Trevor Ludwig all obeyed the formalities but allowed him nothing more; only Professor Adam Piringer, present despite Alison von Guerke's lamentation of the morning, offered him a smile and a handshake, but Eisenmenger suspected that this had more to do with the charm for which he was famous than with any genuine delight at seeing him.

'Welcome, John, welcome. Here, sit down. Have some coffee.'

Trevor Ludwig, a tall, weaselly man with a moustache that was definitely a mistake and intensely cropped grey hair that looked like badger bristles, had eyes that seemed attached to Eisenmenger by lines of force. Only when Eisenmenger, having poured some coffee and taken his seat, quite deliberately returned the stare did Ludwig momentarily allow his orbs some rest from their ceaseless scrutiny and, to cover his embarrassment, he said, 'You're a forensic chap, aren't you?' His voice was sharp and nasal.

'Not by trade, not any more.'

Shaheen was small and appeared too delicate to carry the rather thick horn-rimmed spectacles on his nose for any great length of time. As if to confirm this impression, he took them off as he said, 'But weren't you involved in the Exner case a year or so ago?'

Eisenmenger twitched his lips. 'In a way. Let's just say that I tend not to make much of a living at it these days.'

Piringer flashed a smile at him that Eisenmenger suspected was as well practised as it was meaningless. 'I'm sure John is an experienced surgical pathologist, Amr.' Which somehow left everyone with the impression that his certainty was only on loan, awaiting assurance.

Eisenmenger explained rather tersely, 'I've always been a surgical pathologist, as it says on my CV. Forensic pathology and surgical pathology aren't necessarily mutually exclusive, you know.' He addressed this to Shaheen, and found himself noticing a twitch of a smile cross Milroy's large, rather coarse mouth. Nothing more was said concerning the eternal, unbridgeable divide between surgical pathology – the examination of tissue samples and organs removed for medical reasons from the living – and forensic pathology – the analysis and investigation of those who have died, particularly those who have died in suspicious circumstances.

Alison von Guerke explained, 'We were just discussing the rota.'

It was as Eisenmenger had feared. As a general rule he knew that when consultant pathologists met, it was generally only to discuss rotas, for rotas ruled their lives, and the Western Royal seemed to have more than most. They had rotas for histology, rotas for cytology, rotas for autopsies, rotas for on-call, rotas for the day-to-day management of these various activities (all of which were effectively duties delegated by Piringer), rotas for teaching and rotas for research. Eisenmenger was almost tempted to ask about the rota of rotas in a kind of pathological homage to Bertrand Russell, but felt it was probably too early in his time in the department for such frivolity.

After an hour of discussion Eisenmenger was beginning to discern some of the undercurrents that inevitably develop in departments such as this, amongst which the most obvious was that Milroy appeared to be at war with everyone; suggestions that were made were invariably met by him with arguments that were phrased in the language and tone of contempt, which after a while produced equal and opposite hostility in the others. Piringer, especially, came in for much disdain, being unable to utter a single word without Milroy making some response, often in an undertone and occasionally unmistakably abusive. Piringer met all of this verbal battery with complete tranquillity and undented charm; Eisenmenger found himself at once admiring the man's sangfroid and being rather disturbed by it. It seemed almost unnatural, as if either he were in some way mentally ill or he were dangerously in control; it was Eisenmenger's experience that those who did not react at all at the time of the stress, tended towards extreme reactions later.

After the meeting, von Guerke came to him, full of smiles, and said, 'I know how tedious that must have been for you, but these things have to be decided. At least it gave you a chance to meet everyone. I wasn't expecting Adam to make it back in time.'

Politely, he said, 'It wasn't too bad. Anyway, as I'm going to be here for at least the next three months, I do have an interest in who's doing what and when.'

Her face clouded. 'At least three, and possibly many more, I'm afraid. Victoria's not at all well.'

Again this chimed discordantly with his memory. At medical school she had seemed to him to be well adjusted, resilient and cheerful, not at all prone to stress. 'Was there a particular incident that brought it on?' he asked. In an age of litigation, pathologists were a newly uncovered target for the personal injury solicitors; Eisenmenger himself had come close to being in their sights on one or two occasions.

Von Guerke shook a head that was distressingly unadorned by redeeming features and said only, 'Nothing like that.'

Homer's office was as small as those of all the other senior officers, but tidiness and lack of ornamentation enlarged it so that visitors often wondered why Chief Inspector Homer merited a space that was larger than the Chief Superintendent's. Everything that could be filed was filed, either in box files or wallets or the drawers of his two filing cabinets; pens and pencils were stowed in two mugs, one for each, the pencils all brought to a point of molecular sharpness, the pens all fitted with their appropriate lids; on the desk was a single pad of lined paper, sitting with ethereal symmetry in the exact centre. The only concession to humanity was a single photograph on the dustless window sill, its composition including Homer and the Chief Constable who was caught in the act of congratulating the Chief Inspector on his apprehension of a multiple rapist, thus generating much-needed positive publicity for the force. There were no photographs of family.

Wright did not have his own office, having to be content with a desk in a large room shared with all the other junior members of the CID. This lack of office space had not deterred Wright from making enough mess to fill a room twice as large as Homer's. The desk's surface was hidden by exploding piles of files, aided and abetted by scraps of paper, empty cardboard wallets, sweet papers, pens, pencils and newspapers of varying age and type, all clustered around the keyboard and monitor of his computer (the computer itself was relegated to the floor at

47

his left). Whenever he needed to write anything by hand, he was forced to use his lap, a manoeuvre that only magnified the untidiness of his handwriting, producing yet more irritation within the breast of his small superior. On numerous occasions, Homer had ordered Wright to tidy his desk, but it had never effected a cure, merely a temporary and partial improvement, allowing a small amount of light to fall on the pallid, sun-starved teak of the desktop.

It was only during big investigations that Wright spent a large amount of time in Homer's office, but these occasions were strictly orchestrated according to Homer's instructions; Wright was there only as a scribe and as a surface off which Homer bounced the ramifications of his Idea. Invariably there was an Idea, capitalized and nailed down, the substrate for Homer's ruminations. The Idea was usually acquired early, pursued, chewed and then, not infrequently, eschewed, another one being generated with breathtaking – sometimes breath-snatching – rapidity.

Wright had long ago come to recognize that professional life with Homer was like taking a high-speed train, the driver of which had a weak bladder.

He had, as requested by Homer, pulled all the old files on the Melkior Pendred case and had gone through them, painstakingly making notes on his lap, his desk even more overladen than usual. Wright could now see why Homer was so excited, although he thought there were still problems to be faced. Now he was sitting in Homer's office, the files in three plastic crates beside Homer's desk.

'Well?' demanded Homer. 'Have we missed anything?'

Wright was unsure if this question was a trick, a genuine query or rhetorical. He consequently said nothing, hoping that he was correct, and was relieved when Homer remarked, 'I was right, wasn't I? This murder fits the bill exactly.'

Wright's notes were held firmly in both hands as he sat in front of Homer's desk. It was a standing joke in the station that Homer's feet did not touch the floor when he sat at his desk, which was unjust, although Wright could attest from his present view that only the soles did.

'It would seem to, sir.' Wright had never read Evelyn Waugh, but he would have appreciated the humour had he done so, for this five-word phrase was used to suggest full agreement when only partial was present. Homer, though, rarely heard Wright's words and never listened to them.

'Seem to? It's bloody perfect, even down to the connection. Jenny Muir, née Paget. Part-time whore and Martin's alibi for the fifth murder.'

'But why kill her? He usually only killed people he had a grudge against.'

Homer spluttered in his response to this heterodoxy. 'How am I supposed to know at this stage? Maybe she tried to blackmail him over the false alibi.' He paused. 'Yes. You'll have to check that out.'

He was relaxing on an airbed of satisfaction that bobbed up and down on a sea of self-congratulation. 'It's just a question of whether we pick Pendred up now, or wait until the autopsy's done.'

Wright glanced briefly down at his scribblings. 'There are just a few points, sir,' he ventured, much as Fletcher Christian might once have approached *his* boss.

Homer took a full five seconds to achieve comprehension. 'Eh? What do you mean?'

'Well, there's a slight difference in the MO this time, isn't there?'

Captain Bligh would have offered no less an expression of incredulity. 'What do you mean?'

'Mrs Muir was killed some two hundred metres from her home, then carried there,' Wright explained. They had been alerted to the large, still sticky blood patch by a man who had been walking his dog; the dog's enthusiastic consumption of the peripheral parts of the bloodstain had, they hoped, not destroyed too much of value. From there it had been easy to see the trail of bloodspots that led back to Mrs Muir's house. 'In all the other murders, it was done on the spot.'

He was actually quite proud that he had spotted this, but it was a wasted emotion. Homer was contemptuous. 'Hardly a major change, is it? Hardly invalidates the thesis.' In truth he hadn't spotted the difference, and it disquieted him somewhat, but such was his mental gyroscope that it didn't take long to re-establish stability. 'Don't forget that in the third murder, the pathologist reckoned that a different weapon was used. A much shorter blade, he said. I don't recall Cox shouting about that one being down to someone else.'

49

Wright subsided as so often before, and Homer returned to his own thoughts. 'We have got Pendred under surveillance, haven't we?' He tended to ask the same questions time and again, as if there were fundamental neuroticism within his make-up. Wright reassured him that Pendred was being watched by a team of four officers. A silence ensued and Wright, almost as if hostile forces acted upon his nervous system, found himself expressing another of his doubts.

'You don't suppose that the husband might have anything to do with it?'

Presumably Captain Bligh's facial expression had been identical when cast adrift by Mr Christian, although it is to be debated whether he actually managed such a theatrical splutter. 'The husband?' Homer demanded, his inflexion rising with the grace of a summer swift. 'The husband? What the bloody hell are you talking about, Wright?'

Wright sighed. He was used to both the tenor and the course of this exchange. It was always thus. 'It was just that when I was talking to David Muir, I occasionally suspected that he wasn't always being totally honest. There were a few times when I got the impression that his story didn't hold water.'

Homer stared at him speechlessly, a gaze of such inscrutability it could have hidden an intellect of either gargantuan or minuscule proportions. 'Where's your report?' he demanded eventually. Wright, of course, had not had the time to do this, an omission of duty that he suspected Homer well knew. He shook his head, resigned to what was to follow.

'Well, do it, Wright. You know the rules. Write it down straight away; that's the only way we can make sense of anything.'

Homer seemed to think that this was an end, or at least a pause, to Wright's distressing lack of orthodoxy. In any case, the entrance of Chief Superintendent Call terminated any chance the Sergeant had to press his suit.

Call was of average height and average build but Nature, perhaps tiring of such conventionality, had thereafter abandoned caution and imbued him with ears that were protuberant, eyes that were not quite level and a nose that seemed, like an old vicar's sermon, to go on for ever. To call him ugly gave ugly people a bad name. To call him consequently short-tempered gave a grievously erroneous impression; he was mean to the point of maliciousness.

'Have you seen this?' he demanded of Homer. Wright might have been as insubstantial as a warm, spring zephyr for all the attention he was allowed. Call was waving a paper.

Curiously, of all the detectives at the station, Homer was the one who had the most calming influence on Call. Although not entirely immune to Call's tirades and tantrums, he seemed somehow to endure them better, to shorten them and to cause them to melt away. There was some affinity between them that worked this magic, but its nature remained arcane.

Homer took the paper and read the headline – *Eviscerator strikes again!* Beneath this there was a detailed description of the murder, its similarity with the previous murders, and speculation about police incompetence.

'I'm not surprised, sir.'

Call took a deep breath in preparation for releasing a broadside but, before he could speak, Homer added, 'There were reporters everywhere after about an hour. We tried to keep things quiet, but this was such a gruesome business there was no way we were going to succeed. The man with the dog, the neighbours, even the husband could have blabbed.'

'But the link with the previous murders! How did they get hold of that?'

Homer shrugged. He suspected that it was probably a police source that had given the information away, but he didn't fancy goading Call with that particular stick. Call said, 'We've lost control, Homer, and I don't like it. There shouldn't have been any public mention of the Pendred case until we had had a chance to determine whether or not it's relevant.'

'Oh, it is, sir. It is. The MO's identical.' He stared briefly at Wright who, not being of a suicidal mind, said nothing.

Call sat down for the first time, thus allowing Homer to do likewise; Wright remained standing. 'So you were right, then. About Melkior, I mean.'

Homer smiled graciously at this admission of his superiority. 'I'm afraid so, sir.'

Call nodded. 'I had a call from Cox. He's heard, too.'

'Really, sir?'

'Yes. He sounded worried. I couldn't reassure him.'

'No, sir.'

Call's voice was sad; he and Cox had been colleagues of similar rank for a long time. 'This isn't going to look good for him, if there's a stink.' He sighed. 'Still, at least he's retired.'

'That's something, sir.'

Call was furrowing brows busily. 'What was the name of the girl on the case? She made quite a name for herself, didn't she?'

'Wharton, sir. Beverley Wharton.'

Call looked up in surprise. 'Wharton? Was it her? She was the one who screwed up the Exner case, wasn't she?'

Homer tried a bit of brow-furrowing as well. 'I think it probably was, sir.'

Call stood up. 'Well, if that's the case, she's done for now.' He returned to more immediate matters. 'What about Martin Pendred?'

'We've had him under observation, pending the autopsy results – just in case there's a bit of a surprise.'

'Well, you'd better get him in straight away. The last thing we need is some hack getting to him first and giving him a hundred thousand for his exclusive story.'

He left, leaving the door open. Homer turned to Wright. 'You heard the man, Wright. Bring Pendred in.'

Wright left the room, at the same time leaving a very happy Chief Inspector.

Gary Ormond was a thug. The four-letter word not only delineated him, it sufficed in description of him so that no other datum was required. To think of a thug was to think of Gary Ormond. He made a career of it and, unlike much of modern, disaffected and aimless youth, he chose his role in life early, evincing a penchant for cruelty before he was evincing verbally at all. In the years that followed he asserted his character in the usual ways – bullying, thievery, boorishness, bigotry – and at all the usual venues: home, pub, football matches, work. It was the last that led him into contact with the Pendred twins.

The Pendreds were never going to end up in normal occupations. It was unfortunate that they exhibited none of the *idiot savant* tendencies so famously, but infrequently, associated with their condition; as a consequence, there was nothing that anyone could think of to do with them. They were not unintelligent, but their almost total lack of communicability meant that they were incapable of carrying out the vast majority of occupations successfully. It was with a certain degree of inevitability that they ended up working in an abattoir.

Which was where Gary Ormond spent his days.

Ormond was king of that particular hill. He had no especial authority, other than that which intimidation gave him, but an abattoir is a place of noise and motion and nooks and crevices, where an unofficial authority can be exerted. He had his lieutenants and he had a nice line in pilfering that he wanted protected. Those who did not actively participate were required to hold silence dear; Ormond wanted only two groups, those who did, and those who did nothing.

Ormond did not really understand the Pendreds. Their reactions were not normal, their expressions did not convey the emotions he expected; indeed, they expressed nothing at all. They were large and well built – clearly capable of violence – but they did not respond in the ways that he had come to expect – indeed, they did not respond at all. Thus it was three weeks into their time within the abattoir before he finally decided to discuss with them their place in the world to which they had come.

The abattoir was at its busiest. There was a symphony of noise composed of an undercurrent of background animal noise – smothered by distance but still recognizably distressed – upon which the higher register of numerous melody lines – gates clanging, water echoing, human cries and coarse, cruel laughter – played chaotically. There was also the characteristic palate of odours – blood both fresh and drying, disinfectant, bone dust burnt by the saws – from which this vision of hell drew depth and piquancy. These wailings for a darling's loss and uncleanly savours were a continuous, unchanging soundtrack to the work of the slaughterhouse.

Martin Pendred, buttoned white coat, bright-red rubber gloves, white cap, white wellington boots and face speckled with blood, was leaving for his appointed twenty-minute break. He had taken off his long rubber apron, and it now hung from a hook, glinting back a dark-red sheen dotted with occasional gobbets of fat and flesh. The way out was between the two large refrigeration rooms, down a long dark corridor that was always cold and draughty, even in summer. It was poorly lit, although the walls were quite clearly smeared with blood new, old and ancient.

Ormond was coming the other way, accompanied by a tall, thin youth called Askin; Askin looked stupid and for once appearances didn't lie. In another age or another culture he would perhaps have been cannon fodder or profitably mutilated for begging purposes. Being born into the late twentieth century, though, had allowed him to escape such socially useful fates and pursue the occupation of all those of like disposition – cruel, mindless violence.

'Out of the fucking way,' he commanded Martin over the shoulder of his commandant, for the corridor was not wide enough to allow two men to pass without one of them twisting sideways. Martin may or may not have heard; if he did, he made no external sign. He did not even cast a glance at Ormond which, from Ormond's perspective, was akin to spitting in his face. Instead he stopped forward motion and stared at the door ahead of him.

Ormond also stopped, because he had to – a change in the game plan that didn't improve his mood. He decided to take this opportunity to present a little dissertation on the Rules. The Rules were a code of conduct by which all those round him conducted themselves; they involved deference to Ormond in all things, co-operation in his meat-smuggling sideline, willingness to provide an alibi when he needed one. To his mind, neither Martin nor his brother was sufficiently au fait with them.

He put out a hand, grabbed Martin by the throat, and then kicked him very suddenly and very hard between the legs. Martin then did two things that annoyed Ormond even more; he declined to groan and he declined to convert his facial expression from its habitual one of calm to one of anguish. He did at least drop down to the floor.

By now really rather irritated, Ormond stepped over Martin, who was on all fours, breathing only slightly harder and more frequently than his usual barely perceptible respiratory effort. This meant that he and Askin now blocked off both escape routes.

'Right,' pronounced Ormond, a job well started. 'I think it's about time we talked about the Rules.'

Martin at this point attempted to rise. There was something implacable about this gesture, something that suggested indomitability. To Ormond it also suggested that he hadn't been hit nearly hard enough or often enough. He, with Askin doggedly following the current party line, proceeded to correct this lapse. Their method involved use of their steel-capped boots and the introduction of the Martin cranium to the wall, thereby adding to the bloodstains.

It was during this process that Melkior came out of the abattoir for his break. He stopped, the door open, his face adorned with an expression identical to that of his brother. Ormond had his back to Melkior; he heard the door open but knew that whoever it was would obediently turn, leave and shut it again, forgetting what he had seen. Askin was having too much fun to bother with using his brain to see who was there.

It had taken several seconds for Melkior to identify the object of their attention. When he had done so, he backed out of the corridor and shut the door, his face still betraying no obvious concern.

Feeling that he had made his point, Ormond ceased operations, restraining Askin who, having entered slaughter mode, was quite happy to continue until Martin was no more than seedless strawberry jam with crunchy topping. Ormond bent down to the bloodied ear of Martin.

'Now,' he whispered. 'Perhaps you understand. There are Rules around here. Rules that you have to obey.'

Again the door opened behind him, but Ormond was fully confident that it would again close upon the back of its opener.

His confidence was misplaced. True, it closed, but whoever was there did not scurry away. Instead the intruder walked briskly along the few metres of corridor that separated door and thug. Askin looked up first, then grunted to Ormond. By the time Ormond had begun to turn his head, the trio had become a quartet.

A hand grabbed his long, coarse hair, pulling so hard that for a moment Ormond was off balance and rising against his will. Before he could regain control, his head was jerked back and a knife was pressed to his throat. In his right ear came a soft voice, a hush of breath. The words were slow and hesitant, as if the speaker were using a foreign tongue. 'Let my brother go.'

Ormond's eyes flicked from left to right while his brain wondered if he could somehow reverse his misfortune, but he could feel just how sharp and mean was the blade at his neck. The abattoir had no blunt knives, just as it had no keen minds.

'Back off,' he commanded Askin. The words were uttered through a mouth that did not move and with a tongue that lay dormant, lest the blade slip. Askin had been staring hungrily at Melkior, as if he had just conceived a brilliant plan to free Ormond and turn back the situation, but he did as he was told.

Martin rose shakily from the rather bloodied floor. His face was already swollen and bruising behind the bloodmask. Another might have taken the opportunity to exact some revenge, but not Martin. His eyes were for Melkior only, although no words were uttered. Then he turned and pushed past Askin, apparently continuing his quest for a cup of tea.

Melkior again whispered into Ormond's ear, and again the words were unfamiliar orphans in the world. 'Askin – go.'

Ormond hesitated but the bite of the knife grew just a little bit sharper. 'Fuck off,' he hissed at his lieutenant. Askin departed reluctantly.

They were alone now but Melkior was in no hurry. He waited, impassive and seemingly unconcerned by the possibility of interruption for three minutes; if these seconds were long for Martin, for Ormond they were interminable. The dark, oppressive corridor with its blood-smeared walls and gloomy light seemed now to resembled a burial place, but he remained silent and still in Melkior's rigid grasp for all of it.

Without a further word, Melkior ended the situation. He did so by drawing the knife across Ormond's throat in a smooth and steady stroke, but also he did so with a butcher's care. The edge cut deeply enough to score the flesh but leave the larynx untouched. It was agony and it bled, but it did not kill.

Only at the demise of the stroke did Melkior pull the blade that little bit deeper, so that the external jugular vein was nicked. The blood fell freely and copiously, but Ormond was not to die from the wound.

He fell from Melkior's grasp, gasping, terrified, in pain and profaning.

Melkior left him and walked out to take his break.

That eternity in the still quiet, held by an implacable and alien force, had its effect. Ormond always refused to divulge who had so easily held his life and delivered judgement; nor did he feel it necessary to teach the Rules again to the Pendred twins.

Martin Pendred was arrested at eight thirty that evening. There was no masterful deduction or fantastically complex police operation that brought about this triumph, merely the ability of the four officers who were watching the front and back of Martin's house to remain awake, for when they approached him, he did not run, or even look startled. He merely turned at the sound of his name, as passive as ever. When he was led away, it might have been a daily occurrence for him, a regular trip out with friends.

'What's the problem?'

Peter owned a large detached property on the edge of a deer park. The area was gilded with elegance, perfumed with comfort. Oak trees shaded the end of a long, lawned garden that undulated down to the brook that marking the boundary. Three of the six high-ceilinged bedrooms gave varying views over green spaces, the others looked over a high-walled garden split by a gravel drive. The residue of traffic noise that reached Beverley's ears retained just enough structure for her to hear the haughty tone of executive saloons and four-by-fours.

They were in the dining room, the french windows open and a scent of cut grass stealing in with the crepuscular light.

'The phone call.'

Peter smiled. He had a wide, generous mouth and a smile that somehow consumed most of his face and made his eyes, already humorous, issue an irresistible offer of trust and companionship. 'I had already guessed that, Beverley.' He never abbreviated her name, a habit that ought to have conveyed cool formality but that ignited only warmth within her. 'It was bad news, I take it.'

She sighed. They were sipping wine over a large glass dining table that reflected bright lights from crystal pendants on the ceiling lights. 'You remember the Pendred case?'

He nodded. 'Of course. The Eviscerator, wasn't it?'

'It was my first big case.' Beverley laughed. 'Hell, it was the biggest! Nothing in this country has ever compared with the Pendred case.'

'That's right. Had a funny first name, didn't he?'

'Melkior. Melkior Pendred.'

'Some sort of psychotic.'

Beverley said in a voice that suggested she was quoting verbatim, '*Borderline Autistic. Severe Asperger's Syndrome.* Basically they're disorders of perception. Both Melkior and his

57

twin brother, Martin, had the same problem. Neither of them saw the world as the rest of us do.'

Peter refilled her glass. 'So what's the problem?'

'Well, as you said, Melkior became known in the papers as, the Eviscerator, and for a very good reason. He had had training as a mortuary technician, and all of the victims were murdered by having their throats slit, then they were, literally, eviscerated. It had clearly been done by someone with experience, for the bodies were then professionally sewn up. The brains were removed, and so expertly was it done that you wouldn't have known.

'Then the organs and brain were usually hidden in places nearby; it was a sort of sick game – Hunt the Organs. Sometimes it took us hours to find them.'

'There were how many murders? Four?'

'Five. All of them had crossed or upset either Melkior or Martin in some way – usually Melkior. Both Melkior and Martin had the opportunity to commit the first four, but only Melkior could have done the last.'

'Why was that?'

'Martin was given an alibi by his girlfriend, Jenny Paget.'

'But you said the murders showed experience at autopsy work. Surely if Melkior was the one with such training . . .'

Beverley shook her head. 'They were both appropriately trained. They worked as mortuary technicians at the Western Royal.'

Peter might not have been a criminal barrister, but he still had an incisive grasp of detail, and cause and effect. 'I don't mean to appear rude, Beverley, but it can't have been too difficult to track the killer. You yourself said that the deaths were clearly done by someone with training in post-mortem techniques. There can't be many of those around.'

She sighed. 'You'd be surprised.' More wine. 'I was just a sergeant then, newly transferred to CID. I was working with Chief Inspector Cox – he was a nice, gentlemanly sort of copper. Everyone said that he was 'Old School' – which meant that he said sorry after he'd stabbed you in the back – but I could have done a lot worse. He protected me, led me through the times I could have screwed up big time, and taught me a lot.

'He was methodical to the point of madness, but watching him you had to admire him. He told me to make a list of everyone, but everyone, who might conceivably have the knowledge or ability to do such a thing. He told me to compile lists of surgical and funereal suppliers, then to check them all to see if anyone out of the ordinary had ordered anything recently. He himself checked all the hospitals within a hundred-mile radius, making lists of everyone, male or female, who was either still working or who had ever worked in a position where they might have seen a post-mortem.

'All this was in addition to the meticulous enquiries he made into the victims' lives. Who they were, whom they had known, whom they had disliked, those who had disliked them.' She paused to look at him and he was once again enchanted by her eyes and wide curve of her mouth. 'We hit lucky, we thought, straight off. Charlie Merrick. He was an undertaker, running his own small operation, and making a tidy sum by ripping off the customers. Usual things – selling an expensive box but actually using some chipboard monstrosity; over-inflating the costs; charging outrageously for "sanitizing" the body when all he did was sprinkle on some talcum powder and slap on some lip gloss.'

'Do they all do such things?'

She smiled. 'Not all.' He raised his eyebrows at her tone but said nothing more. She continued, 'Anyway, Charlie Merrick emerged early on as a good fit. He had been originally trained as a mortuary technician, but he had been sacked because he attacked one of the porters at the hospital with a very long knife, trying to slash his throat, and that was only the culmination of a lifetime's worth of violence and conflict, all of which demonstrated quite clearly that he had a temper like a polecat with piles. Eventually he set up the funeral directorship, but that was basically achieved by bullying his wife into giving him a small inheritance. By that time he was already a drunk and she was already bearing the trophies of it.

'The first of the Eviscerator's victims was an old colleague of Merrick's, the second drank in the same pub. We had the psychologist's opinion, for what it was worth, that he was a good fit for the Eviscerator, and we had his knowledge of autopsy techniques. The third murder happened and we felt he had to pull him and start interrogation.

'Unfortunately for us, thirty-three hours in, the fourth murder happened, identical in every way to the first three, and we had the so-called perpetrator in our custody.'

'So you had to let him go.'

She sighed and finished her wine. They were due at a party by nine and they would have to hurry, but Peter didn't seem bothered, despite the fact that it was an occasion that she knew he wanted to attend, something at which he wanted to be seen. She felt touched that he seemed to be elevating her problem over his own political aspirations. 'Which left us looking fairly stupid, a situation that wasn't helped by William Homer.'

Peter seemed to be concentrating as if noting all this down for future reference. He asked, 'Who was?'

'My colleague, also then a sergeant. He had his own ideas right from the start. Essentially he ran an investigation of his own inside the official one.'

'Must have made him popular.'

'You get the idea. He and Cox were at each other's throats for much of the time. The problem was that he had said all along that it wasn't Merrick, and he had made sure his views were known, so when we had to let Merrick go, things almost degenerated into open warfare.

'Then we established the link between the Pendreds and the victims. The Pendred twins were employed at the Western Royal at that time as mortuary technicians. All of the dead could, in one way or another, be shown to have given cause for offence to the Pendreds. When we found that their alibis were dodgy, it seemed that once again we were close. The only problem was, which one of them was the murderer?'

'Couldn't it have been both?'

'Up until the fourth murder, yes, but that one was definitely only one man. Two witnesses interrupted him as he was removing the brain. He ran for it and it was too dark for a description, but there was definitely only one perpetrator.

'Anyway, Cox and I were keeping an open mind but Homer knew better. Homer always knew better. He had decided that his detailed analysis of the crime suggested that it was almost certainly Martin Pendred, Melkior's twin brother. Only trouble was, the fifth murder occurred under our noses, and Martin had an alibi. A prostitute, Jenny Paget, said that he'd been with her.'

'And Melkior?'

'Melkior didn't have such a witness.'

'What about forensic evidence?'

'We never found any, on anyone. We reckoned Melkior was

using hospital blues stolen from work, then burning them. A certain number go missing every month, usually because of wear and tear. They're only lightweight and burn to nothing but a small amount of ash. It was also likely that he was returning after each murder to the hospital to shower. We looked for blood traces in the mortuary showers but never came up with anything. The same was true of the Pendreds' house.'

Peter was silent. He, too, had finished his wine and was now examining the stem of the glass minutely, as if he could see a flaw within. Just for a second, Beverley felt a faraway chill, then it was gone. 'So what's the problem?' he asked.

She suddenly had the feeling that he was asking the question on two different levels, and she saw clearly that he was a barrister as well as a lover. Careful of her words, and feeling strange because of it, she said, 'Melkior was found guilty and sentenced to life five times over. If he'd tried a mental health defence, I think he might have got away with it, although the effective result would have been the same. As it was, he tried to argue against our case and lost. He never stopped arguing his innocence.

'He died seven months ago, still a long way from release.'

She stood up, feeling very, very tired. Peter was watching her from eyes that she could not read, saying nothing.

She admitted at last, 'And now the murders have started again.'

He came to her then and held her. She felt so relieved to have such a man on whom to rely.

Relieved and happy.

Eisenmenger had arranged to pick up Helena at seven thirty but was slightly late because of the consultants' meeting. When he rang her doorbell, there was a wait of no more than eight seconds before the door was opened and, in distinct contrast with generally accepted social convention, Helena said curtly, 'You're late.' She then left him alone at the door.

Her brief appearance had told him not only that she was angry but also that she was still in the process of making up and, as he closed the door and made his way into the sitting room, he was left to contemplate the delightfully hypocritical thing that was a woman's mind. Another seven minutes passed into temporal oblivion before she re-emerged from her bedroom, her preparations this time apparently finished.

She was wearing a wrap-around dress of the palest blue silk, upon which was pinned a delicate silver and diamond brooch that he had bought for her two months ago on her birthday. She was, he decided, a most desirable person; a companion of his dreams.

Except that he could see in her eyes that yet again she was troubled. *What the hell is wrong with you these days?*

He knew from a relatively short but relatively intense experience that Helena's temperament was stormy, that she was fiercely independent and fiercely protective of an inner core that burned brightly, safely and softly, hidden beneath an armoured and icy exoskeleton. He knew also that he was allowed beneath this shield, but solely on her terms, at her discretion; entry to her private self was on a strictly monitored basis.

He had never considered trying to change her, would never even have considered considering, but he was getting fed up with seeing coldness in her eyes.

'How was Paris?'

She was looking for her purse. Or perhaps it was her scarf.

'French,' she said to a rather nice porcelain figurine that refused to melt beneath the terseness.

Or perhaps it was her good humour, reflected Eisenmenger.

'But surely . . . Paris in the spring . . . ?'

'Paris, like all big cities, is full of people who think that they're special because of where they live.' She found a pager and put it in her clutch bag. Turning to Eisenmenger, she added, 'It is also full of dogshit.'

As he followed her out of the front door, he asked, 'You're not on call tonight, are you?' Helena was on a duty solicitor rota; while it wasn't likely that she would be called to help someone in police custody, it would certainly dampen the occasion should it occur.

Her reply was not so much a means of conveying information as a challenge. 'Yes, I am. Problem?'

Knowing what was good for him he murmured only, 'I didn't realize.'

She relented, although it was the slightest of movements. 'Dan's ill. I said I'd cover.'

There was a brief silence in the lift and then, as they were getting in his car, he ventured cautiously, 'Do I take it that it wasn't a good trip?'

She paused in the act of buckling her seat belt. 'It was a conference on the Human Rights Act, John. It was like most other conferences.'

She sounded tired, almost depressed, he decided. Mind you, he usually felt depressed in the hours following a conference; something to do with the remorselessly sickly buffet food, the endlessly cheerful but false reunions, the interminable lecture presentations. He made a vow to attempt to cheer her up during the course of the evening.

It was as he was driving her around the corner from her flat that he saw the headline of the evening paper on a placard by the entrance to a shopping arcade and his vow was temporarily subsumed by his own thoughts.

Eviscerator strikes again.

The Eviscerator? Melkior Pendred? But he was dead, wasn't he?

Helena had also seen the headline and perhaps it was the momentary look on his face that broke through her previous introspection. 'Didn't you work on that case?'

When he replied it was from the past. 'Five murders, all identical. Melkior Pendred was sentenced to life for them. He died in prison some seven months ago. Kind of makes it difficult for him to have struck again.'

'The constabulary got it wrong? Surely not.' Helena's cynicism wasn't so much withering as mummifying.

Eisenmenger was still not in the present as he said quietly, 'Yeah.'

His mind was thinking of the officers on the case; specifically it was dwelling on Beverley Wharton.

Eisenmenger was a patient man – a trait of pathologists – but the evening had proved a strain. The restaurant was one that they both liked but was neither cheap nor ostentatious; on their previous visits, Helena had visibly enjoyed its ambience, allowing it to smooth out the sharper corners of her personality, but not tonight. Tonight she remained resolutely thorny. Rarely had his efforts at sparking sparkling dialogue succeeded beyond the four-line stage, and Helena's side of the exchanges usually involved single syllables seeping into the world either already sickly and dying, or with a pH low enough to dissolve precious metals. He had thought that she might be interested in his reactions to his new job, his new colleagues, but his attempts to introduce the subject made no image on her radar. All she seemed interested in was carping. Her final offering – a rather tart, 'You don't say,' issued in response to his opinion that the dessert (a confection of whipped cream, meringue and fresh peaches) was very sweet – proved beyond his endurance.

'What the bloody hell's up with you, Helena? You're being about as sociable as a conga eel.' He tried to temper the enquiry with a slight lightening of tone but the acerbity showed through nonetheless. And, having started, he decided that there was little point in temerity. 'As a matter of fact, now I come to mention it, you've had a problem for months now.'

He saw at once from her expression that she was going to protest, deny, become outraged, so like all the wisest combatants he carried on. 'Something's been bugging you ever since you got out of hospital in Scotland. You've been denying it, but it's been there, gnawing at you, making you cold company.'

Her mouth had opened and it had remained open when he finished. There came a pause and the universal clockwork failed to tick. Perhaps a million fairies died while she stared at him as if affronted by his effrontery, before her gaze dropped and she mumbled, 'I'm sorry.'

He waited and for a long moment it seemed that he waited in vain, but eventually she looked back up at him. 'I'm not the forgiving sort, John. Judgemental, too, I guess. Quick to condemn.'

'Soon be on the bench, then.'

She returned his smile ruefully. 'Yeah.' Then, 'I went to see Beverley after that business on Rouna.'

Somehow he had known that Beverley would be at the focus of this problem. 'And?'

But she seemed to have lost her way for her next remark appeared to him to be slightly off the subject. 'She's a bitch, isn't she?'

Before he could reply, her pager began to sound. Eisenmenger raised eyes heavenward as she looked at the message then rose to find a phone. That this had fearful symmetry and was somehow in keeping with the whole tenor of the evening did not assuage his exasperation.

When she came back she at least looked apologetic. 'I'm sorry, John. I've got to go.'

He sighed. 'What is it? A drunk driver or a loony?' These were the commonest reasons for the duty solicitor to be summoned.

'Neither. Martin Pendred's been arrested.'

Helena was convinced that the smell – the stench was a more apposite term – of the cells clung. Her move towards criminal law had resulted in an increased amount of time spent in such surroundings, but that she was relatively recently come to this life meant that she was yet to be inured to it. She had to resist constantly the feeling of uncleanness, of degradation and defilement, aware that such emotions were not only imaginary and unwarranted, but also a barrier between herself and her work. How could she serve these people if she hated the place in which she found them, in which she joined with them?

Yet the smell was the least of it; and not even the uncomfortable seats, the scratched and chipped table top, the bleakness of the dull, green-painted walls and the forlorn inadequacy of the dirty windows with their frosted glass and their stern, protecting bars, were the most of it.

No, the most, the worst, was the attitude of the police. Helena had been brought up in the middle class, a mythic world where crime rarely happened and where the police were on her side, displaying an amalgam of deference, good humour and discreetness. Even the trauma of her parents' death and its terrible consequences had not served to destroy entirely this construction, yet the last six months had introduced her to a totally different view of the constabulary and its ways.

True, there was still something that could be called deference but it was now spiked with contempt and hostility. Each utterance was rounded with the apparently appropriate title, yet the word 'Miss' could be made to sound so supercilious and disdainful that it became almost an insult, as if her single status implied either callowness, or stupidity, or both.

And their looks were made by eyes that signalled hostility, set in faces that transmitted something near loathing.

She knew that she had to harden herself to all this, and outwardly she had, but that did not mean that she did not feel it, did not hate it and wish desperately that it would not be so.

She waited now in the interrogation room, a pad of paper and a pen in front of her on the table, her handbag leaning against the scratched and battered tape recorder that was screwed down against the wall. She was not nervous – not as she had been when first she had been duty solicitor – but she was far from relaxed.

The door opened in front of her and Martin Pendred came in, followed by a constable who immediately shut the door and left them alone, leaving a lingering smirk behind him. Pendred stood there, his eyes passing over Helena as if she were just another item of furniture.

He's actually quite attractive.

Helena checked herself with a sharp question – *Where did that come from?*

And yet she could not deny that there was truth in this impertinent judgement. He was tall and well built and muscular; his eyes were dark, his chin strong. All these alone conspired to create something that she could see was quite alluring, but there was more. Pendred's very detachment seemed to represent an attractive imperviousness, a challenge. It evoked within her the query, *I'm attractive, so why are there not the usual signs that he notices?* It was an unsettling realization that normal rules of sexual interplay did not apply with this man; it was even more unsettling to wonder which other rules did not apply.

She forced herself to speak, almost as if the lengthening silence in the cold room was a shelter from which she did not wish to venture. 'Mr Pendred?'

But Martin Pendred did not want to be tied by the conventions of dialogue. Instead of replying, instead even of reacting in any meaningful way, he began to pace the room, from corner to diagonally opposite corner, muttering; Helena soon realized that he was counting his steps.

'Mr Pendred?'

Nothing.

'Mr Pendred?'

The counting and the pacing continued. His face wore a look of concentration that would not have been out of place on an examination candidate. Suddenly aware of the reason for the constable's parting smirk, Helena said, 'Martin? Martin!'

And miraculously he stopped. Didn't look at her but at least he stopped.

'Martin, my name's Helena Flemming. I'm the duty solicitor; I've been asked to come here and give you advice on . . .'

He had stopped his locomotion, but there was plenty of movement left inside him, leaking out in the twitching of his eye muscles, and rhythmic clenching of both his fists. He was standing directly in front of her, but staring just above her head at the wall behind; he could almost have been caught and wriggling in amber.

Except that then he said, 'I didn't do it.' It was no more than a whisper, but it was more than gibberish. She saw that he was shaking slightly, but only slightly.

'What?'

But he had said what he was going to say and he wasn't interested in reprising the performance for the audience. He merely resumed staring. She felt frustrated to have been tossed a morsel and missed it.

'Did you say that you didn't do it?'

But this call for an encore was condemned to be unanswered. Helena sighed, then decided that if dialogue was impossible, and she would have to perform a soliloquy, then so be it.

Now he was on to nursery rhymes. There was undoubtedly something touching about this big, not unhandsome forty-year-old man reciting 'Jack Sprat'; there was something chilling about the way he kept repeating it, and about the blankness of his features.

'What didn't you do, Martin?'

Nothing.

'They say that you murdered someone.'

He didn't even turn his head. She might have suggested that he had tripped someone up.

'Did you murder someone?'

Mr and Mrs Sprat continued their complementary gustatory habits, but the frequency now increased, and Helena suddenly understood. *He's seriously stressed.*

For a moment she wasn't sure what to do. It was from a feeling of rising panic that she rose and came round the table to him. He suddenly seemed huge and the fact that he was shaking gave the impression of increasing pressure, like a large boiler about to explode and lay waste to all around.

'Martin?' As if it were infectious, she noticed that there was now a shake in her own words.

'. . . would eat no fat, his wife would eat no lean . . .' The words were speeding up now and at the same time his breathing was becoming faster.

'Martin?'

'. . . between the two of them, they licked the platter clean. Jack Sprat . . .' The feeling of something careering beyond control was growing as he streamed the words faster and faster.

She reached out her hand.

'. . . could eat no fat, his wife . . .'

If he doesn't stop soon he'll collapse. Her fingers rested lightly on the sleeve of his shirt. It was frayed at the cuff and there was a smear of grease on it.

'. . . and so between the two of them . . .'

'Martin?' She used a louder voice and at the same time pressed slightly down on his arm. His arm was solid, almost oaken, under the grubby material of his shirt.

'. . . Sprat could eat no . . .'

'Martin, it's all right. There's nothing to worry about . . .'

'. . . could eat no lean . . .'

'I'm here to help you. You don't have to . . .'

And suddenly he stopped, and at the same time he became literally animated, moving with shocking speed from automaton to human, from unresponsive to over-responsive, from passivity to sudden action.

His other hand shot out, grasping her wrist (not hard, but unbreakably), but just for a second, forcing from Helena a surprised squeak. With the noise of a crying, barking seal (Helena realized only later that it was a sound of sobbing), he suddenly enveloped her, the nursery rhyme banished from his lips, tears coursing down rough, unshaven jowls.

Within the space of a second, she was lost within him, clamped by what was suddenly a giant of a man, power and strength embedded into every contact point, his breathing intense and loud. Odours of sweat and dirt and mustiness filling every breath, her mind wondered, shrieked, *What the hell's going on?*

But then the panic subsided because he did nothing more than hold her and in that holding did nothing more than weep.

Eisenmenger waited in the parking area at the back of the low square police station, shadowed from the neon lights of the main road by its concrete ugliness. Listening to Radio Four's late evening analysis of the latest political tediousness he dozed off, woken an hour or so later by Helena climbing back into the car.

'All done?' he asked.

'For tonight.'

He started the car and drove on to the road, taking the right-hand lane at the traffic lights. 'And?' he enquired.

She was silent in the semi-darkness for a moment. 'I shouldn't really tell you.'

Eisenmenger thought that she at least owed him something for the wasted evening. 'I'm not likely to rush to the nearest phone and sell the story to the tabloids,' he pointed out.

More pausing. 'He's been arrested on suspicion of murdering Mrs Jenny Muir.'

'Hence *The Eviscerator strikes again?*'

She nodded.

He had stopped at traffic lights. 'Did you get any details on the murder?'

'No. The police aren't obliged at this stage to provide any information. Only when, if, he's formally charged will it become a little clearer.'

He moved the car forward slowly as the lights became green. 'So what are they doing?'

'Questioning him.' She knew that he would want more, so she added, 'Mainly about his relationship with the dead woman, and his whereabouts last night.'

'And where was he last night?'

She sighed, the kind of noise that an exasperated mother makes when its child won't stop asking inane questions. 'I don't know, John. He wasn't answering questions.'

He noticed that the unexpected intrusion of work into the evening at least seemed to have lifted her mood, and for that he was thankful, even if the meal had been ruined. 'Now, that's familiar. The Pendreds were never hot on verbal communication – not hot on communication at all, as I recall.'

'Martin hasn't said a word yet.'

Which presented him with a puzzle. 'How come he asked for a solicitor?'

'He didn't, but the officer in charge got one anyway. Obviously wants it done by the book.'

Waiting to turn right he said, 'So Martin's saying nothing, and you're going home. What happens now?'

'Now Martin has eight hours' rest before it starts again.'

A taxi was behind their car and didn't want to be. This induced silence in Eisenmenger. Helena asked, 'Why the interest?'

It was a question he had found himself posing, found himself struggling to answer. 'Several things, I suppose,' he said at last. 'As I said, I worked on the original murders, so if they've started again, it's not unnatural for me to want to know what's been done.' He ended on a note of slight uncertainty that she would not allow to last.

'And? What else?'

They were nearing her home and drove past a cast-iron statue of King George the Something that had been draped with an American flag; pigeons had defiled both the king and his unlikely apparel, thus perhaps applying some cement to Anglo-American relationships. He took his time formulating his reply. With some care he said, 'It was always an odd case. Now it seems to have got quite a bit odder.' It wasn't the truth – or rather, not the entire truth – but it was an approximation. Helena didn't pick up on the minuscule evasion because it was then that they arrived at her flat.

He had assumed that she would want to be alone with whatever had been bothering her, but she asked at once, 'Will you stay?'

Of course he would – he was a man, after all.

He didn't find the opportunity to ask further about what had been bothering her and she didn't tell him. They drank coffee and brandy, then went to bed. He made no move to make love because she made no signal.

They both slept soundly.

Beverley dreamed of Jeremy Eaton-Lambert that night and found herself wondering why as she lay awake in the morning light; never before had she allowed Helena Flemming's stepbrother into her subconscious, there to summon the twin ogres of doubt and guilt. What, after all, did that case – the brutal murders of Helena's mother and stepfather by Jeremy, his subsequent suicide in prison – have to do with anything now?

70

The past ought to die and, having died, stay dead, yet it never seemed to manage it; like a poorly executed murder, always there were some clues, some traces left uncovered that smouldered and rotted in the light and heat of the present. Sometimes Beverley felt that she carried the past around in her soul, a dead weight that whispered of the horrors of the grave.

She and Peter had returned from the party early and her mood had been further diseased by the news on the radio that Martin Pendred had been arrested. Peter had affected not to notice, and she had affected not to notice his pretence; a metastable artifice that had stretched her nerves.

Even making love had not helped, not least because for the first time in their relationship she had had to ask for this comfort. Peter had caressed her as softly and excitingly as always, his tongue had explored both inside and outside her with just as much expertise and sinful knowledge, but even as she climaxed with his long, slow entry, she had known that there was a small part of his mind that had somehow mutated, that a step change had occurred sometime last night.

And yet when he had woken her that morning he had been as loving and cheerful as ever, and when he had left to go to an early chambers meeting, he had displayed no external clue that there was within him a worm of something, a small maggot born of doubt.

So why did she feel certain that it was there?

She rose from the bed and pulled on a thin red gown. In the large, well-appointed, designer-built kitchen she found the radio playing to neatness. Peter had eaten some fruit and toast, neatly packing his dirty cutlery and crockery in the dishwasher, his easy tidiness seeming not small-minded but casual and right. He had made some coffee and it was left heating through for her (he knew better than to try to wake her with it); she poured some and then sat with the cup in front of her while, merely for something to do, she began to pick her way through *The Times*.

It didn't require much picking to find the article on the latest exploit of the Eviscerator.

She read it through, hoping that this second-, perhaps third-, hand account of a few facts and a surfeit of speculation would provide her with evidence to counter her growing dread that she had made a monumental balls-up when Melkior Pendred had been charged with the murders.

Yet she found none.

As she looked up to the pendant light above the central island, the prayer on her lips was taken by the news report on the radio, where again the macabre murder of Jenny Muir figured prominently.

She began to laugh, a sound as soft as it was sad, the irony becoming clearer by the moment.

She hadn't even tried to frame Melkior Pendred. Just for once, it seemed that she had made a genuine mistake, and that it would be this one that would finally destroy her.

Piringer was serpentine.

The word sprung into von Guerke's mind and she knew at once its rightness. Yes, she decided, *serpentine*. Not reptilian, but serpentine; cold-blooded and without normal mammalian reactions, but also supremely contained. All movements were tightly controlled, muscular and intentioned; Piringer did not waste effort on irrelevant activity.

And quite obviously he did not possess appreciable emotions. Oh yes, she acknowledged, he smiled; often he expressed anger and, she had heard, he had been known to appear to be concerned. Yet these were nothing more than aspects of feeling, little better than syntheses of what people expected a human to show, produced for effect, displayed as a mask. Piringer was a snake who acted the part of a man, who fooled them all.

'What do you think of Eisenmenger?'

This question was typical of Piringer, asked as it was in an educated, apparently amused drawl, and displaying enough gilt-edged superciliousness to have inflated a large dirigible.

'I think we're lucky to get him, given the shortage of pathologists in this benighted country.'

Piringer, of course, smiled, and thereby emitted coldness like a full moon in the polar night. 'He has a reputation, you know.'

He used the word with an inflexion that post-war housewives used when describing the more vivacious members of their sorority. Von Guerke marvelled at the malleable nature of the English language – one word with two contradictory meanings, probably a hundred shades of interpretation. She opted for ingenuousness. 'As a forensic pathologist, he was highly respected. Admittedly, he hasn't quite the same *reputation* . . .'

She could not stop herself placing an emphasis on this word, '. . . in surgical pathology, but most people I've spoken to say he's good at that, too.'

Piringer had good looks and charm aplenty, if you accepted charm as something akin to veneer – good to look at but often hiding cheap, inferior materials. 'That's not quite what I meant.'

Von Guerke and Piringer had weekly meetings to discuss managerial matters. Piringer had instituted them as soon as he had been appointed and, although the principle of such meetings could not be faulted, it had soon become obvious to von Guerke that they were actually a means whereby Piringer would find out what von Guerke had done, criticize where she had made mistakes and plunder where he thought credit was to be gained.

'And what did you mean?'

Piringer rose from behind his desk. His room was large and long with a view from its windows. Most of the offices and laboratories in Pathology looked either on to traffic-filled roads or the blank brick walls of the neighbouring buildings; only Piringer had an office that, being on the top floor beneath the eaves, was high enough to rise above the thronging multitude and catch a smog-ridden glimpse of heaven's home. He leaned against a low cupboard next to an ancient microscope, a gift from the Greek Division of the International Academy of Pathology.

'He asks questions. Even as a forensic pathologist, he was different, I understand. Not like the rest of us – do the autopsy, find a cause of death, write a report. He had a habit of seeing deeper than that.'

Alison von Guerke could have worn a Versace original and she would still have looked little better than a gift-wrapped bag of baking potatoes; that she wore shapeless dark clothes possibly retrieved from the bottom of the remainders bin at a jumble sale was a testament to acceptance of one's lot in life. 'Isn't asking questions a good thing in a pathologist? I know to most of us this job is little more than pattern-recognition and regurgitation of facts, but those who go a little further tend to be the best.'

Piringer nodded slowly, his expression suggesting agreement with her words, even while he hid his disappointment that she did not possess the intellectual machinery to comprehend the deeper meaning. 'How true, how true.' He considered. 'But I'm not referring to his abilities with the microscope or scalpel, Alison, more to his tendency to investigate relationships.'

She frowned but it was no more than a rehearsed move in the social play. 'Meaning?'

'He's a troublemaker. He might be a competent pathologist, but he's not a team player.'

Her dealings with a variety of professors over the years had produced in Alison von Guerke a mental container made of something akin to compressed diamond; it was into this that, at times such as this, she screamed. *Team player! My God, the hypocrite!* Her face, however, remained unchanged, apparently listening with nothing more than a willingness to be complicit in her departmental head's warnings.

'Does that matter?' she enquired. 'He's only a locum.'

Piringer's head rocked slowly from side to side with perfect precision, a signal of caution. 'He may be a long-term locum. We don't know how long Victoria's going to be off.'

'Anyway, I don't quite follow your concern. I know he's helped the police on a couple of occasions . . .'

Piringer sighed, upset that he had actually to approach enunciation of his worries. 'He won't have the loyalties that we have for each other. He may, perhaps, be more critical than we are.' He let this float gently down from the heights of his wisdom, then explained, 'It's not for me, you understand.' When she still didn't appear to be on board, he added, 'But I would suggest that we should be on our guard. Careless talk and all that.'

'You make him sound like a fifth columnist.'

He smiled at her witticism. 'I don't suggest that he has a hidden agenda, but I do suspect that he does not share our hopes and plans for the future.'

She caught a whiff of something. She asked, tiredly, 'Sleeping dogs . . . ?'

He was fulsome in his pleasure. 'Exactly. You and I both know that there some things best left undisturbed.'

For once she let her anger show. 'Meaning?'

If Piringer was perturbed by her impudence, he didn't allow it to alter that perfect smile. 'Look, Alison, all I'm suggesting is that perhaps we should all guard our tongues in front of Eisenmenger.'

'I haven't got anything to hide.' Somehow the unspoken question, *Have you?* echoed this pronouncement.

The smile, if anything, broadened. 'Nor I, Alison, nor I.' He took in a breath then, almost sadly, 'But what about Trevor?'

Von Guerke at last caught up with the Professor. She said quietly, 'Oh.'

Piringer nodded. 'Exactly. I wouldn't want to see Trevor unnecessarily *inconvenienced*. Especially now, at such a *delicate* time.' The theatrical emphases rolled from his lips to help von Guerke appreciate the problem.

She considered, her face made even less attractive than usual by the frown. 'But I don't see how we can do anything.'

Piringer shrugged, appearing to consider that he had done his bit merely by bringing the matter to her attention; how she managed things thereafter was her problem.

'Anyway,' he said, standing to communicate that she should leave, 'I'm sure you'll think of something.'

She took the hint and left, her face troubled. Behind her, Piringer's face bore a feline smile.

'Is she certain?' Homer wasn't quite hopping from foot to foot and clutching himself with ill-suppressed glee, but the pitch of his voice suggested either this or a whiff of helium in the atmosphere.

Wright's gesture was all things to all Chief Inspectors, being something of a nod, something of a shrug and something of a denial. He knew from innumerable embarrassing occasions in the past that identification evidence was not just the first step on the road to the fiery realm, it was a hop, a skip and a jump towards it. The last thing he needed (apart from an overlarge mortgage and a superior who thought he knew where Don Quixote had gone wrong) was to have said superior convinced that Sergeant Wright had been the one who had insisted they listen to Mrs Ethel Greaves, that she was all they needed to nail Martin Pendred.

Not that Mrs Greaves was liable to be any more unreliable than any other eyewitness, even though she was seventy-nine years old and heading rapidly towards deafness. It was just that eyewitnesses tended to see things in retrospect, which, as Wright was well aware, was a mirror that not only magnified, it distorted as well.

'Let me see her statement.'

Wright handed over the two sheets of A4, not surprised when Homer's familiar ritual of tutting, squinting and sighing was commenced as he tried to decipher the ungrammatical scrawl. In the interval Wright decided that a bit more backside-covering was required. 'I thought it important to get the statement as soon as possible, sir. I hope you didn't mind not being told at once.'

He was aware that he sounded as if Mrs Ethel Greaves was liable to shuffle off her mortal coil at any moment (she was frail but not to Wright's eye terminal), but it occurred to him that it would be wise to suggest urgency was a factor in his decision to proceed without the Chief Inspector.

Homer, deep in the jungle of untidy penstrokes that Wright produced in lieu of writing, grunted only, 'Fine, fine.' He had been stuck in a long and rather uncomfortable press conference, following which the Chief Superintendent had insisted upon what he called a 'debriefing', but which Homer found indistinguishable from a 'bollocking'. The entire, unpleasant sequence had taken nearly four hours and left him in sore need of good news; Mrs Greaves' supposed identification of a man she had spotted at about eleven o'clock on the night of the murder – he had been coming out of the Muirs' garden gate and was not, she insisted, David Muir ('such a nice man') – seemed to be a gift from heaven.

'Okay, Wright. First of all, is she sane?' This slightly odd enquiry emanated from a rather awkward incident some eight months before in which Homer's entire case had collapsed when counsel for the defence had demonstrated with frightening facility that the main witness for the prosecution believed that the traffic lights were sending him coded signals from the 'The Great Green Bazoomah'. This no doubt interesting individual evidently resided on Mars and wanted to assassinate Elvis Presley, currently living (heavily disguised) in Chippenham, Wiltshire. The judge had noted all these details with great attention.

'She appears to be, sir.'

Homer stared hard at Wright and decided that he would assess Mrs Greaves' marble quota himself. 'Not registered blind? Not wearing a monocle and an eye-patch?'

Wright shook his head more confidently in answer to these queries. A groaning noise, quite strikingly deep and prolonged, escaped from his unbreakfasted interior.

'And she states categorically that she had a good look at this individual?'

'That's what she says, sir.'

Homer sat back in his chair to consider matters while before his desk Wright waited. After a while Homer asked, 'Anything of interest been found in Pendred's house?'

'Nothing, sir.'

Homer sweetened his disappointment by reflecting, 'Well, we never did have much luck with forensics in this case.' The Chief Inspector indulged in more contemplation while Wright's mind wandered stomachwards. He wondered what his chances were of filling the void and sadly decided that they were not good. Abruptly Homer sat upright, looked at his watch and said, 'Okay. Mr Pendred's stewed long enough. Get his solicitor along and I'll have another crack at him. Then I want you to arrange an ID parade for Mrs Greaves. Make it for four o'clock.'

Wright felt compelled to ask, 'Shall I get his solicitor in?'

'Of course. I want this done by the book, Sergeant.'

'Yes, sir.' As he saw lunch following breakfast out of the room, Wright could not prevent a certain sadness – completely missed by Homer – creeping into his words.

By the early afternoon of his second day in his new job, Eisenmenger was beginning to gain some sense of the space in which he was required to fit, the geometry of its angles, the tensions within the confining threads, the colours of the nuances within its walls. It gave him a feeling of confidence, but it also showed him that the Department of Histopathology at the Western Royal was a far from happy place. Not that he was greatly surprised by this. Most histopathology departments held tensions and antagonisms because most histopathologists were not only smart but also egotistical; the greater the number that were forced to work together, the stronger became the forces at work between them. It wasn't quite particle physics, but there were similarities.

Moreover, if such was the case in departments within district general hospitals, it was an order of magnitude worse in academic departments for a reason that Eisenmenger had never quite managed to identify. No, the situation at the Western Royal Infirmary did not come as much of a surprise.

The morning had consisted of supervising one of the four specialist registrars while he did the day's surgical cut-up – not a particularly onerous task since the registrar was in his fourth year and therefore quite experienced – after which Eisenmenger had spent a tedious hour checking slides and reports for the breast multidisciplinary team meeting. The meeting itself occupied a further and even more tedious two hours over lunch, the only relief being the provision of sandwiches, fruit and coffee. Now he and the registrar had just finished checking slides from the previous day's cut-up, ensuring that the reports that went out were factually accurate and grammatically correct.

As the registrar departed Amr Shaheen came in, bearing a tray of slides.

Shaheen was a small, dapper man with curly, close-cropped black hair, tiny (not to say minute) moustaches and fine, delicate fingers. His dark brown eyes were constantly flicking from side to side, as if he lived in fear of attack, but beyond this he exuded a sense of great dignity and even greater superiority; that he was barely thirty-five and had only just been appointed as a consultant meant that he consequently came across to Eisenmenger as a pretentious prat.

'I was wondering if I could have your opinion on this case, Dr Eisenmenger.'

'John, please.'

Shaheen acknowledged this concession to informality with a nod of the head that was perversely formal. Then he said, 'A sixty-five-year-old woman. An ovarian tumour.'

Eisenmenger took the proffered slide tray and put the first slide on the microscope stage while Shaheen stood somewhat stiffly by the door. For the next five or six minutes, there was silence as Eisenmenger went through the slides, fourteen in all. At last he looked up at Shaheen. 'It looks like a granulosa cell tumour to me, although the mitotic rate's worryingly high in one or two places.'

Shaheen nodded again, this time more enthusiastically. 'That is what I thought. Possibly it will behave aggressively.'

The behaviour of granulosa cell tumours was notoriously difficult to predict from their microscopic appearances. 'Perhaps,' he agreed cautiously. 'Why don't you show it to Dr Ludwig?' Although all consultants looked at and reported all types of cases, each of them also had a specialist interest; Ludwig's was gynaecological pathology, von Guerke's was gastro-intestinal, Milroy's was skin and lymphoid, Shaheen's was urological and Victoria Bence-Jones' (and therefore now Eisenmenger's) was breast. This subspecialization meant that there was a reservoir of expertise within the department for most cases.

Shaheen's reply – a rather vague 'Of course' – intrigued Eisenmenger, but he said nothing more. Shaheen left then and Eisenmenger wondered why the message had been so at odds with the words. Presumably another tension within the department that he had yet to categorize.

At five thirty he rang Helena to suggest that he would make dinner. 'I doubt I'm going to get away until late,' she warned.

'Martin Pendred?'

'Interesting developments. They've found a neighbour who claims to have seen someone coming out of the Muirs' garden late on the night of the murder. Trouble is, when they put Martin Pendred into an identity parade, she failed to spot him. To make matters worse for them, he seems to have an alibi, although it's far from unbreakable.'

'What alibi is that?'

'He was seen drinking at his local pub at least until nine o'clock. That makes it improbable he could have intercepted Jenny Muir getting off her bus, not unless he hitched a lift or something.'

'Oh, dear.'

'I'm trying to pressurize Homer to let him go, but he's resisting at the moment.'

Dinner alone, then. He was about to leave when Wilson Milroy came into his room. 'Heard the news?'

Eisenmenger confessed that no, he hadn't.

'They've arrested Pendred for the murder of that woman.'

Eisenmenger didn't bother to explain his peripheral involvement and was more intrigued as to why it should matter at all to Milroy. He asked, 'Is that of significance to us?'

'Not directly, no. But it's bad publicity for the hospital. They get enough from the way they treat the patients without the staff going around slaughtering the local population.'

'He works here? Still?' Eisenmenger remembered that the Pendreds had been the mortuary technicians at the Western Royal when the murders had started before, but he hadn't realized Martin Pendred was still working there.

'Not as a mortuary technician.' Milroy made a face, adding, 'Thank God. He and his brother always gave me the creeps. I wasn't in the least surprised when they were pulled in for ripping people to bits. No, he was working as a general porter. I used to see him around the hospital quite regularly; never acknowledged me, of course, even though we worked together for years. No, just looked straight through me.'

Something small and almost unnoticed flicked gently inside Eisenmenger's head as he digested this news, but then he lost it and said merely, 'I see.'

Milroy asked then, 'Going to the lecture?'

Eisenmenger, not knowing that there was a lecture to which he could go, raised his eyebrows.

'There's one every Tuesday in term time. It's open to the whole medical school – held in the main lecture theatre. Usually bloody boring, but Piringer expects the juniors to attend and it looks good if we go. Must get some brownie points from our Beloved Leader.' He pronounced the last two words with a brightly glowing dose of sarcasm. 'It's on something about genes, of course. Bloody things. Never understood 'em and never will. Wish they'd never been invented, myself.'

Having now nothing better to do, Eisenmenger assented to go, although he could not, in truth, persuade himself that it was because of the company. Was there no one in the department who had managed to retain a vestige of decency within their personality? Eisenmenger tidied his desk, then they stepped out into the main corridor running through the Histopathology Department.

The Western Royal Infirmary had grown over two hundred years within the confines of the city centre. This had meant that most of its expansion had been by the acquisition of surrounding buildings, the consequence of which was that busy roads and thoroughfares now separated all the major departments; a site redevelopment was planned but had been held up in a planning enquiry for two years.

The fabric of the building through which they were walking was either decaying or decayed. Once it had been a large lingerie store – one of a chain of sixteen supplying camisoles, corsets and (in a discreet subdepartment) incontinence pants to the better-off women of the thirties, forties and fifties. Its conversion into pathology laboratories had been fifty years before; not enough (in fact hardly anything) had been spent on maintenance during those five decades and, with the prospect of demolition and starting again so tantalizingly close, no manager was going to start now. Thus the paint was either faded or peeling or both, there was a curiously stifling odour of damp, the linoleum was pocked with holes and fraying rips, and the lighting was so feeble that all work within the building, no matter how hi-tech, was conducted in a curious, sepia-tinged twilight, a crepuscular, aged world that begged for nostalgia, demanded muted respect.

Milroy seemed somehow to belong to this place, this time past. He was clearly close to retirement, both because of his looks and his attitude. Eisenmenger had seen a similar picture before – weariness, world-weariness and worldliness summed together into a kind of faded hauteur, an arrogance because he thought that having done the job for forty-odd years, he seen it all and therefore knew it all.

Trouble was, medicine knew more, and had a habit of proving it.

Still, Milroy seemed to be one of those people who like talking (or are at least afraid to stop talking) and Eisenmenger had a strong suspicion that this verbosity would not be limited by personal loyalties when it came to extending the subject matter to include his colleagues. They had gone less than ten metres from Eisenmenger's office when Milroy asked, 'And what do you think of our happy family?'

Eisenmenger, guessing that this was no more than an oblique way for Milroy to spread some poison about his colleagues, said helpfully, 'I get the impression that there are some real characters amongst them.'

Milroy's laugh was an unpleasant braying sound, a trumpet of vindictiveness and dark knowledge. 'You could say that,' he remarked in a tone that didn't so much suggest as broadcast.

Eisenmenger held the door open for him, then said, 'Professor Piringer seems to be very competent.' He said this with a hint of innocence, shrewdly judging that Milroy was the kind of man who would always have the last word, the trumping card.

'Yes,' he agreed, but then spoiled it by continuing, '*Seems* to be.'

Eisenmenger spotted a couple of the registrars up ahead of them. They were waiting for the ancient lift to clack and clank its arthritic way up to the top floor where Histopathology was located. He didn't respond to Milroy's insinuation but then he wasn't required to. As they turned right to go down the stairs, Milroy remarked, 'The trouble is that there just aren't enough people of the right standard these days. It's symptomatic of the state of histopathology in this country.'

Eisenmenger said mildly, 'But I thought Adam Piringer was held in quite high esteem.'

Milroy smiled. 'Yes, I suppose he is,' he admitted, but it was merely a tactical ploy for he carried on at once, 'but look at what he's being compared with! Academic histopathology has been in decline for decades now. Not only is the money better in the district general hospitals, but they're usually located in far nicer and cheaper places. No wonder we can't recruit decent people into them.' He snorted and Eisenmenger reflected that here was a speech well rehearsed. 'There are no world-famous pathologists left in this country, so we're making inexperienced and frankly second-rate people into professors.'

'But Adam Piringer published some quite highly regarded stuff on early colo-rectal cancer, didn't he? He identified some of the genetic changes that may be of use in diagnosis and screening.'

Milroy sighed, clearly amazed at Eisenmenger's naivety. 'His name was on the papers, but just because he was in the right place at the right time does not make him a candidate for the Nobel Prize. Anyway, what's he done since?'

It was a fair question and one that Eisenmenger could not answer.

'Precisely. Nothing.'

They had reached the ground floor and Milroy led them out through a side door on to the street. The rush hour traffic was heavy and loud and fumed. They crossed between stationary cars and then walked down a narrow alleyway to emerge on a broad straight thoroughfare where Milroy turned right.

'I managed to get a sneak look at his CV when he applied for the job here,' he confided to Eisenmenger. 'Strictly unofficial – it so happens that I know the Medical Director – but it was quite revealing.'

'How so?'

They were now entering a large and imposing building with twin revolving doors, made of brass and wood, set into a pillared portico. This was the main part of the medical school.

Milroy dropped his voice and leaned towards Eisenmenger as he spoke. 'He's published only thirty-one original articles. A few book chapters and suchlike, but of the proper research, hardly anything.'

'Really?'

Milroy nodded; his whole demeanour was now one of a man who kept sanity to himself with a firm clutch while the world tried desperately to pluck it from him. 'I mean, I've got nearly seventy. I expect even you have more than thirty.'

Eisenmenger murmured only, 'Possibly,' observing that Milroy seemed entirely oblivious that he had just fired off an insult.

Milroy had guided them through the main foyer (a porters' lodge, one hundred and one noticeboards, sundry discarded medical students and an unwholesome amount of gloom) then on to the main lecture theatre. This was large, capable of holding perhaps three hundred, and semicircular; it was steeply banked and lit by a single large cluster of bulbs, each in an opaque spherical shade, that hung from the high ceiling by a brass rod. It was rapidly filling up with people of various ages, clothing styles and degrees of dignity, a typical audience of senior medics, junior medics, students and researchers.

They sat at the back, high up and almost level with the lighting, but the view was good because the tiering was so steep. In front of a large projection screen at the centre of the theatre a middle-aged man in jeans and T-shirt too young for him was fiddling with a laptop. On the screen behind him the software was doing its thing. Eisenmenger recognized Piringer far below at the front; he looked totally at ease as he chatted with his neighbours who were presumably also citizens of professorial note. Occasionally Piringer would glance around behind him as if checking that his wish that other members of Histopathology should attend had been obeyed.

'Look at him,' said Milroy, his voice suddenly filled with loathing. Eisenmenger had the suspicion that he didn't realize he was voicing his thoughts. 'Cocky young bastard. What gives him the right . . . ?'

He stopped abruptly, aware that Eisenmenger was looking at him. For a moment he looked almost confused, then he smiled, his wide, thick-lipped mouth crowding creases on to his cheeks. 'Forgive me. I have an ulcer and sometimes it makes me rather ill-tempered.'

It was then that the Professor of Medicine, who was hosting the meeting, tapped gently upon the microphone to begin proceedings.

'You'll have to release him.'

Had Superintendent Call suggested Homer should paint himself purple and insert his head in a condom, the Chief Inspector could not have affected more surprise. 'Release him?' he said, the words venturing into querulousness.

'That's right.' Call knew Homer's histrionics well and had adopted his customary antagonistic pose.

'But he did it.' This confident assertion rang a somewhat forlorn note.

Call frowned and Wright, who was in a corner of Homer's office and wishing that he were better camouflaged, noted just how unpleasant Call could make his face. There was a definite resemblance to a gargoyle, he decided.

'Don't be a prat till the day you die, Homer,' suggested Call tiredly. 'It doesn't matter diddly-squat whether or not he did it. You haven't got the evidence to hold him. You have a witness who can't identify him – in fact who said it definitely wasn't him in the presence of the defence solicitor – you have no forensic evidence to link him to the crime, and he has an alibi . . .'

Homer was almost trembling, as if frustration, like caffeine, were giving him palpitations. 'It's hardly an alibi,' he interrupted. 'No one can say with certainty that he was in the pub past nine, and the pub's only a couple of miles from the Muirs' house. He might just have made it.'

'How? By putting on his jet-pack?'

Unwisely, Homer persisted. 'He could have run all the way.'

The gargoyle, somewhat against the odds, became even uglier. He breathed heavily and gave the distinct impression that deep within him dark and drear forces were at work. Then, after several seconds he swung round and his facial gruesomeness fell upon Wright who, if he didn't actually squeak, made a sort of gulping sound.

'What do you think, Wright?' This was posed in a tone that incongruously mixed the silky with the hectoring. 'Do you think we've got enough to charge Pendred with murder? Or should we let him go?'

It was one of those occasions that came too frequently in Wright's life; in fact, existence seemed to Wright to consist of a series of such occasions, separated by all-too-brief moments of boredom. Enjoyment had seeped away some decades before, probably at about the time of puberty. He hesitated, knowing that whatever he said would upset one of them to a greater or lesser degree. He excavated for the small reserves of diplomacy with which God had endowed him. 'I can't see that the CPS are going to consider our case strong enough at the moment, sir,' he began, addressing Call but aware that behind the gruesome countenance the figure of Homer was listening with interest. 'But, like the Chief Inspector, I'm sure that Pendred did it.' The figure relaxed and Wright began to congratulate himself on a nifty bit of footwork.

'So what do you suggest?'

This question, in a similar but somewhat softer and therefore more sinister tone, was most unwelcome to Wright. It caused him to stare fearfully at the Chief Superintendent, his nervous system temporarily paralysed. 'Well,' he began, knowing not where he was going, 'we could be releasing a depraved monster . . .' This last was for Homer's benefit, although he could detect no sign that it was appreciated.

Call nodded slowly. 'So?' he enquired.

Another pause. 'So . . . perhaps we should release him but only under strict, constant surveillance . . . ?'

Call ignored the hint of question, breathed out, straightened, and turned back to Homer, temporarily coming between the Chief Inspector and his Sergeant. 'See, Homer? Some initiative. I'm glad someone around here has got some. Why didn't you think of that? Turn a setback into an opportunity. That's the kind of thinking we need in the modern police force.'

He walked to the door and, like the ending of a solar eclipse, the shining light of Homer's incandescent anger was turned full upon the miserable Sergeant.

From the doorway, Call instructed, 'Now kindly arrange it, Homer. At once. Understand?'

Homer nodded, but his eyes never once left Wright who wearily wondered how and why he inevitably ended up in the shit.

Pendred emerged from the depths of the police station, passing through the heavy steel door with its clunky combination lock and its lower half that was scuffed and dented. In doing so he traversed a barrier between guilt and innocence, between an unreal nether region and the boring, predictable world of normality. And yet Helena noticed that even this momentous transition left Pendred unaffected; most people she had known in such a situation expressed something of relief, or exhaustion, or shock, but not Pendred, not this large, taciturn, imperturbable man. As if robotic or perhaps disengaged to an extreme, he passed through all experience, all emotion and noticed not one whit.

He might not even have noticed Helena had she not stepped forward and said, 'Mr Pendred?'

The gaze – always so serene and distant, and yet so correspondingly chilling – passed from its usual hidden realm to Helena's features. Nothing on his face or in his eyes altered but something about the fixity of his attention told her that he recognized her.

'Do you understand what's happening to you, Mr Pendred?'

He continued to stare and she thought that she would have to go through the usual useless reiteration, but then he nodded slightly. His eyes did not move from her face but he said in a low monotone, 'They released me.'

'That's right. You're on bail, but they are letting you go. There are certain conditions . . .'

'They say I killed her.'

She was aware that the Desk Sergeant was listening with unconcealed amusement. 'I know they do, Mr Pendred, but you've got an alibi.'

'Like the last time. They said it was Melkior.'

'I know, but you must . . .'

'They took Melkior. They'll take me.'

She shook her head, stretching her face into a reassuring smile. 'No. No, they won't. I'll make sure of that.'

'I didn't do it.'

'I know.'

'I didn't do it. I didn't do it. I didn't do it . . .'

And try as she might, she couldn't interrupt this pentasyllabic tongue-twister, uttered with the eyes fixed upon her face. She looked across to the Desk Sergeant, a mute appeal, and he raised his eyebrows in teasing query before sighing and reaching over the counter and tapping Pendred hard on the shoulder. 'Okay, Polly Parrot. You've made your point.'

Pendred stopped. Anyone else might have taken exception to being treated thus, but not this strange man. For a few seconds he was silent, then eyes still fastened on Helena, his large, hard-skinned hands suddenly reached out and grabbed her left hand, enveloping it, smothering and losing it. For an instant she thought that he was going to assault her, but was even more surprised when with surprising gentleness he brought it up to his lips and kissed it tenderly.

But all the time, his eyes stared at her from a face that assumed no expression.

When at last she was released and could take her leave, she did not see Pendred go to the window of the police station and look out as she walked away through the car park and then along the busy street.

He left the building almost at once.

'Can I have a quick word, Peter?'

He was on his way out, but he was not about to upset the Head of Chambers with appointments to the judiciary pending and influence to be gained or lost by a careless word, the wrong remark, an unintended slight. 'Of course, Benedict.'

He followed the old man into his office, the largest in the building. Seated with a small glass of a rather nice vintage port (Benedict's favourite tipple), Peter waited and wondered, watching the completely bald pate in front of him reflecting the evening light.

'I've been meaning to have a chat.'

Such chats were the foundations of many a legal career, Peter reflected. It was with cosy assurance that he sipped his drink, complimented Benedict on its quality, and asked, 'What do you want to talk about?'

'I'm led to understand that you are . . . seeing someone by the name of Wharton. Beverley Wharton.'

Caught by surprise to such an extent that he was temporarily and quite unusually speechless, Peter took a while to react. 'What?'

'She is a police officer, I believe.'

Peter frowned. Suddenly the port wasn't quite so good. 'Where is this leading?' He knew Benedict – knew that he was a bastard – and so wasn't surprised that his Head of Chambers didn't seem in the least embarrassed to say, 'She's not good enough for you. Drop her.'

Peter Anderson had been a barrister for a long time. Such views were, he knew, far from dead in the higher echelons of the Bar. He sighed. 'Thanks, Benedict, but I think that I can look after my own affairs.'

He stood to go but Benedict barked, 'Sit down!'

Somewhat shocked, he complied, a puzzled look his only sign of consternation. Benedict said more gently, 'This isn't snobbery, Peter. This is a question of your preservation.'

'Really?'

Benedict leaned forward conspiratorially. 'I have no idea about her intellect, her breeding, her habits. I have no idea and I have no wish to find out. However, I do know that she has already been involved in one unfortunate 'incident' involving a miscarriage of justice . . .'

'She told me all about that.'

'. . . and another is unfolding as we speak.'

'The Pendred case? Is that what this is about?'

Benedict nodded. 'The word coming from the more senior ranks of the police is that Martin Pendred is guilty and that she was instrumental in the miscarriage of justice that resulted in the wrongful imprisonment – and death, I may remind you – of his twin brother.' He fingered his glass. 'I don't want you to be connected with the publicity that will inevitably follow; indeed, that is already starting to arise.' A slight smile as he said, 'Not with candidates for higher office being sought by the Lord Chancellor's Office.'

Peter Anderson smiled back, but it was born largely of cynicism. 'Supposing she was right? Supposing Melkior Pendred was guilty?'

Benedict shook his head. 'I really don't think that's very likely, do you?'

He was forced to concede that it wasn't and he had, in truth, been slightly anxious about the fall-out from the latest killings. He said, 'But I love Beverley.'

Benedict's smile widened. 'Of course you do, Peter. Of course you do.' He drained his glass. 'But that's not enough, is it?'

'What can I do for you, Helena?'

Helena rarely visited her general practitioner. She told herself that this was because she was rarely ill – and there was more than a little truth in this – but it was also because she hated the necessary surrender of privacy that medical intervention in her life entailed. Not least of her dislikes was what she saw as the astonishingly impertinent presumption that someone – even a medical professional – had the right to use her first name, as if they were childhood friends, often given to partying together. This young woman (probably two or three years younger than Helena) was no more than a vague acquaintance, a name and a face without further distinguishing detail.

For a moment Helena found the embarrassment of the circumstances almost unconquerable. Then she said as simply and unselfconsciously as she could, 'I've found a lump.'

Dr Carolyne Ackermann had large, sympathetic eyes set in a face that somehow took youth and turned it from callowness to enthusiastic assuredness. Something about Dr Ackermann told her patients that her lack of years meant only that she could shoulder their diseases with impunity, and that because she was obviously fresh out of training, she knew all the latest treatments.

'A breast lump?'

Helena nodded.

A note was made on a small sheet of blue-lined paper, one of several held together by a green tag. To Helena's eye, they had always looked so inadequate to hold her entire medical life with safety.

'Which side?'

'Left.'

'When did you notice it?'

'Just a couple of days ago.'

'Any discharge from the nipple?'

Helena shook her head as she said, 'No, nothing.'

'Is it painful or tender?'

Another negative.

Dr Ackermann had been too busy writing to look at the patient while this was going on. Only now did she look up again. On her face was a look not quite of compassion, more of care, as if she were aware that she needed to tread softly. 'Any other lumps or bumps?'

'No. I don't think so, at least.'

'Nothing under the arm? Is the other breast okay?'

Helena's nods seemed to allow Dr Ackermann some relief. 'Good,' she said. She resumed writing, then paused and began to look back through the notes. Helena felt her life being read by eyes that were essentially a stranger's. Then, 'You're on the pill.'

Unsure if that was a question but assuming that it wasn't, Helena said nothing.

'Are your periods regular?'

'Usually.'

'Lost any weight recently?'

'Unfortunately, no.' The good Dr Ackermann allowed her lips the freedom of a minuscule twitch accompanied by the faintest and shortest of faraway laughs at this joke she had heard so many times before. If Helena had felt herself relaxing into the consultation, the process terminated then.

'No new aches or pains?'

Helena merely shook her head.

When this last answer had been translated and transcribed, Dr Ackermann looked up, smiled a broad smile beneath blue eyes and said, 'I'd better have a look at you.'

She rose from the desk in front of her, went to Helena's right where there was an examination couch and a small stainless steel trolley which she then drew a curtain around. She held the curtain aside for Helena to enter this pseudo-private space, saying in a professional, almost bored voice, 'If you could take off your blouse and bra, then just sit on the side of the couch.'

Helena closed off mental shutters as she complied with this command, following contradictory thoughts of subservience and rebellion, chasing away her fears. She was astute enough to follow the reasoning behind most of the questions and could draw some relief from her negative answers, but the fact remained that both she and Dr Ackermann were wondering if this was a cancerous lump.

From the opposite side of the light-green curtain, in the real and unfettered world where once Helena had not worried about dying from cancer, came Dr Ackermann's educated voice. Shorn of a face, it sounded worryingly immature. 'You haven't been attending for your cervical smears.'

Helena said nothing, might not even have heard from the lack of physical response.

'Perhaps we could take this opportunity.' This was phrased not as a question but as something more than a suggestion. Helena's face phrased distaste. Her intense need for privacy did not sit well with the intimate acts necessary to obtain a cervical smear.

The curtain was drawn aside and Dr Ackermann appeared. She wore a smile that seemed to Helena to be as plastic as the curtains the general practitioner now stood before. 'Ready?'

Helena found the examination less intolerable than expected, much as she might have found amputation of one finger preferable to amputation of two. It commenced with a scrutiny of her breasts and this, somewhat unexpectedly, she found the worst part of it. There was a sense almost of voyeurism and exhibitionism in this tableau, with the general practitioner standing before her, now not smiling but frowning, while Helena sat as commanded before her – first with back straight, hands on hips, chin up, but then with arms held straight up, as if grasping for the ceiling.

The next stage was an examination of her right breast, causing Helena to begin, 'But – '

Dr Ackermann said at once, 'I need to examine them both. Find out if there is any asymmetry.' Clearly she was well used to this reaction.

The examination was done using only the fingertips of both hands, and again it was done with Helena adopting two poses at the doctor's request. It was as asexual as it was possible to be; at no time did their eyes meet or a sound pass between them. A light examination of the armpit sated the doctor's curiosity for the right breast.

There then followed a repeat of this sequence for the left breast, but this time there was the lump, and it was when Dr Ackermann met this that she betrayed the first sign of interest, her hands (previously moving smoothly and almost autonomously) coming to a halt, like foxhounds catching a scent. On her face passed the briefest and weakest of frowns, but one that Helena, watching from eyes that had not left the doctor's face, did not miss.

The lump was in the upper, outer part of Helena's breast. She had been unable to leave it alone since then, her fingers finding it whenever they were given the chance, whenever her guise of reassured unconcern was weakest and most ragged. She had felt it again that morning as she had dressed, once again fighting the fearful suspicion that it was just that tiny bit bigger than it had been the last time.

Dr Ackermann played it with it interminably. Squeezing it gently, rolling the skin over it, pushing it this way and that. *What did she think it was – a marble?* Eventually she seemed to tire of this game and progressed through the remainder of the investigation with relative speed.

'There,' she said, the smile back, no more genuine in Helena's eyes. 'You can put your stuff back on now.'

Helena began to comply without voicing the question that was screaming in her head. Then Dr Ackermann said, 'It's a good opportunity to take a smear . . . ?'

Helena hesitated, wanting not to have to do this thing, knowing that she should. She thought of what John would say if he knew that she was refusing this potentially life-saving test.

She sighed. 'I suppose so.'

'They've lost him, sir.'

It was such a simple concept, yet it appeared that Homer could not grasp it, for he said first, 'What?' then, 'What?' and finally, after a perfectly judged pause, 'What?' The tone rose in perfect harmonic intervals, and became synchronously louder.

'They've lost him,' repeated Wright. Then helpfully and, as it turned out, unwisely he added, 'Pendred.'

Homer exploded, an incandescence to outshine a supernova. 'I know who you mean, you idiot!' he screamed. Wright, who had had the phone wedged between his ear and his shoulder, winced, jerked his head away from the verbal assault that it had been dealt, and thus dropped the receiver. He therefore missed the start of Homer's follow-up to this overture, a dramatic piece that began its main theme with a sustained crescendo but unfortunately never really developed a secondary, quieter theme so that it lacked contrast.

In short, Wright was given a right royal bollocking, which he rather resented, given that he had not been in any way connected with the surveillance team that had done the losing. The sense of injustice was increased by his presence at work at nearly nine o'clock in the evening, while Homer had been at home for three hours.

'I've got everyone available out looking for him.'

'So I should bloody well hope.' A rather grumpy acknowledgement, then a pause before Homer began again. 'How the hell did you manage to lose him, Wright? He's not exactly small, is he? He's not exactly inconspicuous.'

I didn't lose him. Someone else did.

But when he began with the words, 'It was while Cooley and Neumann were on duty . . .' Homer interrupted at once with, 'It's no good passing the buck, Sergeant. You were in charge of the surveillance operation.'

Was he? Wright could not recall having been specifically allocated the responsibility. True, he had organized the rotas, but Homer had okayed the arrangements.

But before he could argue the point, Homer had moved on. 'Where did you lose him?'

'At the Bell, sir. He must have slipped out the back, or something . . .'

But Homer had found more cause for remonstration. 'I don't believe it! You're not telling me they just sat out the front and waited, are you? Even PC bloody Plod in Toytown could organize a surveillance operation better!'

'Yes, sir . . .'

'Have you checked his house? The hospital? Other pubs in the neighbourhood?'

'Yes, sir.'

'And?'

'Not a peep.'

Homer breathed the way a bull with inflamed testicles might breathe when it sees something to charge at. 'I see.' Wright heard the implication and could only console himself with the memory of hearing it a thousand or more times before.

Homer's next words came from the phone in an almost ghostly, ethereal manner. 'Do you realize what Superintendent Call is going to say when he hears this news?' It was much as a damned soul might ask the question.

Wright found it difficult to pitch his voice right. 'I think I can, sir.'

Homer's only response was a simple, 'Yes.' This single syllable was hissed and low, telling of extreme anger and

93

extreme foreboding. Then he added in a forlorn tone, 'God knows what he'll say if there's another murder now.'

Wilms had heard of Martin Pendred's arrest with neither surprise nor sorrow. It had always been his opinion that the Pendred twins were inseparable both by looks and temperament, and that if one of them was a killer, then the other was too, much as there were some bitches that littered dogs that were just plain mean. When Wilms had been retired from the army he had landed a job in a security company and in that profession he had come to learn a lot about mean dogs; not the ones that you could train and use, but the ones you couldn't. The ones that were just so mean and vicious and beyond human control that there was only one fate to be given to them. That was how he thought of the Pendred boys.

Patrick Wilms was not a religious man, but he did believe in evil, in punishment, in fighting for goodness; he believed that there were some who were agents of malfeasance and darkness, and in the Pendreds he believed that he had seen something akin to the incarnation of this darkness. He had been too young to fight the Nazis but he had seen and fought plenty who were just as bad, merely dressed in different skins and speaking in different languages. He wasn't surprised to discover members of the species in his neighbourhood.

Nor was he surprised that no one but he recognized the danger. Over the years he had written a regular series of letters to a variety of authorities about the Pendreds, all ignored (as, indeed, were all his other letters, written on a rich and diverse collection of topics); even the arrest and trial of Melkior had not brought forth recognition of his attempts to warn society before tragedy occurred.

But even if this deliberate slight on the part of the powers-that-be was what he had come to expect, he still felt resentment at his treatment. Sometimes it seemed to him that scum like the Pendreds got a better deal than he did. The news of the release of Martin Pendred that evening only confirmed his opinion that there was not a single aspect of the Establishment that was not corrupt, or incompetent, or both.

He spent the day composing a literary expression of his opinion upon this latest instance of police stupidity, sitting at his dining-room table in the front room that looked out directly on to the street, and that had photographs of his comrades on the walls and a ticking clock that had been his mother's favourite because she had received it for long service to the local train company. The rumble of traffic was ever present now – not like when he had first moved in – and it made it difficult for him to concentrate. Because of this he did not finish it that day. Evening had come and he was aware of the pains of hunger in his belly, so he decided that its completion would wait until tomorrow.

It was Tuesday and therefore a good day for fish and chips, a meal that he always looked forward to. One of the few, these days. His appetite had dwindled with the girth of his legs and as his teeth had grown longer. He now rarely ate more than bread and jam for breakfast and frequently nothing at all for lunch. Only in the evening did he make the effort, and this was done according to a strict rota, a habit that clung to him tenaciously from his army days. If the day was good, however then it would be fish and chips – and not just any fish, but always haddock. Preceded by a couple of pints of Guinness.

He put on the brown mac that he always wore, that he had worn for over forty years. It did not occur to him to change it for another, nor did it occur to him that for many people in the streets around it helped to define him as he trudged along the pavement, his angular frame bent habitually forward, his gait rapid, his nose and chin leading.

He slipped out through the front door, unaware that he was being observed by two police officers sitting in a dark green saloon parked fifty metres down the street, almost exactly halfway between two streetlights. He marched off towards the centre of town, purposeful as ever.

Helena tried to feel unmolested and unviolated as she sat again before the desk and waited while Dr Ackermann wrote and wrote and, it seemed to Helena, wrote; she did not entirely succeed, but she could not dwell on this because of the crescending anxiety about what was coming next. Then the writing stopped and, for Helena worse than anything, there was a pause before the head came up and she could look at the countenance and try to gauge what the news would be.

She did not think that it was good.

'I think it would be wisest to refer you for an expert opinion.'
What does that mean? But, of course, she thought that she knew already.

'What do you think it is?'

Another pause in which whole medical texts were being written by Helena's imagination. 'I can't be sure . . .'

But?

'. . . but I am concerned by some of the features.'

Helena was not the kind of person to allow for blurring. 'Meaning?'

But there was no immediate answer. *How many more pauses must I endure?*

'It might be a small cancer.' And then, with a rush that contrasted sharply with her previous hesitancy, she rushed on, 'But, if it is, the signs are good. There's no sign that it's spread and it's relatively small.'

But it's cancer.

She knew that there were a million questions to be asked, but she could think of only one. 'So what happens now?'

'I'll fax the Western Royal. I know one of the breast surgeons there personally. I'll try and squeeze you in as soon as possible.'

'Tomorrow?' Helena heard the desperation in her voice and felt shame but it wasn't enough to overcome the fear.

She was denied complete satisfaction, however.

'I'll try the best I can.'

And as Helena left the surgery she could draw no comfort from the imminency of the truth of her diagnosis.

'John? John?'

The lecture had finished, and Eisenmenger and Milroy were making their way through the crowd as it left the theatre. From Eisenmenger's point of view it had not been a particularly enlightening talk – too full of gene microarray slides that consisted of chaotically arranged red, green and yellow dots which, by statistical sleight of hand, were forever being rearranged into larger, vaguer splodges of the same colours – but he felt at least that he had taken on board something of what had been said. He turned, as did Milroy beside him. Through the scrum of established and would-be academics came a familiar figure.

'Isaac! Good to see you!'

Isaac Bloomenthal, a good head taller than most of those around him, was easily seen. As he approached and shook hands with Eisenmenger, he said, 'And to see you, John.' He had a smile that lost something as he turned to Milroy. 'Wilson,' he said, the neutrality of the tone almost insulting.

Milroy returned the smile, a mirror image of conventional politeness. 'Isaac.'

Before anything could become too obvious, Bloomenthal turned back to Eisenmenger and continued, 'It's been three years, at least. What are you doing here?'

Eisenmenger's reply included not a trace of his interest in the exchange between Milroy and Bloomenthal. 'I've just started a locum in Histopathology.'

'Really? I'd heard they needed a locum, but I didn't realize they'd fooled you into accepting the poisoned draught.'

Bloomenthal flicked a look at Milroy, then back to Eisenmenger, who had the distinct impression he wasn't just missing something, he was missing a whole history. Milroy grimaced and said sharply, 'Your department's hardly a nest of singing birds.'

Before Bloomenthal could respond, Eisenmenger murmured, 'There are plenty of draughts in the department, but none is noticeably poisoned.'

Bloomenthal smiled at the pun, Milroy ignored it, but it at least had the effect of partially defusing the situation. Milroy said, 'Well, since you two clearly know each other and I've got to get home, I'll leave you to chat.'

He went at once, joining the by now thinning crowd moving past them.

'Got time for a drink?' asked Bloomenthal. Eisenmenger thought of the empty house awaiting him and said that yes, he did. 'Good.'

Bloomenthal led him on a short walk to a compact but apparently convivial pub in a small, narrow street just opposite the entrance to the medical school building. He ordered two pints of best bitter and took them to the small corner table where Eisenmenger had sat. The pub had a single, rather narrow bar room and was decorated with pictures of horses and horse races from the eighteenth and nineteenth centuries. The patrons seemed to be mostly medical students, nurses and other assorted medical personnel.

'Did I detect a certain frisson between you and Dr Milroy?'

Bloomenthal laughed. He had friendly, extensively creased eyes and a mouth that was large but not unpleasantly so. When he grinned he showed enough perfectly formed and symmetrical teeth to cause a small heart murmur in on-looking dental surgeons; there seemed to be no end to them, causing Eisenmenger to wonder if, somewhere near the back of his neck and the base of his skull, they met and shook enamelled hands.

'Well, you know as well as I do that there's always rivalry between a forensic and a diagnostic department.' Although closely linked, forensic pathology and diagnostic surgical pathology were entirely separate departments at the WRI, leading to a certain degree of generally benign competition.

'Really? Is that all it was?'

Again the laugh, this time not quite so loud or long or, indeed, amused. 'Maybe there's a bit more to it.' He sighed. 'It really isn't a happy department that you've ended up in, you know.'

Eisenmenger shrugged. 'I'm only there for a few months.'

Bloomenthal said only, 'Ah, yes. Poor Vicky.'

Eisenmenger had been about to have a drink, but the four words had been obviously so weighted with hidden implication it was a wonder they hadn't fallen into the ashtray in the middle of the table. 'What do you mean by that?'

Bloomenthal shrugged, taking a drink himself.

'Oh, come on, Isaac. You can't say things like that and expect them to be ignored.'

The barmaid dropped a glass. She was young and extremely attractive – probably a medical student or a nurse – and Eisenmenger wondered whether the landlord accepted the odd broken glass as a reasonable cost for maintaining a pleasant landscape.

'I don't *know* anything, John; no facts with which to build a case.'

Eisenmenger persisted. 'But . . . ?'

Bloomenthal leaned forward in a conspiratorial but theatrical manner. He didn't look around to make sure that no one was listening, but that was the only cliché missing. 'As I said, I don't know anything for certain, only rumours.'

'Tell me the rumours, then.'

'Well, for one thing, there have been an awful lot of Adverse Clinical Incidents of late.'

'Reporting errors? Made by Victoria?'

Bloomenthal shrugged. 'Who can say?' Before Eisenmenger could dismiss this as groundless, he went on, 'Then, there was some mysterious business between the Medical Director and Wilson Milroy.'

'What's that got to do with Victoria?'

Bloomenthal bobbed his head into his beer, rather like a ducking bird. 'My dear boy, don't you know? The Medical Director is Geoffrey Bence-Jones, her husband.'

'Oh, I see.'

'There's no love between Dr Milroy and the Medical Director, just as there is none between Dr Milroy and his professor.'

'Does he like anybody?'

Bloomenthal laughed. 'If he does, I've yet to meet them.' He drained his glass. 'As far as the good Professor Piringer is concerned, I can give you chapter and verse as to the origin of his peculiarly venomous attitude. He was up for the chair, you see. He was even told, I understand, that it was his for the taking. Unfortunately these were siren voices, whispering lies for whatever reason.'

The appointment of professors in a medical school was a notoriously deceitful process. Potential professors were courted unofficially, told that they could have whatever they wished, and that they were the favoured candidate, all simultaneously. In this way a good shortlist was guaranteed, thus enhancing the reputation of the medical school.

'He should have known better.'

Bloomenthal concurred. 'Well, of course he should, but he was desperate. He's been a reader now for fifteen years, and he's due to retire in two. I also understand that he's been stuck on a small number of Discretionary Points for over a decade. He wanted that appointment to boost his pension.'

Another familiar story. Discretionary Points were salary increments handed out by the Trust for achievement in management, research, audit and teaching – effectively performance-related enhancements that were pensionable.

'Piringer rather rubbed it in,' went on Bloomenthal, 'By overlooking Milroy when it came to Deputy Head of Department, and preferring Alison von Guerke. Ah, what joy, what joy. Another one?'

'I'll get them.'

When Eisenmenger returned, Bloomenthal said, 'And the fall-out from that particular debacle was Dr Milroy's pathological dislike of Amr Shaheen.'

'I did rather get the impression that there was a problem there. Why should Dr Shaheen have earned Milroy's displeasure?'

'He was Piringer's appointee. Practically followed along tied to his coat-tails.' Once more the conspiratorial style descended. 'There are rumours that their relationship is more than professional.' Bloomenthal waggled his eyebrows while showing his dental immaculacy.

'Is Piringer married?'

'My dear John, Adam Piringer is far too much in love with his image of himself to allow any single *individual* to have sole property rights.'

The barmaid was having trouble with the till which clearly hadn't succumbed to her beauteous charms and was refusing to open when she wanted it to.

'Of course Professor Piringer hasn't exactly gone out of his way to help matters.'

'Meaning?'

'Well, his personality hasn't helped, for a start. He came in with big ideas and didn't see why he had to listen to what the others thought.'

'So he's hurt their feelings? He wouldn't be the first newly appointed professor to forget to be polite to his new colleagues.'

Bloomenthal shrugged. His own professor had abraded a few egos when he had taken up his post. 'I don't pretend to know all the plots and treacheries that have gone on in that department, but you see now why I described it as a poisoned draught.'

'I don't suppose it's any worse than half the academic departments in the country.'

Bloomenthal merely showed an inordinately large number of incisors, canines and molars. Then he said, 'Enough of this particular rats' nest. You've heard, no doubt, about the murder of Jenny Muir.'

Everyone, it seemed, wanted to tell Eisenmenger either about Victoria's research prize or about the murder of Jenny Muir. 'I did hear something.'

'I've got the case.'

It was Eisenmenger's turn to smile. 'Ah.'

'You did the earlier murders, didn't you?'

'You know bloody well I did, Isaac.'

Bloomenthal sighed through his over-dental grin. 'It would appear, then, that Melkior didn't do them,' he announced provocatively.

Cautiously Eisenmenger said, 'So you're happy Martin Pendred's guilty?'

Waving an airy hand, Bloomenthal said, 'Oh, yes.'

'Identical technique?'

'Pretty much.' Bloomenthal couldn't resist more teasing. 'I seem to recall you were fairly certain it was Melkior.'

Which wasn't entirely true. Eisenmenger had proffered no opinion, other than to confirm that it could have been Melkior, just as it could have been his brother. He asked, 'What does "pretty much" mean?'

Bloomenthal grimaced and bobbed his head from side to side. 'There are some problems,' he said cautiously. Then, as if afraid that he was giving the impression that he wasn't toeing the party line, he added, 'But they're only minor ones.'

Neither for the first nor the last time, Eisenmenger found himself contemplating the question, *Why can't people be objective?*

'But you're convinced that the same hand did this one as did the first five?' he asked, as much for sport as for information.

Bloomenthal nodded at once, the good team player. 'Oh yes.'

Eisenmenger found himself intrigued. Things in pathology were rarely so well defined, so easily categorized. He asked, 'I don't suppose I could have a look, could I? For old times' sake?'

Bloomenthal considered. 'Well, I don't see why not. I'm sure Homer wouldn't mind. After all, the more minds that are brought to bear, the less likely it is that we'll miss anything.'

The mention of Homer's name brought feelings of cynicism to Eisenmenger. He recalled the officious little man, so certain of his cause, so antagonistic to those who doubted him. Bloomenthal went on, 'I'm stuck in court most of tomorrow – another bloody drug death – and then I've got reports to write. How about tomorrow evening? Say half six?'

'Fine. Have you got copies of my reports?'

'Of course.'

'Five thirty it is, then.'

They finished their drinks. The barmaid was in deep and presumably intimate conversation with a patron who, from the

101

evidence on show, had more tattooed than untattooed skin. They went out into the street just as two police cars sped past, lights flashing, sirens excruciating.

'Late for the pub,' murmured Bloomenthal.

'Or dying for a piss.'

They went their different ways into the neon darkness.

Wilms strode the darkened cemetery, a portion of deep fried fish and chips wrapped in newspaper swaddling beneath his right arm. There was a fresh wind blowing down the by-now-dark gravel path, one that he guessed heralded rain. Not that it mattered to him particularly, for he would be home in less than fifteen minutes.

The path was an effective shortcut between his house and the fish and chip shop, shaving ten minutes from the journey time. It was broad and lit by widely spaced neon lights that illumined only the first two rows of headstones and memorials, leaving the rest of the sepulchral audience in darkness. Many people found the path uninviting after nightfall, even with the lights, but not Wilms. He had moved down far more dangerous paths in his life, expected perhaps he might have to again; the well-lit gravel path through a burial ground was not for him something to fear, possessing as he did little in the way of imagination.

He passed the ruined chapel that was situated in the approximate centre of the cemetery. He knew it to be a favourite place of hooligans, a location for drug dealing and drug taking, for tramps sleeping away their alcohol and for those with nowhere else to go to have a quick but uncomfortable fuck. Indeed, he had written about it on more than one occasion, demanding that it should be demolished, that it was a sore and an insult to the dead. He expected one day to be laid to rest in the cemetery, and he had made it quite plain in his missive to the local council that he did not want the chapel still there when his time came.

Sadly, he was not to get his wish.

A torch shone through a gap in the boards on the windows where a rotting plank had been pulled away. Wilms saw it quite clearly as he drew level with the building. Then a giggle sounded, girlish and soft, but unmistakable.

Wilms did not hesitate. Through his well-ordered, angled but somewhat tram-lined mind suspicion set off and transmuted instantaneously and without obvious effort on his part into certainty. Phrases such as *Bloody disgusting, Little tart* and *Bet they're taking drugs* flicked easily through the well-worn paths of his obsessions.

He walked purposefully towards the chapel and saw at once the main door had been broken and that it was ajar. This only increased his outrage and decreased his caution. Without any consideration of personal danger, he pushed the door further open and stepped inside.

Instantly the torchlight vanished and he was forced to stop to allow his eyes to adapt. In the meantime he used the interval to call out, 'I know you're in here, and I know what you're up to.' He was pleased to hear that his voice betrayed no fear or hesitation.

Gradually the neon light that found entry through the half-open door and the various chinks in the boarded windows allowed him to see the interior. He saw pews, some tipped over, ranked across the chapel, in the main facing towards an altar table to his left. On the table was a large stone urn. Much of the periphery of the chapel was in complete darkness.

The giggle again, still soft but undoubtedly coming from the vicinity of the altar table, probably from behind it where there was quite a large well of darkness in front of an extensively broken stained glass window.

'I know where you are,' he boasted but, for the first time, he noticed that his voice was perhaps unnecessarily loud. 'Come out now.'

Nothing but a further giggle, almost a sigh. The voice that made it sounded very young but also very sly; Wilms thought for some reason of the sirens who had called sailors to their deaths.

'All right, then,' he announced, putting determination in the place of such stupid irrelevancies. One thing above all else he knew, he could not allow himself to turn around now for to do so would have forced a mirror to his life and his beliefs and his certainties, and perhaps found them decayed into mould. He stepped forward into the gloom, kicking as he did so a crushed drinks can. The noise was absurdly loud, as if he were listening to it through a hollow metal chamber, and it made him pause and listen and wonder.

Another giggle.

It was then that he began to wonder.

Is there something odd about that giggle?

He was already moving forward again, the question adding curiosity to bravado. A few long strides and he was at the altar table, just barely seen in the few shards of light that found their way into the chapel. He took a moment, but then he saw something next to the urn.

It was a black, rectangular box.

He reached out and dragged it forward just as the giggle came again, this time unmistakably from the box.

He had to lean forward, his face close to the box to see the details, but at last he discovered what it was.

A cassette tape player. One that was playing.

He frowned, and this was the last voluntary movement made by his muscles.

For then someone slit his throat from behind, the blade running first through both right jugular veins and the right external carotid artery, then the trachea (incising but not transecting the oesophagus), then out through the external carotid artery and the jugular veins on the left side.

He was lost in a dying maelstrom of torment, a gush of warm, glutinous fluid, and choking asphyxia as he drowned in his own blood.

Part Two

Dayne Sturge had genital warts but it wasn't about to stop him shagging Melanie 'I'm not a fucking bicycle' Day. Only penile amputation was going to prevent the latest stage in her seduction on that particular Tuesday night. He had been after Melanie for weeks, spurred on by the jeering insults of Rod, Dayne's rival in all things, but especially in the shagging league – an informal but highly competitive tournament between not only Dayne and Rod, but also four other young men who had the privilege of working for Hashimoto's Foundry. Rod, who had taken Melanie (he claimed from behind) on the top floor of the number thirty-six bus, had made it plain that he considered Dayne to be incapable of a similar victory. Dayne was thus determined to prove him wrong and to come home with proof of his success (which, according to custom, was the young lady's knickers).

He had planned his tactics with great care, plying Melanie with not only food (chicken and chips from the Royal Oak) but also drinks (Melanie liked Bacardi and Coke, but was given that night Bacardi, vodka and Coke). As far as Dayne was concerned, this combination had had a satisfactory effect, in that Melanie had lost the ability to walk in a straight line and the feeling in her lips.

'Where are we going?' she asked as they stepped out into the neon night; coincidentally they were passing the gates of Hashimoto's.

'For a walk.'

No one could deny that there was truth in these three words, but not enough to have filled a fairy's thimble. Melanie burped and found this unaccountably and hysterically amusing;

Dayne's smile was broad but for different reasons to those of his consort. They were holding hands and there was a fine drizzle in the air that had moistened the pavement and that made rings and rainbows around the streetlights.

'Where to?'

Dayne was tall and rangy, his Adam's apple almost pointed, his permanently grimed fingers long, his legs appearing absurdly delicate as they emerged from his trouser bottoms. He wasn't ugly (or so he considered, as he shaved in front of the small, chipped mirror on the bathroom cabinet) but his was not a conventional attractiveness, he had to admit. He was unaware that Rod (who had no doubts about his own handsomeness) described his face to others as *a fucking road accident*. Still, whatever the merits of his features, Dayne was well pleased with his success in the Hashimoto Shagging League, even if Rod was marginally ahead.

'I don't know,' he lied. He dropped her hand and put his arm around her shoulders.

'Well, it won't be much fun just walking around the streets,' she opined. They were approaching the gates to the cemetery and Dayne could not have asked for better timing.

'Okay, then, let's go in here,' he suggested.

Melanie cast him a quick, suspicious glance through the ethanol. 'In the cemetery?' she demanded. 'I hope you're not up to no good.'

It wasn't clear whether she fully followed the tortuous double negative as it emerged from her anaesthetized mouth. It was starting to become quite cold and this combined with the laciness of her blouse to produce an effect on her nipples that was proving quite magnetic for Dayne. Melanie was a well-endowed girl who adopted the 'less is more' strategy for dressing, but paradoxically preferred 'more is more' when it came to cosmetics, so that she tended to resemble a study in oils. Not that this bothered Dayne, who was planning to spend the minimum possible amount of time on anything above the shoulders or below the knees.

'I don't know what you mean.' The injured innocence was fairly well done through not infrequent practice, but he was not dealing with an ingénue in the tactical game of courting. Melanie gave him a long, adamantine stare and then said firmly, 'I'm not a fucking bicycle, you know.'

Dayne's heart exploded with joy. Certain well-informed sources had told him that Melanie's *I'm not a fucking bicycle, you know* speech inevitably heralded a willingness to engage in sexual congress. Neither Dayne nor his informant was interested in the psychology of this idiosyncrasy. They did not care to consider that she might have a problem with her behaviour, that it might be creating deep within her psyche conflicts between what her id commanded and her superego deplored.

No. Dayne was more interested in getting her legs apart and his 'pork truncheon' (as he so colourfully put it) inside her.

'Bloody hell, Mel,' he expostulated, the rhyming scheme neither planned nor appreciated. 'Of course you're not.'

Once again, there was something missing in the palate of colours used in his tones of innocence, and once again she cast him a look, but this time there was something less suspicious, more playful in it. 'That's all right then,' she sighed and they walked into the cemetery through the small door beside the large iron gates. He said softly, 'I really fancy you, you know.'

He squeezed her shoulder gently and she responded by moving closer to him, although she said nothing. He allowed his fingers gently to massage the side of her neck and she made a small sound of pleasure, while in the deeps of his mind Dayne crowed. Once again his information had proved accurate; Melanie found great ecstasy in the sensual manipulation of her neck. Even, his informants assured him, to the point of losing all control, if the manipulation were done skilfully enough.

Inside the cemetery the air seemed colder and the drizzle damper; it wasn't easy for Dayne to assess the nipple state of Melanie because she had pulled her coat together, but his imagination – in other matters so barren – supplied him with tumescent images. He hurried her along the wide gravel path, past the cemetery's uncomprehending sleepers, mouldering beneath their unnecessarily ornate marker stones. There were irregularly spaced lampposts along the way, tall and thin, beacons of metallic stoicism in the darkness of the cemetery that gave light on the heterogeneous population of tombstones in their vicinity.

'Where are we going?' she asked in a hoarse whisper that, in the silent night of their location, was far more penetrating than a normal tone would have been. There was a small chapel in the centre of the cemetery that had long ago fallen into disrepair; it was Dayne's intention to introduce Melanie to the delights of sexual congress on the altar that resided therein. Maybe, he fantasized (given Rod's information), he could persuade her to bend not only backwards, but also forwards.

'Don't know,' he said, his face a badly drawn picture of disingenuousness.

'We'll have to get out of this rain.'

It was certainly getting far heavier, for which Dayne was silently thanking his hazy idea of a Supreme Being. 'I think there's a place somewhere up here. On the left.' He hurried her forward and presently the chapel emerged from the moist darkness. It was very, very uninviting, offering as far as she could see little more than somewhere out of the now-rising breeze; she wasn't even convinced that it had an intact roof.

'Is that it?' she demanded.

What the bloody hell do you want? A fucking four star hotel?

'It'll be fine. It's dry.' Which by now neither of them was.

Again the suspicious glance, but he hurried her towards the building and she didn't resist. She seemed to have slipped into acceptance of events.

There was a lamppost directly opposite the chapel casting faint illumination. By its light the red paint of the door could just be seen to be irregularly blanched into artistic shades and fades from pink to crimson, and overlain with cracks and scratches. The colour reminded Dayne of his gran's house, for it had been painted a similar colour; Gran who had been his sanctuary when his mother was incoherent with drink and his father comatose with it. Gran, who had died of a growth in her belly, lying there on the sofa and crying in agony, while her loving cunt of a son felt sorry for himself in the Queen's Head two streets away.

'How do we get in?' Melanie's enquiry, couched in a curious partnership of relief and disappointment, brought him back to the task at hand. Brought him back to the wet as well. Melanie's enquiry was now as damp as her blouse, spurring her enthusiasm for the project.

'There's an open window round the back.'

She reacted at once to this rather quick reply. 'Is there now? Know your way around here, don't you?'

'I used to spend time here when I was at school. Good place to go for a smoke in the lunch break.'

Which, as far as it went, wasn't a total lie.

She went to push the door.

'It's locked,' he said.

Melanie pushed anyway and the door opened. 'No, it's not,' was her unnecessary comment. Dayne was understandably surprised; never once in all his illicit visits to the chapel had this door been unlocked. Melanie was progressing cautiously inside, sniffing loudly as if fearing unmentionable unpleasantness might lurk within, but obviously preferring that to the rain. Dayne followed her, noticing as he did so that the door had been forced, something that would take a considerable amount of effort, given the thickness of the door.

From inside, Melanie's voice echoed surprise. 'It's not too bad. Bit dark, though.'

'Try this.'

Dayne produced a torch from his jacket pocket. The torch was small but powerful and it produced enough dispersal of the darkness to reveal three small rows of pews, an altar and some feeble attempts at classical church architecture. It also revealed a florid sprinkling of detritus – empty beer cans and bottles, waste paper and rubble. Melanie didn't look at it too closely but she guessed that she wouldn't have to search too long before finding needles and syringes.

'Charming.'

'At least it's dry.'

She sighed and sat down on the front pew, holding herself tight. For a moment there was silence, then she said, 'Well, you'd better come and sit next to me. Keep me warm and dry.'

Dayne needed no further encouragement. He noted a certain hint of promise in her words and moved swiftly to her side; the cold darkness amplified the ill-defined echoes around them. He leant the torch on the corner of the narrow shelf in front of them, angled so that it shone upwards above the altar towards a simple stained glass window that had been used for stone-throwing target practice for years and consequently suffered grievously. Putting his arms around her, he hugged her and she, gratifyingly, responded. She sighed appreciatively.

He waited all of two minutes before beginning his campaign upon her erogenous zones, first with his fingertips then, following on from Melanie's rather exciting wriggling, with a gentle kiss just below her right ear.

The effect was better than he could ever have expected; had he written the script (an unlikely prospect), he would not have thought to make Melanie actually shiver with excitement, suck in breath and giggle. Not surprisingly, he did it again, this time with just a hint of tongue. This lingual touch, he reasoned, might be a good thing to add.

In the event it took him perhaps a minute to realize that he had been proved correct, these sixty seconds being occupied with fighting through the surprise, for Melanie 'I'm not a fucking bicycle' Day was suddenly all over him, apparently deciding to get him to forsake the ambulatory lifestyle and start pedalling. Her mouth took on an exceedingly soft, wet and voracious aspect, applying itself with an astonishingly high degree of suction first to his mouth, then to his neck.

His delight lagged behind his astonishment at this metamorphosis, but only by a moment; he joined in enthusiastically, first by paying some more attention to her neck (on the grounds that if once was good, twice would be brilliant), then by paying attention to disrobing her. She, in fair and proper payment, set about doing likewise to him.

She had nice breasts, she had to admit; nice breasts and no bra – what more could a young man want? Reaching into her blouse his hands enjoyed their soft, fragrant warmth and the deliciously erect nipples. Not perhaps as gently as a gentleman should, he tried to prise one out, and might have ripped a couple of buttons from her blouse had she not breathlessly undone them. Having done this, her hands returned to burrowing into his trousers where she was treating his engorged penis to the kind of attention that under any other circumstances would be considered battery.

Their noises filled the chapel and bounced back indistinctly, turning them into the unconsidered sounds of rutting animals. Smelling her flesh and her perfume and her sweat, his hands feeling her buttocks and her crotch and her readiness to fuck, he suddenly became aware of how uncomfortable he was. The pew was narrow and, in common with all its brethren the world over, hard; their legroom was distinctly limited.

'Over there,' he gasped at the first opportunity, meaning the altar. Melanie, who had given up using her hands on his penis and therefore had her mouth full of not only Dayne's throbbing gristle but also his genital warts, took a moment before replying incredulously, 'On the altar?' Her parents were religious and,

110

although she did not share their strict observance of Christian morality, she did find the thought of copulation on the altar 'not quite right'.

'Yeah. Where else?'

He disentangled himself and, while he held his trousers up with one hand and she failed to keep her breasts covered, he led her to the flat, dusty altar. It was about a metre wide and two metres long. The altar cloth was long gone but in the middle was a heavy stone urn, perhaps half a metre high. As soon as they got to it, he started on her again, following the well-trodden path of neck, breasts and pants. She leaned back, parting her legs while doing the sucker-thing with her mouth. More echoing, this time more obviously human with its added element of soft moans and syllables.

Dayne whispered, 'Lie back on the table.'

Melanie looked back over shoulder, then did as she was bid, but in the semi-darkness misjudged the distance to the urn. Her head knocked it hard, nearly tipping it over and moving it close to the edge. 'Shit!'

'Come on, Mel,' was Dayne's idea of empathy, mainly because he could feel juices stirring in his groin. 'Don't muck about.'

This distinct lack of compassion led Melanie, rubbing the back of her head and wincing, to opine, 'It's all right for you, you bastard. You've got me for a cushion. I'm the one lying on bare wood.'

It was here that Dayne produced his masterstroke, an uncharacteristic act as masterstrokes had not thus far in his life been Dayne's strength. 'Not if you lean forward,' he said in a tone that to his ears was entirely reasonable, and then adding in a seductive whisper, 'Do it from behind.'

And, incredibly, wonderfully, breathtakingly, she giggled. 'From behind?'

'Sure,' he said. He moved his hand between her thighs while kissing again her breast. 'It'd be good.'

The light from the torch was localized and angular, so that he didn't see the smile, only heard it in her moans.

'Come on, Mel. From behind, eh?'

And she sighed once, long and hard, and then without a word turned to bend forward obligingly with her forearms on the altar.

He pulled her short skirt up, her knickers down. When he

took them below her knees and tried to remove them completely, she said peevishly, 'Get on with it.'

Wisely opting to leave souvenir hunting until later, he contemplated her backside and found that it met with the approval of both him and his penis. He dropped his trousers, thrust his hips forward and found warmth and lubrication within the pleasure of Melanie Day.

She made appreciative sounds and this encouraged him to use the time-tested method of alternating forward and backward motion, giving himself not unpleasurable sensations and apparently giving Melanie something she rather enjoyed. He grasped her hips, increasing both frequency and strength.

The altar began to shake with each thrust. Not that either of the two participants in the drama cared. In their little world, neither the darkness nor the cold nor the decay mattered. Suddenly the fact that they were surrounded by detritus, that it was raining outside and that they were alone in a shadow-laden, dilapidated building was without interest.

A killer might have been lurking in those shadows, watching them fuck – perhaps enjoying them fuck – but they did not then care.

Dayne slipped into the familiar rhythm and both blood and brain did their thing. The altar was shaken regularly and it wasn't long before he began to mutter the usual, time-honoured phrases while Melanie produced similar groans of encouragement. During all this, neither of them noticed the urn edging further and further over the far edge of the table.

At last, after increasingly violent thrusts (and a couple of accidental 'disengagements' due to his eagerness to please), Dayne slid home one last and emphatic time and held himself tightly clamped, the target acquired and autonomic muscular contractions of which he knew nothing doing wonderful things. Melanie, meanwhile, although not quite at orgasm, but joining in with the spirit of the thing, jerked up and down and made the best of things with a few words of sighed appreciation.

It was these final movements that put paid to the urn and it crashed off the altar to the stone floor, fragments splaying out in front of Melanie.

Which was why she suddenly gasped, screamed a rather incoherent, 'Oh my God!' and backed away, scrabbling across the table and therefore pushing into Dayne. This produced an initial sensation of pleasure in the region of his groin, but when he was involuntarily disjoined from her, and when he nearly fell over because Melanie kept reversing, this dispersed. He opened his mouth to protest, but Melanie by now was screaming incoherently, continuously and loudly (and regardless of her state of dishabille), such that he couldn't actually make himself heard. It was only when Melanie grabbed him and then pointed towards the darkness behind the altar that he comprehended that she had seen something.

He edged forward, putting his habit straight while Melanie, having given up on screaming as a form of self-expression, was merely sobbing and moaning. He leaned over the altar.

It was dark back there; dark and dusty.

So it took him quite a while to see the pieces of brain now spread liberally on the floor.

It had taken a long time for Eisenmenger to feel wholly comfortable with Helena, to overcome the feelings of trepidation and frustration that her mood swings and the intensity of her personality evoked. Intrinsically, he was stable, varying little from an even temper and only when circumstances grew so extreme that there was no other option but to show his emotions. He had seen too much of the destruction wrought by anger to want to allow it freedom within his own personality, and neither did he want to see it in anyone else, especially someone to whom he had become so close. Yet Helena without the passion, the fire and the unpredictability would be a very different beast indeed – perhaps not even Helena at all – and so he had to accept that she possessed deep within her a fire that he could do nothing about, that, whether he liked it or not, was as much an integral part of her as her eyes, her tongue and her soul.

But even with all that as a given, as a boundary within which they had to dance, he knew that her mood that night was atypical, a subtle variation on the usual theme; yet, subtle or not, it was as obvious to him as would have been the loss of one of her eyes.

They had been that night to a small jazz club not far from Eisenmenger's mews house. Helena had developed an interest in jazz over the past six months and, whilst Eisenmenger did not share her enthusiasm for the music, he did not abhor it either. It passed him by, much as the sound of birdsong; pleasant but not, as far as he was concerned, communicative.

They had eaten at the club and drunk slightly too much, and then returned to his house where they now sat side by side, their bodies softly touching. They had not been aware that they were being followed.

Helena had talked throughout the evening whenever he might have expected her to, but always what she had said had been just short of normality, answers given to satisfy his need for conversation rather than to engage in any meaningful dialogue.

He had held off asking about Martin Pendred because he knew that she disliked talking idly about current cases, but he ran out of topics at about the time of coffee, his desperation growing in tandem with his concern. Eventually he asked, 'Is it true that Martin Pendred has gone missing?'

Helena nodded and then said in a tones that were only partly mocking, 'Obviously he didn't think much of his legal adviser.'

'More likely he didn't think much of his chances of getting a fair trial.' He put his hand on her wrist. 'Anyway, I'm intrigued. What did you make of him?'

They were drinking brandy, the blade-sharp, air-light glasses on the coffee table in front of them refracting meaningless, distorted brightnesses. Helena stared at them as if there were truths to be found in their depths.

'He was . . .' She hesitated, and then when she completed the sentence it was in a voice that was odd, as if she were pulled between fear and affection, admiration and abhorrence: '. . . fascinating.'

He thought then that he had unexpectedly uncovered the reason for her strange mood.

He thought wrongly.

'Fascinating? That's an odd word to use. Most people would say things like "odd", or "frightening", or even "evil".'

She reached forward for her glass before replying. 'He's certainly odd, and he's certainly frightening – probably because he's odd – but evil? I'm not sure you could say he's evil.'

'Some would. Some do. Just like his brother was.'

She shook her head, her face an expression of consideration. 'Doesn't evil imply a will to destroy, to negate? Martin Pendred just struck me as a vacuum.'

'So a psychopath's not evil? After all, they're just you or me without the conscience.'

Surprised, Helena asked, 'Is that what he is? A psychopath?'

'No. The Pendreds had Asperger's.'

'Which is?'

'The jargon term is Autistic Spectrum Disorder.'

'And the term that makes sense to those not in the know?' There was a definite sound of cynicism in her question. She put the glass back next on the table and then leaned back next to him.

'Autism is thought to be a disorder of perception, or perhaps perception processing. They see, hear, feel, smell and taste just as you or I do, but there is some distortion in what happens to the information thus received. Maybe they see the world as we do, but can't react normally: maybe they see the world differently and act accordingly. No one knows, but it's clear that their view of the world is very different to that of the rest of humanity.'

'But you said he had something else . . . Asperger's?

'Asperger's is part of the Autistic Spectrum Disorder. It's thought to be a less severe form of autism.'

'And what's the difference between this and psychopathy?'

'Psychopaths see the world exactly as the rest of us. They just lack the desire to care. They do what they want because they want to do it.'

'So autistics can care?'

He didn't know quite what to say. Eventually, 'I don't think they ever get the chance. The world to someone with autism or Asperger's is a strange, frightening place; a jumble of fractured sounds, sights and other sensory perceptions. Nothing ever gets synthesized into a whole, so that they look at a face and they see two eyes, a nose, a mouth. They see these things in the correct orientation and they see them on the front of a head above a body; they may even hear a voice come from the mouth, but something happens – or perhaps doesn't happen – and it doesn't become the construct of a human face with all its connotations. We care because we see objects that mean things to us. Autistics never see those objects. They really are strangers in a strange land.'

'But are they violent?'

At once he shook his head. 'No, not usually. They may exhibit self-destructive behaviours, but generally they are too inert, too aghast at what they find themselves lost in.'

With something that perhaps wanted to be quiet triumph, as if they were playing a game, she asked at once, 'So how do you explain the Pendreds?'

He smiled, pleased that she seemed now for the first time that evening to be lightening in her mood. After a sip of brandy he said, 'Martin and Melkior Pendred were born forty years ago, identical twins. As far as I can ascertain, their parents weren't very bright. Maybe they were good parents, maybe they were bad – I don't know – but I think it's fairly obvious that they didn't have the faintest idea about their sons. Not that that was unusual at the time.'

'Meaning?'

'Meaning that human nature being what it is, if you're unlucky enough to have an illness before the medical profession has recognized it, then at best you'll be left to fester alone, at worse you'll be condemned to a life of misery as a freak, a witch or a monster.'

'It doesn't say much for doctors.'

He smiled but his voice was a long way from humour. 'It doesn't say much for humanity, I think.'

She accepted the loss of a debating point without argument. He went on. 'Autism and Asperger's are examples of conditions that are all around us, only they're invisible until we look. Almost certainly that's why the incidence of autism is apparently rising; we're recognizing it more.'

'For a pathologist, you know a lot about psychiatry.'

He shrugged. 'This isn't a new case for me, remember. I learnt a lot about autism and Asperger's the last time around.'

Pathologists weren't required to learn about the psychiatric problems of perpetrators, despite the popular misconception. Helena knew that Eisenmenger had an intense curiosity and a deeply analytical intellect that required answers, but even she was surprised to hear that he had taken his involvement to such an unorthodox extent. When she expressed this, he explained, 'As I said, autistics and Asperger's patients don't commit violent crimes. When they came into the frame for the murders, I was intrigued. I looked into it a little bit more.'

'And?'

He leaned forward, picking up his glass and cradling it with two hands. 'There's something about these conditions; something wonderful and terrifying, something that reveals how strange, how God-given the brain is.' He took his time over a small sip of brandy. 'In the Autistic Spectrum Disorders, there's something wrong with the hardwiring of the brain, but it's something subtle, something beyond the present level of our understanding. In fact, it's so subtle that it can act as a background for other psychiatric diseases. Autistics can be psychopathic, depressed, neurotic or obsessive-compulsive. They can also be schizophrenic – as was Melkior.'

Helena considered this. 'And it was his schizophrenia rather than his Asperger's that led him to murder?'

He shrugged slightly. 'That's the theory.'

After a pause she asked, 'What did you mean about autism being wonderful and terrifying?'

'Because of *idiots savants*.'

'I've heard of them. Children who have some incredible talent despite being otherwise retarded.'

'Not retarded – severely autistic – but you're right about the talent. It might be an ability to play a piece on the piano perfectly despite having heard it just once, or it might be the ability to reproduce perfectly with paper and pencil a complex scene, perhaps only glimpsed for a second. It makes you think that whatever is wrong is perhaps not all bad.'

'But those children are incapable of independent living; they need constant help. And don't people with autism have low IQ? How could the Pendreds have coped all these years?'

'Severe autism is completely disabling, but there's a broad spectrum of the condition, and most people with Asperger's cope in society tolerably well. And the myth about autism and mental inadequacy is a myth. For a start, the IQ test is just not capable of assessing their intelligence; it's like using weighing scales to measure height – not a suitable instrument. People with autism or Asperger's can be bright, possible very bright, even genius. Some of history's greatest artists probably had Asperger's.

'And the Pendreds weren't stupid – very far from it. If they hadn't had Asperger's, they would probably have had the chance at good careers. As it was, they grew up in a poor family with parents who didn't have the knowledge or ability to recognize that there was anything wrong with their twin sons other than cussedness.'

117

'Even so, if Melkior was schizophrenic and they both had Asperger's, it was amazing that they managed to live alone and apparently unknown to the psychiatric services.'

'Their parents refused help. As far as I can tell, they preferred to take the head-in-the-sand option. To a certain extent that worked. The father was a mortuary technician at the Western and he got the boys jobs there as well. They weren't capable of doing the paperwork, but they excelled at evisceration and at body reconstitution.'

'*Idiots savants?*'

He smiled. 'Something like that.'

'Even so, what a thing to be expert at!'

Eisenmenger drained his brandy and then leaned back next to Helena. His head was stretched back on the sofa as he turned to look at her. 'I told you, autism is a wonderful and terrible thing.'

She didn't seem to find quite as much black amusement in the concept as he did. He continued, 'It gave them a simple, structured life, which is basically what sufferers from Asperger's need; they go to pieces when the props of regularity are removed.

'And then their parents died. A double road-traffic accident, Something that would have stressed most people to the point of breakdown, so you can perhaps imagine what it probably did to the Pendred twins.'

'Not good?'

'The best guess was that it was the point at which Melkior's schizophrenia began, except that they slipped through our wonderful social security net. Nobody noticed them. They lived their lives in our modern society and, amazingly, it came to no one's attention that they were there, and that they weren't coping.'

'So Melkior went bonkers and started to kill people.'

'That was the explanation that the police clung to.' He sounded not at all convinced.

'But?' she asked.

'It was a good theory, as far as it went.' This with a long, thoughtful sigh. 'But I was never sure it went far enough.'

She knew that she ought to have been used to his habit of thinking ten things and articulating one, but then she knew that she ought to stop eating chocolates. 'Would you care to explain?'

'Part of the case against Melkior was his schizophrenia; that

118

and the alibi given to Martin for the last murder. Yet schizophrenia, like Autistic Spectrum Disorder, has a strong genetic component. If the situation stressed Melkior enough to give him a schizophrenic breakdown, then there was a good chance that it would have done the same to Martin.'

'But wasn't he given some form of psychiatric assessment?'

'No. Why should he have been? When Melkior was arrested, he was given one, but no one ever looked at Martin. He was never formally charged with anything.'

'So Martin could be as mad as his brother?'

It was when he didn't say anything and just kept staring at the empty glass on the table that she guessed. 'Or perhaps you think that Melkior was innocent? Perhaps it was Martin all along?'

His smile was long and lazy and broke from something enigmatic. 'To be honest, I was never really sure who did them. But I was only the pathologist. My opinion didn't matter.'

'Oh, shit.'

It was perhaps the hundredth time that night Wright had heard Homer mutter this particular imprecation under his breath, but he had lost count and couldn't be absolutely sure. There was no doubt that whenever he wasn't issuing loud, peremptory and occasionally impractical or contradictory orders to the assembled throng, Homer was repeating this over and over again to himself, his eyes filled with much the same sense of doom as had probably drowned poor Captain Smith's eyes when the iceberg slid slowly by on the starboard side with a loud crunching noise.

He was clearly a man who saw stormy weather ahead and no umbrella immediately to hand.

The small chapel had grown no warmer, despite the temporary lighting that had been erected and the crowding together of perhaps twenty-six bodies (only one of whom was dead). Neumann, Cooley and Fisher were there, running various duties including cataloguing forensic specimens, assisting Bloomenthal and SOCO, and general gophering. The main foci of activity were behind the altar and the back of the chapel, the former the site of a rather disturbed and distorted human brain surrounded by shards of ugly pottery, the latter the site of a mound of rubbish under which had been discovered the eviscerated remains of Patrick Wilms. His non-neural organs were still AWOL, whereabouts unknown.

Wright left Homer to his preoccupied and peevish supervision of the forensics team (who were minutely examining and bagging up a rich and infinitely varied array of used condoms, needles, syringes, silver wrappers, pieces of chewing gum, and paper tissues soiled in various ways, as well as many other examples of what the human race produces merely to discard), and went over to Bloomenthal, notebook in hand.

Bloomenthal, dressed in a white one-piece that did nothing for his figure and that positively distressed his complexion, glanced up from his contemplation of the less-than-complete former soldier. 'Do you appreciate how clichéd you are, Sergeant?'

'I beg your pardon?'

'The notebook,' explained Bloomenthal, gesturing with a sky-blue disposable scalpel held in a hand that was clad in a thin rubber glove. 'Hasn't the Thin Blue Line entered the twenty-first century yet? Why aren't you jotting down your no-doubt astute observations and astounding deductions in those interesting things known, I believe, to the cognoscenti as "palm-tops"? Make your notes, hurry to the police station, download it all into the central computer and, within the hour, correlations are made, cross-references established, the perpetrator caught.

'That,' concluded Bloomenthal, 'is what you should be using.'

Wright, lost in a grey fog of doubt as to whether the pathologist was serious or joking, mad or erudite, rude or witty, took a moment to establish communication between ear, brain and mouth. Once this was achieved he contented himself with a simple, 'Yes, sir. But what happens if the battery runs out?'

Bloomenthal stared at him for two seconds before uttering a short, braying laugh that was as affectionate as it was scathing. 'Do you know, Sergeant, I can't decide whether you're a troglodyte or a visionary.' He paused and stared into the darkness of the high ceiling above them. 'Which I suppose makes you worthy of immortalization.'

Wright by now was on the point of calling in a psychiatrist – if not for Bloomenthal, then at least for himself – but Homer hove into view then and appeared to have managed to repossess some semblance of normality. 'What have you got for me, Doctor?' he demanded.

Bloomenthal switched smoothly from transcendental to

mundane (leaving Wright lost and slightly miffed). 'Oh, the usual, my dear Homer, the usual. One corpse, much fuss.'

Homer was far from the mood needed to take this flippancy with reasonable grace. He said curtly, 'I don't need an overpaid butcher to tell me that. Can you tell me if it's the same as last time? Is it Martin Pendred?'

Bloomenthal, for whom Homer's anger was as meaningful as a pimple on the tongue, concocted a patronizing smile. 'There is a single anterior incision in keeping with that normally used for evisceration, but since it has been sewn up I cannot say with certainty.'

'Why else would anyone make an incision like that?'

'I am a pathologist, not a psychiatrist. I am merely pointing out that until I reopen the incision, I cannot be certain that the organs are no longer in situ.'

Exasperation took a little walk around Homer's face, then settled around his mouth in a sort of pout. 'Well, at least you can deduce that his brain's been removed, I suppose? I mean it's over there behind the altar, so you'll allow that it's not in his head?'

Bloomenthal might have been completely serious, might have been completely facetious, so finely drawn was the distinction as he said simply, 'There is certainly a stitched incision around the back of the head and, as far as I can determine, the top of the skull has been detached, but I fear that at present, Chief Inspector, I cannot join you in the confidence that all is as simple as it seems.'

'What?' Plaintiveness vied with incredulity for supremacy, the result a tie.

'Is it not entirely possible that the brain over there is nothing to do with the body over here? Perhaps somewhere in the vicinity is another body, another dissection. Until we resort to the wonders of modern DNA technology, we can only hypo-thesize that yonder organ was once in this cranium.'

He smiled sweetly while Homer opened his mouth and widened his eyes. After several moments of this catatonia, Homer abruptly collapsed his expression and turned away, more profanity readily at his lips. In sympathy, Wright whispered in his ear, 'I don't know about you, sir, but I think Dr Bloomenthal's gone mad.'

In an unnecessarily loud voice Homer replied, 'He hasn't gone mad, Wright; he was always mad. He's a pathologist – look at what he does for a living – they're all just sickos in suits.'

He did not look back to see Bloomenthal's smile widen into a grin accompanied by the slightest of acknowledging nods. Instead he asked Wright, 'Have we got anything to identify him yet?'

Wright looked at his trusty, non-battery-powered notebook. 'He had a bus pass in his left-hand trouser pocket in the name of Patrick Wilms.'

Homer showed a sign of hope for the first time that late, late evening. 'Wilms? Do we know that name?'

Wright frowned but decided against showing ignorance. Homer was thinking, driven by a scent of success. It did not take him long to cry, 'Wilms! The neighbour!'

'Sir?'

'Patrick Wilms is the Pendreds' neighbour. A bloody trouble-maker but, give him his due, he always knew the Pendreds were murderers.' His Sergeant was busily writing this down. Homer said, 'Get over to Wilms' house. If you can't get an answer, break in.'

'Is that wise, sir?'

'Just do it, Wright. You can always use the pretext that you were worried about his safety.'

Wright's 'Yes, sir' was marinated in the kind of suffering only an owner of a boil on the buttock normally knows.

'Who found him?'

'A couple, sir.'

A not unreasonable answer, or so Wright mistakenly thought, but he had momentarily forgotten that he was in the presence of a man who felt in mortal peril and who was therefore not in a conciliatory mood. 'A couple? A couple of what? Dogs? Aliens? Paedophiles?'

'A young lad and his girlfriend, sir.'

'Well bloody well say so, next time. Names?'

'Dayne Sturge and Melanie Day.'

'Where are they now?'

'In one of the cars.'

Homer said nothing more as he left Wright in search of the witnesses; Wright glared at the small man's back but even that solace was tainted when he saw Bloomenthal's broad smile.

Making love had not yet lost for them the pleasure of discovery. When, later that night, she began to kiss him as they both lay naked beneath plain white sheets, it was for him still shot through with the thrill of the new, with disbelief of his good fortune. He was tired but he responded readily, first kissing her on the shoulders, then moving down her body, part of his thoughts still treasuring her sleekness and enjoying her responses.

He didn't notice when, as she lay back and he took her left breast in his hand, her nipple between his second and third fingers, she gently moved away and distracted him by inviting him lower and deeper, where he moved slowly and languidly, his whole world suddenly found in her softness and perfumed smoothness and, when she allowed him between her thighs, the knowledge of their intimacy.

The unfamiliarity could still cause small moments of awkwardness, when the rapport born of mutual experience was still too weak, but that night it seemed to him that there were no such instances. Helena and he were choreographed, movements complementary, response and reaction perfectly timed; she seemed to immerse herself in what he did to her and, when the time came, in what she did to him, appearing to find enjoyment in a way that he had never before known in her. Finally, when he had tasted her and she him, when they had come as close as they could to holding, possessing and consuming each other, she bade him lie back. She knelt astride him in the semi-darkness, her silhouette half-formed against the orange streetlight shining against the curtains of the window.

She began to gyrate slowly, sumptuously, her back rod-straight, her breathing soft but urgent. The movement – a single fluid thing – became more pronounced and with this, she began to flow gently up and down, up and down. He took her hips, trying to help, trying to co-ordinate the flux of their engagement, but she was becoming more unrestrained now, her mouth no longer closed, her back beginning to arch.

The fingers of his left hand moved between her legs and with the first touch she increased her movement and he found himself starting, gloriously, to lose control. For a few seconds that disguised themselves as minutes, she continued her increasing frenzy while he simultaneously excited her and tried to restrain her, then she abruptly stopped, her back so curved it might have been willow, her belly forward, her breasts sloping. He was so close then as he jerked his hips upwards again and again until at last he came, holding himself as deeply within her as he could manage, and it was just at the end that he reached up with both hands and grasped both her breasts.

He held himself there for as long as he could, enjoying the touch of her breasts, unaware that she had changed, that she was suddenly back from their act of love, back in a present that had been momentarily banished. Even as he relaxed and she climbed off he did not appreciate what was happening, nor even that there was anything happening at all. He lay on his back, pleased, assuming that she was also pleased, that she was lying on her side away from him for no particular reason.

Homer opened the passenger door of the police car and got in without proffering introductions to the passengers in the back.

'Right, you two,' he said, looking over his shoulder. 'Names?'

Homer could see that his witnesses were cold and shocked, but he could also see that his bollocks were on the railway line and the locomotive was approaching. The girl was trying to stop crying and doing it badly. When Dayne had given his name (in a voice, Homer noted, suggesting that he was used to such formalities) she began again to weep and it was left to Dayne to inform Homer of her identity.

'So why were you in the chapel?'

'It was raining. We were sheltering in there.'

Homer sighed like a pantomime dame. 'I see.' He waited for few seconds, staring at them in turn before asking, 'What was it? Drugs?'

Dayne reacted at once. 'No!' Even Melanie managed a decisive shake of her head.

'Well, it's hardly on a main road, is it? What were you doing in the cemetery in the first place?'

Dayne, though, had decided to make sure that Homer was clear on the drugs issue. 'I don't do drugs. I've got nothing to do with that shit.'

'So why were you in the chapel?'

The hesitation told Homer everything. 'Having a shag,' he said tiredly, rather like a careworn parent. Dayne smiled in a mismatched marriage of sheepishness and arrogance, Melanie began to cry again.

'So how did you come across the body?'

Dayne said, 'We noticed it.'

This artless response failed to hit the spot for Homer. 'Noticed it? What does that mean?'

Dayne shrugged and his next remark might just as well have been flying a big banner labelled, *I'm hiding something.*

'We happened to look behind the table and saw it there.'

Homer's patience was on a short lead and he had reached its full length and was about to snap it through. 'Oh, for Christ sake.' he said. 'It was found on the floor in a million pieces of cheap pottery. Which means that it was originally in the urn on the altar. Which means that somebody knocked the urn off. There was the murderer who put it in the urn, and there was you who found it. Now please don't make me go looking for someone else in this investigation, eh?' He had gradually mutated his tone into one of reasoned pleading. 'You knocked the urn off the table, and that was when you discovered the brain, right?'

Dayne might have been about to deny this concoction of supposition, but Melanie suddenly found coherence and used it. 'That's right.'

Homer smiled. 'Good,' he cooed. And, as if giving them a poisoned fillip for her honesty, he decided, 'And I won't ask what you were doing to knock the urn off.'

Melanie's eyes, as they dropped precipitously to the darkness of the floor of the car, were eloquent enough. Dayne said suddenly, 'The chapel door was open.'

Homer turned an interested face to him. 'I was wondering about that. How were you expecting to get in?'

Dayne had caught the mood of confession. 'Round the back. There's a window you can prise open.'

'The front door's usually shut and locked?'

Dayne nodded.

'But tonight, you say it wasn't?'

Now Dayne shook his head. 'Someone had kicked it in.'

'What time was this?'

Dayne chose this moment to voice protest. 'We've already told people this.'

It was one of the irritations of becoming more senior in the police. By the time Homer got to see people, they had already answered all his questions (and probably five hundred more) three or four times. 'Humour me,' he said. It was phrased as advice, much as Caligula might have proffered it.

Melanie said, 'Maybe ten.'

'Can't you be more exact?'

Dayne offered in an irritated tone, 'It was five past ten, okay?'

Choosing not give him a small piece of trouble, Homer asked then, 'So you were walking from . . . which end?'

'Haddow Street.'

'And did you pass anyone as you walked?'

Two heads shook almost, but not quite, in perfect co-ordination.

'Was there anyone that you noticed in Haddow Street?'

There was a knock on the car door then. Wright's face appeared from the darkness, but if Homer was thinking to bollock him, he was soon diverted from that course by Wright's apologetic explanation.

'Sorry, sir, but I think you'd better come and see this.'

'See what?'

Wright glanced at the couple in the back of the car before replying. 'We've found the rest of the body, sir. It's in an unexpected place.'

Eisenmenger woke from satisfied sleep, his thoughts troubled but by what he could not at once say.

It was some seconds before he heard Helena's quiet, almost silent weeping.

'Oh, shit!'

The only appreciable difference in Homer's somewhat repetitive use of profanity was that now the tone was one of awe.

'Oh, shit!'

Or perhaps it was dread.

They were standing beside a grave located some hundred metres from the chapel. It was of interest because it had been desecrated. Someone had expended considerable energy digging a deep hole. When Homer had looked into the hole with the aid of a torch, he could just make out that it reached to a rotting coffin lid on which was resting a clear plastic bag; within the bag were clearly seen a heavy mass of human entrails.

Around them, temporary lighting was being set up, run off car batteries. As if by some unseen playwright's stage direction a spotlight shone down upon them at this point, and the grave and its stone stood out with painful brilliance.

Homer groaned and for long moments just stared, before he turned to Wright like a man who has just seen the future and that future had murder in its eyes. 'Can it get any worse?'

Wright was about to reassure his superior, but then he spotted what Homer had not, and there settled on his calm, slightly confused face a look of deepest sympathy. 'I'm rather afraid that it can, sir,' he advised sorrowfully.

Even as Homer turned he knew what he would see, and for one surreal moment the sight of Chief Superintendent Call making his stately way through the headstones and assorted police personnel bore in his dread-filled vision the appearance of a demon from the nethermost pit of hell. The look in Call's eyes – intense, smouldering and malignant – suggested, more-over, that it was not a happy demon, that it was one who was coming for his soul.

'Homer!' There was a touch of thunder in his stentorian call, a strong suggestion that painful dyspepsia was wrestling with a pulsing headache and producing titanic ill temper.

Homer stepped forward, his face as passive as he could make it. He was at once aware that all other work had ceased around him, that his subordinate officers had silently formed an inter-ested and probably partisan audience. 'Sir?'

Call continued his approach, eventually coming to a halt directly in front of him. It was cold enough to cause the moisture in his breath to condense and he therefore appeared to be breathing smoke. 'What the fuck have you done now?' Call shouted this,

'There's been another murder,' Homer replied in a voice as normal as he could make it. 'The same MO, the – '

'I know what's happened, you idiot! I know and the Chief Constable knows! And by morning the bloody press will know!' He paused for breath. In the bright arc lights the colours were washed into bleached shades, but it was clear that the emotion and exertion had turned his face an inter-esting and abnormal colour. 'You lost him, didn't you? You let him go, and then you lost him, and now he's massacred some other poor bugger!'

This was such a monumental distortion of facts and responsibilities that Wright found himself compelled to defend Homer. From somewhere behind his right shoulder, Homer heard Wright say, 'It wasn't the Chief Inspector's fault, sir. We – '

It was like watching the guns of Navarone swing round to pound seventeen types of excrement out of a small rowing boat. Call moved his fiery gaze from Homer to Wright and shouted, 'Who the fuck asked you, Sergeant? Where the fuck do you think you get the right to interfere in this matter? Eh? Eh?'

Wright, by now not so much holed beneath the Plimsoll line as in the water and clinging to small pieces of wreckage, opened his mouth but could only manage a slightly tardy, 'Sorry, sir.'

'Well piss off, and do some policework. Try and find the fucker, why don't you?'

Wright nodded and said, 'Yes, sir,' and then walked away with as much dignity as he could.

Call turned back to Homer, gesturing over his shoulder at the grave. 'What's going on here, then? Why aren't you at the scene of the murder?'

Homer felt dissociated from the events that were happening around him and to him. He heard his voice say, 'In accordance with his previous habit, the body has been autopsied and the organs removed. The brain was in an urn that had smashed on the floor, but there was no sign of the rest of the organs in the chapel. A search subsequently turned them up here, sir.'

Call didn't exactly cease hostilities but he did at least tell the gunnery officer to stand down for the time being. He looked at the hole dug down into the grave. Because of their relative positions, he could see nothing else.

'Down there?' he demanded.

Homer nodded, breathed once deeply, then said tentatively, 'There's one more thing, sir.'

Call eyed him suspiciously, the guns coming round to bear again; something on his face suggested that a target had been acquired. 'What?'

Homer moved aside so that Call had an unobstructed view of the headstone. An unobstructed view of the name inscribed thereon.

Melkior Pendred.

Homer had actually shut his eyes, a natural but he thought wholly inadequate defence mechanism against the coming onslaught, but nothing came. No abuse, no shouting, no screaming, no heavy breathing. When he opened his eyes it was not upon the angered demon but upon an experienced policeman.

Call was staring at the writing, but there was now only a questioning look on his face. 'Why?' he asked. He turned to Homer. 'Any theories?'

Homer had had barely enough time to take in the facts, let alone extrapolate into theories, but he had been coppering long enough to wing it convincingly.

'Two possibilities, sir. The first is that it's merely a smoke-screen, designed to make us think that it's the ghost of Melkior come back to life – '

'We're hardly likely to think that, Homer.'

'No, sir. But I know Pendred, sir, and it might just be the kind of thing that *he* might believe. He doesn't think normally, don't forget.'

Call weighed this, then accepted it. 'The other?'

'That it's a tribute. A tribute to Melkior. Perhaps he's saying sorry.'

'Sorry? What for?'

'Melkior took the rap, don't forget. Martin never said anything when his twin brother was banged up on five counts of life.'

Call raised his eyebrows. 'Bloody hell, Homer. I know he's a sick bastard, but even so . . .' He appeared to shudder.

'He is, sir. Very sick.'

Call said nothing more for a while, then, 'There's another possibility.'

'Sir?'

'That Martin's only taken over from where his brother left off. That we were right the first time, and Martin's just following the family tradition.'

At once Homer was starting to protest, his mouth open, but Call shut him up. 'I know, I know. It doesn't fit your pet theory, but there are other dimensions to this.'

'Meaning?'

Call was a Chief Superintendent and, as such, half his job was political, but Homer had never shown any aptitude for such considerations. It was the main reason why Call doubted that he would ever rise any higher in the police firmament. Exasperated at the other's obtuseness he said, 'Think about it, Homer. If it turns out that Martin is merely copying what his brother did, the police are off the hook. We don't look like plonkers for nabbing the wrong man. A man who, may I remind you, died in prison.'

'Protesting his innocence.'

'Oh, for God's sake, Homer! Are you planning to let out every convicted criminal who bleats a lie about his guilt? Try and use some sense.'

Aware that he was goading a gorgon, Homer said nothing more and merely nodded.

'Right.' Call took a deep breath and turned away from the grave where SOCO was now busy at his happy work. He could be heard complaining loudly of everyone and no one that he couldn't get decent pictures of the organ mass because the hole was so deep.

Bloomenthal came towards them through wet grass and past a huge yew tree. His white all-in-one suit made him almost glow against the night's background. 'Good evening again, Chief Superintendent. I understand our felon is living up to his usual standards of appallingly sick behaviour.'

Call did not respond to this, saying merely, 'Evening, Doctor,' this coming out as little more than a grunt. When Bloomenthal was by the grave, standing with his hands clasped in front of him (almost an attitude of pleasant anticipation), Call moved away with Homer following. When they reached the gravel path and another oasis of light, Call said, 'They're such funny buggers, these pathologists. Give me the creeps.'

'I know what you mean, sir.'

Call recollected his thoughts. 'I don't need to tell you that we've got to find Pendred, and find him fast.'

'Absolutely, sir. Unfortunately, at present we've got no witnesses. The couple who found him saw no one else.'

'You'll start house-to-house?'

'It's too late now, but first thing in the morning.'

'Have we got an identity yet?'

'Patrick Wilms. Pendred's neighbour.'

'Has someone gone over there?'

'Yes, sir.' Strictly speaking, a lie.

'Good.' Call lapsed into introspection, then looked up at

Homer. 'This is going to hit the papers, Homer. It's going to hit them like a bloody explosion in a sewage works. We've got to find him before he does this again.'

Homer really meant it when he said, 'Don't worry, sir. I will.'

The woman who was sitting beside them in the waiting room was dying, radiating her long descent from life to death and thence into oblivion to become lost not only to the world but also to the world's memories. Helena saw it at once – saw it and sensed it and, she was sure, smelled it; the scent of death's interest, of life's tiredness. The woman was slightly pinched, perhaps early in her fifties but clothed in skin that had the sallow transparency of someone in her nineties; her breathing was stertorous, almost as if each lungful fired pain into every cell, as if this were yet another task she could well do without. Her head lay back against the wall, her grey, lank hair exactly covering a patch of grease and dirt on the emulsioned plaster; her eyes were closed, her lips not closed.

Eisenmenger appeared not to notice any of this. He stared at the picture on the wall opposite (an abstract commissioned by the League of Friends, abstracted not just from recognizable form but also from all recognizable artistic merit) and dug into thoughts that were his own. He seemed relaxed, might have had Helena believing that this was a correct impression, but for her knowledge of him; Eisenmenger, she knew, was a long way from relaxed. She herself resembled something twisted so far beyond its normal configuration that she felt that she might at any instant either tear or whip back and maim whatever, or whoever, was in the way.

Eventually, after perhaps fifteen minutes, the door opened and a middle-aged woman came through. Although she was not dressed in a uniform, she wore a name badge that informed the reader that she was Bridget Fallot and that she was a Breast Care Nurse. Like all outpatient nurses, she looked as if the last thing she needed was another bloody sick person.

'Mrs Southern?' The sallow woman, thus addressed, moved her head forward as her eyes opened. Helena was at once struck by the similarity of this action to a doll she had once had when she was a six-year-old. For hours she had rocked the small, slightly grubby thing with its blue satin dress and coarse nylon hair, back and forth, watching the eyelids moving up and down as she did so, from wide awake through drowsy, to apparently peaceful sleep. Like that doll, Mrs Southern said nothing as she sluggishly came back to the present, gathered herself for the effort of movement, and stood up. Only the breathing – continuing through all this exactly as before, as independent of her as the ticking of the quartz clock by the window – marked her from the pathetic, plastic toy of Helena's childhood. She disappeared from the room past the nurse slowly and without obvious joy. The door closed and the room's silence resumed, each of them with their thoughts, each of them with their fears.

Helena stole a look at Eisenmenger, but was caught and his eyes flicked round before she could retreat into solitude again. He asked softly, 'All right?'

She nodded, although even then the lie was evident. He smiled encouragement and she was grateful for that, despite wondering why he was not sitting next to her but one chair away. She dropped her gaze from his, finding the carpet and a prominent footmark by the outside door.

Why hadn't she taken his advice and gone private? He had assured her that he could get her seen as a courtesy but she had refused, full of entirely rational reasons why not, and now she was slipping into regret. Oh, she had been seen quickly enough, and probably by the same surgeon who would have taken her private money – but this depressing place, this run-down room with its run-down furniture, set in a run-down hospital and understaffed by overpressed and run-down people!

She felt nausea creep up on her, looking to join its partner, anxiety.

The lump has grown.

How do you stop a thought? You can't. You can only muffle it newborn, stop its cries for attention; but it's there, it exists having come from nowhere, and no amount of wishing or striving will make it otherwise.

The lump is bigger.

And of course, there followed in the shadows its meaner, nastier brother.

It must be cancer.

John had tried to comfort her when at last she had told him of this certainty within her head, telling her that it was probably her imagination, that even if it were slightly more prominent than before, then it was almost certainly because of an accumulation of fluid or inflammation, or something harmless.

Probably.

It was all very well until she noticed his use of that word, and then his support had been revealed as nothing better than spun sugar, brittle and sweet.

My God! Cancer!

These seemingly random, certainly consciously unprovoked phrases had become part of her daily existence, bursting into her thought streams, sometimes one after the other, like flickering fireflies of worry. While the majority of them would burn away and die (to be reborn again and again), occasionally she would grab one, or perhaps it would grab her, and she and they would wrestle with each other, testing willpower and nerve. The word *cancer* was the meanest, the one that was least forgiving in its demand for attention and play.

Cancer.

She'd come across it before, in film, in literature, in her imagination, but never in her body; it wasn't supposed to crop up there, not in *her*. Articles describing the statistics, the biology, the feelings of sufferers, the feelings of the bereaved – she'd read them, but until now read them as someone on the outside, someone interested because one was naturally interested in such things, because it was a part of modern life.

But never a part of *her* life.

Until now.

Now she was suddenly there, hoisted above the barricade, strung out against a bright white background, the target for a word that carried more weight than even death itself, for it bore also the burden of pain and suffering, of wasting and surgery, of deterioration and decay.

The door opened again and Helena, sunk deeply into this nihilistic reverie, experienced an absurd shock as the Breast Care Nurse addressed her. 'Miss Flemming?'

It took her a moment to relocate the normal, then she said, 'Yes,' standing as she did so. She thought how small and afraid her voice sounded. She looked to Eisenmenger who proffered another smile to encourage bravery, then walked through the doorway. Eisenmenger followed.

'You don't mind, do you?'

Ludwig made a face that he presumably thought was ingratiating, but that Eisenmenger scored as ten out of ten on the scale of repulsiveness. It didn't help that Ludwig's tone suggested he could not possibly have cared less whether Eisenmenger minded or not. With a shake of his head, Eisenmenger said only, 'No.'

'Good.'

Perhaps it was Eisenmenger's calm acceptance that prodded Ludwig to say, 'This back of mine has been quite a problem of late. It's getting worse, despite physiotherapy twice a week. Bloody orthopods – carpenters with BMWs, that's all they are.'

The noise from Eisenmenger was possibly interested, possibly bored.

'It's only the post-mortems I can't really manage, you see. Everything else . . .'

Eisenmenger had been trying to authorize some reports when Ludwig had come in without knocking. His request that Eisenmenger should take his turn in the mortuary for the day had come without any preamble, almost as if it were his right to expect acquiescence.

When Eisenmenger said nothing to these explanations, Ludwig left without a further word. As the door closed, Eisenmenger sighed and abandoned the computer. He could, he knew, have said no to the request, but in truth he had wanted to visit the mortuary and this at least would provide a legitimate reason for him to be there and ask a few questions.

He left the office and walked down the stairway. The mortuary was in the basement, a dark and uninviting place, run through with pipework and draughts. He had yet to explore it properly, having been there only once, on his first day when he had been introduced to Kevin Lewy, the mortuary technician.

There were three autopsies to be done, an unusually large number and, Eisenmenger presumed, the reason for Ludwig's sudden onset of back problems. He sat in the small office and read through the notes while Lewy made some coffee.

This was not a public mortuary and so there were no coronial post-mortem examinations carried out there, only hospital autopsies and there were few of those following the problems at Bristol and Alder Hey. Since hospital autopsies did not attract a fee, they were not particularly attractive to pathologists, being long and often difficult. The majority of coronial cases involved relatively little in the way of preparation (the only history provided by the stalwarts of the Coroner's Office usually consisting of nuggets such as 'Found dead,' 'Collapsed in street' and, by far the most entertaining, 'Stopped breathing'), whereas hospital autopsies always involved trawling through large quantities of notes. Theoretically these were in a logical order, but the logic must have been from a non-Euclidean, parallel universe where time looped around on itself and where some days did not exist at all. Invariably, it took a long time to know what was required of the pathologist in a hospital autopsy. All of which would not have been a problem for a consultant, the work normally being done by the specialist registrar on the rota for post-mortems, but it so happened that the named individual was on annual leave that day.

Just as it so happened that Ludwig had back problems.

By half past ten, Eisenmenger was in the middle of the second case and he felt that he had established some sort of working relationship with Kevin Lewy.

Lewy was young to be in his position and it soon became obvious that he wasn't the brightest star in the firmament, but that suited Eisenmenger. Bright people, he knew well, thought too much; the less intellectually endowed had the oral cavity bypass switch welded into the open position.

'You're on your own, then.'

Lewy was weighing the organs of one Mr Matthew as Eisenmenger dissected them from the 'pluck'. He was wearing bright yellow gloves, the type worn by happy housewives on commercials for washing up liquid, but somehow there was no urge to snigger. Perhaps it was the muscles, or the tattoos, or the way he handled the knives.

He looked up, the comment failing to connect. 'Eh?'

'In the old mortuary there used to be four of you, didn't there?'

'Oh, yeah.'

'What happened to that place?'

'It was condemned. They amalgamated the public work with the mortuary in Christmas Street and converted this place just for the hospital work. I've been here for three years now.'

Eisenmenger placed seventeen slices through a liver with as much mechanical precision as the best of master butchers. It was fatty because the poor bugger had been diabetic.

. . . And bronchitic.

. . . And a cardiac cripple.

. . . And in renal failure.

The problem was not so much determining why he had died, as trying to twig why he had lived so long.

'So how long have you been a mortuary technician?'

Kevin Lewy made a face. Eisenmenger was beginning to notice that whenever he was required to think, Kevin Lewy made a face.

''Bout five years.'

Eisenmenger, who knew full well how long Kevin Lewy had worked in a mortuary, professed interest at this illuminating return. His tone suggested connections newly made as he said, 'You must have known the Pendreds.'

If he considered this a question that was in any way unusual or loaded, Lewy concealed it well. 'Oh, yeah,' he said brightly. 'They were working in Mole Street when I started there.'

'Mole Street?'

'Where the old mortuary was.'

'What were they like?'

As far as Lewy was concerned, the situation had changed. Whereas before he had been subordinate, now he was the leader, the one with the knowledge, with Eisenmenger the seeker, the one who was disadvantaged. He had a small moustache and short, black hair, so that he looked like an army recruit. From what Eisenmenger had seen he was an adequate mortuary technician, nothing more.

'Oh, they were weird. No doubt about that. Bloody weird. I knew as soon as I saw 'em that they were weird.'

Of course, Eisenmenger reflected ruefully, there was a downside to interviewing the less intellectually endowed. Much of what he was going to learn from Lewy was going to be strongly coloured by hindsight, perhaps obliterated by it. He resisted strongly the desire to make absolutely sure that Lewy thought they had been 'weird' and instead asked, 'How long had they been working here when you started?'

'Three years, I think.'

'Did you get on with them?'

Lewy had finished weighing the organs and was now wholly immersed in his recollection of the Pendreds. Eisenmenger was opening the pulmonary arteries and major bronchi prior to slicing the lungs. 'I suppose. They weren't really the kind of guys you ever got to know. They hardly ever said a word, for a start. Plus they never looked you in the eye. Made 'em look bloody shifty.'

The lungs had been badly abused despite having been owned from new by only one person. There was severe anthracosis throughout, the dust spots appearing in a lepine manner as he sliced. 'But they did their work okay? They were good at the job?'

'Well, they could dissect, all right. Bloody good at that, both of them; they could have the pluck out inside three minutes, the brain out in another two. But they weren't no good at the admin. Not the booking in or the rest of the paperwork. Joe had to do that.'

'Joe?'

'Joe Brocca. He was in charge then.'

Eisenmenger had turned to the heart. At six hundred and thirty-eight grams it was impressively ox-like. Regular transections of the coronary arteries showed them to be narrowed by atheromatous plaques, sometime down to pinholes. Lewy said, 'They also had trouble with sewing up. At least Martin did.'

Eisenmenger looked up at him. 'Trouble? What kind of trouble?'

'There were a few complaints from undertakers when his stitching came undone.'

Eisenmenger considered this. 'What happened?'

But Lewy didn't know. He shrugged. 'Joe sorted it out.'

Eisenmenger returned to the heart. He took a large pair of scissors and with them followed a snaking pathway through its muscle, cutting first through the right atrium to the right ventricle (and thereby through the tricuspid valve), then up through the main pulmonary artery; in this way he effectively separated the heart into two halves. A similar procedure followed, this time taking the scissors through the left atrium, through the mitral valve and down the back of the left ventricle. The heart muscle here was thickened but pale and flabby. Blood clot hung leech-like to the inner surface.

'When the murders started, did you suspect them straight away?'

Eisenmenger could see that Lewy was pulled one way by an

urge to boast, another by a vague attachment to objectivity. Human nature won. 'I did wonder. I think I told Joe, in fact, but he told me to shut up and keep out of it. Anyway, then they arrested the other bloke, so I thought that maybe I'd been wrong.'

Charlie Merrick, the funeral director.

Eisenmenger moved to the sink to wash from his gloves and apron the blood and small gobbets of flesh that inevitably became stuck there, then went to the small alcove where the dictation machine was located. He recorded his report (concluding that death was due to, 1a, Cardiac Failure, caused by, 1b, Ischaemic Heart Disease, caused in turn by, 1c, Coronary Atheroma, with Chronic Obstructive Airways Disease as a contributory factor) as Lewy picked up the sliced and opened organ remains in their two silver bowls and tipped them back into the body cavity.

Having finished, Eisenmenger came out of the alcove to start on the last case. 'So presumably it was a shock when Melkior was eventually arrested.'

'I suppose.' Lewy shrugged. There were small shaving nicks on his chin and they moved slightly as he made a face. 'Still, as I said, I'd had me suspicions all along.'

'About Melkior? Or about both of them?'

This made him pause. 'Both of 'em, I guess. You couldn't really separate 'em. They looked pretty much alike and they sure behaved the same. Either of them could have done it.'

Eisenmenger felt again something unsettling fluttering in the back of his mind. *But Martin had the alibi*, he reassured himself.

Except that something was wrong, and perhaps always had been.

'Presumably you talked to the police then.'

'Bloody 'ell, I should say so. It was bad enough that they'd had Martin and Melkior in and out of the station for days on end, leaving me and Joe to do all the work. Then, they arrest Melkior and spend near enough a week going over this place looking for evidence, and grilling me and Joe. Took us fucking weeks to get straight and clear the backlog.'

'Did Martin continue in the mortuary after it all happened?'

Lewy smiled, although at least one of its unmarried parents had been a leer. 'Nah. They used the crap state of the place to close the mortuary; they'd already been planning the amalgamation, so they took the opportunity to shift him to portering duties. Joe was due to retire, so he went without much trouble, which left me to carry on here.'

Eisenmenger continued with the last case, a fairly straightforward pancreatic cancer. Lewy was sewing up the second body when he commented, 'They should have known it was him, anyway. After what he did to Budd.'

Eisenmenger looked up sharply. 'Who's Budd?'

'A porter.'

'And what did he do to him?'

Lewy had another story to tell and this clearly pleased him. 'It wasn't long after he started here. Budd said something to upset Pendred.'

'What did he say?'

Lewy's face clouded with recall. 'Something about his parents. Something rude. Budd was a fucking sarky bastard.'

'And what happened?'

'It was never proved.' Suddenly Lewy seemed to be thinking better of his indiscretion.

'What wasn't proved?'

'That Melkior did it.'

'Did what?'

'Somebody jumped Budd one night, when he was going home after a late shift. Knocked him out, then took a knife and ripped his clothes down the front. Then whoever it was used that knife to make a shallow cut in his skin, all the way down from his neck to his prick. Not deep enough to open him up, but it bled like fuck.' Lewy looked uncomfortable, as if the recollection stirred up unpalatable memories. 'Like I said, no one ever proved it was him and Budd didn't have a clue, but no one ever narked the Pendreds again.'

Arthur Cox had no inkling what had happened when the first reporter came to call. With his wife visiting her sister he had risen late and had not even shaved, nor even been long from his bed, and he had not thought to put a radio or the television on. Thus he was completely unprepared for the onslaught that followed. Alas his confusion and ignorance, when transcribed and viewed through the appropriate journalistic prism, were ripe for misinterpretation.

'Chief Inspector Cox?'

Cox knew at once that it was a reporter although he had never to his knowledge met him before. He began to erect his defences at once, an automatic reaction learned long before, but the mechanism was rusty and he was far from practised.

'Yes?'

A Dictaphone appeared from his pocket and was at once under his nose. 'I wonder if you have any comment on the news?'

'News?'

'Yes, sir.'

'What news?' He was in fact already forming suspicions as to the nature of this 'news' but he needed to know more before he could respond appropriately. Unfortunately, this ignorance was translated as indifference.

'Don't you know?' There was something of the incredulous in this enquiry.

He was shaking his head as the reporter, a youth so callow he might not have been long from his mother's nipple, went on, 'There's been another murder, exactly like the first. Exactly like the ones you put Melkior Pendred away for.'

Cox closed his eyes, feeling the weight of age like a yoke on his shoulders.

'Chief Inspector? Have you any comment to make? How does it feel to have put away the wrong man? Are you ashamed that he died in prison an innocent man?'

'Go away,' he said tiredly. He was trying to close the door but like all good journalists, his visitor had placed his body in the way.

'Are you saying you don't care?'

'Please, go away.'

'Surely you feel some remorse . . .' The Dictaphone was being waved around in the gap as if in encouragement.

The door was pressing hard on the reporter's thigh now, but there was no sign that it was having any effect on its owner's eagerness to get answers. 'I can take it then that you're not bothered about having not only the wrongful imprisonment and death of Melkior Pendred on your conscience, but also now the deaths of Jenny Muir and Patrick Wilms?'

When another shove made no noticeable dent on the reporter's devotion to his job, and with all these questions being fired at him, all implying a guilt far from actually proved, Cox suddenly erupted. He gave up trying to crush the reporter's leg into nothingness and suddenly flung the door wide.

'Go away!' he shouted. 'Get off my property! Leave me alone!' Far from being surprised and far from being inclined to follow these strictures, the reporter actually smiled at this lambaste. He opened his mouth, presumably to goad Cox further, but didn't need to.

'You parasites! You vultures!'

The smile only grew. 'Can I quote you?'

Cox began to push, to push as he used to, when he was young and when he was not stalked by chest pain. 'Go away! Please, go away!'

The reporter had partially retracted his left leg, but his foot remained, its steel toecap preventing any serious damage to the foot within. 'Just give me a quote, Chief Inspector. Then I'll go.'

But Cox knew the press. Knew that they were worse than the most vicious of the criminals he had encountered because they pretended amicability. He took a huge breath and felt the first twinge of a deep and familiar pain, but he hoped to finish things before it grew as he knew it might.

'Look, I've nothing to say, okay?'

'But surely you're sorry about the new deaths?'

'Yes, of course . . .' He stopped, but it was too late. The sides of the trap had clicked shut without an audible sign, only the satisfied smile on the reporter's face alerting him to his fate. It was too much.

'You bastard!' He opened the door wide and was coming out, his face bearing the details of what his whole body was signalling. The reporter began to retreat, the smile gone to be replaced by a look of supercilious admonishment.

'There's no need to get violent.'

'Yes, there is, you jackal. You're no better than a vampire. You're the lowest of the low. You're scum. You're just fucking scum.'

He abhorred bad language, had often reprimanded his junior officers when they used it in his presence, but twice now he had felt its use necessary. He was still advancing and the reporter was still retreating down the path through Cox's neatly tended front garden with its roses and its cotoneaster and its small bay tree in the centre of the lawn. The pain in his chest was growing but he wasn't bothered about that now; a couple of tablets under his tongue would soon take of that.

They reached the gate and the reporter turned and was through it quickly. Once on the pavement and therefore no longer on Cox's property he seemed to draw again from the well of audacity. 'Any final quotes, Chief Inspector?'

Cox lunged forward, but it was more of a gesture than a serious attempt to reach his tormentor. He was becoming short of breath and the pain was snaking lazily up into his neck and around his left shoulder, like a lover's jealous caress. The journalist skipped back and then turned to walk away. 'I'll take that as a no, then,' was thrown over his shoulder in a deliberate final goad.

But Cox didn't care. The pain was stealing his breath, his anger at this outrage gradually being leached from his body as he became aware of his heart beating itself against his chest wall and his skin melting in warm clamminess.

He turned away and stumbled rather than walked back to his house. As he closed the front door, he saw a car stopping and a man and a woman getting out. One had a Dictaphone, the other a camera.

After he had showered, Lewy offered Eisenmenger a cup of tea. They sat in the small office (on second-hand and tattered chairs) and ate chocolate digestive biscuits while they talked of trivia; this consisting first of points of common experience, with Lewy asking questions about Eisenmenger's previous jobs, but inevitably the conversation turned to Eisenmenger's new colleagues.

'What do you think of 'em?'

Eisenmenger had known quite a few mortuary technicians in his professional life and he knew that they craved gossip, which they then used as currency. Because their job inevitably brought with it a degree of loneliness and estrangement from the rest of the hospital staff, they used this currency to buy their way into the mainstream.

Eisenmenger knew better than to proffer his opinions too early and too cheaply. 'An interesting bunch,' he said with a smile that was at least in part knowing.

'I'll say.'

'Do they give you much trouble?'

Lewy considered. 'The Prof. does occasionally. You know, sounds off about things not being tidy, that kind of thing, but it doesn't bother me.' Lewy was clearly the kind of person who wasn't going to be worried by anything said by a mere professor. 'Anyway, he's hardly ever down here. Only when we're doing the Membership exam.'

The practical part of the examination for Membership of the Royal College of Pathologists.

'So who's your line manager?'

'Dr von Guerke.'

Eisenmenger bit into a biscuit. 'Not too much trouble with her, I'd guess.'

Lewy heard the conspiratorial edge and responded. 'Nah. She's a sweetie.'

There was a lull in the conversation, with Eisenmenger drinking tea and Lewy staring at the upturned top of a skull that he kept paper clips in. Then, he added, 'Bit more than a sweetie to some, I've heard.'

Eisenmenger hadn't consciously worked out how to make Lewy talk, but instinct had led him to prepare the ground well. 'Really?' he said, his voice draped on a skeleton of salacious interest.

'Oh, yeah. Haven't you heard? Everyone knows.'

But Eisenmenger had been either too stupid or too deaf apparently.

'She and Dr Ludwig have had their moments,' explained Lewy.

Eisenmenger frowned and with a patina of innocence asked, 'He's married, isn't he?'

Lewy's eyelid dropped shut over a wide smirk. 'Not just to anyone either. His missus is loaded. Father-in-law is George Krabbe, the property developer.'

'Bloody hell,' whispered Eisenmenger appropriately.

Lewy sighed and it became clear that his mind had wandered. 'Makes you think, don't it? Christ knows what it would be like shagging her. Bloody tits probably knock you out cold if she got on top and started jumping about.' Eisenmenger had to admit that the image was arresting. 'Difficult to see what he sees in the old Zeppelin, other than jugs the size of piglets,' continued the mortuary technician. 'Mind you, it's just as hard to see why she'd want to shag him. I mean, he's one of the ugliest bastards I've ever seen.'

'"Zeppelin"?'

Lewy was by now totally happy talking to Eisenmenger. 'That's her nickname. Von Zeppelin.' He made a gesture indicating two large bosoms.

'Ah. I see what you mean.' He thought for a moment. 'How do people know? They haven't been caught, have they?'

'A couple of clinches here and there. I saw 'em once down here. It was in the pathologists' changing room. They were just coming out. Earwig said there was a spider in there that he'd got out for her. I reckon he got something else out for her, if you see what I mean.'

Having fathomed that Earwig was Ludwig, Eisenmenger did. 'Is this still going on?'

Lewy shrugged. 'Far as I know.'

'And everyone knows?'

'In the department they do.'

'But not Mrs Ludwig.'

Lewy shrugged. 'Serve the old cunt right if she did. He's an unpleasant bastard. Hardly says a word to me when he comes down here. Always grumpy and forever bollocking the junior doctors. I was quite pleased when you turned up instead of him. The less I see of him, the better, is the way I look at it.'

Eisenmenger didn't feel particularly well disposed to Ludwig either, but he didn't feel it entirely appropriate to agree too enthusiastically with the mortuary technician. Changing subjects he said, 'And what about the others? What about Dr Shaheen? How do you get on with him?'

Lewy had finished his tea but wasn't in any hurry to get back work; Eisenmenger knew that he could be doing more productive things, but curiosity was one of his vices.

'When he first started, he was a bit of stuck-up prick,' opined Lewy candidly, 'But when you get to know him, he thaws.' He considered and then with a nod, 'Yeah, he's all right for an A-rab.'

Eisenmenger closed mental eyes at this racism but overtly did not react, an omission that the freethinking liberal part of him found unforgivable. He said, 'Is it me, or is there something between him and Dr Ludwig?'

With complete seriousness and entirely without irony, Lewy

gave judgement upon Trevor Ludwig. 'He's a fucking racist, isn't he? He thinks Shaheen's nothing better than a camel-fucker.'

Trying to ignore the explosive charges of hypocrisy that had detonated around the last statement, Eisenmenger assimilated this datum. It certainly fitted what he had observed and deduced. Lewy, however, was giving forth again. 'I've heard him say some pretty nasty things about the Shah to the registrars while he's been down here.' Lewy apparently had a nickname for everyone, leading Eisenmenger to wonder about the nature of his own sobriquet. 'How he's no good, how he's only got the job 'cos of who he is, that kind of thing.'

'And who is he?'

Delighted to be once again in the possession of facts unknown to Eisenmenger, Lewy leaned forward. 'Well, that depends on which story you believe.' His pause, Eisenmenger had to concede, was masterful. 'There's the one that I heard Earwig telling Zeppelin – that his dad's a shipping millionaire. Owns more bloody boats than the Royal Navy – not that that's hard. Anyway, Daddykins gives Piringer money for his research; it's something to do with some sickness he's got. And when Daddy's little boy comes along and asks for a job, Piringer says, "Yes. No problem." Need I say more?'

'And have you heard other stories?'

Lewy squirted air through pursed lips beneath widened eyes. 'I should say so.' He lowered his voice so that the multiple listening devices would not catch what he now imparted. 'Milroy made it pretty plain that he reckoned the Shah and the Prof. were a couple of windjammers.'

The vernacular found Eisenmenger temporarily bereft of bearings before he understood. 'Homosexuals?'

Lewy's broad grin went up and down in affirmation.

'And Milroy told you this?'

'In great detail. Bloody spitting venom, he was. Hates 'em, you see.'

Eisenmenger stood up to wash his cup in the small sink by Lewy's desk. He said, 'Wilson doesn't seem to have a good word for anybody.'

Lewy had been tempted by one more biscuit. 'He thinks his colleagues are all a load of wankers. Keeps on about the old days, and how none of this present lot are worth anything more than used bog paper.'

A thought occurred to Eisenmenger. 'What about Victoria Bence-Jones?' The question was deliberately ambiguous, left to spin slowly round and point in whichever direction Lewy fancied.

Lewy frowned. 'That was a bit funny. When she first started, he couldn't say a bad thing about her. Then suddenly it all changed. He came down here one day and she was just signing a cremation form; as soon as she saw him, she came over most peculiar. Her face dropped, became almost a sneer. She couldn't get out of here fast enough.'

'Really? I wonder why.'

'Dunno.'

'And what about Dr Milroy? What was his reaction?'

'He just laughed. When she'd gone, he said something about her being menstrual.'

'When was this? How long ago?'

Lewy considered. 'Maybe a couple of months ago.'

Eisenmenger said nothing more and left shortly after with the patient's notes and the tapes of his autopsy findings under his arm. As he climbed the steps, he tried to work out why he was intrigued by this last piece of information. Perhaps it was the timing, he decided. Victoria Bence-Jones had gone sick with stress some three weeks after the incident with Milroy.

Not particularly significant, he was forced to admit, but still something worried at him as he sat in his office and stared at cobwebs in the corner of the ceiling.

Piringer was returning from a meeting at the Royal College of Pathologists when Wilson Milroy accosted him in the corridor outside his office. Since the top floor of the department was occupied only by a photocopying room, a secretarial office and Piringer's rather palatial lair, the Professor had difficulty working out quite where Milroy had been lying in wait.

'Wilson! What can I do for you?' Piringer always employed a hearty tone with Milroy.

'Can I have a word?'

Rather than pass through the secretary's office, they entered Piringer's office through the door directly off the corridor.

Once settled, the Professor behind his desk, Milroy on a considerably smaller chair opposite, Piringer asked, 'What can I do for you, Wilson?'

Wilson Milroy smiled. It was far from the first time that Piringer had faced this unpleasant spectacle, but repetition provided no robust defence. He tried not to avert his gaze.

'I thought that we should talk.'

'Of course.'

The smile refused to make an exit. 'About Amr.' The smile was a fixture, it seemed.

Piringer asked politely, 'What about him?'

'He has an older brother.'

Piringer did not then understand but was understandably suspicious. 'Has he?'

Wilson shifted position, crossing his legs, but still the smile remained; the Cheshire cat would have been dead impressed. 'Yes, he has. He says that his little brother is gay.'

Piringer looked down at his hands that were grasped on his lap. When his gaze again found Milroy, it was just a moment or two too late. 'And?'

Milroy's eyelids dropped briefly, a gesture of tired exasperation. 'Do I really have to be explicit?'

Piringer felt that his head was suddenly too small, ten thousand thoughts too small, but he was wise enough not to show anything. He opted for the standard indignation ploy. 'What the hell are you talking about?'

And still the smile wouldn't shift. 'About Amr Shaheen and how he got appointed, Adam. About why he got the nod over me.'

Piringer raised his eyes to the ceiling and he too joined in the general smile-fest. 'That again.'

'Don't be so dismissive, Adam. It's still a question worth asking. After all, the appointment of a consultant is an important thing. It needs to be as open as possible to scrutiny. Any queries must be openly dealt with.'

'As I recall, you were the only one to have any queries, Wilson.'

At last Milroy lost his sense of humour. 'Just as well, then.'

Piringer asked lazily, 'By which you mean?'

Milroy's snort was a classic of its kind. 'We're both intelligent men, Adam. Do I really have to spell things out?'

'Perhaps you should. I appear to be dense today.'

Milroy shrugged. 'You're gay too, aren't you?'

Piringer's head jerked up at that. For a moment as fleet as a mayfly's love his face showed first shock, then anger, then control returned. In a voice too neutral to be anything other than a pretence he said, 'What does idle speculation about my sexuality have to do with anything?'

But Milroy wasn't interested in Piringer's efforts at bluster and obfuscation. 'You worked with Shaheen before, didn't you?'

Piringer was too wary to rush into reckless denial. Instead he admitted in a low voice, 'For a while.'

Milroy snorted. 'For four years.'

'I have worked with a lot of people, Milroy.' Piringer had moved on from the use of the first name, a sign of how things stood between them.

Milroy leaned back in his chair, as if they were in the club after a particularly good dinner. 'How about this? You're gay and he's gay. You've worked together for a few years and over that time you've grown close. So close that when you land the job here, you feel obliged to help him out. Perhaps you're still lovers, for all I know.'

Piringer's whole demeanour now was stiff, as if his muscles were pulled tight by a vicious puppeteer. His face was pale, his lips merely wire cords stretched over his teeth. 'That's a lie.'

'Which bit? Who are you living with, anyway?'

'That is none of your business. It is no one's business but mine.'

'It is if you've decided to make an appointment based on how you feel about someone. I deserved better than that.'

Piringer finally found movement. He stood, jerkily almost, but none the less menacing. 'Get out! Get out of my office!'

Milroy showed no sign that he was perturbed. He stood up as slowly and insolently as he could, then declared sweetly, 'Of course.'

He turned to go and behind him Piringer shouted, 'There's no proof. If you repeat this defamation outside this office, I'll ruin you, Milroy. Remember that, I'll ruin you.'

It wasn't until Wilson Milroy had made his stately way to the door that he turned to respond. 'I rather doubt that, Adam. You see, I have proof.'

He left at once, leaving the door open upon Piringer's face. There was a look of startled dread upon it.

'You're late. Is there something wrong?'

148

Peter at once shook his head and hastened to reassure her. 'No, nothing.'

Which to Beverley's ears was one negation too many.

They ordered coffee and Danish and sat at a small table in the window of the shop. They talked of inconsequential things but Beverley felt as if they were standing in front of a man taking a belt to a child and admiring the buckle. She said, 'You haven't asked.'

He feigned surprise. 'About what?'

It would have been better, she considered, if he hadn't asked that. 'The Pendred case.'

'Ah.' He looked into his cappuccino before asking, 'And how is it going?'

She felt sadness like a deep dark pit beckoning. 'Badly.'

As soon as they entered the examination room, Helena knew. She did not need to hear the words delivered with a smile that Mr James Angelman, Consultant Breast Surgeon, might have considered reassuring, but that to Helena was patently false, plastered there because that was what you did when you are about to give someone the worst news that they'll probably ever hear. She wondered how many people had had to endure what he was about to say and decided that it was probably in the thousands.

Thousands of poor sods who had heard the words she was about to hear.

'Sit down, Miss Flemming.' The smile was fixed, as if tiny hooks were pulling it wide. There was a glance for Eisenmenger, a slight nod of acceptance that he was her chosen partner and therefore entitled to some peripheral inclusion in this vignette.

For some reason her breast was becoming painful again. An hour earlier, Mr Angelman had first passed a needled syringe, and then inserted a rather thicker, more menacing trocar. The surgeon had claimed to inject local anaesthetic, but Helena had wondered at the time and then it had started to throb with the kind of deep, chiming pain that she remembered from a laceration she had once received after putting her hand through a window as a six-year-old child.

'I've got the results of some of the tests back.'

Of course he had. Why else would they be back here, in the

small room with its desk and its anglepoise lamp, its three chairs and its complete lack of character?

He rose and went to a white box affixed to the wall behind them. It was fronted with white plastic and had two switches at the bottom right-hand corner. Clipped to the front were two X-rays, which were illuminated when the surgeon flipped the switches. It was almost theatrical, the way this prop had been prepared.

They were looking at mammograms, as Mr Angelman explained. In fact they were two X-ray views of Helena's left breast. They had a kind of beauty, somewhat at odds with Helena's recollection of how they had been acquired.

She had expected to lose dignity, certainly to lose control, but she had not expected the degree to which she would be expected to accept passivity. This was Angelman's world and, to a lesser extent, it was also John's; it most certainly wasn't hers. She was the visitor here, the centre of attention but that particular role required something that she was finding it difficult to supply. The ultrasound had been bad enough – the horrible, cold gel and the intrusive pressure of the probe – but the mammogram had surpassed even this. Placing her breast upon a cold metal plate, having it handled in a completely dispassionate way by a stranger who then had the temerity to squash it beneath Perspex, all this had only contributed to the impression that she was merely a number, like a single cow in a large herd.

Mr Angelman pointed to the spectral image. 'You see that?' She nodded and at once wondered why, because she could see nothing at all that was different about the area he indicated. 'Stromal deformity and some hard microcalcs,' he proclaimed confidently and obscurely.

She realized that she must have looked perplexed because beside her John murmured, 'Microcalcifications.'

Mr Angelman had turned away from the X-ray, forcing them back to the chairs in front of the desk. Once settled he looked up from her notes that were new and thin, making her wonder if they would soon grow much fatter and more dog-eared. 'We won't get the results from the biopsy until the day after tomorrow.' He cast a glance at Eisenmenger, aware that he was a pathologist. 'But we do have the cytology and ultrasound results.'

It was the pause that told her, told them both.

'The indications are that it's a small malignancy.'

She hadn't known what she would do if, when, she heard those words and, having heard them, she still didn't know. Strangely it was John who seemed to find some pain in this single and oh-so-peculiar word. He swore softly but most distinctly, making her look across to him and see that his eyes were closed.

Mr Angelman knew better than to allow too much time for contemplation. 'I know that this is a shock, but I can assure you that the prognosis is excellent.'

It was John who recovered his voice first. 'How big is it?'

The surgeon consulted the notes again. An ultrasound photograph was stuck into them. 'We've measured it at fourteen millimetres.'

John said at once to her, 'It's not big.' She nodded but she was lost in thoughts of her own by now. 'What happens now?'

Mr Angelman said at once, 'I take it out. Wide local excision.'

'Not mastectomy?'

He smiled. 'Goodness, no.'

'What about the axillary nodes?' John's voice beside her was still anxious.

'I can't feel any positive nodes.' He aimed this at Helena. To John he said, 'Sentinel node.' And, almost like a well-rehearsed music-hall routine, back to her he explained, 'I inject some dye and a radioactive tracer into the tumour at operation, then we track where it goes along the lymph channels. The first node that becomes positive, we take out. If that's negative, then we can be sure that all the others will be.'

'Radioactive?'

'Very low dose. It's gone in six hours. No more radiation than a chest X-ray.'

She considered, as if she were fully in possession of the facts and the implications, as if she were objective and calm and thinking about where to go on holiday. She was very far from any such state.

Mr Angelman was continuing. 'I'm afraid I can't say at this stage whether you'll need any adjuvant treatment.'

What is he saying now? Adjuvant? What does that mean?

Again it was John who explained. 'You may need radio-therapy or even chemotherapy.'

Thoughts of hair loss, vomiting, tiredness and a million other unpleasantnesses filled her head.

'I'll have to check, but I think I can get you in at the start of next week.' The surgeon who appeared so kind was looking down at a list. He nodded and made a mark, then stood. The appointment was at an end. She had turned from a woman who had no health worries at all to one who had suddenly to contemplate death, but his part in the proceeding was temporarily done.

'There's no need to worry unduly, Helena.' Suddenly they were on first name terms, it appeared. 'The Breast Care Nurse has some leaflets for you.' As if leaflets were a cure for cancer.

Now they were standing but she felt as if she were floating. Floating into oblivion.

John took her hand and led her out.

'Where are we then?'

Refusing to allow the phrase 'in the shit' to distract him from what Homer wanted to hear, Wright said, 'Second murder in two days, sir.'

'Connections?'

'Not directly, but both were known to Martin Pendred.'

Homer was sitting at his desk, looking morose. He always looked slightly down when he was thinking, but today he had definitely declined into morose. He was leaning forward, his forearms on the desk, his hands clasped, almost in supplication to a god. Wright, remembering what Call had said to Homer, tried not to let his eyes linger too long on his superior's face.

'What else?'

'Well, the MO's the same.'

'*Apparently*, Wright. Apparently. We haven't had the post-mortem on the second case yet.'

Wright was sitting in the chair opposite the desk. His bladder was rather full and he was tired and he had a pain in his left big toe. He suffered from occasional bouts of gout and he was afraid that this presaged an attack.

'Oh come on, sir,' he urged. 'The poor bugger was sliced just like Jenny Muir, and his organs were removed just the same. They were hidden in the same macabre way as well.'

Homer said after a pause, 'Yes, I suppose so.' He suddenly looked across at Wright, where before his eyes had been on his desk. 'But we must never jump to conclusions, Wright. That's bad policecraft.'

There was so much hypocrisy associated with this advice that perhaps Wright, who merely nodded gravely, missed it completely, much as an ant might miss an elephant.

'When's the autopsy on Wilms being done, sir?'

Homer's head had sunk down slightly, his gaze back upon the small space of desk between his arms. 'Tomorrow morning. Eight o'clock sharp.' He did not need to say that he wanted Wright's attendance; indeed he sounded distracted as he said it, the idea already written into history's scroll. He asked, 'Is it possible that I'm wrong? Is it possible that Pendred's not guilty?'

Wright was momentarily unsure whether he was required to respond, since Homer had a fancy for rhetorical enquiries, but then Homer jerked his head up and looked at him with a demanding, 'Well?'

'Uh, well, I suppose there's a faint possibility . . .' He paused because the signs were ominous. Homer had begun to frown and, like the good party worker that he was, Wright changed his pattern of thinking accordingly. 'But I can't really see it, can you?' Homer failed to nod, so Wright drove a little way on. 'The evidence that it was one of the Pendred twins who committed the first murders is overwhelming.' Homer's facial expression, previously in stasis, had melted slightly at this, so Wright had a crescendo of confidence as he continued smoothly. 'We know that Melkior Pendred's dead, so that leaves Martin. These murders have all the same hallmarks of the previous murders – in fact, they're identical, and any slight differences we can surely attribute to the time that's passed.'

'Maybe.' Homer said this with a face that was straight and a voice that was smirking.

'Well, if you take into account that both victims were known to Martin Pendred and that no sooner do we let him out of custody, he goes missing and then another body turns up, I can't see how he didn't do it.'

He didn't quite invite three cheers, but Wright felt he had done fairly well and Homer, although still appearing to probe for problems, was also clearly pleased. 'But what about his alibi for the Muir killing?'

That was easy. With confident stride, Wright stepped forward and smote it mightily. 'He hasn't really got one, in my view. I don't think any jury's going to fret too much after what happened last night.'

Homer nodded slowly. It was then that there seemed suddenly to occur to him a genuinely uncomfortable thought, a flaw in his theory. 'But why?' he asked almost plaintively. 'Why did he suddenly start again?'

This was trickier; a slower ball and one that was moving deceptively in the air. Wright felt distinctly uncertain of what to do with it, but he put up a stout defence. 'He is mad, sir.' It wasn't a pretty stroke, but it was effective.

'Yes,' said the Chief Inspector, 'he is, isn't he?' Apparently satisfied with this explanation, ignoring the anguished squeals of a million dead psychiatrists, he moved on. 'Right. Who's on house-to-house?'

'Sergeant Kaplan. He's got four teams of two.'

'Pendred's house is still being watched?'

'Fisher and Neumann. And Clark's gone to check on Wilms' house.'

This brief burst of activity, apparently so optimistic, died into depression when Homer suddenly sighed and said, 'Not that he'll turn up there.'

'He might, sir,' said Wright, more out of encouragement than expectation. 'He is unpredictable.'

It didn't work. Homer continued to brood. At last he said, 'We've got to find him. Call made it clear that if we don't find him, I might as well buy a mop and start practising for a janitor's job. The rest – the forensics, the autopsy, the house-to-house – is just detail.'

It seemed to Wright to be a fair conclusion. 'But where do we start?' he enquired. 'He's got no family left and he never had any friends. The only places he ever went were work, home and the pub.'

Homer stared at him hard. Had Wright just strangled a kitten in front of him, it would not have been a more disgusted expression that Homer wore. Wright mumbled defensively, 'You never know, forensics might give us some clue as to where he's hiding.'

'Oh, yes? Like a type of soil found only in one particular street? Like a scrap of a library card giving just enough information for you to brilliantly deduce his present whereabouts?' He snorted. 'Do me a favour, Wright. This is real, not Hercule

154

bloody Poirot. Forensics were no bleeding use on the first murder, were they? This time round there was enough rubbish and shit around to have buried an oil tanker, so I hardly think I can rely on a smoking gun, can I?'

Wright said resignedly, 'No, sir.'

As if to prove his point, Homer demanded suddenly, 'Where are the forensic reports from the Muir killing?'

Wright fished them from an impressive pile of similar documents that tottered from a blue box on a desk beneath the window. They were weighted down with a large pebble on which the words *Weston-super-Mare* had been obscured by a sticky label bearing Jenny Muir's name.

Homer leafed through it but his gloom did not depart. He threw it down with something very close to disgust. 'Where's the autopsy report?'

Wright obliged, but Homer's patience with this was even briefer. 'Why does he have to talk like this?'

'Like what, sir?'

'This medical bullshit. *The incision was eighty-three point five centimetres long and began at a point two centimetres above the anterior prominence of the thyroid cartilage, ending on the pubic symphysis at a point two point five centimetres anterior to the anterior commissure.* What does that mean?'

'Don't know, sir.' This was uttered merely to keep Homer satisfied.

Homer turned to the back page. 'Even his bloody conclusions are gobbledegook. *The presence of the small glioma (necrotic and therefore most probably glioblastoma multiforme)* . . .' Homer struggled with this last and in fact got the pronunciation almost completely wrong. '. . . *can be considered an incidental finding, as can the not insignificant degree of atheromatous coronary stenosis found in the proximal part of the left circumflex artery* . . .' He threw the report down. 'Why can't he just say that she died when that mad bastard Pendred sliced her throat from ear to ear?'

Wright merely shrugged now and Homer, finding even this brief storm of indignation to be of only scant comfort, flung himself back in his chair, his hands on his face. There followed a minute of silence, perhaps in tribute to a policeman's unhappy lot. Wright waited, the obedient sidekick as ever.

Suddenly Homer found inspiration and enthusiasm. He stood up (slightly surprising Wright who had closed his eyes for a moment). 'Okay. This is what we're going to do. You're going to find the biggest bloody map of the area around Pendred's house that there is. We're going to start house-to-house in a widening circle, and we're going to search any and every empty property as well. I want the Western Infirmary searched from top to bottom, and I want all the staff who've had contact with Pendred interviewed. I want them asked if they remember anything that might tell us where he's gone. The same for the pubs where he drinks. Got that?'

Wright was struggling to scribble down these instructions. It seemed to him to be a massive and probably hopeless task, but at least it was not inaction. Eventually he said, 'Got it, sir.'

'Right. I'll get on to Call. We're going to need huge numbers of bodies for this. Also, we're going to go public. Tell them who we're looking for. Get his face on the telly and in the papers. Get it known.'

'Is that wise, sir?'

'The public need to be made aware, both for their own safety and so that they can help us.' He paused and his face broke into a smile that was long removed from amused. 'Anyway, I think it's about time people knew the truth about the Pendred case, Sergeant.'

The reporters and photographers knew Beverley and she knew them, but there was no room for sentiment; they were still playing the game and the rules were the same, but the roles had changed. She was now quarry rather than uneasy ally. They were waiting for her outside the station following her interview with the Chief Superintendent and, like a piece of ageing meat past its sell-by date, she felt thrown to ravenous dogs.

'Beverley? Beverley?'

There were only ten of them, but then there were only four horsemen of the apocalypse and at that moment she felt as if the end of the world had truly arrived.

'What have you got to say about the murders, Beverley? Is this another one of your cock-ups?' The background to this query was in irregular staccato of camera shutters.

She was pushing through them. She had intended a dignified silence, knowing that this was the best of a poor set of options, but she felt that plan go wrong almost at once. 'Fuck off,' she advised them tiredly. 'Just fuck off.'

'Is that a quote?' asked one of them, his face bearing a grin that broadcast his contempt.

'Do you want to tell us how you got it so wrong again?' enquired another.

'What about Jenny Muir's husband? Do you feel sorry that because of you, he's become a widower?' a third wished to know.

They were dancing around her across the car park outside the station. She was aware that a few of her erstwhile colleagues were standing and staring at this strange street entertainment. She could not see whether they wore expressions of sympathy or enjoyment.

Nearly at her car. 'What about Melkior Pendred? Do you feel ashamed of what you did to him?'

She turned at that one. It was so far below the belt she expected to see blood and grit on his knuckles. She opened her mouth to reply but the hungry look in their eyes warned her. She clamped her lips closed, got in the car and drove through them. None, she noted disappointedly, was killed.

She hoped that would be last of it. They would not get past the entrance foyer at the block of flats and she had no reason now to go anywhere for a day or two. She had only to sit and brood.

'Well, that's that, then.' She hadn't meant to say it, words from her mind, thoughts filling it and diverting it. She glanced across at John, could tell that he knew exactly what she was referring to. Of course he did. You don't get told you've almost certainly got cancer and then start fretting about the price of tomatoes or the state of public transport.

He said at once, 'No, it's not.' This was definite, assertive. In a tone that was slightly more giving he went on, 'It's not the happiest of news . . .'

She laughed but the sound might have withered a fragile flower. He drove on through this scornful noise. '. . . But it's *not* the end. It's *not* a death sentence.'

They were driving away from the hospital and the traffic was still heavy from the rush hour. She sat next to him in the front passenger seat, still and straight, her face, she knew, set into rigidity. She had tried to analyse what she was feeling and decided that it was predominantly anger. If she probed deep enough there was fear (if she stayed long enough she smelt real terror), but her reaction was essentially anger.

She felt able to say nothing to his reassurances.

'It's a small lesion and it's resectable without mastectomy. There's nothing clinically in the lymph nodes. All those are good prognostic factors.'

There were a few seconds of quiet within the car when the noises of the engine and street outside invaded their space. Helena had not looked at him during his encouragements and he, of course, could do nothing other than stare at the road outside as they sparred with the traffic around them. Only when they were halted by a red light did she see him from the corner of her eye look across at her. He put his hand on her arm. 'The survival rate from breast cancer is increasing all the time, especially here in the UK . . .'

There was no warning, the bile and the bitterness erupting from her, an occurrence as unexpected to her as it clearly was to him. 'That's the point, you idiot! That's the whole, bloody point! *Survival!* Suddenly I've got to become a survivor! Suddenly, I'm facing death when less than a week ago I was just normal!'

She had shouted this and wanted to quieten her voice but there was no way for her to make it happen. She continued, 'God, you make me sick! You with your talk of statistics and prognosis and treatment. What do you know of how I'm feeling?'

The lights had changed but he didn't notice until the car behind sounded its horn. As he hurriedly put the car in gear and moved off, he tried to intercede. 'I don't . . .'

She could feel herself beginning to cry now, beginning to feel the fear, as if this outburst were draining her fury to expose her terror, but she couldn't stop. This was now a rupture rather than a controlled release. 'No, you don't. You think you do because you're a doctor, because you've been to lectures and clinics, because you've seen operations, because you've lorded it over the poor bastards who've come to you for help or come to you for dissection, but you don't. You don't really.'

She had to stop for breath but he knew better than to try to intercede again. When she began once more there was the sad moisture of tears in her eyes and her voice was gradually ebbing and breaking as it did so. 'You can't do. Not until you've gone to the doctor because you've found a lump somewhere or because you're losing weight or coughing too much. Then, when you've waited while they've done their tests and you've caught glimpses in their expressions of what they suspect but won't say, when they've finally taken a deep breath and put those smiles on their faces because they're about to blow your world apart, then you'll understand what I'm feeling now. Then you'll have the right to talk to me and comfort me.'

She was openly crying by now. They were almost back at her flat and there was yet more rain threatening. Her next few words were snatched between sobs. 'Statistics are no good for me. They might give you some comfort, but for me they're just the cruellest of lies.' Before she broke down completely, she managed one last sentence, a cry of anguish. 'I don't want to have this, John!'

He pulled into the parking area by the side of her apartment block a few seconds later. He parked and at once tried to put his arms around her, not even turning the engine off, but she couldn't respond. She had to get out, get away, as if by running she could outpace her cancer. She ran from the car and up to her flat, not bothering with the lift but taking the stairs. Once she stumbled and nearly fell forward on to her chin. When she got to her front door, she opened it and rushed at once to the bathroom where she began to try to vomit into the basin. Her stomach was empty and there was nothing to come except verdant, acidic mucus, but again and again she retched and gagged.

When Eisenmenger came into the flat through the still open front door, he stood in the hallway silently before turning and leaving.

The eyes that watched Helena enter her apartment block were in themselves no different to billions of others. They were dark eyes, the whites no longer as bright as a newborn's, the bottom rim of the iris just beginning to pick up the silver-greyness of age, but they were anatomically correct. There was nothing intrinsically within them or about them that was different.

But different they were.

Different in perception, different in comprehension, and different in intention.

Martin Pendred turned away, his travelling gaze fixing briefly upon the man who followed her. He had waited a long time for the solicitor to return and, although he did not articulate it, he had been undecided until that moment as to what to do, what to say.

All he had known was desire.

His decision to follow the man might have been made for him, a thought placed in his mind from without. Whatever its source, he acted upon it without question.

Eisenmenger was just getting into the car when he caught sight of the large man on the opposite side of the road, heading towards him. He thought that he recognized him, although it was a hazy recollection, without detail or definition. It was only the peculiar gait of the man, the curious robotic demeanour that caused him to call out speculatively, 'Martin? Martin Pendred?'

The sound of the name, or perhaps just the sound, caused the other to pause. His eyes were fixed upon Eisenmenger, but there was no humanity in them, no emotions playing around them. He stopped in the middle of the road, his hands deep in the pockets of his buttoned jacket, the cold of the night impotent upon him.

'It is Martin, isn't it?'

Eisenmenger didn't feel afraid. Curious, perhaps, but not afraid. He closed the car door and came around the back of it.

With that, the large man turned and began to walk rapidly away.

After a momentary hesitation, Eisenmenger began to follow.

Dennis Cullen enjoyed night fishing for many reasons, not least of which was the solitude and the quiet. Having been made redundant from his job as a bus driver three years before, he had managed only a part-time job as cleaner in a factory that made steel shelving. It was an extremely noisy working environment that invariably left him with a headache, and fishing, he had found, was the perfect way to soothe the stress; since he was long since divorced from his wife, he had no need to spend much time in his small maisonette.

Not that he ever caught much, but that wasn't the point. The occasional perch, a few tench, nothing spectacular. The lights from the footpath behind him weren't really strong enough and he knew that he should have invested in expensive high-intensity lamps if he wanted to do things properly, but he couldn't see the point.

Half the time he dozed anyway.

Eisenmenger was walking as quickly as he could to keep up with Pendred. He did not call out again and was now more interested in following him to see where he went. Why, he wondered, had he been outside Helena's flat?

The route Pendred was taking led down to the river. He saw his quarry about a hundred metres ahead turn right on to the towpath which thankfully was reasonably well lit. He hurried after him.

Dennis Cullen was quite well hidden in the scrub and small trees by the water's side. He heard footsteps hurry by on the path behind him. He took no great notice but he did happen to glance to his right to see the figure of a large, hunched man walk rapidly into the shadow of the road bridge about twenty metres beyond.

His interest was tweaked, though, by the sound of more hurrying footsteps passing behind him. When the cause of these became visible, it occurred to him that the second man – considerably smaller and thinner – was following the first.

'Aye, aye,' he murmured. Occasionally he was witness to a variety of illegal activities such as drug dealing, and once he had had a spectacularly ringside seat to a prolonged and exhausting bout of sexual intercourse on the grass not five metres from him, and it looked as if something was going to happen tonight.

Eisenmenger saw Pendred hurry into the shadows, unaware that he was participating in a spectator sport. He rushed on into the shadow of the bridge and, just as his footsteps began to echo and the sounds of flowing water to magnify and clarify, he realized that Pendred was no longer ahead of him.

It was then that something came out of the darkness to his right and grabbed him around the shoulders from behind. The grip was immediately crushing and although he struggled it was completely useless. He cried out but that was at once stifled by a hand that seemed then to be as big as a bear's paw. He began to thrash out, mostly with his legs and lower body, but despite this he felt himself being pushed towards the water. No matter how hard he tried to resist, the movement continued until he was on the very edge of the path.

The cry was short and sharp but given a sense of peril by the acoustics of the bridge. Dennis Cullen was torn between interfering and being, as he saw it, sensible. He didn't react at once but instead listened, the sounds of shuffling and rustling coming to him from the shadows. He also saw occasional flashes of a trouser leg or a shoe as they were thrust briefly into the dim light that reached furthest under the bridge.

Something serious was happening, that much was obvious to him. Perhaps an assault, perhaps worse. What should he do?

He was no great hero, but he liked to think of himself as an ordinary, decent man: the average citizen, the one by which a country is measured. It wasn't so much courage that decided him as hatred of the thought that the country's moral fibre had degenerated to such a degree that violence and possibly murder could be ignored. He got to his feet and began to hurry up the short bank to the path.

Eisenmenger felt himself falling into the water and, absurdly, his first thought was how cold and wet it was. His descent, though, was controlled, the arm around his shoulders and the hand over his mouth easily taking his weight; he felt almost childlike in such a hold. Then, again with adamantine strength, the arm around his shoulders was removed and he was held just above the water's surface by the hand over his mouth before his head was brought back to collide painfully with the concrete of the path's edge.

He thought about struggling again, trying to free the grip now that he had two hands of his own to use. That thought was confined to the recycle bin when the knife appeared in his peripheral vision to his left.

It began to move towards his throat.

Cullen hurried along the path, squinting into darkness. He could just make out a man crouched on his knees apparently peering over the edge of the path into the river.

In his left ear, Eisenmenger heard breathing and then, indistinctly, he heard a sound, a sibilant word that he couldn't quite comprehend and then was gone. He couldn't speak because of the hand. He couldn't move his head because it was clamped so hard against the edge of the path that sounds of grating were being transmitted through the bone of his skull. All he could do was try to reach up with his hands and grab hold of the wrist that was now coming towards him, vicious blade held towards him.

Cullen's approach slowed. What was the bloke doing? And where was the other one?

It was then that he realized the crouching figure was holding something in the water, and a dead heat with this was the recognition of what that something was.

He was watching someone being drowned.

He opened his mouth, took in air and was about to shout out, try to stop the crime by surprise. Then he stopped.

He caught sight of a bright glint of silver moving above the water and the realization of what it was terrified him.

He began to run.

Eisenmenger had caught hold of the arm but he might just as well have been trying to stop the piston of a steam engine. The knife came on anyway. Despite the limitations, he tried to move his head away, a futile gesture.

The knife caught his skin and began to cut.

Dennis Cullen charged forward, recklessness now the only captain of his actions. His one plan was simple and he executed it perfectly. He ran as hard as he could into the crouching figure and collided with it.

Afterwards, he remembered that the impact was a little like

163

running into a brick wall, but it had good effect. The crouching figure lost balance, rolled away and fell into the water.

Eisenmenger's release was abrupt. Simultaneously the knife was jerked up, causing a jagged cut under his jaw, then taken away. He slipped down under the water as he heard movement and a muffled splash to his right. He found himself choking on dirty river water, his chest suddenly angry, his stomach sick. He thrashed around and came back up into air, coughing and nearly vomiting. At once a hand reached down to him and he heard a hoarse voice say, 'Come on. Quickly.'

Eisenmenger was cold and wet and the laceration on his throat was bloody painful. He sat at Dennis Cullen's dining-room table and sipped hot chocolate while Constable Fisher asked him questions and his rescuer sat opposite and spent much of the time frowning.

'You're sure it was Martin Pendred?'

Eisenmenger shook his head. 'Not for certain.'

Fisher scratched his eyebrow with his pencil. 'But you said – '

'I *thought* it was Pendred. I can't be sure – I haven't seen him for four years, and even then it was only briefly at the trial of his brother. The man I saw sure looked like Melkior, though.'

Fisher had with him a clipboard and he picked this up to show Eisenmenger a photograph. 'Is this the man?'

Eisenmenger nodded, much to Fisher's satisfaction. He noted this down. 'Where did you first see him?'

'In McArdle Street.'

'And you followed him from there to the river?'

Eisenmenger hesitated before answering affirmatively. A more experienced or more astute interrogator might have noticed this, but Fisher was neither of these.

'Where he attacked you.'

'Vicious, it was.' Mr Cullen's opinion was accepted with polite interest by Constable Fisher, although he decided not to make a note of it.

Fisher again applied pencil to eyebrow. 'I wonder why he attacked you.'

Eisenmenger shrugged. 'He didn't like being followed, I suppose.'

Fisher considered this and found it not inconceivable, a judgement he signalled by a grave and slow nodding of his head. He said then, 'Well, I guess that's about all I need at the moment, Dr Eisenmenger.'

Eisenmenger finished the beverage and put down the mug; it had a picture of Winston Churchill on it. He said tiredly, 'Fine.'

Fisher stood up. 'You'll have to make a formal statement. Can you come to the station tomorrow?'

'What time?'

'Whenever's convenient.'

Dennis Cullen clearly felt excluded. 'What about me?'

Constable Fisher's diplomatic skills proved sadly inelastic. 'What about you?'

'Don't you want a statement from me?'

Fisher's first impulse was to dismiss the idea, but caution prevailed. He had learned that, with Homer, there could never be enough paperwork. 'Okay,' he conceded grudgingly. 'You'd better make one, too.'

Eisenmenger added to the pleasure thus engendered by saying, 'Thanks for what you did, Mr Cullen. I really can't thank you enough.'

He stood up, the movement making him aware of how damp his clothing still was. The towel on which he had been sitting was completely wet through. Fisher asked, 'Would you like a lift, Dr Eisenmenger?'

His host put in, 'You can spend the night here if you like, on the sofa.'

As enticing as that was, Eisenmenger declined. Not only was he still wet through but his chest felt bruised, and he wanted to be alone. Reluctantly, Mr Cullen let him depart with Fisher.

His car was only a few streets away and as soon as Fisher dropped him off, he got in and began the drive home. He did not think it for the best to disturb Helena.

Several things about the evening's events bothered him. What had Pendred been doing when he had first encountered him? It had seemed as if he had been approaching Eisenmenger, perhaps following him, but for what reason? To attack him, as he had done under the bridge? If that were so, then for what reason?

165

Perhaps revenge. Eisenmenger's part in the conviction of Melkior had been relatively slight, but not insignificant. Yet surely there were others in front of him in the queue for Martin's vengeance?

And then there was the peculiar way he had first approached Eisenmenger, then run from him. What was that about?

He shook his head and sighed. Too many questions, most of them contradictory.

He turned into the mews where he lived, parked the car and stepped out. As he put the key in his front door, another question occurred, equally perplexing. What word had been whispered into his ear as Pendred had held his head to slice his throat?

He felt that he ought to know, felt also that it was important to know, but no amount of effort could bring about his enlightenment.

Fisher's report back to Homer sent the Chief Inspector scurrying to his map.

'A mile and a half away from the cemetery,' he concluded ruminatively to Wright. He turned. 'What do you think?'

Wright thought that it meant little. It was near enough to be suggestive of vicinity to the murder scene, far enough to be dismissible. He said carefully, 'I'm not sure, sir.'

Homer nodded slowly. Then, 'Why did he approach Eisenmenger?' A pause. 'Why did he attack him?'

Wright cast about for inspiration. 'Revenge?'

Homer made a face. 'Maybe, but why didn't he just go for him in the middle of the street? Why did he go towards him, then run off?'

'Perhaps he wanted to draw him away from a well-lit area to somewhere a little more secluded and darker.'

Homer liked that one. 'Yes,' he decided. 'You may well be right on that, Sergeant.'

The call from Beverley had been full of mixed emotions for Eisenmenger. She had rung him at home the night before, just after he had got home and while he remained in wet clothes. Her slightly husky voice had brought back emotions that he found both exciting and guilt-ridden, but even then he had thought that she sounded stressed. When he had asked why she wanted to see him, she had been initially reticent, subsequently eloquent, as if the need to talk had fought and conquered the desire for self-containment.

They're throwing me to the wolves, John.

The cliché somehow didn't sound too outrageous. And when he had asked what she meant, she had replied, *The Pendred case. They've seen the headlines and they're threatening to suspend me. This is the end for me if Homer proves me wrong.* She wasn't crying and her voice didn't sound as if she were holding back tears, but it wasn't normal either.

Yet he didn't at once reply. It was perhaps cruel of him, but it wasn't done deliberately. While she was forced to wait, he was forced to wonder about the wisdom of making contact yet again with Beverley Wharton.

She said into his silence, 'Remember what I did, John? Remember how I saved Helena in the fire?'

He almost smiled. He couldn't blame her; emotional blackmail was the last weapon in the locker, the one that everyone used eventually.

'I remember.'

'I know you don't owe me anything, John. I know that I've been a bitch, but I'm asking for your help, John.'

He took a long while to point out lazily, 'There are some who are saying that you screwed up again, Beverley.'

'No, I didn't, John. Not this time.'

They were at the ends of the telephone line and he suddenly realized that they were as intimate as lovers. He was finding himself being sucked into culpability.

A pleasurable culpability.

'So you say.'

She responded at once. 'Let me prove it. Let me talk to you.'

He didn't know what to do or say.

Yet he knew how weak he was. He wanted to see her again. 'Where and when?'

She seemed almost surprised by this, as if she had assumed that he would be a tougher challenge than he had proved. 'Well, how about now? You could come here, to my flat.'

He could at that.

But he knew better.

'I think not.' Even as he carried on, his thoughts were back to the last time and he hoped to beg time. 'Tomorrow.'

'Where?'

Even as he said it, he knew that it was perhaps a mistake. 'Here?'

She accepted at once, asking only the time and address.

The Department of Forensic Pathology resided, along with the Coroner's Office and the Coroner's Courtroom, above the Public Mortuary, in an entirely separate building to the rest of Pathology. This spatial separation reflected the philosophical divide that existed between those in forensics and those not.

Eisenmenger, who had started his career as a forensic pathologist before a nervous breakdown, could not see the need for a division, perceived any differences as illusory. He found it tiresome that forensic pathologists chose to emphasize the difference between their craft and that of other histopathologists when everyone was using the same skills and training, everyone was looking to uncover why people die.

The traffic was terrible and therefore a small piece of Eisenmenger's world was unchanged and, deep within him, he was just a little bit reassured.

Just a little bit.

The morning had not been easy. His chest felt inflamed and angry, showing its displeasure by producing a hacking painful cough with great regularity. The jagged cut on the side of his throat was sore, although the collar of his shirt hid most of the dressing. Numerous people had joked about cutting himself shaving, a conceit that he had taken readily as camouflage. Helena, though, when he had been round to see her first thing that morning, had not even noticed it. Clearly depressed and preoccupied, she had been barely responsive to his attempts at ladling reassurance into her. He had been able to tell her, and tell her with almost total truth no less, that her prognosis was good and that, even if she did require further treatment after the surgery, it was unlikely to be chemotherapy and probably only hormone therapy. He told her that it was a small lesion, that it was easily resectable, that it would almost certainly not have spread, but all this had proved an ineffective nostrum. For, though she had listened, asking questions about various aspects of the disease, of the treatment, of her prognosis and what side effects she might expect, her mood had not changed one quantum. She had heard it all and she had considered it all and, despite what she said, he knew that she had somehow rejected it all. No amount of optimism was going to break down the barrier in her mind, the barrier that had composed itself of six letters, two syllables and incarnate fear enough for a lifetime. She could not, in short, get past the single word that was her diagnosis.

She had left for work apparently no more cheerful than when he had arrived.

Somehow the Department of Forensic Pathology had cadged or stolen or even, perhaps, been legitimately given, enough money to live in a building that did not bear the marks of its previous life too obviously. Whatever trades, legal or otherwise, had once been conducted in Number One, Chalazion Street, the evidence was now smothered by a sand-blasted exterior and an interior that had been coated with concrete, plaster, wood panelling and the cheapest of chrome fittings. It reminded Eisenmenger of a private company that was doing quite well; not very well, but quite well.

The girl who came to the window when he rang the bell in the small foyer wore a ring through her nose. Eisenmenger found that he was old enough to notice, young enough not to care. He smiled as he always did but found it a stiff, almost sapping task, as if he were having to construct it from a memory long distant.

'I'm here to see Dr Bloomenthal.'

'And you are?' This was expressed rather as if she could not believe he was daring to interrupt her.

'Dr Eisenmenger.'

He was left without a further word, presumably so that she could phone and check it was all right with Isaac, but for all he knew it was to go and have a coffee break, or even to emigrate to Australia. It was typical of life in the city in general and the public's attitude to the medical profession in particular.

His hypothesis that she was emigrating was destroyed by her sudden reappearance at the window. She looked no happier to have to be confronted by the visage of Dr John Eisenmenger once again. 'He's in the mortuary. Lower ground floor.' Mortuaries were usually subterranean or at best on the ground floor, a subconscious reminiscence of the grave; somehow the concept of a mortuary above the head of mortal man chimed uneasily and discordantly.

She waved him through a door on his right which was now buzzing as if angry. He pushed it open and was confronted with lift doors flanked by stairs that ascended on his left and descended on his right.

Isaac was waiting for him at the bottom of the stairs. He was dressed in theatre-style blues, a surgeon's disposable cap on his grey hair. He ought to have looked ridiculous but decades of thrilling medical dramas on the small and large screens had somehow forced the observer of such sights to feel respect and awe.

'John. Thanks for coming. Sorry about yesterday.'

'No problem.'

They walked on into the fridge bay, the biggest that Eisenmenger had ever seen, and capable of holding eighty-eight bodies. Eisenmenger put on gown, gloves and disposable overshoes and they went into the dissection room, where Patrick Wilms lay, and steadfastly stared at the ceiling and not down at his opened body cavity.

Not that Eisenmenger blamed him.

Bloomenthal, as only a pathologist can, ignored his patient completely, going to the metal bench that ran along the far wall. On it were various files and photograph albums; the latter were not of sun-soaked vistas or happy, smiling children.

Most certainly not.

'The first murder this time around was that of Mrs Jenny Muir, a forty-two-year-old married housewife. Husband of forty-seven, single son of three. The forensic evidence indicates that she was killed some few hundred metres from where the body was found. She was returning home from her evening job as a cleaner. Death was by a single left to right incision, fourteen point five centimetres long, commencing superficial and lateral to the jugular and terminating in the equivalent place on the opposite side. Almost perfectly symmetrical, in fact.'

He leafed through a photo album, showing Eisenmenger a tasteful shot of Jenny Muir's neck. He flicked on a couple of pages to a close-up; she would have been horrified to see the brown warts, of which she had been so ashamed, so prominently displayed. Their eyes, however, were on the rather ugly gash that was being exposed by the gloved hands of an unseen helper (actually, the mortuary technician) that held the head back. The darkness in the circular hole of her upper trachea was clearly seen, as were the severed carotids.

'An artist,' remarked Eisenmenger drily.

'Of sorts,' concurred Bloomenthal. 'On its journey the blade severed most of the major neck structures.'

'Any clues as to the type of blade?'

'At least ten centimetres, possibly a lot more. And very, very sharp.'

'Like a PM40?'

'Maybe,' conceded Bloomenthal. A PM40 was a fixed-bladed, extremely sharp knife favoured in many mortuaries. 'Or a carving knife, or a filleting knife.'

'Or any sharp knife.'

'Precisely.' The perennial problem of forensic pathology was that it could often only give indications rather than accuracies; if a blade was found, they would be able to say if it couldn't have done the crime, but probably no more. 'The main incision is of interest.'

Running down from the middle of this was another incision that disappeared out of view at the bottom of the photograph. It was accompanied on either side by a row of red punctations where the incision had been sewn up with thick thread.

'The incision's high,' said Eisenmenger at once. For the first time he sounded genuinely interested, intrigued.

Bloomenthal's words suggested agreement, his tone otherwise. 'A bit.' Then, 'Presumably it was a question of convenience. Where else to start it than off the transverse cut?'

Eisenmenger was looking intently at the photograph but he was also aware that Bloomenthal was scrutinizing him with equal concentration as he said, 'The thing that intrigues me is that it isn't particularly straight.'

He flipped over to the next photograph, not quite so close-up and lower down the torso. The incision continued in a vaguely undulating fashion. 'See what I mean?'

When Eisenmenger said nothing, he remarked, 'It was dark. It can't have been easy.'

'Maybe,' was Eisenmenger's only comment.

As if provoked, Bloomenthal turned to another of the photo albums. 'Here's the general scene. You can see just how dark it was.'

Eisenmenger made a noise that might have been agreement but might well not have been. Bloomenthal gave him a copy of his report. While Eisenmenger read, he said, 'It's not the best evisceration I've ever seen. The pelvic organs in particular were badly done by – the bladder was slashed anteriorly, the rectum cut too low.'

'And the aorta's been cut a couple of times.'

'Small nicks, nothing more.'

'But sloppy, nonetheless.'

Bloomenthal hesitated. 'It was an experienced eviscerator who was out of practice, and who was working in a hurry and in poor light . . .'

'Pendred?'

Bloomenthal's head bobbed from side to side, glad to hear some apparent concurrence of opinion. Unfortunately, Eisenmenger said then, 'Or it was the work of an inexperienced eviscerator.'

Which rather upset the tall, toothy pathologist. It was with a huffy tone that he said, 'I'd say that given the conditions under which he was working, it could easily have been Pendred.'

Eisenmenger was frowning as he looked up from his reading and murmured, 'I suppose I couldn't deny that.'

If Bloomenthal heard anything but confirmation of his opinion, his reaction suggested otherwise. 'Good, good.'

Eisenmenger, though, was off on an intellectual sidetrack. 'What knot was used to tie the stitching?'

Bloomenthal was clearly disconcerted by this knight's move. It took him a little while to locate a photograph that showed in suitable close-up that a hitch knot had been employed. Eisenmenger accepted this without reaction. After another pause Bloomenthal said, 'The brain was taken out through a standard, single incision in the back of the scalp and a wedge excision of the skull. There was some trauma to it but, again, I think that was because of the constraints of time, lack of practice and darkness.' He waited for Eisenmenger to emerge from the report, which he did with a sound of surprise.

'She had a brain tumour!'

'Yes. Bit of a surprise, really. The histology is glioblastoma multiforme, actually.'

Bloomenthal saw a look he knew on Eisenmenger's face. 'It's a bit of a coincidence, but I can't see anything of significance in it. In a way, Pendred did her a favour – she was likely to die in a few months anyway.'

Eisenmenger was back reading the report, leaving Bloomenthal to wonder what was going through his mind; Eisenmenger had a habit of seeing things that weren't obvious to others. Eventually, though, Eisenmenger merely looked up from the report and asked, 'And what about the second victim?'

Bloomenthal would have wanted more, but he was forced to turn to the body cavity behind them.

'This is Patrick Wilms, the latest victim. Found on Tuesday night in a disused chapel in the middle of the cemetery. The body was killed and prepared in exactly the same way as Jenny Muir. It was hidden in some rubbish. I haven't got the SOCO photographs yet, unfortunately.'

They approached the body, Eisenmenger staring at it quite intently, as if here were a work of great beauty, the highest artistry.

'The brain was in a stone urn on the altar; unfortunately it got knocked off the table by the couple who discovered the body, so it suffered rather grievously.'

Eisenmenger leaned forward over the neck, one hand angling a light that was suspended over the dissection table so that he could see more clearly. The transverse slit was identical, as was the incision for the evisceration. He asked, 'And the knot?'

Bloomenthal sighed. 'What does that matter?' he asked irritatedly.

Eisenmenger gave him nothing more than a shrug.

'To be honest, I'm not sure I remember.'

'Will you let me know?'

'If it will please you.'

Eisenmenger smiled his gratitude and Bloomenthal, after a short intermission to make sure that his audience wasn't going to ask any more stupid questions, said, 'The main organ mass was quite some way from the body – outside the chapel completely, actually. In a hole, resting on the coffin of Melkior Pendred.'

He was gratified by Eisenmenger's surprised reaction. 'Really?'

'That's not the half of it. For once the body cavity wasn't empty.'

'What was in it?'

Bloomenthal tried to keep the smile from his face and his voice. 'A neatly wrapped parcel of haddock and chips.'

Eisenmenger stared at him for a long, almost uncomfortable time, as if Bloomenthal had just broken some social taboo. He made no comment save for a murmured, 'How interesting.'

'Pendred always was a joker, wasn't he? Mrs Muir's brain was in the freezer.'

Eisenmenger was back at the neck with its now-blackened adornment of coagulated blood, but he glanced briefly up at this news. Bloomenthal went on, 'As for the evisceration, it's pretty similar. Not the best, but he was again working in near-darkness, save from light coming in through the boarded windows and maybe a torch.'

As if he weren't listening, Eisenmenger asked, 'How did he cut the ribs and the skull?'

'Presumably a tenon saw. The ends of the ribs indicated a straight serrated edge rather than a curved one as you'd get from an electric saw.'

'And anyway the noise of an electric saw probably prohibited its use.'

'Presumably.'

Eisenmenger stepped back slightly from the body, his lips pursed. 'So there's nothing to indicate that specialized equipment was used. The whole job could have been achieved with everyday tools, the kind of thing everyone has access to.'

Bloomenthal nodded. 'Not that I imagine that Pendred would have had a problem obtaining post-mortem instruments. He could easily have sneaked into the mortuary while on duty as a porter; and that's assuming that he didn't have some secreted away from four years ago.'

Eisenmenger had stepped back up to the body and was again examining the primary incision and row of holes on either side of it. Bloomenthal said, 'This one's straighter than Mrs Muir's. Presumably he was getting back into the swing of it.'

'Or he had more room. After all, it must have been fairly cramped in the front garden, but presumably much less so in a chapel.'

Bloomenthal nodded slowly and murmured, 'Yes, I suppose so.'

He sounded oddly discomforted and this caused Eisenmenger to look across to him. 'You're fairly convinced that Pendred did these, aren't you, Isaac?'

Bloomenthal waved his hand in the air and protested, perhaps a shade too quickly, 'Not at all.' He didn't allow much time to flow past his words before he went on, 'Muir and Wilms were killed by the same hand – that much is clear. The only question is, can we link these deaths with the first five? I'm fairly certain from reading your reports that there is such a link, but you're the only one who's really in a position to compare the characteristics of both sets of murders and confirm that they probably were committed by the same man.'

'Mmm . . .'

Bloomenthal frowned at this less than enthusiastic response. 'Oh, come on, John. What's your problem?'

At this somewhat brusque enquiry, Eisenmenger smiled and, cautious as ever, said, 'I haven't got one, Isaac, but you may, if I come to the wrong conclusion.'

'Is that likely?'

Eisenmenger shrugged. 'I don't know. After all, you've had much longer to consider the matter; I haven't seen the original reports for four years.'

Bloomenthal nodded slowly. 'Why don't you take my reports and compare them? I'm sure you'll soon see that the similarities are quite striking.'

Eisenmenger said nothing, his attention once more upon the body of Patrick Wilms. Bloomenthal mistook this hesitation. 'I'll clear it with Chief Inspector Homer, and I'm sure we could arrange a fee.'

The fee, Eisenmenger reflected, would come in handy, but in truth his delay in answering was something deeper and closer to the bone. He had given up forensic work, given it up because it had changed him, because it had taken him by the hand and shown him the horrors of the human world, the worst that there is. The death of little Tamsin – incinerated by her mother to die in his arms as she whispered from cracked, charcoal lips – had been the trigger for his decision, the subsequent self-immolation of his then girlfriend Marie had precipitated a complete breakdown.

He had found himself not just wanting but needing to get away from murder.

Yet murder kept coming into his life, and events kept seeming to demonstrate that of all the things that he knew, he knew murder best. He had a talent for it, or at least a talent for dissecting (both physically and intellectually) its entrails, its aftermath. It wasn't a

talent that he would have wished, and it had few other applica-
tions, but he had to admit that it was something at which he
excelled. He had a skill and he knew that he should be grateful but,
like Cassandra, he endured it, no more.

And now it had come knocking again, a persistent visitor, not
to be refused entry.

He asked resignedly, 'Why not?' The question was almost
plaintive.

'Excellent!' Of the three of them in the room, only Isaac
Bloomenthal displayed any elation.

'Could I speak to Mr Anderson, please?'

'Who's calling?'

'Beverley Wharton.'

Did she imagine the faint sound of a small sigh? Certainly she
saw in her mind a picture of a slight grimace and definitely she
heard the changed tone as with little delay came the answer, 'I'm
sorry. Mr Anderson's busy.'

'I see.' Beverley could feel no huge surprise at this – indeed it
merely confirmed her suspicions – but that did not preclude
disappointment. 'Is he busy just because it's me, or is he busy for
every caller?'

With some asperity the secretary (Beverley had met her once
and had then noted her attitude of almost proprietorial disdain)
responded, 'Mr Anderson is busy.' Such repetition was not
going to cause balm to flow over Beverley's exasperation.

'So you said. Well, I'd like to leave a message for Mr
Anderson, then.'

'Yes?'

She tried to choose her words with care and her manner with
calculation. 'Could you tell Mr Anderson that Beverley Wharton
just called for the last time. Could you also tell the limp-wristed
prick that the next time I see him – and I will see him, he can be
sure of that – I'm going to make sure that the whole world
knows what a complete bastard he is.'

The secretary said nothing and, since the line went dead,
Beverley was left unsure if she got the message down accurately.

As it was lunchtime Eisenmenger had slipped out to the local

176

supermarket; he had said that he would cook for Helena before he had discovered that his refrigerator was possessed only of one of small slab of strong Cheddar, half a dozen eggs, two and a half slices of ham and some semi-skimmed milk. He was returning with two full bags and the rain was just beginning again when he saw, sheltering under the awning of a delicatessen, a young woman whom he vaguely recognized. She was tall, with long blonde hair pulled tight to her skull by a wide, crimson hair band. Her face was broad with eyes that were deeply set and a nose that was long and thin and pointed above a mouth that was thin and straight.

'Victoria?'

If he had planned to surprise her, he couldn't have done so more successfully. Her reaction was so extreme it suggested more horror than amazement. For a second she just stared at him so intently that he began to wonder if he had made a mistake. Perhaps it wasn't really Victoria Bence-Jones after all. He had not infrequently made mistakes like this before; they were always embarrassing moments, born (he hoped) of an endearing absent-mindedness.

After all, he reflected now that he was close, this woman was older than he had thought; her eyes were larger, her mouth thinner.

He had just decided that a tactical withdrawal would minimize humiliation when her face and attitude changed. 'John? John Eisenmenger?'

Even as he accepted her hand and she smiled and apologized that she hadn't recognized him at once, he was aware of the wrongness of her response. It seemed to him that she did not want to see him, no matter how hard her words tried to persuade him – and perhaps herself – otherwise.

'You haven't been well, I hear.'

Once again he seemed to discomfort her, a habit in the making. She frowned and was almost afraid to ask. 'How . . . ?'

He smiled. 'Didn't you know? I'm doing your locum at the WRI.'

That he should know so much about her was clearly not welcome. 'Really?'

'How are you? Are you any better?' He followed the convention of avoiding any mention of that pejorative word, 'stress'.

Another tricky pause that was short but all the worse for that. 'Not really.'

Is that all?

The thought was almost involuntary but indicative of how the atmosphere was congealing. It was nearly an act of masochism to suggest, 'Are you due somewhere else? Why don't we have a quick drink? Talk over old times.'

Judging from her expression, she didn't appear to hear those words. The way her eyes widened, she perhaps thought that he had asked for a sneaky peek at her knickers.

More silence.

A car sounded its horn nearby, causing them both to look up, he with curiosity, she with desperation. Already she was moving away from him, her face filled with relief.

'I'm sorry. It's Geoffrey. He said that he'd pick me up.'

She was already leaving him, entering the rain that by now was falling heavily. She turned briefly. 'Good to see you, John. I expect we'll meet again soon.'

The car was big and expensive – a Mercedes or something. It didn't just park outside the delicatessen, it made derogatory statements about it. The only feature that he could discern of the man inside who beckoned Victoria Bence-Jones was his glasses.

She didn't look to the side as she was driven away but her profile was just as strained.

Which left Eisenmenger to the rain and to his wondering.

It was a sordid little flat but then, Alison von Guerke reflected, it was a sordid little affair; perfect camouflage, perfect synthesis of place and act. The ceiling had at one time been liberally coated in bright white emulsion, inexpertly applied; age had withered it, a hundred thousand cigarettes smoked beneath it had left it as nicotined as an old whore's fingers. The walls hid their cracked nakedness in woodchip paper, once magenta, now greased and dirtied. Even their bed was old and ready only for disposal.

Like its present occupants. Two decrepit lovers making a love that had slowly become itself decrepit.

She heard Trevor moving about the bathroom next door and could tell just from the sounds that made their way through the thin walls that she was listening to a man who was ageing, no matter how much he might pretend otherwise. There was in what she heard a slight but certain loss of co-ordination, a feeling of ever-present unsteadiness.

Not that she could criticize or mock.

She looked down at her body. Once, when she had been young and when minutes passed like minutes and not half-seconds, she had been proud of her large breasts. She had been no great beauty (she had once overheard a male colleague describe her face as 'bovine' and for days after had been so distressed that she had formed feeble thoughts of suicide until a sense of proportion had reasserted itself) and age had done nothing to help. Gravity, too, had proved inimical and her once impressive bosom now struggled with infirmity. It either hung pendulous and bag-like or, when she lay flat, flopped to either side like sherry sacks over a donkey's back.

She smiled. Trevor, though, liked them. He called her his 'milk-mother' and found them an endless source of pleasure and fascination, especially when she crouched over him so that they brushed his face. When he sucked them she had often thought how like a baby he looked, an observation that awoke at the back of her mind Freudian thoughts of what his mother had been like. She found that particular avenue slightly uncomfortable.

'Are you getting up?'

He was naked and she had to admit that his state of undress did not make him any more a thing of beauty. Yet it was his ugliness that seemed to attract her. In a paradoxical and counter-intuitive manner, she had found that she wanted him because he was so patently unattractive. She had never been able to explain it other than by assuring herself that, if not Apollonian in looks, he was certainly distinctive in them.

He sat on the side of the bed and began to pull on his socks. He had lost his erection by now. 'I've got to meet Molly at seven.'

She lay there unmoving.

As he got up to pull on his stylish red boxer shorts, he looked around and asked, 'Are you all right?'

Knowing that she had to say it now or it would never be said, she turned her head and said, 'I think that we may have a problem, Trevor.'

With a deep frown he give up struggling with his left sock and sighed. 'Oh. How serious?'

She hoisted herself up on her left elbow, causing the bed and

179

consequently Trevor Ludwig to oscillate gently. 'To be honest, I don't know. Adam Piringer's worried, but . . .'

'Piringer?' He was perplexed, outraged almost. 'What does Piringer know about us?'

It took her a moment to grasp. They were talking about different things. 'It's not about us, about this.' She gestured at the somewhat tawdry decoration. 'It's about work.'

He was still frowning, though. 'Work? Work? What about it?'

She reached forward with her right hand to touch him. 'There's been a complaint.'

At once she saw the distress of an aged man. Not that she hadn't always known something along that line, but the context then had been one of mutual ageing and their love affair. For many more years than she could accurately remember they had been coming here to his grubby little flat in this grubby and dubious locality for sex. Somehow neither his wife, Molly, nor her husband, Richard, had ever discovered this infidelity or, if they had, it had never bothered them. She wasn't sure which possibility depressed her more – that they were blind or that they were uncaring.

'Complaint?' he repeated as if he still didn't understand, although she knew that he did.

She nodded. 'To Geoffrey Bence-Jones.'

'Saying what?'

'That your practice is substandard.' She felt as if she were visiting some form of ritual humiliation upon him as the words came out, one after the other. 'The letter cites particular instances.'

He was growing older as she watched. It felt to her as if time had raced ahead in front of her eyes, as if the universe were taking a terrible revenge upon him. It was merely an old man's show of cynical indifference when he asked sneeringly 'And is he shocked to hear that I make mistakes? Presumably he's heard that Piringer is perfect, never been wrong. Beside such a godlike presence, mere human frailty must look sickening.'

She agreed with him, patting his hand, and perhaps momentarily comforted he continued to dress in silence. When he was nearly dressed, she got out of bed and padded to the bathroom. When she returned he had left the bedroom and she dressed alone.

She found him in the lounge tying his tie in the large mirror over the ugly gas fire. He had originally rented out the flat to medical students. although not since the affair had started. It hadn't been redecorated in all those years and probably many before that, and consequently was tatty and unwelcoming and dusty; the perfect scene for their regular acts of adultery. She had never poked around the place, half-fearful that she might uncover some dirty dishes left there by the last group of students, covered in a mould that would never yield anything as useful as penicillin.

He said into the silvered reflection, 'Would I be right in supposing that I am not entitled to know which of my colleagues is the Brutus amongst them?'

Do you really see yourself as Caesar? she wondered as she replied, 'Piringer said that he didn't know, but he wondered about Eisenmenger.'

He seemed surprised. He turned away from the mirror and said, 'The locum?' He considered, then decided, 'Well, it's possible I suppose, but he wouldn't be top of my list.'

'Who is?'

'Isn't it obvious? That little shit, Shaheen. He knows I'm on to him.'

She had heard his opinions many, many times before but had still not grown used to them. 'It might not be him,' she pointed out somewhat feebly. 'You shouldn't be too certain, not without evidence.'

He considered, then conceded, 'Maybe.' He held out his hand to her and she went to him. They kissed, and he asked, 'But if not Shaheen, then who?'

She smiled weakly, almost a death mask. 'I find none of our colleagues particularly pleasant.'

He said at once, 'Oh, I don't know. Milroy's not too bad . . .' He stopped at once, his face showing his embarrassment. 'Oh, Alison. I'm sorry.' Her face hadn't changed but its very fixed-ness was a testament to pain. 'I forgot.'

She shrugged as he held her. 'It was a long time ago.'

She was desperate not to cry because it was so stupid to do so. She was in her sixties, long past the age of child-bearing. What did it matter now that she was sterile? She whispered, 'What really hurt was that he didn't ever let me see some remorse.'

'I know, I know.'

'He just said that it was bad luck. Nothing to do with him.'

He tried to calm her, to wipe away the tears that would not be denied their entrance. They hugged in silence while she thought again for the thousandth time of what might have been.

The last time she had drunk his wine, the way things had ended still brought a feeling of shame tinged with guilty pleasure to Eisenmenger. As they sat at the table by the window that looked out on to the bricked road surface of the mews, he tried to see in her eyes what she remembered of that night. It was with a start that he realized yet again how deep and beautiful those eyes were.

'It's always good to see you, Beverley, but as always I'd guess you're here for a reason.'

He had expected her perhaps to laugh or at least to acknowledge the pleasantry, but she merely smiled tiredly. Not taking his eyes from her face, he offered, 'The Eviscerator strikes again?'

She grimaced. 'I always hated that name.'

'So how does this involve me?'

She didn't want to put any inflexion on what she said next, but it crept in like dry rot. 'If it's shown that Melkior Pendred was innocent, I'm finished in the force.'

He had been hypothesizing one or two reasons for her presence, but not that. He was genuinely incredulous. 'Why?'

Her tongue wet her lips as if her mouth were suddenly dehydrated. 'Ostensibly it's one mistake too many. You'll have seen the papers, of course. "Another miscarriage of justice. Will the police ever get it right?" That kind of thing.'

'So?'

'So, I'm a bad smell under the noses of the powers-that-be. That plus the fact that the man in charge of the case doesn't particularly care for me means that I'm squarely in their sights and number one for the drop.'

'But you weren't even the chief investigating officer, as I recall. It was Cox.'

'Who's now retired. Anyway, his record was pretty good – he didn't have a big black blot of ink on his record named Nikki Exner.'

She was looking directly at him as she said the name. *Your fault*, she was signalling.

'What about what happened on Rouna – the Sweet case? They can't fault you there.'

She was shaking a weary head. 'Too many deaths, too much carnage. Anyway, who got arrested? We never actually proved anything, so there was no trial, no conviction. We're measured by our convictions, John. That's why the police need criminals.

'No, there was little kudos to be gained from that one. Which leaves me one step away from the cesspit with this case threatening to push me in.'

'It's Homer who's running this one, isn't it?'

'Unfortunately.'

'And you don't get on?'

She leaned back, her long fingers gently caressing the stem of the wineglass. Eisenmenger felt strange things as he watched this manipulation. 'Homer was a sergeant like me on the original case. He disagreed that Melkior was the murderer. Managed to make himself fairly unpopular.'

'So he has a score to settle?'

'When Melkior was convicted, Homer was carpeted. He's spent the last four years working his way back and, give him his due, he's managed it pretty well.' She offered him a tight smile. 'He's a CI, after all. What am I?'

He didn't proffer consolation and she didn't seem to want any. She continued, 'Anyway, this is a gift from the gods as far as he's concerned. Now he can prove that we were wrong and he was right and stick the knife into me at the same time.' She looked up at Eisenmenger. 'We kind of fell out over it.'

He knew her well enough to guess that perhaps she had been more than an interested observer in the decline of Homer.

'What about Cox? He was a good detective, wasn't he?'

'And he was brilliant. He was probably the best chief I've ever had. The perfect copper – professional, insightful, patient and fair.'

'And now he's retired?'

She emptied her glass with a long, almost theatrical flourish. 'Lucky bastard,' was the verdict as she put the glass back on the table. 'Beyond their reach.'

He reached forward to fill her glass again, aware that she was beautiful, that he still felt drawn to her, that he could not allow himself to fall for her again. 'All of which is interesting, but what is it to me?'

She took in a deep, deep breath, frowned, looked down to her hands, then directly up into his face. 'There was no funny business, John. No planted evidence, no mistakes. Melkior Pendred was the murderer.'

In his mind there floated the words, *But you would say that, wouldn't you?* as he said, 'It was always a close call, Beverley. Whether it was Melkior or Martin wasn't clear for a long time.'

'Martin had the alibi for the last one, John. Melkior didn't.'

He drank some wine. 'Alibis can be manufactured.'

The shake of her head was emphatic. 'He did it. I knew it then, I know it now.'

Someone walked past the window coughing and sneezing.

'So how do you explain what's happening now? Who's doing the killing this time?'

She said at once, 'Two possibilities. Maybe someone is mimicking the original murders and Homer's completely wrong in thinking that Martin's guilty.'

'And the other option?'

'Martin and Melkior were identical twins. They both had autism and Melkior was schizophrenic; if he was schizophrenic, why shouldn't Martin be the same? Perhaps Homer's right and Martin is committing these murders, but that doesn't mean that Melkior wasn't guilty the first time round.'

Eisenmenger nodded in appreciation. He had known that she was smart but he had to admit that he was impressed by her analysis. 'Quite possibly,' he conceded. He said no more and for the next few moments they just stared at each other, a game of silence. It was he that yielded. 'And so?'

She tried a smile; on anyone else it wouldn't have worked, but Beverley Wharton was cursed with stunning beauty. 'And so that's why I'm here.'

It actually came as a shock but at once he knew that he should have guessed. 'You want me to help you investigate these murders?' He tried to keep incredulity – or perhaps it was fear – out of his voice.

'Why not? We're a good team.'

Possibly too good.

He enquired gently, 'What can I do?'

She leaned forward, not quite imploringly but it gave him a pleasant view of cleavage. 'Don't you see? I need to show that these killings are being done by a different hand, that there are points of difference.'

The irony of his situation was almost delicious. He thought of the files that Isaac Bloomenthal had given him, sitting no more than a metre behind her; given to him because Bloomenthal and the police wanted to prove exactly the opposite, that any differences were explicable by circumstance. He wondered should he tell her – it would be the decent thing to do – but knew that he wasn't going to. He hadn't forgiven her for her betrayal on the Exner case.

'I couldn't pay you,' she said.

He didn't show his smile as he said merely, 'I wouldn't expect anything.' The last thing he needed was a conflict of interest of that sort. 'That's not why I'm hesitating.'

She snorted. 'Helena.'

Which it was, partly.

'She won't be happy.'

Beverley shrugged her shoulders. For some reason it was only then he smelt her perfume, the same that she had worn that night so long ago. 'She owes me. I saved her life, remember. Anyway, she's representing Martin Pendred. It would be in her interests to prove exactly the same thing.'

Except that Martin Pendred had disappeared and he wasn't quite sure where that left Helena. He leaned forward. 'What about you? What are you going to do?'

'I'm not going to sit at home and mope. I'm going to find Martin Pendred.'

'Why don't you leave that to Homer? He'll have more resources.'

She smiled. 'Because Homer's a dolt, and I'm not. He'll do it by the police manual, plod through the standard procedures one by one. I'll use some brains.'

He didn't point out that it was because she had never gone by the manual that she was in her present position. He merely said, 'Okay. I'll look into it.'

He hadn't appreciated how tense she was until that moment when she suddenly seemed to let out some breath, to thank some unknown god. 'Thank you.' Then, 'Can you get hold of the files? If you can't, I should be able to swing it – I still have some friends left.'

He thought again of the paperwork that was so close to her

and a smile broke through. 'Don't worry. I know Isaac Bloomenthal. I'm sure that he wouldn't mind letting me have a look.'

She finished her wine and stood up. As he went with her to the door, she stopped and at once they were close. Very close.

'I don't have to go, John. I've got nothing to occupy me now.'

Her perfume again. That and her eyes and her bright, shiny lips. Despite himself he found physiology doing haemodynamic things.

'No, Beverley. I don't think so.'

She paused a long time, looking into his face. Perhaps she saw things that he wanted hidden, for the smile that spread from her mouth to her eyes was sly. 'Shame.'

The morning was cold but Beverley didn't notice; she was feeling consumed by fire. Not a wild, unregulated conflagration, but an intense, focused flame, a torch of white, bright heat; a thing to cut or weld or, perhaps, to maim. The road was empty at the moment, although during the forty minutes that she had waited, a variety of executive and luxury-class cars had left nearby drives, the milkman had made his deliveries and a paper boy had housewards cycled his weary way no fewer than twelve times while in her view. Some of those she had observed had, in their turn, cast covert and not so covert glances at the attractive blonde who leaned against the car and who seemed to be doing not very much at all. She had ignored them while enjoying, as she always did, their attention. Beverley didn't mind whether they were male or female, young or old; their awareness was what mattered, the assurance that she was still riveting, still to be envied.

Just as a jet crawled across the clear blue sky, so high that it was merely a silver glint and its vapour was white and misty and beautiful, the front door of the house in front of her opened and Peter came out.

He was smartly dressed, ever the barrister, immaculately groomed, face calm and handsome, radiating security in his intellect, his position, his future. The sight of it only made her angrier.

He didn't see her at first. The locks on the dark blue Mercedes had clicked open and the boot had obligingly flipped up as if the thing had been imbued with artificial intelligence before he happened to look up. His face barely registered but she knew him well enough to know that he was, to say the least, discomforted.

She pushed off from the side of her considerably less expensive car and walked across the road and up the drive, the gravel loud and insistent as she made purposeful strides towards her quarry. When she reached him, he had put his two briefcases in the boot, closed it and was standing with his arms folded, a pensive expression his only defence.

'Beverley.' There was a definite undercurrent of apprehension.

She stopped in front of him. She was wearing long black leather boots with heels that brought her up to his height. She said nothing, merely looked at him, almost curiously.

'I can guess why you're here.' Which was hardly an impressive display of intelligence.

Still she was silent.

'You have to see my point of view, Beverley. It's not that I don't love you, it's merely that in my position . . .' It wasn't clear whether he thought his position so obvious it transcended mere words, or whether he was embarrassed.

Not that it mattered.

The corners of Beverley's mouth moved up slightly, small concentric arced creases forming as they did so. 'You have to see my point of view as well, Peter.'

He began to nod. 'Of course, of . . .'

She had taken from her pocket a glass bottle. He had stopped speaking because she had unstoppered it and stepped to the car. The liquid poured out over the beautiful metallic blue paintwork, a slightly viscous and, it was immediately obvious, pungent fluid.

The paint bubbled immediately.

She turned back; he hadn't moved – he wasn't the kind of man to risk action when words were still available – but there was definite anger on his face, at last. She said, 'You're a fucking bastard, Peter. If I could get away with it, I'd cut your dick off and force-feed it to your mother.'

He was looking at the car again, almost as if he were grieving, but still there was no movement from him. There was now an acrid, almost choking smell coming from the stain on the car and the bare metal was becoming visible. The paint stripper had run down to the rear bumper and was dripping on the drive. 'I could have you charged for that,' he said, not looking at her.

'You could, but you won't. You wouldn't want the publicity about you and me.'

He bowed his head briefly, then looked up at her. 'I think you'd better leave, Beverley.'

At last a real smile broke out on her face. 'Bye, Peter. It was good for a while.'

She turned away without waiting for an answer, but stopped again after three paces. She still had the glass bottle in her hand. It seemed an afterthought as she threw it as hard as she could against the passenger side of the Mercedes. It left a noticeable dent and a few more bubbling spots of paint stripper.

The day had clouded, the sun now obscured by greyness. It wasn't warm and it wasn't cold; a nether region of mediocrity, an oblivion of averageness. Nothing seemed to connect with happiness.

Helena had arrived at her normal time, and had merely passed like a disinterested passenger through her appointments with an accused shoplifter, a convicted fraudster (suspended sentence but appealing) and a sixteen-year-old girl who had just been arrested for the one hundred and forty-third time. Their problems had been genuine but they had been mundane. A sixteen-year-old arrested once was a tragedy, but arrested a further one hundred and forty-two times and Helena had difficulty summoning sympathy. That this particular teenager brought into the office her three-year-old daughter who pulled half the leaves off the rubber plant did not help.

A working lunch had followed, a discussion amongst all of her colleagues on housekeeping matters involving the whole practice; Helena had not been able to feign interest but given the nature of the subject no one around the table considered her attitude odd. At two o'clock in the afternoon Helena was at last alone and therefore unable to prevent her thoughts from making their intrusive way into her world. Once there they would not be silenced; had Lord Lucan himself entered her office it could not have banished them.

She opened her briefcase and found the letter.

She was invited to attend in two days' time for the operation that would save her life.

She ought to have been able to find a background of comfort, even if the foreground was one of anxiety. After all, someone was going to do something; if what she was told and what she had read were correct, she was going to receive optimal treatment. But no such relief was to be had because there was still the bigger picture, the sky behind the scenery, that could not be ignored, that negated whatever succour she might have expected.

She was possibly going to die from this.

She read the letter once more, for perhaps the sixth time. Unconsciously she put her hand to her breast, a frown on her face. She imagined that she could feel it, couldn't tell if perhaps she really could. A spasm of anger flared, a welcome and unexpected feeling, accompanied by an indignant question: *How dare this thing happen to me?*

She was startled by the thought; startled and pleased. The anger was a welcome change, a spark, a return to the norm. It often felt to Helena as if she had been angry all her life and sometimes she had found herself depressed by the realization, yet it was with some relief that she greeted its return.

She considered this. Put her hand again to the lump. 'You bastard,' she whispered.

It was after six fifteen when Trevor Ludwig began his investigations into who had accused him of professional incompetence. He didn't really expect to find anything – after all, there need not necessarily be written evidence – but it was an itch that bothered him. He knew that it was Shaheen who had done it, a petty revenge for the fact that Ludwig had seen through him, had spotted him for the incompetent spear-chucker that he was, protected only by Piringer's patronage. He had often wondered why Piringer, who was in other matters not noticeably stupid, had such a blind spot where Shaheen was concerned, had confided this to Milroy once, only to be met with a harsh laugh and nothing more.

It still perplexed him.

Shaheen had left at five, another habit of which Ludwig disapproved. Clock-watching was not the habit of a professional, and to Ludwig's mind it was yet more proof of how unsuited he was to be a consultant. It would be easy to look through his room since none of the offices was ever locked, and he was fairly sure that his other colleagues had all departed by six.

Yet, despite knowing that he was unlikely to find anything of value, when he came away empty of the proof that he sought, he was dissatisfied. His prior realization that he might not find anything was proven most definitely not to have been acceptance, merely delusion, and he was therefore left with a feeling of incompleteness. He was forced by this to look elsewhere. After all, he reasoned, no one else was around, so why not?

Eisenmenger had been given Victoria Bence-Jones' room, which was next door. It was a logical place to start, but he found little to satisfy his craving there, apart from a tin of biscuits in one of the drawers, two of which he took, and a photograph of a small girl of perhaps six years – a niece, he presumed.

He moved then next door, to Wilson Milroy's room. The brief-case was open on the floor beside the desk, which made him pause. Clearly Milroy was still around, probably on some private business of his own since Ludwig knew that he also had a habit of making other people's business his own. He knew that wisdom dictated that he should leave well alone, but curiosity was an insistent counter to this. He had often wondered just what Milroy got up to when he came in early and left late, and he was also quite keen to see whether there was any evidence for Milroy's whispered insinuations regarding various members of the department.

And anyway, it wasn't beyond the bounds of possibility that he had been the sender of the letter.

He looked both ways along the corridor, then entered the room, making straight for the briefcase. He squatted down on all fours and began to rummage within, gently and quietly.

It didn't take him long to come across a copy of a letter written seven days before to the Medical Director. It was long but packed with information, all of it concerning the incompetence of one Trevor Ludwig. He read it with a growing sense of incandescence. He had known that Milroy was fuelled by an unassailable certainty of injustice with regard to a variety of matters, that he had a need to pry into the affairs of others, to manipulate and control, but he had never really believed . . .

'Satisfied?'

Milroy's voice was so infused with disdain it almost fell apart in his mouth. Ludwig's immediate reaction was one of guilty shock, but it didn't last longer than a single, stuttered syllable as his head jerked round. What right had Milroy to be indignant? He straightened up. 'Not really, no.'

Milroy came into the room from the doorway. He walked past Ludwig, shutting the briefcase as he did so, then sat in his chair. Ludwig asked, 'Why?'

Wilson replied simply, 'Because it's true. You're becoming incompetent, making errors that should not be made. Sooner or later, someone will suffer because of it.'

'And you don't ever make mistakes?

Wilson grinned. 'You're mistaking the trees for the wood. Yes, I make errors, but people see them against a background of capability and efficiency.' He sighed. 'Yours are viewed in a different light. People see you as old and failing. Everyone thinks that you're a joke.'

Even as he was indignantly denying the words, Ludwig was aware of their truth. People *did* now see him as old and, by a construction of logic that was superficially easy but he knew fundamentally flawed, they therefore saw him as incompetent. No matter how well he performed for most of the time, they were judging him now by his lapses, by the criterion that *young is good, old is bad*.

But that didn't mean that Milroy had to.

'I've worked with you for twenty years,' he pointed out. 'How could you do this to me?'

Milroy couldn't be bothered with contempt. 'Easily,' he said simply, the word couched in something close to tiredness. 'Easily. Why not? Why not screw everyone else? It's not money that makes the world go round, it's A screwing B, who screws C and so on, right back round to A again. The economics of treachery.'

Ludwig thought that he saw partial understanding. 'Sally,' he said.

Wilson's reaction was scornful. 'Oh, please, Trevor. don't bother with the amateur psychology. My wife's decision to run off with an accountant isn't the reason why I've decided that I can no longer stomach your incompetence.' He broke into a weak smile. 'You and I have never really liked each other, have we?'

Ludwig was surprised by that. They had never exactly been bedmates, but he had assumed that there had been a good working relationship. 'I wouldn't quite have said that.'

Milroy went on, 'No? I would but in any case I had hoped for better treatment when the chair came up.'

'I don't understand.'

'Don't you? You've got a short memory then, Trevor. Perhaps another sign of your agedness.'

Despite his anger, Ludwig was finding himself increasingly fascinated by Milroy as layer upon layer of emerging bitterness was displayed. 'Humour me, then. Tell me how I mistreated you over the chair.'

Milroy leaned forward, elbows on his desk, fingers of one hand clasped in the other. 'When the vacancy arose, I was the natural choice. I was a reader, I was the internal candidate, I have a track record in research. The post of Professor was mine.

'Yet I didn't get it. Piringer popped up and suddenly he was the wunderkind, the one everyone wanted for the job; I was just the also-ran, which led me to wonder what had happened. Why was I no longer a serious contender? Accordingly, I began to ask discreet questions in the University Senate. Do you know what answer I received?'

He paused and looked at Ludwig, as if expecting an answer. When none was proffered he said, 'Someone – no name was given – in this department had actively lobbied against me.' He stopped on a note of revelation, as an actor might proclaim a significant line.

Ludwig asked after a short pause, 'And you think it was me?'

Milroy threw himself back in his chair. 'Oh, please, Trevor!' he pleaded in a disgusted tone. 'Have the grace not to lie.'

Ludwig found his anger again. 'I wouldn't bother to lie, not to you. If you want to know, I told them the truth, which is what they wanted of me. I told them that you were a good histopathologist and, as far as I could tell, you were a reasonable researcher. Unfortunately, the job description also requires leadership. I didn't feel able to recommend you on that criterion.'

Milroy broke into a sneer, his head nodding slowly. 'I knew it! I knew that you were the bastard responsible!'

Ludwig let out an exasperated sigh. 'Don't kid yourself, Milroy. In the first place, I hardly think my contribution carried sufficient weight on its own to render you unappointable, do you? In the second, all I did was give my view as I saw it – I didn't make anything up or embroider the facts. In the third, I would wonder about the motives of your source. Perhaps I'm just the scapegoat.'

Milroy said at once, 'Nice try, but I know what happened. You couldn't bear to see me succeed. Jealousy, that's all it was. Nothing but old-fashioned jealousy.'

Ludwig found himself suddenly tired; tired of arguing, tired of standing, tired of defending himself against accusations born of delusion. He said, 'Have it your own way. I know what I did and I know that it was fair.'

He turned away and went to the door but Milroy said loudly, 'Is that it? No apology?'

Ludwig managed to laugh as he turned back. 'Why should I? I told you – I did the right thing.'

Milroy raised his eyebrows. 'Which is all I'm doing, Trevor. We must always do the right thing. My letter to the Medical Director was nothing more.' He smiled. 'Equally, the letters to each of the patients concerned will be motivated merely by an overpowering sense that justice must be done.'

Ludwig's eyes widened, his skin became pale. 'You wouldn't!'

Milroy affected puzzlement. 'Why not? Don't they have a right to know?'

Ludwig was becoming submerged by panic. 'But that would be a gross breach of confidentiality. The Trust would dismiss you . . .'

Milroy waved this aside. 'Haven't you heard, Trevor? Whistle-blowing's okay now. Anyway, anonymous letters – who's to say that I sent them? No one else knows and as far as I'm concerned this conversation has never happened.'

Ludwig found his jaws clamped together, the glue a mix of anger and fear. He wanted to break Milroy's neck, or perhaps beat his face to a haemorrhagic pulp, but he did not move. After several breaths, he whispered, 'You won't get away with this, you cunt.'

Milroy didn't even bother to reply. He shrugged, his expression one of total unconcern. Ludwig left unsatisfied despite having had the last word.

The Medical Staff Committee met and, having met, moved on. Composed of all the consultants and staff grade doctors in the Trust, it crept through life talking and deliberating, being informed and pretending to inform, making much noise, little wind and no discernible effect on the world. It discussed the Grievance Policy, the Acting Down Policy, the Trust's ever-imminent financial meltdown and (always a fraught topic) parking in and around the hospital. The deliberations produced no result other than to vent feelings and opinions; the Trust's senior management (although the Medical Director and the Chief Executive habitually attended and made great play of listening) had far more powerful drivers than the disgruntlement of the consultant staff guiding its actions.

It was, in short, a waste of time, space and energy, a black hole of debate.

There was, however, a quaint custom of serving wine after this monthly group expulsion of carbon dioxide (and probably methane) and it was thus that Eisenmenger found himself standing next to Geoffrey Bence-Jones, the Medical Director. They were introduced by Alison von Guerke as Eisenmenger found himself observing not only that Alison von Guerke's main role in life seemed to be making introductions, but also that the wine was quite simply awful.

'John's doing Victoria's locum,' explained Alison.

Bence-Jones wore spectacles that were so thick it hurt Eisenmenger's eyes just to look at them, as if they actively sucked in light from onlookers, causing optorrhoea and headache. Eisenmenger briefly saw liquid eyes like cold water anemones before he had to look slightly to one side, to the balding fair hair, the rounded face and the wide, grinning mouth.

Bence-Jones, it became apparent, grinned a lot.

His handshake was firm but brief, as if he had a limited supply of grip and wasn't about to waste it on lesser mortals like a locum consultant. 'Really? Well, I must express my personal gratitude, then.'

He did not, however, actually *thank* Eisenmenger, leaving a short gap into which Eisenmenger commented, 'How is Victoria? I knew her at medical school.'

Bence-Jones made a non-committal noise that might have been 'Okay,' but might also have been some belligerent morsel of partially digested food making its presence known.

Eisenmenger was not feeling particularly diplomatic, or he might not have persisted. 'Stress is a terrible thing.'

Bence-Jones was still grinning but it was below a stare that had a hint of hostility; despite this, his tone was calm and neutral. 'Yes, but I'm afraid that it's a symptom of modern working life, especially in the health service.'

Von Guerke was drinking the wine as if afraid that a drought was imminent. She said cheerfully, 'And such a shame, especially in Victoria's case.'

Eisenmenger picked up an intonation in what she said but couldn't place it. He raised querying eyebrows and she explained, 'The College Research Medal.'

'Ah, yes,' said Eisenmenger.

Except that Bence-Jones was shaking his head and muttering, 'It was nothing.' Which struck Eisenmenger as a bit of a liberty, as he wasn't the one who had actually won it.

'What is her line of research?'

Bence-Jones, still all a-grin, said vaguely, 'Something to do with ribosomes, I believe.'

Someone came past with more wine that Eisenmenger declined but both von Guerke and Bence-Jones readily accepted. Bence-Jones then asked Eisenmenger, 'And you? Do you have a research interest?'

But Eisenmenger had to disappoint him, which appeared, as far as the Medical Director was concerned, to take the shine off him. Von Guerke tried her best – 'John is an experienced forensic pathologist' – but this was a medical school, where there was no currency other than research.

'Really?' There was still the grin but it was now plastered upon the face of a being far, far away.

Eisenmenger decided to leave the field of battle. He put his glass down on a nearby window sill and said, 'Perhaps you'd give Victoria my best wishes.'

Bence-Jones broadened the grin slightly – although still nothing too encouraging – and nodded. 'Of course, of course.' It never seeped up into his eyes, though, and he was already talking of cabbages and kings to von Guerke by the time Eisenmenger had taken one step away.

The warble of the phone wasn't loud but it was nonetheless

intensely irritating to Wilson Milroy as he sat late drinking a chilled Sancerre and listening to early Miles Davis in his small but, he considered, perfect study. Lined by books, it boasted a large oak desk with its leathern surface on which to write, a disgustingly expensive stereo system on which to play his extensive collection of jazz records and, most important of all, a lock. He had made frequent use of the lock in earlier times when his daughter had been at home and his wife remained faithful. Why he still habitually locked it – even though his sole companion was now Eva, his housekeeper, who respected his privacy and had never once interrupted him – was a question that he'd never considered asking, let alone answering.

He tried to hold out against the sound, tried to let Miles Davis play in the kind of adoring silence that such genius merited, but it was no use. The bloody thing would not desist; with surprising speed he found that he could not listen to anything other than the silences between the rings. Even when he increased the volume of the stereo, to his incredulous irritation he actually *strained* to catch it.

Eventually, and almost trembling with irritation, he stormed from the study, leaving behind on the desk the neat pile of papers through which he had been reading with such absorbing interest. The house was large and, since Milroy had refused to have an extension in his study on principle, the telephone far distant. Incredibly it was still ringing when he reached it.

'Hello?' he barked.

'Daddy?'

It was Abigail and at once he was subsumed by softness, his anger lost, forgotten. 'Abi?'

She had moved out last year but still called regularly.

'I've got a problem with the car. Can you come and help?'

Abi now seemed to him to be his last hold on compassion. He had only to hear her voice to feel once more at peace. She didn't sound worried or stressed, but then she never did. Worry and stress were immiscible with Abi. She always managed to calm him down when the worst excesses of his world made him incandescent.

'Now? Straight away?'

He unaccountably knew at once that she was smiling. 'Of course silly.'

He often wondered what he would do without Abi, without

the balm that she gave him just by letting him hear her words. He suspected that the iniquities of his life – that Piringer had stolen his chair, that he was unrecognized in a sea of incompetents and frauds, that professionalism and ability were no longer enough – would have twisted him beyond recognition, had it not been for her.

She asked anxiously, 'Is it convenient?' She was forever hoping that he would start again the courting game.

He sighed theatrically. 'I suppose so.'

With mock seriousness she said, 'Well, if it isn't . . .'

And of course he replied at once, 'You know it is.' Her giggle was helium in his heart.

'Silly.' She had called him 'silly' so many times in their relationship that it had almost become a nickname.

'I'll come straight away.'

She thanked him and somehow that pleased him more than almost anything else might have done.

He went to the large wardrobe in the spacious hall where he kept their outdoor clothes and shoes, selecting a corduroy jacket and some casual shoes. Picking up his car keys from the hall table by the large mirror he patted his trouser pocket for his house keys, then opened the large front door with its stained glass central window.

The evening was just falling lightly with a faint drizzle as he stepped into the large front garden that sloped gently down to a street that was partially hidden by the mature apple and pear trees. He walked across to the wooden doors of the double garage, their paint flaking yet somehow all the better for it. In the poor light he had trouble finding and inserting the correct key into the padlock. While he was crouched over it, he heard the faintest of sounds behind him and within the space of a second this had become incarnate certainty that someone was there. He began to straighten, turning as he did so, no particular thought in his mind as to who it might be.

He hadn't realized how close this person was, certainly hadn't appreciated that the shadow was close enough to reach out and grasp him as early as it did.

The grip was strong but one-handed, the left hand on his shoulder pushing him so that he could not straighten. 'What . . . ?'

He looked up, having to twist his neck to do so.

197

Colossal mistake.

The blade sliced into his skin.

The pain – the agony – found a reflex. Milroy had enough latitude to jerk his upper torso away and to pull round. He managed to get his hands to the arm that was holding his shoulder, but the grip was immense. At the same time he was trying to stand as blood was flowing freely down his neck and chest. He was almost able to forget the torture from the sliced wound.

Which was when the hammer cracked into his scalp and then into his skull and he felt yet more anguish, more agony, except this time there was a ringing tone in his hearing and his vision was rapidly becoming fogged. He carried on trying to stand though, but now his legs were weakening; certainly he couldn't find the strength to release the grip on his shoulder.

His head began to roll, the ringing tone somehow coalescing with the agony in his head and a feeling of increasing pressure behind his face.

He was barely conscious when the grip left his shoulder and his chin was taken and lifted.

Unfortunately he was conscious enough to be aware of the blade being reapplied to his neck, to feel its continuing slow but thoughtful journey deep into his neck.

Homer lived in a new semi-detached house on a housing estate near a golf course. The estate was described as being 'low density', which meant that the gardens at the rear were big enough to house a small greenhouse as opposed to a cold-frame, and that topless female sunbathers could be seen by only four sets of neighbours as opposed to sixteen.

Not that such a consideration bothered the Chief Inspector.

It was, however, neat and quiet and respectable. His immediate neighbours in the small cul-de-sac were an accountant and his family, two professional women who claimed to all about them that they were sisters but who were in reality lesbians, a luxury-car salesman and his partner, and a retired couple (he an architect, she a bank manager). He knew everything he needed to know about them because they had all been vetted to ensure that he would not be embarrassed by living in their proximity. They didn't bother him, and he didn't bother them; all were polite to each other, and all were outwardly happy. So it was a good place to live, with four bedrooms, two bathrooms (one en suite), a kitchen-breakfast room with a view over the back garden and a study (or dining room, depending on the need).

And it had to be faced that he had no need, that there were times in the evening or on Sunday mornings when it came to Homer that it was a big house for a single man . . .

Another bloody long day saw him returning in complete, silent darkness, the kind that only drifts down when the sensible, normal part of the world has long been home and long been fed, when the children are in bed and the watershed has passed into maturity. He had not eaten and was not hungry. He didn't even want a drink, but he got some whisky anyway and went into the lounge.

He had never wanted female company. The obligatory girlfriends at the training college and in his early days as a uniformed constable had convinced him that he was not a natural suitor. Not, he no longer needed to tell himself, that he had a problem with sex; no problem at all. It was merely that he was a loner, that he found life easier when he didn't have to consider what another might want or not want.

Hell, most of the time he enjoyed being alone. The job had always required so much teamwork and camaraderie that for him there was none left for his social life. At such times all he needed was the television and a glass of whisky.

Most of the time anyway, for there were without doubt occasions on which such a simple prescription for happiness was insufficient, when he *did* crave company. Once (he cringed to recall it) he had dared to wonder about Beverley Wharton, had even . . .

She had seemed everything that he wanted; intelligent, sparky and quite stunningly attractive. He had heard the rumours about her, of course, but he had considered it worth a crack; after all, even if she was choosing to sleep her way to the top, that didn't mean that she wouldn't enjoy a proper relationship, one that meant a bit more than drinks at six, sex at seven and then alone at eight. That had been on the first Pendred investigation, when he and she had been, in his eyes at least, in some way kindred and perhaps, therefore, likely to have something in common.

199

He suddenly sighed and lay back in the armchair. There was a photograph of his parents on the sideboard and it caught his attention now. He hadn't spoken with them for weeks, using the pressure of work as his excuse, but he knew that he was doing wrong in being so inconsiderate.

Why did he have to be so bloody conscience-ridden? It wasn't as though he was a Catholic. Perhaps he was genetically pre-disposed to Catholicism, doomed by an accident of birth to be by nurture an Anglican, by nature a papist.

It wasn't so much the rejection as the manner of it that had hurt. After a smoky evening in the pub during the early part of the Eviscerator case – when they were still only two murders in and Charlie Merrick was looking like their murderer so that they were starting to feel stupidly complacent and proud – he had suggested that Beverley might care to come out with him for a meal, just the two of them, that very night.

She had accepted and they had left together for a little Indian place he knew not far away. It had been a good meal, too, and she had been good company and he swore that he had not expected anything further from the occasion. Certainly not sex, not straight away, anyway. When he had suggested that she could come back to his place for coffee (it wasn't far away, coincidentally), he had not been expecting to fuck her. It was perfectly clear in his memory that his intentions had been honourable.

Her reaction, though, had been short, sharp and uttered with a smile as sweet as a humming bird's tongue.

'Forget it, Homer. I wouldn't fuck you if you were a million-aire and had a dick like a truncheon.'

She had left him at the restaurant after that, without even offering to help out with the bill.

And then, of course, Charlie Merrick had proved a bust and they had focused in on the Pendred boys, except that it had soon become obvious to him that it was Martin, not Melkior, who was guilty. Funny thing, though, he could no longer recall quite why it had been so obvious to him.

He was positive, though, that it had been nothing to do with his rotting relationship with Beverley Wharton who had, along with Cox, come to believe that it was Melkior because of Jenny Paget's testimony. She had been lying, and now he had been proved right.

200

So why was he feeling so bloody miserable? Why wasn't he walking on air, commanding respect, all-powerful? He had the opportunity here to guarantee his promotion to Superintendent, if not now then soon. Why, then, did he have the distinct feeling that he was delicately poised above his doom, that he was in serious danger of being destroyed by this investigation? It wasn't his fault that the wrong man had been convicted those four years before, and he was equally blameless for the release of Pendred after the murder of Jenny Muir, née Paget. It was only protocol that held him responsible for Pendred's subsequent disappearance, and who could possibly suggest that it was negligent not to have located him again in the city's maze of by ways and alleys?

It was so bloody unfair!

He went to bed, but only after a lot more whisky had passed his lips, its delights increasingly unappreciated.

Homer, Wright decided, was definitely looking stressed. He habitually wore a look of self-satisfaction that bordered (some would say impinged) on smugness, but that was now eroded, replaced by a haunted demeanour. He had clearly missed out on much sleep over the past days and Wright had the suspicion that he might have missed out on some meals since his collars were starting to pull away from his neck; collars that were now exposed as frayed and less than clean. There was no Mrs Homer – there never had been – but Wright had never before noticed such lapses in his superior's appearance. Homer had always been insistent that there were standards to be met and had been consistent in himself living up to them.

They were back in Homer's office after the early morning briefing of the detective team and before two ordeals that looked likely to test the strongest of men – yet another 'strategy session' with Call, and yet another press conference; either alone would have been sufficient to induce explosive diarrhoea and deep pallor in Homer, but in combination they were potent enough to produce catatonia.

If the press conferences had started as a way of publicizing the manhunt and getting Pendred's face known, they had rapidly become an ordeal in which Homer was asked one question in a myriad of ways and a steadily increasing tone of contempt: *Why hasn't Pendred been caught yet?* It had not escaped Homer's attention that Call, despite his usual unslakeable thirst for self-publicity, had somehow always failed to find his way to these events.

The title 'strategy session' stank to Homer's nostrils of euphemism for yet another bout of bloodletting; long knives would be out and most of the red stuff on the shagpile was going to be his. His only consolation was that thus far Pendred had not committed more homicide but even that, he knew, was almost certainly an ephemeral harbour; Pendred would kill again.

He had gone over every aspect of Pendred's life, had done so repeatedly, but had uncovered no clue regarding where he might have gone to ground or whom he might choose as his next victim. Such speculation had formed his entire perspective for all the hours that he was awake and had informed and deformed his dreams.

He felt like a man given a diagnosis of untreatable malignancy and a cap on his longevity; death was coming and, when it did, he knew that he would be working with the ticking of a count-down in his ear.

The investigation had grown so that now there were sixty detectives working on it. That Pendred remained untraced was in a way a failure for every one of them, but his failure was a summation, perhaps even a synergy, of everyone's. He carried that burden as well as he could, but it was bowing him down.

Only his elation that he had been proved right kept him going. He had been right all those years ago in his belief that Martin, not Melkior, had been the murderer. Jenny Paget had lied – why, he did not know for certain, but he suspected that it was nothing more complex than money – but in doing so she had condemned his twin to prison and thence death. Neither Cox nor Wharton had listened to his suspicions (Wharton had even mocked him), an omission that Homer had heard they were both now regretting. Wharton's suspension had seemed like a fanfare from God, an affirmation of his victory. The irony that, despite his triumph, the atmosphere was very much one of impending nemesis was not lost upon Homer, but it was a mocking, unhelpful irony.

The door opened and Call came in, a man who had no need or desire or politeness. 'I thought you ought to know at once. Arthur Cox died this morning.'

202

Homer's surprise was brief, replaced almost at once by guilt. He heard Wright murmur, 'Shit.'

'How, sir?'

'Heart. I blame the bloody reporters. The bastards wouldn't leave him alone.'

Homer hated the press as much as the next policeman. He told himself that he shouldn't blame himself for their despicable actions. After all, if Cox and Wharton had listened to him, they wouldn't have made such a ghastly cock-up; why should he feel any guilt?

'Shame, sir.' Did that sound sincere? He thought it wasn't bad, and Call seemed to accept it, but Wright was looking at him. He turned away from his Sergeant, irritation flaring. Who did Wright think he was? His conscience?

Call went on, 'Which brings us to the press conference.'

Well, maybe it did, but Homer didn't quite know what that meant; silence thus ensued until Call demanded irritably, 'Well? What are we going to say?'

As with most good questions, the answer was correspondingly poor. 'Umm . . .'

Call raised his eyes to the part of the ceiling where a tile had fallen some years ago, the five blobs of adhesive long desiccated. 'Did you learn nothing on the PR course? Or was it two thousand quid of the ratepayers' money down the drain?'

Homer could not truthfully reply that he recalled much of the five-day residential course. In fact he could not have truthfully replied that he recalled anything of it. He had not wanted to go, had not enjoyed it and had found most of the lectures, tutorials, role-play and feedback sessions to be excruciatingly tedious. He ventured cautiously, 'We put a positive gloss on what we've achieved, sir.'

Call glanced suspiciously at him, then nodded. 'Exactly. We can't claim to have found the bugger, but we can at least tell people about the progress being made.'

Which was all very fine and dandy, but Homer couldn't immediately think of any progress . . .

'Yes, sir.'

Call turned his attention to Wright. 'You,' he barked. 'What have you got to say?'

Wright's expression called to mind a man brought before

Torquemada just after Spain had been knocked out of the World Cup. 'We've traced Patrick Wilms' final few hours, sir.'

'And?'

Wright consulted a typewritten sheet. 'He left his house at five forty-five, called first at the the Bleeding Heart public house, his usual drinking place. The Bleeding Heart is located about half a mile from the cemetery. After about forty-five minutes there, and having drunk two pints of stout, he proceeded to the Fisherman's Friend eat-in or takeaway fish and chip shop. There he purchased haddock and chips with a pickled egg on the side.'

Call interrupted ominously, 'I don't really care what he had on the side, Sergeant.'

'No, sir. His most direct route home from there was through the cemetery. The chip shop owner reckons he left there at about six fifty. We have one further sighting of him at about seven thirty, just as he was entering the cemetery from the northern entrance.'

'And he was discovered when?'

'About five minutes after ten, sir.'

Call turned back to Homer. 'What about sightings of Pendred?'

'Plenty of those, sir, though how many are reliable is another matter. When we weed out the obvious lunatics, we're left with fifty-seven. I'd reckon that maybe half can be considered distinct probables; the problem is deciding which of the fifty-seven those are.'

Call didn't want to hear negatives. 'And is there any pattern to these sightings?'

Aware that presentation was all, Homer replied, 'They're all in the locality around Pendred's house.' Which wasn't surprising, considering that Homer had decided that all sightings over ten miles from Pendred's house were from cranks. He went on, 'We have reports from two people who place Pendred near the chip shop; one at six twenty, the other at around seven.

Call at last looked pleased. 'Good, good. So we assume that he was keeping watch on the chip shop, knowing Wilms' habits. He must have murdered him, then gone directly to McArdle Street. When does Bloomenthal say that Wilms died?'

Homer said promptly, 'He gives a window of seven fifteen to eight o'clock.'

'Good.'

Into this satisfaction Wright put tentatively, 'I don't quite follow what he wanted with Dr Eisenmenger.'

Call clearly found this a detail that was eminently ignorable. 'Presumably he took a dislike to him.'

'But when, sir? And what did Eisenmenger do?' At once he saw that he had goaded the monster a little too unwisely.

'For God's sake, Sergeant! What does that matter? Pendred's completely barking. He doesn't need a reason.' He turned to Homer who was enjoying the sight of someone else taking the brown stuff in the face. 'Why can't these junior officers learn to concentrate on what's important?'

Homer said obsequiously, 'I know, sir. I do try to educate them.'

He did not fail to spot Wright's expression of irritation.

'What about the psychologist? Has he got anything to add?'

'Reckons Pendred will sooner or later revert to his childhood haunts.'

'His house? Surely he won't go back there. He must know that we're watching it round the clock.'

Homer raised his shoulders. 'He doesn't do normal things.'

Call lapsed into contemplation. Then, 'What does Bloomenthal say?'

Wright had the reports on his lap. 'He's ninety-five per cent certain that whoever committed the first five murders is also committing these.'

'Ninety-five? Only ninety-five?'

Homer explained. 'He's asked John Eisenmenger, the pathologist on the first five murders, to check through his findings, see if he agrees. We're waiting on that.'

'He bloody well better agree, because if he doesn't, we're shafted.' There was a note of menace in Call's voice that could not be ignored. 'You're sure Pendred's not hiding in the hospital? It's big, plenty of hiding places.'

'We've searched it thoroughly. Their security personnel have been briefed and there are posters all over the place.'

'Search it again,' Call said simply. He had positioned himself behind Homer's desk (thus forcing Homer to the comfortable visitor's chair, Wright to the perch by the window where there was a perpetual Siberian draught), and he now stood up suddenly. 'Right. That seems straightforward.'

Homer, who wasn't a devotee of cryptic crosswords, didn't follow the meaning of this comment. 'Sir?'

Call was clearly preparing to leave, his job done. 'You know what to say in the press conference – Wilms' last movements, our confidence that Pendred is in the area and will be found, our certainty that Pendred is responsible for the murders both now and in the past. You can also express sorrow that Cox has kicked the bucket and send our condolences to his widow. Also you can say that we're enquiring into what went wrong with the first investigation four years ago.'

He was on his way, with Wright scribbling down what he had just said and Homer trying to spot the good news in it. He had an ominous feeling that he had been given a shield made of papier-mâché with which to defend himself in the press conference, and he could feel the rain coming on.

But then Fisher came in. 'A Dr Milroy's gone missing. Apparently he was known to Pendred.'

Call cast a look at Homer that not even the Gorgon could have managed.

Part Three

Fisher was not an imaginative man and this had served him well thus far in his career as a police officer. He did as he was told, kept quiet when so ordered, ran and shouted as required. He enjoyed the social life, much of which involved drinking to great excess, often in the seedier clubs of the city, and the feeling of camaraderie.

The only slight cloud was his sex life. Jess had been a lovely girl with big brown eyes and nipples that he had always found satisfying, being the longest he had ever seen in his life. Their lovemaking had been times of fascination for Fisher, whether her nipples were in his mouth or between forefinger and thumb; once he had measured them and found them to be over two centimetres in length, while she giggled and squirmed beneath him.

But Jess had not fancied the life of a police wife. She had not really fitted in with the other partners she had met, had not been able to become part of the club. On the few occasions on which she accompanied him to a party or on a trip to the bowling alley, she had been quiet and, although always polite, had not been a hit with his colleagues.

They had frequently rowed after such nights.

The relationship had begun to bleed, exsanguinating as relentlessly as a slit wrist in a warm bath.

And thereafter he had been alone.

Until now.

He had been looking far from where sex eventually came calling.

'Have you never considered other ways?'

The question was couched in what was almost a bored tone and Fisher found surprise replaced by indignation. 'What do you mean?'

Resting on one elbow, Beverley Wharton placed a well-manicured hand of long thin fingers on his stomach. 'Can't you guess?'

Sexual excitement fought with traumatized pride. 'What's wrong with the way I do it?'

She smiled and once again he found himself aroused by her. Every move she made seemed to highlight how stunningly attractive she was as he viewed her from different angles, in different lights.

'Nothing. What you do, you do very well.'

Her fingers had moved. He began to squirm very slightly, partly through ticklishness, partly through anticipation.

'I've never had complaints.'

She said nothing to that. As soon as she had managed to make him appreciate that they were going to go to bed, he had adopted what she regarded as the Neanderthal approach, although she suspected that the epithet was probably unfair to an ancient and dignified race. Foreplay to people like Fisher was a kiss and a belch; the sexual act was penetration and a few heavy-handed squeezes of the breasts (treated like stress balls and still aching), followed by a de rigueur pistoning that ended with a climax – only one, though, and on this occasion, at least, it had certainly not been hers.

Her hand had found his penis already tumescing. He was pleasantly large, which made his technique all the more disappointing. Her grip was soft but strong and he took a sudden, deep breath. 'Sit up.' Not a suggestion, more a command and, with a faint hint of surprise, he obeyed it willingly. 'Lean back against the wall.'

She knelt astride him, bringing her breasts so close he found it hard to focus on them; which was perhaps why he decided in favour of touch rather than vision. She sighed appreciatively. 'There.'

He moved from touch, to touch and taste and she sank slowly and gently down upon him, causing him to pause momentarily in his appreciation of her upper body.

'There,' she whispered again. She took his head between her forearms and began, by contracting her pelvic floor, to squeeze him slowly and rhythmically.

It was from morning radio and television that the public were informed of a third murder, although no name was released immediately. Eisenmenger heard it as he pulled himself from his bed after a late night spent with the reports that Bloomenthal had given him. It did not register as in any way of immediate importance.

He had not intended to stay up until three o'clock but the reports had drawn him into their world, one that whispered enticingly not only of his past, but also of a puzzle. He did not yet know what the puzzle was, but he could sense that it was there, that the surface appearances were nothing more than refractions of reality.

In truth he had not intended even to be at home that night, the night before Helena was due to enter hospital, but she had insisted that she be left alone, not unkindly but clearly without need of argument. He had acquiesced, but unhappily so.

And so there he had been, without purpose and without means of disguising the fact, until the reports had come to mind.

He began by closely reading Bloomenthal's reports on the autopsies of Jenny Muir and Patrick Wilms, making notes as he went, comparing and contrasting; he repeated this exercise with the books of photographs on each crime scene. It took an hour and a half to complete this stage, by which time he had a surfeit of information, a scarcity of understanding. He got up then and poured himself a large glass of beer. For the first time he noticed that it was raining very, very hard.

What to make of these reports?

His medical training had taught him how to analyse problems, if it had taught him little else of use. A not inconsiderable part of the answer was to know the questions to ask; the remainder was to have a method and to keep with it.

So what were the questions?

He could think of only two that interested him. Why hide the Wilms organ mass in Melkior Pendred's grave? Why was it only the external appearance of the corpses that bothered him? He was aware that these were not directly the questions that Bloomenthal and Beverley were concerned to have answered, but he had always had difficulty bending his intellectual curiosity to fit the expectations of others.

It was clear that the autopsies were the work of someone not experienced at them; Martin Pendred had not been a mortuary technician for four years, so it was obvious that he would be a bit rusty.

Wasn't it?

He considered long before deciding that, yes, it was.

Except that, for a reason he was as yet unable to define, he didn't like that conclusion.

He went back to Bloomenthal's reports. They were undoubtedly good reports, logical and full of detail; when combined with the photographs they gave him what appeared to be a reasonably accurate idea of the deaths.

So what did they tell him?

It took him a distressingly long time to decide that they told him exactly what they were telling everybody else. His problem was that for some reason he suspected that he was being told a lie.

He decided that he had to go back four years, to the deaths that had started this terrible sequence, to his reports of the autopsies from that time. He was at once amazed by the familiarity of what he had written. There was no surprise in what he read, though the sentences held no direct remembrance; he was transported by the phrases into a world he had never really left. He felt both comforted and repulsed. He had fought so hard to escape, had been certain that he was happy only when he wasn't immersed in the worst that humanity defeated, yet here he was, somehow warmed by his return to a past that he supposedly hated.

Sheryl Symmers, who had almost certainly realised her full potential in life working as an assistant in a small, independent chemist's shop, only to meet her demise shortly after she had slapped Melkior Pendred because he had grabbed her breast.

Clement Lever, an undertaker who had had a running feud with Martin.

Antony Greenfield, a self-styled artist and inveterate drinker who had one night whilst drunk taken offence at Melkior Pendred's face in the pub.

Benjamin White, who had accused Melkior of stealing his mother's wedding ring from her corpse, and Lynette Morson, the manager at the WRI who had mistakenly instituted formal proceedings against Melkior because of it.

The names brought back the memories of their faces, the incredulity with which anyone and everyone confronted the murderer's handiwork, his own observations and deductions as he gazed for hour upon hour upon it. These last he tried to recapture, magnify, experience again.

His overwhelming thought at the time was of the monstrous insanity of the deaths. To kill by slitting the throat was comprehensible – awful but comprehensible – but the time and effort involved in what followed suggested someone driven, someone who considered the likelihood of discovery far less important than whatever was gained by the evisceration. Therefore this murderer was not interested merely in death but in something beyond it. But what?

To satisfy a need. Everyone has needs to which they are slaves; murderers, Eisenmenger knew, were no different. At the time, Eisenmenger had come to the conclusion that in dissecting the bodies, the murderer was trying somehow to understand them. It had given Eisenmenger the impression of a child taking apart a mechanical toy to discover its secrets only to be confronted by an insoluble puzzle and numerous disconnected pieces, but he suspected now that he had been naive. After all, why stop at removing the 'pluck'? Why not continue until all the organs were separate and in constituent pieces?

The forensic psychologist had been of the opinion that the murderer had suicidal tendencies turned outward, that he or she had wanted to lay bare a terrible secret long suppressed, but it hadn't really mattered, because the case had come down to one of almost classical simplicity. Means, motive and opportunity, nothing else. The means being someone who knew how easy it was to rip the organs from a body, how beautifully compact and economical was the internal layout of God's child. The motive being various slights upon the Pendreds; slights that seen with the eyes of normality were minor, yet seen with otherworldly eyes were worthy of extreme retribution. The opportunity had been unclear to everyone until the end.

Cox and Wharton had been distracted by Charlie Merrick, who was a piece of human excrement. An undertaker and, in the past, a mortuary technician, he had been thoroughly evil, possessed of a bad temper and little conscience; borderline psychopath. He, too, had taken a dislike to Sheryl Symmers and Clement Lever, coincidence that had been too strong to ignore. Only the fact that his alibi had been strong had prevented his immediate arrest; the third murder, for which no reasonable motive could be identified, had saved him.

That same third murder brought attention to the Pendreds.

'I shouldn't be here, I suppose.'

Fisher, having done the dirty deed, suddenly seemed to have started considering the implications now that it was morning. He was wandering around her flat in his underwear, poking through the few ornaments that she had bothered to acquire. Beverley was making coffee with her back to him which was something of relief to her, since she found him a less than edifying sight and she found that she was also a less than edifying sight. Had she really resorted to sex for favours? Her lofty thoughts of such a short time ago came back to visit her and mock her. It seemed that she was doomed to repeat the mistakes of her history.

She asked wearily, 'Why not?'

He became shy. 'Well . . .'

She had poured the coffee and, a deep breath taken, she now turned round, suppressing the desire to close her eyes to remove the image. *Why don't you get dressed?*

'You mean because of the Pendred case? Because Homer's desperate to prove me wrong?'

He nodded but didn't say anything.

It didn't stop you half an hour ago, did it? Didn't make you stop me when I was giving you the best fucking head you've ever had.

'I haven't been suspended yet. I'm still a serving police officer and, as far as I can recall, there's nothing in the regulations that says I can't socialize with my fellow officers.'

'Yeah, I know, but . . .'

'But what?'

His lack of intellect was signalled by the hesitation that followed. 'Well, it doesn't look good, does it? I mean, if anyone found out . . .'

She sat down on the leather sofa. 'Don't you think that you should have thought of that before? Like in the pub?'

She had met him in the Lamb and Goat, which might have been a surprise to him but which was exactly where she had expected to find him. It had taken her a great deal of thought to select someone on the investigation team who was both stupid and gullible, but not too repulsive. The first two qualities had been easy, the third a considerable problem. Not that the pool of candidates was not increasing. The investigation team was growing, by all accounts, presumably because its failure to catch Pendred merited reinforcement; Fisher was the best of a poor selection, both because he was slightly less unevolved than the others, and because he had been on the investigation from its start. He was therefore a connection to what they were thinking, although his junior rank meant that he wasn't privy to the innermost councils. She could not afford, however, to be too choosy.

He sat down opposite her, underpants distressingly obvious, and she was forced to question her wisdom. He didn't actually smell and he wasn't actually ugly, but he was far from her normal choice of partner, being uncouth, arrogant and uninventive.

Still, the ends would hopefully justify the means.

When he didn't say anything, she went on, 'It's not illegal to be with me and, anyway, who's going to know? I'm not going to tell, are you?' He shook his head. She leaned towards him. 'It's just some fun, Terry.'

He nodded and laughed. 'Yeah.'

She picked up her cup. 'Drink up.'

While he was doing as he was told like a good, obedient boy, she asked, 'So how *is* it going? The investigation, I mean.'

A momentary glance of suspicion was wiped from his face when she added, 'Don't tell me if you'd rather not. I don't want to compromise you.'

He shrugged. 'Not well, but I suppose you know that. Everyone else does.'

'I had heard something.'

He laughed. 'Poor old Homer's going nuts. Call's on his back at every turn. He's so frustrated because he knows that Pendred did it, but he just can't find him.'

'No trace at all?'

'Nope. Homer's done all the usual things – known contacts, known haunts – but nothing. Not that with Pendred there were a lot of places to look. He's got no living relatives, he's got no friends and he hardly ever went anywhere.'

'What about the hospital?'

'That was one of the first places we looked.'

'Has he had Pendred profiled?'

Fisher snorted with derision; coming from one so naive and yet so arrogant, it was a juvenile gesture. 'Usual crap there.'

She smiled, 'All the things that you already knew and a few you didn't need to know?' Criminal profilers – no doubt an honourable profession – were something of an open joke in the force.

Fisher nodded. 'Yeah.'

'So what's he doing now?'

'They've issued an e-fit and they're distributing posters; they've booked a slot on the telly to advertise the search. Apart from that, they're continuing the house-to-house and just waiting.'

'And, I suppose, hoping that he doesn't slice someone else's throat.'

Fisher grinned, a rather ugly spectacle. 'You can say that again.'

The rain had eased off but then come back with even greater ferocity, so that it formed a constant waterfall of background noise as Eisenmenger worked. After three hours he had covered several sides of paper with scribbled notes – most of them questions, few of them facts or conclusions – and now he was concocting a table, with the names of the victims down the left-hand side, various aspects of their murders across the top. The column headings, taken from context, suggested impending or enduring madness on Eisenmenger's part, perhaps as great as the murderer's. *Shape of incision, Neatness of incision, Regularity of stitch marks, Style of stitching, Shape of skull segment, Buttonholes?, Organs nicked, Length of carotids, Bladder intact?, Site of the pluck, Site of the brain, Knots.* He had written down remarks under each of these for every victim and it caused him to stare for a long time at the resulting sheet. So long, in fact, that he had consumed the best part of a bottle of Riocha Gran Reserva while doing so.

Eventually he sighed, finished his glass and went to bed. He was going to upset either Bloomenthal or Beverley, he had known; now he was beginning to guess which.

Helena looked out at the rain, her face set into a grim reflection of her mood. Behind her the bag she had packed for her stay in hospital sat on the floor by the sofa. Sandy Denny sang sad songs into the neatness of her flat and the television was on but muted.

214

I will beat this. This is not going to win.

The thought, permutated but fundamentally unchanged by repetition, sounded again and again in her skull, bouncing off her determination. She would not be beaten, she would not allow herself to succumb.

Sandy Denny finished, silence again taking command, defied only by the splatter of rain on the window in front of her, through which innumerable neon lights were displayed. It was a panorama of the civilized twenty-first century, a view unknown in ages past, but it was still one of darkness, one of the night. No amount of electricity could really lift the night, just as no amount of medical wisdom could really lift the burden of disease. Isolated victories did not mean the war was being won; indeed, they merely emphasized the weakness of humanity's weapons.

No!

This was wrong. This was not a fate for her. The darkness might be all around but she would overcome it. Tomorrow was the day of her operation and this night really did feel to her like the eve of a battle. Nothing heroic though, nothing of Agincourt in her mind, no dogs of war to be unleashed. This was a personal, unheralded fight; only she would benefit from victory.

John had offered to be with her, a proposition that tempted but that she had gently refused. He had accepted this with good grace and she wondered whether he perhaps understood that this night she needed solitude in which to find concentration. That he had offered was enough solace for her; he would be with her even if only in spirit.

She closed her eyes.

I will come through this.

She had unfinished business; a murderer still to catch, her parents still to be avenged, her step-brother, Jeremy, still to be proved innocent. Almost beyond her consciousness her hand had gone again to her breast, to *the* breast. With realization came anger and she pulled her hand away sharply.

She turned away from the window, her determination rekindled, the darkness behind her.

From the street below, Martin Pendred watched, the light of love unseen behind his eyes.

215

Or something that passed for love.

When she met Dr Malcolm Pinkus in the early morning at his house in the small dormitory town about twenty kilometres from the city centre, Beverley was astonished at the change that had come upon him. In her memory he was tall and vibrant, dark-eyed and with hair so pale that it seemed somehow magical, only half within this universe. Now, however, he looked worn down, with lost weight hanging from him, eyes too deep within his face, a hunched gait that brought his face level with hers.

Four years before, she could have imagined being attracted by him, by his self-confident ebullience and his charm, had he been ten years younger. What, she wondered, would have happened had that been case? Would she now be secure in her life, Peter merely an unrealized betrayal that would never bother her? She smiled grimly at such romantic wish fulfilment; she did not really believe that such a life could ever be hers, not in this life, nor in an infinity of others.

'Sergeant Wharton! What a delightful surprise.' 'Sergeant' because that was how he remembered her; he didn't know that she was in decline from greater things. He held out a hand beneath a genuine smile; the hand was arthritic and she was at once afraid of squeezing it too hard and perhaps hurting him. She merely held it, feeling its warm, smooth dryness. He stood to one side. 'Come in. Come in. I guessed that someone would be coming to call.'

Of course he had. Malcolm Pinkus was bright, almost luminescent. The best psychiatrist she had ever encountered.

He moved before her into the darkness of the elegant, Victorian house, past neatness that belied his widower status. His movement was slow and clearly painful, and she could hear his breath rasping pain from his throat, as he led her into the front sitting room. The ceiling was high and there was an original fireplace in which a fire had been set but not lit; she sat primly in a high-backed armchair to its left, he in its twin to the right. As he sat painfully down she could see the extent of the damage that the arthritis had done to him.

He looked into her eyes and smiled with something that was almost apology. 'You see that I have lost the blessing of good health.'

She nodded. 'How long?'

'Not long after the Pendred case, as a matter of fact. It was of quite sudden onset – first the ankles, then the knees, then the hands and gradually onwards. In weeks I was in pain that I had never known before, unable to walk, unable even to write.'

'What is it?'

'Just arthritis.' Again the smile, but without any humour. 'What does it matter to me what it's called? Steroids, immuno-suppressants, methotrexate – I went through the panoply in those first few months and none did anything of great merit. Eventually the arthritis got tired of playing with me, I think. It left me alone, or at least stopped advancing, and here I am, three years on. Retired and tired. Tired all the time.'

Beverley didn't know what to say. He had spoken quietly and with an air of something that suggested puzzlement; she had heard no self-pity or anger. He saw her embarrassment and said at once, 'But you haven't come to discuss my problems. You're here because the murders have started again.'

She said, 'You must think I'm dreadful, coming here like this . . .'

He smiled and held up a hand with fingers that bent the wrong way and joints that were slightly too large. 'Please, Sergeant. I'm delighted to be asked. Makes me feel a little less useless.'

'There's no need for formality, is there? It's Beverley.'

His smile broadened. 'And I am Malcolm. Not a name I would have chosen but, nevertheless, I have chosen not to change it. I can offer you tea or coffee but, I should warn you, it will take me considerable time to make it and it will probably not be worth the effort when it arrives.'

She shook her head. 'Thanks for the offer. I'm fine.'

'Very wise.' But his eyes betrayed disappointment and his tone was grave and possibly bore a hint of bitterness. She said quickly, 'You're aware, of course, of what's been happening?'

'More murders in the style of the Eviscerator.'

'So they say.'

He nodded gravely. 'And you have come to me to discover . . . what?'

'You were the man who interviewed both Melkior and Martin for us. You knew them better than anyone else on the investigation.'

'You can't know an autistic, Beverley. You can't know them,

217

and they can't know you. There is a barrier that separates them from the rest of us.'

'But you have more understanding than the rest of us.' At this he shrugged, a slightly asymmetric gesture. 'You know that Martin's gone missing?'

'Who doesn't? Chief Inspector Homer – he has done well, I think – has graced our screens on several occasions telling us that Martin Pendred is wanted for questioning in relation to the latest murders.'

'You haven't been asked to offer your advice?'

His smile became slightly frozen beneath a faint frown. 'Are you here unofficially?'

'Does it matter?' When he hesitated, she admitted, 'I'm not on the case, but that doesn't mean I'm disinterested. It's been made fairly clear that if it's shown that Melkior Pendred was innocent, I'm finished.'

'Just because of one mistake?'

She shrugged. 'It would make a good excuse.'

'And now you'd like to . . . what? Find Martin Pendred before Homer does?'

'Look, Malcolm. If they find Martin, you know as well as I do what'll happen. He'll be hung out to dry because he won't put up a fight, because he won't be able to defend himself properly. He's been lined up for this, because Homer wants to prove that he was right and I was wrong all those years ago.'

Pinkus considered. 'And you? What are your motives?'

'We got it right, Malcolm. Melkior committed those murders. You were happy at the time that he did it, if you remember.'

'Actually,' he pointed out at once, 'I was merely asked whether Melkior was capable of murder and I believe that he was. That didn't mean that Martin wasn't.'

She opened her mouth, a breath caught within her throat before he smiled and added, 'But, if it matters to you, I thought that you were right.'

She continued to breathe, raising an eyebrow. He had been extremely attractive; still was, in some ways.

'So you're protecting him from Homer? Conceivably a laudable aim. How can I help?'

'Give me a clue where he might be hiding.' She was aware that she was making it sound like a game – perhaps hide and seek for grown-ups – with Pinkus as the one who was in charge.

He would have shrugged had he been able. There was a movement of his shoulders that was slight but even that was clearly painful. 'I wish that I knew, Beverley.'

'But you've got a good idea, surely.'

He pursed his lips and there was a gap while she looked at him and he looked into the past. Then, 'Perhaps an idea, but not a good one. Or rather, I can tell you where he hasn't gone.'

She was willing to take anything.

'Autistic Spectrum Disorder imposes strict rules on its sufferers, both in their perceptions, their emotions, and their actions. They are within fences that they cannot climb, they cannot even see over.' When she said nothing, he added, 'He will not run far.'

She couldn't hide her disappointment as she said, 'Old haunts? His house, the hospital? All those will have been checked and checked again.'

He held up his hand. 'Obviously; and equally obviously, he has not been found. But it's likely that what Martin Pendred considers to be a safe or familiar place to hide may not be what you or I or the police would consider as such.'

'How so?'

'Martin, as his brother was, is outwardly mentally impaired – "severe learning difficulties", "special needs", whatever the jargon, politically correct phrase is now. That, most specifically, did *not* mean that he was stupid. I would prefer to say that he was merely ineducable, at least using conventional methods. One thing that I know he did have was an eidetic memory.'

'Eidetic?'

He smiled. 'Photographic. Neither Martin nor Melkior ever forgot anything. Possibly it was part of their madness – those who can't lose unpleasant memories are in a sort of hell, you see.'

She worked through the implications of what he was telling her. 'So you think that he might have gone to hide in a place that perhaps he visited only once but has never forgotten?'

'That must be a possibility.' He clasped painfully destroyed hands together. 'There is another factor to be included.'

'What?'

'He will have run to safety. As I have just said, that will have to include all the places that he has ever visited, even if only once, but you have also to be aware that Martin's idea of what is safe may not be yours. He almost certain has a different notion of what is a "safe" place to hide.'

She had come to Pinkus for help and he had certainly broadened the scope of where she might now have to look, but he had broadened it to such an extent that it was starting to look hopeless. 'Can you give me an example?' she asked, striving for some idea of where to start.

He steepled his forefingers, tapping them against his mouth. 'Well, supposing when he was a child, he went on a bus trip to the city centre, perhaps to go to a museum. Suppose at the start of the trip, they had walked to the bus station, two streets away from where they lived, and when they had arrived there, he and his brother had been overawed at the sight of so many bright red buses, so much activity. It might now be that he has returned to that bus station, although it is only two streets away from where I should imagine the police have spent a considerable amount of time and manpower investigating. He would view it as a place of safety because he associates it with happiness, although he only went there once and it is dangerously close to where he has lived all his life.'

She saw what he was saying but saw, too, that her task would not be easy. Certainly not on her own. Still, perhaps Fisher could help . . .

She smiled and said, 'Perhaps I will have that tea, if that's all right, Malcolm.'

It was clear at once that it was.

Helena had not slept well and had felt sick when she had at last risen from her bed; not that she was allowed to eat or drink anything, anyway. John had called just as she was about to leave, the conversation tense. Yes, she was all right. No, she hadn't changed her mind about a lift to the hospital. Yes, she would ring him if there was anything she needed.

She had booked a taxi for eight o'clock and it was there on time. The driver helped her into the car with her small bag and made inane conversation even when she didn't respond. The traffic was surprisingly light and they arrived in Hippocampus Street only twenty minutes later. She paid him and went into the entrance to the surgical wing of the WRI, unaware that from his distant vantage point, Martin Pendred had seen her arrive.

In the department the day had started without much to indicate its tragedy. When Eisenmenger had arrived (tired but satisfied, with Helena his only worry) he had settled down to work his way through a pile of cervical screening slides, simultaneously comforted and abhorred by the familiarity of what he was doing.

Such mundanities, however, ended abruptly at ten minutes past ten, when Eisenmenger was summoned to Adam Piringer's office without explanation. When he arrived, all the consultants but Wilson Milroy were there; the reason for *his* absence was explained at once by Piringer. 'I'm afraid I have some bad news for you.' He barely paused before going on, 'Wilson Milroy is dead. Apparently murdered by Martin Pendred.'

The reactions around the room were mixed, their only commonality found in shock. Amr Shaheen uttered a faint, 'My God!' and closed his eyes. Trevor Ludwig sucked in a sharp breath, then stared across at Alison von Guerke, who in turn held her hand to her face and looked at once grey with sickness. Eisenmenger turned the corners of his mouth down and bowed his head but he let his eyes look around the room. Piringer, he noticed, seemed to be taking the news with fortitude but then, he reasoned, he had known about it for longer than the rest of them.

'The police will be coming here to talk to us all. In the mean time, I will disseminate the news to the rest of the staff; we will keep working, of course.'

'Where did it happen?' asked von Guerke, almost fearfully.

'At his home. He was found this morning.'

'His throat was . . . slit?'

Piringer had no time for such prurience. 'Presumably, since they think that Pendred did it.'

Ludwig asked, 'Why do they want to speak to us? If Pendred did it, I can't see why we have to be involved.'

Piringer appeared not to know. It was Eisenmenger who explained, 'They'll want to know his movements yesterday. Who saw him last, when he left here, that kind of thing.' He couldn't resist adding, 'Anyway, they'll want to keep an open mind about who might have done it, at least until after the autopsy.'

'I hope nobody's going to suggest that I slit his throat,' warned Ludwig.

Piringer said tiredly, 'Nobody's suggesting anything like that, I'm sure. It's as John said, merely to discover his last movements.'

Amr Shaheen at last found some words, albeit quiet ones. 'I'm glad that he's dead.'

Eisenmenger caught the words, caught as well Piringer's stare into Shaheen's eyes.

'John! Good to see you.' Bloomenthal was hale and hearty, an act (Eisenmenger guessed) for the audience. 'More work for the undertaker, I'm afraid.'

The audience was a good one, although perhaps less enthusiastic than most, possibly because this was not a first night and they had clearly become less than enthralled by having to see the same play yet again. Eisenmenger noticed several faces that he recognized, including Coroner's Officers, SOCO man Moll, Constables Clark and Fisher, and Wright. He looked around for Homer, finding him in deep conversation with someone on the end of a phone. From his face, Eisenmenger had the feeling he was not talking to his lover.

Bloomenthal, dressed in usual mortuary garb, had finished directing the Scenes of Crime Officer, Moll, in the photographs that he required and was in the middle of dictating into a hand-held recorder his findings on external examination. They were, as usual with the Eviscerator, striking. The characteristic sutured incisions down the front of the torso and above the ears were telltale evidence of an emptied body. Eisenmenger went at once to its lower end, where it was knotted. Then, with a soft grunt but an expressionless face, he turned his attention to the head with its ugly wound. 'A deviation from the usual,' he commented.

Bloomenthal agreed. 'Yes. It would appear that Dr Milroy fought back and had to be subdued before the script could be followed as per usual. The carcase was hidden in the garden shed: so well that no one noticed it.'

When Eisenmenger said nothing, Bloomenthal remarked with some anxiety, 'Everything else is as normal.'

And it was. Even the handiwork was improving, as Eisenmenger pointed out. 'Where were the organs put?' he asked.

It was Wright who answered, 'The brain was found on top of the victim's personal computer in his study. The rest of the organs were in a freezer, labelled *The Dog's Dinner.*'

Bloomenthal asked, 'Did Milroy have a dog?' Nobody had an answer and he murmured to Eisenmenger, 'He's certainly a joker.'

Eisenmenger didn't smile, merely replied thoughtfully, 'He certainly seems to be.' He then enquired of Wright, 'I take it Pendred had some sort of grudge against Milroy.'

Before Wright could reply, a voice behind him said loudly, 'Oh, yes. It was Milroy who had him removed from the mortuary after his brother was convicted. He actually wanted him sacked completely – was quite noisy about it, we understand.' Homer had put the phone down looking as if he had been forced to swallow a dung beetle. He came forward. 'It's Dr Eisenmenger, isn't it?' he demanded somewhat rudely. When Eisenmenger bowed his head in admission of this offence, Homer asked, 'And how are you? Recovered from your own particular encounter with Mr Pendred?'

Eisenmenger's throat was healing and no longer required a dressing. The top of the scab peeped above his collar. 'Just about,' he murmured. Homer didn't express much interest in this answer for he was already saying, 'Well, I hope you're going to tell me that you agree with Dr Bloomenthal that all eight murders are the work of one hand.'

Eisenmenger found himself taking a dislike to Chief Inspector Homer. His vague recollection of him from the first investigation was that he had been bombastic and overconfident; like a caricature, these qualities seemed now to have grown into his only recognizable features. He said, 'I'm still considering the matter.'

Homer was stressed. He had just had a roasting from Call because Call had had a roasting from the Chief Constable. The leitmotif had been incompetence bordering on negligence; there had been a not-so-subtle subtext of suspension if Pendred wasn't caught quickly. He didn't need smart-arse pathologists refusing to tell him the things he wanted to hear.

'Well, bloody well get on and consider it more quickly. This isn't some abstract intellectual exercise to amuse you, it's a murder investigation with people having their throats cut by a fucking lunatic.'

He may not have been particularly tall but he had picked up the knack of being authoritative; he called it man-management. Eisenmenger, however, had picked up the knack of not being interested in policemen who shouted at him; he called it bloody-mindedness. He said, 'Fair enough. Since you ask so politely, I'll tell you what I think. I may be wrong, but I don't think that all eight were committed by one man. I think that there are two distinct murderers here.'

If he had accused Homer himself of the atrocities, he couldn't have produced a more extreme reaction. Homer actually did something close to a double take before widening eyes that were filled with incredulity. 'What?' he demanded. Then, just in case its loudness had not been appreciated, he repeated it, only at a higher frequency and greater amplitude. 'What?'

'These murders are not being committed by the same hand as the first five.' It was patient and it was slow which only made it more painful. His words were a blade drawn slowly across flesh for pain and enjoyment. He turned back to Isaac Bloomenthal. 'I know you think otherwise, and I might well be wrong, but you asked me for my opinion . . .'

Bloomenthal suddenly seemed to have the same dung beetle problem as Homer. 'I don't see how you can say that.'

Eisenmenger shrugged. 'I was asked for my opinion. I'm giving it. Do you want a written report?'

Before Bloomenthal could answer, Homer said loudly, 'No, thank you. I'm sure that Dr Bloomenthal can make up his own mind.' He looked pointedly at the pathologist. 'Can't you?'

Bloomenthal looked even less happy as he nodded slowly after a brief pause.

Homer turned to Eisenmenger. 'Thanks for your contribution. We won't be needing your help any more.'

Eisenmenger left not a friend behind him as he departed.

Despite Professor Piringer's pious and inevitably unrealistic hope that they would all keep working, no one managed anything particularly productive that day. The news of the murder spread rapidly, a nauseous liquid that was into every crack and corner of the hospital before the second circumcision had been commenced in the urology theatres, the five-day stool collections had been perused by the gastro-enterologists and the

Chief Executive had taken his second valium; his third followed shortly after hearing the news. There came upon the department a sort of suspension, a moist fog of inertia, infecting everyone with a mindset that precluded useful labour, that bred only whispered, almost shocked horror and a feeling of dread.

Piringer, himself, was unable to follow his own dictum. He spent most of the morning gone from his office, with interviews first with the Chief Executive, then with the Clinical Director of Pathology and finally with the Dean of the Medical School. By the time he had finished with these, someone called Sergeant Wright was waiting to speak to him. This interview lasted twenty minutes and was followed by a meeting of all pathology staff, in which Wright announced that police officers would be talking to all of them, and in which he warned them against discussing the matter with anyone other than the police.

Eisenmenger listened and sort of took notice but, as the day wore on and he learned more of the rather perfunctory interviews that the police conducted, he started to realize that the advice was not for him. Wright himself talked to Eisenmenger, and as was always the case with the Sergeant he was polite and attentive, but Eisenmenger heard only a policeman following procedure. He was asked how well he had known Milroy, when he had last seen him, if he had thought that there was anything bothering him; doubtless questions that added to mankind's knowledge and perhaps helped to ensure his ultimate well-being, but to Eisenmenger in the present context without relevance.

'Have you seen Martin Pendred recently?'

Eisenmenger bit on sarcasm, finding the flavour sour. 'No,' was all he could manage.

And that was that, except that as Wright was leaving, Eisenmenger said, 'He didn't do it, you know, Wright.'

Wright stopped and turned back to him. 'How can you be sure?'

'The same way that you know when a witness is lying. I've looked at the autopsy reports and I *know.*'

Wright shook his head. 'Dr Bloomenthal doesn't think so.'

Eisenmenger sighed. 'Do you know what *folie à deux* is, Sergeant?'

'Can't say I do.'

'Well, it's basically what happens when a sane man is locked

225

up in an asylum, when he isn't allowed to peep out into reality any more. Sooner or later, he'll be subsumed by the logic of the asylum, he'll fall into it with all the fervour of the lifelong lunatic.'

Wright's smile was small and all but mirthless. 'Is that what we are? Lunatics?'

'No. But you're wrong.'

Wright shrugged and as he turned to go said, 'Chief Inspector Homer doesn't think so.'

To his back, Eisenmenger said, 'One of the hardest tricks to master is to stop making the facts fit the theory and allow the theory to grow from the facts, and policemen sometimes have more trouble than most.'

Wright didn't turn back or appear to react at all, which meant that Eisenmenger didn't see the worried frown on his face.

'It's not relevant where Pendred is.'

Eisenmenger had arranged for Beverley to meet him in the pathology seminar room after work. It was uncomfortable and sparse but he considered it safer than a rendezvous at his house or her flat. He had just called the ward to be told that Helena was out of surgery and sleepy, but the operation had apparently gone well.

The police had gone now, leaving the department to mourn its loss, a process that was proving remarkably unstressful as if no one could believe (or no one could care) that Wilson Milroy was now part of the choir invisible. Eisenmenger had worked on through the afternoon, buoyed by the news about Helena.

When, however, the pathology reception staff had telephoned to say that he had a visitor, and when he had caught sight of her looking up at the poster on the wall (an electron microscopic study of adrenal carcinoma), he was ashamed (and yet somehow delighted) to feel familiar feelings of desire and attraction within him.

'Thanks for coming.'

She smiled. 'Always a pleasure, John.'

They walked together back to his office, passing Ludwig as they did so; his stare was gratifyingly envious. Safely ensconced, he asked, 'Coffee?'

'No, thanks.' He saw her looking around his office, her eyes bright and curious. She caught his study of her and smiled lazily. 'I hope you've had more success than I've had.'

'Well, I don't know that you could call it success . . .'

'But you've got something?'

He went to his briefcase that was under the window. From this he took the chart that he had made and put it on the desk in front of Beverley. As she leaned over it, he stood behind her and watched the cotton of her blouse tighten around her shoulders, smelled the scent of her bright blonde hair. For a few moments he was back in his old flat and things that might have been were played out in his head.

'What's this?' she asked, turning around to him. They were deliciously close, or at least it seemed so to him. Perhaps there were a few more skin creases, a couple of extra blood spots in the whites, but somehow it didn't matter, somehow it even made him even further in her thrall.

'I know it's a bit like schoolboy revision, but it was the only way I could see to work things out.'

She looked back down at it. Some of the headings seemed to be finding her lost. She asked, 'And?'

He stood up straight as he said, 'And I can't be sure but I think we're dealing with two killers here.'

Her head jerked round, hope just winning the battle with dignity. 'Really?'

At once he was shaking his head. 'Don't get me wrong, Beverley. This is a theory, nothing more. No proof, no promises. It's only what I think.'

Her face didn't change. 'Fair enough.' Then, 'But if I'm going to run with this, perhaps I should hear what makes you think that Homer's wrong and I'm right.'

It seemed a fair enough proposal. He walked around the desk and sat opposite her. She was studying the chart again, but when she looked up at him and found him looking at her there was at once a sly grin on her face as if she knew, as if she always knew, exactly what he was thinking.

'Tell me,' she suggested. She had on pale pink lipstick, bright and shiny. She could, he reflected, have made a man cross his legs as she read out a shopping list.

'I suppose the main point is that there are obvious differences in technique between the two groups of murders.' He pointed at the chart. 'First and foremost to notice is that the technique used

227

in the first five murders is assured, that used in the second three is relatively poor. The murderer's primary incision isn't as straight, there are more accidental cuts in the organs, everything's more ragged and poorly done.'

'But isn't that because Martin Pendred hasn't done any dissection for four years? He's bound to be rusty.'

Eisenmenger didn't reply directly. 'If you look at the details of how the dissections were done four years ago, then compare them with the latest round, it becomes even clearer. For instance, the carotids were all cut long four years ago, this time they're all short.'

When she clearly didn't understand he explained, 'The carotids run up on either side of the neck from the arch of the aorta to the base of the brain. You have to cut them off somewhere along that span and, as a general rule, the same dissectionist will cut them at approximately the same length every time.'

'So a different length implies a different murderer?' She considered this, then doubtfully, 'It's not much.'

'It wouldn't persuade a jury,' he admitted. For a moment there was silence with Eisenmenger watching her, partly out of delicious pleasure, partly because he had a whole lot more to say but he wanted her to reach the same conclusions as him without too much leading.

At last she asked, 'Hang on. You say that it's almost like a signature? What about Melkior, then? Did he cut them long or short?'

Once more she was to be disappointed as he failed to answer. 'The neck structures are amongst the hardest to remove, primarily because for cosmetic reasons you have to stop the skin incision below the collar line; that means that you have a problem because you need to remove the neck structures and the tongue. Generally speaking, the better you get at evisceration, the longer you will be able to cut the carotids.'

She didn't follow him but he hadn't finished. 'I mentioned the poor quality of the evisceration and you, like Isaac Bloomenthal, put it down to his recent inexperience, and there may well be something in that, but I can't see that it explains everything; certainly I would expect him to get up to speed very quickly. For years Martin Pendred was performing two or three eviscerations a day; he must have performed thousands in total. I can accept that he might have had trouble with Jenny Muir's dissection, but I think that thereafter you would see a pronounced improvement.'

'Even in the dark, with the body on the ground instead of a dissection table?'

'The conditions were no worse than with the first five murders.'

She was looking directly into his eyes now. 'What are you driving at?'

He sighed. 'When you sit down and look at all of these factors – all of the factors I've listed at the head of the columns – I think it becomes obvious. Look at the stitching; with the first murders it was regular, almost to the nearest millimetre, but on these three it's all over the place. Then there are the hiding places for the organ pluck and the brain.'

She was used to Eisenmenger, his method of explanation and it was with a resigned tone that she asked, 'Tell me about the hiding places.'

'For the first group of murders they were bizarre. To the normal mind they were inexplicable – Lever's brain under a pile of washing, Greenfield's organ pluck in a water butt. It occurs to me that this time round, though, they've been somehow more *calculated*. This last murder, particularly, rings false; the brain on the computer? A bag labelled *The Dog's Dinner*? It's as though we're dealing now with someone pretending to be mad, rather than a bona fide madman.'

He could see she was there but he carried on anyway. 'And both Melkior and Martin cut the carotids long.'

There was no apparent reaction and he let his last datum fall with something that amounted to sadness. 'And the knots are different.'

It took a short while but it wasn't, he had to admit, an inordinate delay before she said, 'The knots? You mean the stitching?'

He nodded. 'In the first five murders, the knots were double hitches. All of the knots this time around have been single hitches.'

For a moment she said nothing at all, then slowly and deliberately and through a slight smile she said, 'So it's definitely someone different.'

He took a while to reply. 'It's somone who wants us to think that the Eviscerator is at work again, but it's someone different.'

She leaned back, chin down on her chest, eyes staring at the paper in front of her. Suddenly she stood up. 'Is there a bar around here? I need a drink while I think.'

The student bar was too tawdry so he took her to a café-bar by the Ophthalmology Department. It was expensive because it wanted to attract the right clientele but in fact to Eisenmenger's eye the strategy had merely resulted in the place being filled with well-heeled rather than unheeled louts. They sat at a small low table in the corner by the window, with late night shoppers hurrying past, and the varying stages of courtship being enacted around them.

'Let me work this through, John.'

Fair enough. He sipped the wine – Pouilly-Fumé – and waited. It would be intriguing to see if she reached the same conclusions as he had done.

'If what you say is true, then we have a series of murders designed to look as though they're the work of the Eviscerator. It works because of the uncertainty that existed in some people's minds about whether Melkior was really guilty.' He noted laconically that she was not even bothering to name Homer. 'But it's a blind. The murders are not the work of the Eviscerator, and so the motive is different.'

As if she had reached the first checkpoint she glanced up at Eisenmenger but his attention was caught by a nearby couple. They were standing at one of the pillar-bars, each drinking beer from a bottle. He was tall and dressed to impress with slicked-back hair and a smart suit; she was short and dressed to impress with a cleavage that could have accommodated an A4 envelope.

'But we still have the problem of the technique. It's not just anybody who can disembowel a corpse – '

'Or perhaps more pertinently,' Eisenmenger interrupted as he looked back at her, 'sew it up again.'

Her face showed dawning comprehension. 'It's the same problem as before. We have only a small pool of potential murderers – those who have the necessary skills to do what the Eviscerator does.'

The wine was really rather pleasant, he decided. Not far away Slicked-back Hair had put his hand on Cleavage's shoulder.

Beverley continued. 'And amongst the three murders, we have a pathologist.'

Eisenmenger murmured. 'Yes. It's quite intriguing, isn't it?'

Beverley took a sip of wine, then said, 'The murderer is trained in evisceration. If it's not Pendred, we have only a narrow field of pathologists, mortuary technicians and maybe funeral directors – the same pool we had last time – and the third person to be murdered is a pathologist.' She raised wire-thin eyebrows at Eisenmenger. 'Misdirection? You want to murder a colleague so you make him part of a series, all done in the style of a serial killer who, in the eyes of some members of the police, was responsible for five others four years before.'

He took his eyes from the courtship ritual next door. 'That's what I think. Pendred's the fall guy. Someone wanted someone murdered and they've used the uncertainty that surrounded Melkior's conviction to throw suspicion on Martin. As you've said, only someone who's got some experience of dissection could be the murderer, and it beggars belief that the real target is anyone other than Wilson Milroy.'

'Which means we have how many suspects?'

'Adam Piringer, Alison von Guerke, Trevor Ludwig . . .' A pause. 'Lewy, the mortuary technician . . .' It was almost as an afterthought that he remembered, '. . . and Victoria Bence-Jones.'

'Five, then.'

'Assuming that we don't have to include specialist registrars who've passed through the department over the years. And any old consultant colleagues that I don't know about.'

She finished her wine. 'We'll concentrate on the five to start off with.'

We? The thought resounded briefly as he asked, 'And that means?'

'Motive and opportunity,' she explained simply. 'It's hardly rocket science, John. Do you know of any reasons why one of the five might want Milroy dead?'

'He certainly wasn't popular. In fact, he was a miserable, vindictive bastard, as far as I can tell. If what I've heard is true, he made Piringer's life hell because he thought that he should have had Piringer's chair, and he hated Amr Shaheen because he saw him as Piringer's protégé. I don't suppose it'll take much digging to discover a few more reasons why people might have disliked him.'

'Can you work on that, while I check out where they were when the murders were committed?'

'How will you do that?'

She grimaced. 'You could say that I have a source.'

He didn't pick up on the subtext. 'Shouldn't we tell Homer? He's still looking for Pendred.'

She snorted. 'He wouldn't want to believe us, even if we tried.' She stood up, as if she wanted to get started right away. 'Anyway, someone has to find Pendred. All the time that he's not in custody, the real murderer might decide to commit a couple more killings, just to bury Milroy's death even deeper. The killings will have to stop if Pendred's arrested.'

She didn't add just how difficult she suspected that might prove. They went to the door of the bar. Behind them Slicked-back Hair had his hand on Cleavage's thigh. Eisenmenger suspected that it wouldn't be long before Slicked-back went looking for A4 envelopes.

He called in at the surgical ward as soon as he parted from Beverley. Helena was in a four-bedded ward, the main lights turned down, the patients in ill-defined oases of light. She was sleeping but apparently lightly for she awoke as he stood at the end of the bed. It took her a second or two to focus on him, to come back into the world.

She looked almost as if she had been assaulted, the victim of surgical muggers, their identities hidden by silly masks and disposable hats. Under the nightie there was a slight asymmetry around her chest and bandage peeped out at the neckline. There was a rubber drain tube running from her armpit down to a glass bottle on the floor by the bed that was filled with bloody, yellow fluid. Dextrose saline ran into her left wrist, the bag half-empty.

'Oh, hello.' She might have come round from a hundred-year coma, woken by the kiss of a hero, except that the words were carried by a tone of weariness rather than delight. She didn't move.

'It went well,' he said, coming to the side of the bed. He put his hand over hers and bent to kiss her cheek. It was cold.

'Did it?' She yawned, almost as if she were drifting away. 'They should look at it from my side of the fence.'

232

He had only been allowed into the ward at such a late hour because he had quite deliberately used his medical title and begged the nurse in charge to let him see her. A strict limit of five minutes had been the quid pro quo.

'I'm sorry I couldn't get in earlier.'

Her closed eyes were immersed in a grimace of pain when she attempted to shrug her unconcern.

'I can't stay,' he said.

For the first time she came to him rather than having him chase her. She opened her eyes and turned her shoulder and said, 'Thanks for coming, John.'

He kissed her again. 'I'll be back in tomorrow.'

He left, aware that there were tears in her eyes, aware also that she would not want him to see them.

'Who'd have fucking thought it, eh?'

Eisenmenger was perfectly well aware of what Lewy was 'fucking thinking' but decided against allowing this information to reach the mortician's ears. Lewy had taken a liking to Eisenmenger, presumably because, as was Eisenmenger's habit, he did not treat him as either a moron or a piece of excrement. In consequence of this, Eisenmenger was being fed a supply of cremation certificates – those long-winded, repetitive, tedious and ultimately useless pieces of paper that were supposed to ensure that bodies confined to the fire were not required as evidence in a murder trial – along with the not inconsiderable fees that accompanied them.

'What's that?'

Lewy was nursing a cup of tea (not that the tasters of the East India Company would have recognized the curiously viscous, darkly staining liquid he was currently swirling round in his Get Yer Jugs Out mug) and admiring the view. It seemed to Eisenmenger that he took some form of sustenance from spotting and verbally admiring the bust sizes of any woman between the ages of seventeen and sixty who walked past.

'The Eviscerator taking out poor old Milroy.'

The first part of the cremation certificate was to be filled out by one of the doctors who had been looking after the unfortunate when he or she died. That usually meant a junior and, in turn, that usually meant the forms were incorrect and this one was no exception. As Eisenmenger fought feelings of incredulity that intelligent people could be so stupid, he said to Lewy, 'As far as I understand it, Martin Pendred just "takes out" those who happen to have upset him in some way.'

Lewy laughed. 'Well, there's a fucking good chance he'll have been upset by Milroy. He pissed off most people.'

'He was a bit abrasive . . .'

Lewy took his eyes from a double-D cup and explained tiredly, 'I told you. He was a bitter bastard. He reckoned that the world hated him, and therefore he hated the world. And that meant he hated you and he hated me, and he hated every other poor cocksucker that he met.'

With deliberate and, he hoped, innocent obtuseness, Eisenmenger said, 'He wasn't that bad.'

Lewy found that most amusing. 'You're kidding! Once his missus had decided that his best friend had a bigger cock than him, he was only interested in screwing the world as much as the world had screwed him. No one was safe. If you'd been around much longer, he'd have started on you.'

'I didn't realize he had in it for Dr Ludwig.' It was the name that seemed to him to be least likely to have earned Wilson Milroy's spite.

Lewy shrugged. 'Ludwig didn't need Milroy to make life difficult. If the rumours were true, he was already doing that perfectly well on his own.'

'I'm sorry?'

Lewy waved a custard cream dismissively. 'He was past it. He was making cock-ups practically on a weekly basis, apparently. When he could be bothered to drag his arse down here I used to have to lead him by the hand; point out the pulmonary emboli or the rip-roaring peritonitis that he was tending to overlook.'

'So nobody's going to miss him, then?'

Lewy finished his biscuit. 'I certainly fucking won't. Tight cunt never gave me anything for putting the crems his way.'

Taking the hint, Eisenmenger promised, 'Don't worry. I'll see you're suitably reimbursed.'

Lewy nodded in satisfaction. As he rose from the table, Eisenmenger remarked, 'And I can't believe Milroy would have had any sort of argument with Victoria Bence-Jones.'

Lewy was back assessing the talent unconsciously parading before him. 'Don't bet on it,' he murmured. Then he looked back at Eisenmenger. 'In fact, I'd say he hated her more than the rest of them.'

'Really?'

'Oh, yeah. For some reason I could never fathom, he really wanted to destroy her.'

Fisher had bought the latest round of drinks and was therefore in good odour with his colleagues, which meant that for perhaps two minutes they didn't bait him or tease him or swear at him. Clark was looking more butch than ever (Cooley reckoned she was really a man, claimed even to have seen her in the female showers at the Sports Club and swore that she had a prick as big as a baby's forearm) and Neumann was rapidly running down the road marked 'Totally Pissed'. It was seven o'clock and they were all off duty and police officers off duty tended to abandon the finer feelings of life.

'Christ, you're a fucking ugly cow, Mandy,' opined Neumann in a judicious manner.

Clark was well used to such comments, especially from Neumann who fancied himself as a ladies' man and was still smarting from the memory of the occasion when, shortly after she had been posted to the station, he had attempted his customary seduction techniques only to be publicly humiliated as Clark had poured a pint of stout down his trousers and called him 'Tiddler'.

She smiled sweetly. 'Why don't you go and fuck yourself, Colin? You're not going to pull anyone else.'

Neumann was already halfway down his pint. 'I've got no problems in that department,' he boasted, somewhat vaguely. 'I'm all lined up for the night.'

'Who with?' she demanded scornfully.

He hesitated briefly but tellingly before saying, 'Trish Koplick.'

But Mandy found this so highly amusing that she spilled her lager top on the pitted wood of their small table. 'Trish?' she screamed. Several people looked up at her from nearby tables. The pub was their local and they were well known in it – indeed, over half of those present were coppers – and Mandy Clark's extrovert personality was infamous. She began to laugh, loudly and, it had to be admitted, rather coarsely. 'Did you hear that, Terry?' she asked of Fisher. 'Trish Koplick!'

'What's so fucking funny?' Neumann asked this somewhat fearfully. He looked to Fisher who was grinning broadly. 'Terry?'

Under cover of Clark's raucous cackling, Fisher explained, 'Wrong choice, mate. Trish Koplick's even more bent than Mandy. They've been sucking each other out for the past six months.'

Neumann raised his eyes and cursed his fate. Mandy patted his hand. 'Never mind, Colin. You'll strike lucky one of these days. Everyone does. Look at Terry.'

Glad to have someone else the centre of attention, Neumann joined in with this tack in the conversation with enthusiasm. 'Yeah, that's right. Who is she, Terry?'

Fisher suddenly felt himself blush. 'No one you know.'

Mandy Clark was herself enjoying the pleasant relaxation brought by three pints of lager top. 'Little Terry's very shy about his new love,' she told Neumann in a stage whisper. 'Mind you, she must be quite a goer. Most mornings this week he's looked as if his knob's been worn down flat.'

Fisher retreated into his glass and Neumann joined in. 'Is she a copper, Terry?'

When Fisher didn't respond, they looked meaningfully at each other, nodding in unison. Back to Fisher, Mandy asked, 'Do we know her?'

Slamming his glass back down on the table, Fisher asked plaintively, 'Why don't you two just mind your own business?'

A noise like a rising whistle escaped from their mouths and they drew back in mock alarm. 'Touchy, isn't he?' asked Clark of Neumann; 'Suspicious,' decided Neumann in turn. 'Very,' she agreed. They turned to Fisher who was becoming increasingly agitated. Suddenly Clark had an inspiration. 'She's not a superior officer, is she, Terry?'

Fisher found that a question too far, or rather too close. Abruptly he stood up, spilling the glasses that were, thankfully, empty again; the ashtray emptied its contents in Neumann's lap. 'Why don't you shut the fuck up?' he demanded and walked out through a now-silent pub.

Outside in his car, he tried to calm himself before his date with Beverley. It was obvious he couldn't keep it quiet for ever and that he ought to end it now, but he was too weak, he knew. The sex was fantastic and it appealed to his vanity to have Beverley Wharton receiving his favours. Not that he was so entirely smitten that he had been blind to all the implications of their pact; he wasn't that stupid.

Beverley Wharton wanted more than regular rogering from the liaison; she wanted information about Homer's investigation. At first he had been outraged and refused, but she had proved persuasive. After all, she had argued, she was still technically on the force. She had a moral right to know what was going on and, since she did not believe that Homer was after the right man, to attempt to solve the case on her own.

They were not completely compelling arguments but she had a way with her tongue that made him swell just to think of it, and in an hour it was highly likely that she would be reminding him yet again of just how great it was to have sex in a shower . . .

So if what it took was a few files borrowed from the thousands that they had amassed – files that were not even central to the case – and answering a few questions, then it was a price that he found eminently affordable. Except when people asked questions and the enormity of what he was doing was so painfully inserted into his nose, and except when he remembered that if any of his superiors were to find out what he was doing, no amount of Beverley Wharton's knob-sucking would be adequate protection.

He could only hope that he would not be found out, but until that moment he was having the most enjoyable time he could ever recall.

'Victoria!'

She looked up at the sound of her name and at least this time she recognized him. She was just outside Wilson's room, in conversation with Piringer's secretary, a small woman of Far Eastern extraction who, like so many of the secretaries and PAs that Eisenmenger had met, had somehow come to the conclusion that because her boss was important, so was she. She left with a reproachful glance at Eisenmenger.

'John! I wasn't expecting to see you!'

The conversation was fast becoming overpopulated by exclamation marks and it was with some relief that a few interrogatives entered the fray.

'What are you doing here? Not out of a job, am I?' He asked these with a smile on his face to indicate jocularity, a sign of reassurance, and he was rewarded with a laugh, but all the while he was wondering, *Why should you be surprised to see me here?*

'Good grief, no! I had to meet Geoffrey and I thought that I'd come into the department. After the shocking news about Wilson . . .' She trailed off while Eisenmenger wondered what else she was going to say and, it transpired, so did she.

Eventually he took pity on her. 'That was thoughtful of you.'

She smiled. She had been pretty when he had first known her; frail and small with features that seemed not so much functional as ornamental; fragility spun into beauty. Now, however, there was a slight tarnish, a subtle weathering, as if the universe, as it will, had seen this pulchritude and been jealous.

'There's hardly anyone here, though.'

He tried the smile again. 'It is well after five, you know.'

She took surprise. 'Is it?' A glance at her watch and then, 'You're right! I must be going. Geoffrey will be wondering where I've got to.'

She smiled and for an instant he saw the young girl he had known at medical school, the one he had coveted but never dared to ask out. She walked away up the corridor and he watched her, a plethora of thoughts entrancing him: what would have happened had he had the courage to act back in medical school, why he was worried about her near-imperceptible fall from unblemished comeliness, why he had a feeling of sorrow in his abdomen.

He turned away and went back to his office, waited another thirty minutes, then re-emerged. Surely everyone would have departed by now?

He made his way to Milroy's room, trying not to creep stealthily and finding it almost impossible. He pushed the door open and disappeared inside, closing it as quietly as he could.

The room was a mess. Three of the four walls were covered in shelves broken only by the door through which he had entered and a large window on the far wall. All of these were piled haphazardly with papers, files, books, boxes of wax blocks and glass slides. Cupboards ran underneath the shelving leaving floor space that was really only large enough for a desk and two chairs at the far end near the window, as well as two squat stools which flanked an aged wooden table on which a small double-headed microscope sat. A fan heater covered in dust stared at the chair behind the desk.

It could already have been searched, perhaps a hundred times, or it could have been pristine. An idle thought crossed his mind: had Victoria Bence-Jones just been in here? He sniffed the air, finding only dust and old books.

Where to start?

He walked across to the desk and sat behind it; best to view the problem as Milroy rather than a visitor. The room he now saw was still cluttered and disorganized, but there was one other aspect that was at once clear. No fewer than four photographs were turned towards him, all of the same attractive woman. She was young, perhaps with West Indian blood, sorrowful and shy. She looked at the photographer with wide eyes that could well have been adoring.

On either side of the desk were unlocked drawers deep enough to accommodate suspension files and he spent the next forty minutes rifling through them with no result. He now knew all about Milroy's external quality assessment performance (adequate), his attendance at the Regional Audit Committee (patchy) and his record of Continuing Personal Development (unsurprisingly good), but he knew nothing about why someone might have been willing to kill two other people as a cover to murdering him.

Eisenmenger stopped and reordered his thoughts and looked again around the room.

On the top shelf were numerous box files. Their labels were untidy, written in either black marker or blue biro; some were obvious, some were cryptic. He got up and began the laborious search through every one of them by taking down the nearest one on his right-hand side.

It took forty-five minutes and a slow and tedious trip halfway around the room before he found some reward. On the second shelf down were box files named after organs and organ systems. Somewhat disproportionately, five were devoted to *The Anus*, and in the file marked *The Anus (1)* were photocopied sheets of Adverse Clinical Incident reports, all of them involving Trevor Ludwig. There were four in each of the previous two years, six so far in the present year. Also in the file was a letter to Geoffrey Bence-Jones and what appeared to be an undated draft of one to the General Medical Council.

Not only that, there was a signed affidavit from a private detective detailing the affair between Ludwig and von Guerke.

Place, dates, times were all listed. Almost threatening by their very presence were the names, addresses and telephone numbers of their spouses.

Potential motive, indeed, for murder.

The Anus (2) beckoned and in it Adam Piringer's life was displayed for Eisenmenger's delectation. Early success after working in the US at the Armed Forces Institute of Pathology had brought an unfeasibly early appointment as Professor of Pathology at the WRI. Eisenmenger was forced to concur with Milroy that the appointment had come early – perhaps too early. A single success in research when under the wing of some of the greatest pathologists in the world was not proof of great academic prowess. Eisenmenger could begin to appreciate how galling it must have been for Milroy to be cheated of his lifelong prize.

But if he could begin his appreciation, he could not see it through as he read on. Adam Piringer might not have been top-grade material as a professor, but he deserved better than the destruction of his character that followed, the main thrust of which was that he was homosexual and that he was having an affair with Amr Shaheen.

That the affair had occurred seemed fairly conclusive – Milroy even had photographs of a candlelit dinner for two in which they were holding hands – but what was not present was anything particularly damning. Homosexuality was not going to worry anybody, although clearly Shaheen and Piringer had not wanted their relationship public, and only if some consequence of the relationship could be proven would Milroy have something he might consider valuable.

There was nothing of that sort in the file.

The Anus (3) contained Amr Shaheen's life, including a less than complimentary résumé of his academic achievements (he had failed the membership exam of the Royal College of Pathologists three times) and a list of previous lovers. There was nothing new for him in it.

The Anus (4) contained the life and times of Alison von Guerke, replete with Adverse Clinical Incidents (although not as many as Ludwig) and her affair. Yet more potential grist for a blackmail mill, but nothing else.

Lastly came *The Anus (5)* and in it lay Victoria Bence-Jones, Problem was, it was exemplary. Had it been a file in anyone else's possession, it would have been a testament to her fitness to practise, for there was nothing to argue against her; somehow, in this company, it suggested dissatisfaction.

Milroy had looked for dirt, it appeared, but found none.

'What the bloody hell are you doing in here?'

Eisenmenger twitched and nearly dropped the file. He turned quickly around to discover an angry Amr Shaheen standing in the doorway. He saw that the little man was noticeably shaking and that his fists were clenched; his face was drawn into an expression of outrage.

Eisenmenger said calmly and simply, 'Looking though Dr Milroy's files.'

Eisenmenger found himself struck by a faint comicality in the other's indignation as Shaheen advanced into the room and exclaimed angrily, 'How dare you!'

Eisenmenger shut the file and put it back in its home. He said as he did so, 'I didn't realize you were the chosen curator of Dr Milroy's estate.'

'I'm not.'

'So what is it to you if I happen to be looking through his files?'

To which for several moments Dr Shaheen failed to provide a very good answer, saying only lamely, 'I don't think it's right to go through his stuff like that. Not when he's barely cold.'

Eisenmenger walked back to Milroy's desk and very deliberately sat down at it. He then pointed out, 'That's a solid door behind you and I was making no noise to speak of, so what are *you* doing here?'

'I . . . I wanted to look up a reference. One that I believe Dr Milroy had in his possession.'

Eisenmenger smiled. He suggested helpfully, 'Try the files marked *The Anus*. His most interesting references are in those.'

Shaheen gave him an odd, almost fearful look but went to the files as Eisenmenger suggested. To his back, Eisenmenger suggested, 'File number three is the one most relevant to you.'

A glance over his shoulder told of increasing anxiety. He pulled out the file and opened it. For a few moments there was silence save for the traffic in the street below. When at last Shaheen looked at Eisenmenger, his face was pallid and all attempt at bluster had withered. He looked ready to vomit.

'You read this?' he asked.

241

Eisenmenger had the idea that this was more out of hope than expectation and didn't bother to reply. He said quietly, 'He hated your colleagues just as much.'

Shaheen tried to laugh but his heart wasn't in it and what reached Eisenmenger's hearing was more of a moan. 'I was the one he really couldn't stand. Him and Ludwig, the bastards.' He came and sat down before the desk. 'They started on the first day I arrived. Snide little comments about my qualifications, about conditions in the hospitals where I trained, that kind of thing.'

Eisenmenger was wondering how much of this was real and how much reconfigured in memory.

'Of course,' and here Shaheen really did manage a laugh, 'I didn't appreciate the full extent of it until Lewy told me.'

Lewy? Once more Eisenmenger heard the name and wondered. Lewy had not seemed the type to worry about a spot of victimization.

'What did he tell you?'

'What Ludwig was saying about me. The names he called me – Spear-chucker, A-rab – and Milroy's rants about how I got the job.'

'What did he say about that?'

Shaheen's gaze darted up to him, suddenly wary, but then it dropped, and he seemed to reach a decision. 'If you've read what's in the box file . . .'

But Eisenmenger wanted Shaheen's side of things, not Milroy's obsessions. He asked, 'Is there any truth in it?'

'No!' There was a little fire in his belly for a brief time, but that was soon guttering, for he then continued in something of a whine, 'Adam and I are friends and colleagues. Close friends, I admit, but nothing more – not lovers.' The last word was uttered with an accentuation that might have been intended as disgust but sounded more fearful. When Eisenmenger said nothing, he was forced to rush into more explanation.

'I know that it looked bad, but for God's sake why can't people believe that two heterosexual grown men can be good friends with shared interests?'

Eisenmenger leaned across the desk and pointed at the box file. 'And that?' he enquired.

Shaheen picked it up and thrust it at Eisenmenger. 'Lies!' he hissed.

Without saying anything, Eisenmenger rose and went to the other files. He pulled out number two, opened it, picked out the photograph and gave it to Shaheen.

For a long, long breath there was absolute silence while Shaheen looked at it intently, his face completely impassive. Eventually he said to the image, 'I didn't kill him.'

Eisenmenger said drily, 'Nobody's saying you did.' He waited.

'He used awful words. Arse-bandits, Sausage-jockeys, Cottagers. There was a whispering campaign about us, one that he instituted and fed. So what if Adam and I have a relationship? I still say that my appointment was entirely on merit; there was a properly convened appointments advisory committee, and all the records are still with Human Resources.'

Eisenmenger was experienced enough and cynical enough to know that records from appointments advisory committees were, like magazine advertisements for haemorrhoid cream, unlikely to be read and even less likely to be the whole truth and nothing but the truth.

'So you were at the theatre with Professor Piringer when Milroy died.'

Shaheen was at once defensive. 'What does that matter? We all know who killed Milroy.'

'Do we?'

Shaheen's face showed confusion and suspicion and fear, each flowing into the other. 'It was Pendred. Wasn't it?'

Eisenmenger leaned back in the chair, his eyes still on Shaheen. 'Apparently, but then you come in here looking for Milroy's evidence about your relationship with Piringer, and that makes me wonder. Could it be that you and Piringer were getting a bit nervous about Milroy's insinuations? Perhaps you took the opportunity to bump him off in the style of the Eviscerator, then you came in here to destroy the evidence linking you to him.'

'That's rubbish! I admit I came in here looking for anything he might have, but I didn't know what he had. I didn't even know that he definitely had anything at all. I just figured that he might.'

Which was possibly the truth; not that Eisenmenger could prove anything either way. Knowing that he was losing any advantage he asked wearily, 'Did you ever hear Milroy say anything against Alison von Guerke or Trevor Ludwig?'

'He thought Ludwig was incompetent.'

And with that Eisenmenger thought that he had gained all he could from Shaheen, which was why he was stunned when Shaheen said, 'And Alison von Guerke hated him with a vengeance.'

'Really? Why?'

Shaheen appeared unaware that he was exploding bombs around Eisenmenger as he said, 'Because about twenty years ago, he made her pregnant, then dumped her. She had to have an abortion; it made her sterile.'

'And how is Helena?'

Beverley asked the question without a hint of interest and Eisenmenger, knowing that Helena would not want Beverley Wharton to know what was happening to her, said only, 'Still unwell.'

'Give her my regards, won't you?' The tone echoed down from somewhere north of St Petersburg. Before Eisenmenger could say anything she went on briskly, 'Right, to business. I hope you've made more progress than I have, John.'

They were walking in the crematorium at lunchtime. The weather was cold but the only clouds were high and wispy so that the shadows in the weak sun were sharp. There was a sprinkling of people around them, including two dishevelled and unwashed men swapping talk and lager as, rising above the trees, the hospital looked over their shoulders.

'Possibly.'

She barked out a laugh. 'Same old John. Never the straight answer.'

'You misjudge me, Beverley. I tend to give straight answers when I possess them. Unfortunately, at present I see only probabilities and possibilities, improbabilities and impossibilities.'

She sighed. 'Well, I'm afraid all I can do is add to your impossibilities.'

'Meaning?'

'According to the reports, they've all got alibis.'

'All of them?' It was unusual for every suspect to have an alibi; normally there were one or two who couldn't or wouldn't remember, or ones who really did spend the time in question reading a book alone.

She indicated a bench on the side of the path. A Victorian monstrosity – all seraphim, cherubim and unfeasibly long trumpets – reared up before them on the opposite side of the gravel. 'I've made some notes from the files.'

She handed them to him and he asked, 'How are you managing to obtain this stuff?'

She said only, 'Don't ask.' The bleakness of her tone and her face told a story he decided that he didn't want to hear. While he read the notes, she said, 'The only oddity that I can spot is with Professor Piringer's and Dr Shaheen's stories. Piringer claims to have spent the evening at the same theatre as Shaheen, although neither of them admits seeing the other.'

Eisenmenger looked up from his reading. 'That's because they're lovers.'

Understanding dawned rather attractively on her face. 'And they want it kept quiet? Why?'

'Because of the suspicion that Shaheen only got his job through Piringer's influence.'

She considered. 'So they were at the theatre together but can't admit it. The least dangerous path is to adjust their alibi as little as possible, merely to deny that they were at the theatre together.'

'I guess so. I don't suppose there's a small chance either of them can't remember what the play was, or what happened in the third act? Perhaps there was a fire alarm that emptied the theatre which one or both of them failed to report?'

She shook her head with mock gravitas. 'I wish it were so.'

He had found notes of a statement from Victoria Bence-Jones. 'They've even interviewed Victoria,' he said, surprised.

'Chief Inspector Homer is nothing if not thorough.' He could feel his eardrums being abraded by her words.

'Her husband gives her an alibi.'

'You don't really think that this is being done by a woman, do you?'

A problem that, he had to admit, he had not considered seriously until that moment. 'Well, the main problem is going to be removal and carriage of the main organ pluck. It weighs maybe ten kilos. By no means impossible for a woman.'

But even as he was saying it, he knew that it wasn't the whole picture. The bodies were on the floor which meant that getting to the back of the head to cut the scalp for removal of the brain would have necessitated heaving the body up and putting something under the back. Could Victoria Bence-Jones really have done that, even if she had been capable of manipulating the organ pluck?

He conceded, 'But I have a problem with Victoria doing it. Alison von Guerke's old but she's built like a carthorse; she could possibly have done it, but again it's a difficult scene to visualize.'

'Well, maybe we can forget the two female suspects, then.'

But something was nagging at him. 'Maybe,' he said cautiously. 'But I'd feel a lot happier if I knew what she found so stressful about the job.'

'It's irrelevant if we can exclude her on physical grounds.'

He didn't say anything, bending his head back down to read the notes. Alison von Guerke had been visiting her mother, Trevor Ludwig had been with his wife and children at a rugby match and Lewy, somewhat surprisingly, had been at church.

'I must say, Lewy has never struck me as the religious type.'

Beverley shrugged. 'Homer's had someone check all of these accounts. In Lewy's case, his alibi is supported by the priest.'

Which left them with nothing. Eisenmenger sighed, then handed the papers back to Beverley. 'You'd better keep those.'

As she put them back in her case, she asked, 'So have you found out anything helpful?'

He told her of the files in Milroy's room and what they contained. She whistled. 'My God! What was eating him?'

'Crossed in love, apparently.' He related his conversation with Shaheen.

'But why take it out on his colleagues?'

'Because it was work that drove her away, I think. Because he was spending all his time doing his service work and his research and his management duties so he didn't notice that she was first unhappy and then that she was having an affair. After she'd left him, his work was all he had left. When Piringer took from him what he considered to be *his* chair, I think he just decided that all his colleagues had somehow betrayed him. He had nothing left to live for, other than nursing his prejudices.'

'Poor bastard.'

Two children cycled past, shouting obscenities. A helicopter flew high over their heads and strummed the air with deep beats.

'Whatever. It leaves us with a large, if not insurmountable problem – namely, all our suspects have alibis. What do we do now?'

She patted his knee which, had it been done by anyone else, would have had no sexual connotations at all. 'We do what all good policemen do. We keep our options open.'

'I'm sorry?' he asked, sounding distracted. *What were they missing?*

'We neither assume that we were wrong, nor trust that we were right.' But she could see that he was thinking of other things and hadn't caught the meaning of what she had said. 'We don't rely on the alibis being truthful, but we have also to look further abroad. I'll need the names of everyone who's worked with Wilson Milroy during his career and who might be capable of dissecting a human body.'

'Would you like their National Insurance numbers as well?'

She stood up, brushing down her skirt as if it needed such attention, as if it didn't draw attention to her legs and the tightness of the fit. After doing this in silence, she bent down and kissed him lightly, delightfully, on his cheek. 'Only, where relevant, their prick lengths,' she whispered with a smile.

'This isn't strictly legal.' Beverley's words were barely audible under the sound of the gravel beneath their feet. If there was an implication of trepidation in what she said, the smile she cast to Eisenmenger told otherwise. She was enjoying this.

'So why, exactly, are we doing this?'

She didn't look at him; in fact she was looking everywhere but at him. 'Because Dr Milroy clearly had a serious problem; not so much a chip on his shoulder as an entire potato farm. If he kept files like that in the office, who knows what he kept locked away in the security of his own house.'

'And is there no other way of finding out?'

At last she looked at him. With a smile that told him he was being stupid she said simply, 'No.'

She dismissed him from her mind for a while until he asked, 'Tell me, Beverley, which do you prefer – upholding or breaking the law?'

She laughed. 'Definitely breaking it, John. It's far more arousing.' She squeezed his hand.

It was the middle of the following day and the sun was again shining brightly. Although Milroy's house was relatively secluded, there was a chance that they would be seen, so they were walking as unostentatiously as they could up the driveway, holding hands and apparently without any sinister intentions.

'And arousal is everything, right?'

Her sigh was long and deep. 'Oh, John. Just think what might have been.'

To late-middle-aged neighbours they could easily have been a courting couple, which suited them fine.

At the front door, Beverley produced a labelled bunch of keys from her handbag. Eisenmenger asked drily, 'Would I be wise to ask how you managed to get hold of those?'

She gave him a long, deep look from bright, wonderfully coloured eyes. Her lips were caressed by lipstick that was bright and shiny. 'No, John. You would not.'

She didn't want to tell him what she had had to do obtain this particular prize; how unkeen Fisher had been to provide her with such dangerous contraband, how much she had had to promise.

The door was double-locked. As she turned the key and the front door opened, he asked, 'Who's the next of kin?'

'Sally Milroy. They were never divorced.'

The house had six bedrooms and was built in the style of a large executive-style home. It was new enough not to show the decay of age, although here and there Eisenmenger noticed the decay of poor building – the gaping settlement cracks, the damp patch in the porch, the off-centre light fittings on the wall. It was also quite clearly the abode of a single man.

'Not houseproud, was he?' With the door shut behind them, there was a distinct relaxation in their demeanour and Beverley's voice was abruptly and shockingly loud. She bore an expression of some distaste as she took in the dust and the clutter and faint odour of old, cooked food.

Eisenmenger's eyes were looking around constantly as he trod carefully forward into the house. Beverley said almost to herself, almost to the house, 'Why do I never get to search places that I like?' To Eisenmenger she called, 'Are we looking for anything in particular?'

His voice came back from a farther room. 'I assume that he

wasn't hiding anything, so my guess is that we're looking for a box file and it's most probably in the study, but we shouldn't take that for granted.'

For room after room they found nothing other than neglect. It seemed clear that most of the cupboards and drawers had not been opened for months, if not years. The only things of significance that they found were photographs, all of the same attractive young woman; in the main bedroom there were no fewer than four. Beverley picked one up. 'Attractive bitch, isn't she?'

Surprised, Eisenmenger asked, 'Bitch?'

'I don't mean that as an insult, John.'

She lay on the bed and he tried not to look at her. 'Why don't we take a break?' she enquired of the ceiling. He was looking in the wardrobe, discovering that it was full of women's clothing and shoes. He said calmly, 'I'm not sure that we have the time, Beverley.'

'I'm sorry? I didn't catch that.'

He looked around just as she rolled over, so that she was up on her elbows, her eyes innocently asking nothing too demanding, nothing too damning. He had to find a couple of moments to repeat, 'I don't think we have the time.'

She just stared at him with the smallest yet most knowing smile he had ever beheld, holding his gaze for long enough to signal something as complex as quantum mechanics, as simple as a thump in the balls. Then she murmured, 'Ah, well,' and rolled off the bed. She seemed to take a delicious for ever to straighten her skirt and top.

They went into the study, once a bedroom, now a mess, for files and papers were piled all over the floor. In front of the window was a desk on which were a keyboard and flat-screen monitor. A sofa and low coffee table were at the other end of the room positioned in front of a small television set, beside which was a stereo system. The walls were lined with shelves on which were books and yet more files; it was partly a celebration of Wilson Milroy's professional achievements, certificates were everywhere, all framed, and each telling of some success in his life. Eisenmenger looked for it, but didn't spot the cycling proficiency badge and could only assume that Milroy had never learned to ride a bike.

'My, he was proud of himself,' remarked Beverley. She found

another photograph of Sally Milroy, this one next to a portrait of a teenage girl, and said thoughtfully, 'But he certainly loved you.' Eisenmenger glanced across, surprised by the wistful tone. She put down the photograph perhaps a little too hard, then walked across to the sofa, examining the base of it.

'It's a sofa bed,' she said. 'He lived in this room, I bet. Apart from making occasional meals and using the bathroom, he used no other part of the house.'

Eisenmenger was looking at the files. They seemed to be merely old research papers, clippings from journals, records of experiments and lecture notes. As Beverley began looking through the files on the floor, she asked, 'What about the computer?'

'I don't think Milroy had entered that far into the digital age. All his files at the hospital were old-fashioned longhand, so I'd guess if there's anything else around here, it's going to be in this lot.'

It took twenty minutes to find it at the bottom of a particularly ancient pile of lecture notes on diseases of the Organ of Zuckerkandl, presumably hidden there deliberately by Milroy. Beverley, who found it, brought it to the desk where they stood side by side to examine the file.

On the top was a letter, a single handwritten page signed by someone called Yvonne Havers. According to its contents, Yvonne Havers had been laboratory assistant to Victoria Bence-Jones and it had been she who had assisted Victoria in her awarding-winning research. The letter stated quite bluntly that, in her opinion, Victoria Bence-Jones had fabricated the results, since it was her recollection that the research had been going nowhere. It offered to meet with Wilson Milroy to compare her laboratory notebooks with the published results. Tied to the letter were two sets of notebooks, one written by Victoria, the other by Yvonne Havers.

'Well?' demanded Beverley. 'Is this what we're looking for?'

Eisenmenger nodded reverently. 'Oh, yes.'

'Tell me, then.'

'This is devastating, Beverley. It claims that Victoria Bence-Jones was a charlatan. If this is true, Victoria undertook systematic and deliberate falsification of experimental results so that her null hypothesis was disproved and thus her initial premise vindicated.

'She basically created her success from nothing, and she's been given the most prestigious pathology research prize in the country for it.

'And Milroy knew all about it.'

'This research prize is really that big?'

'Not in terms of money, but in terms of kudos for an academic pathologist, it's the bee's knees. It'll certainly help your career to win it; obversely, it'll seriously hurt it to be discovered to have cheated to win it.'

They were now sitting on the sofa bed, mulling over the significance of the find.

'And these support the claim?' Beverley indicated a mass of documentation that had been underneath the affidavit. They were photocopies of research notes and experimental results.

'I'd guess so. Milroy obviously thought so.'

'How?'

'It'll take quite a long time to check it all, but I suspect that if you compare these results with those she published, you'll find significant differences.'

'Which suddenly makes her a strong contender, I suppose.' Beverley sounded as if he had just let it slip about the Tooth Fairy. He didn't say anything in reply, content merely to frown at the pile of papers. Tiring of his passivity, she straightened up and said, 'Well, while you're contemplating the navel of the universe, I'll carry on.'

'What do you mean? We've found what we were looking for.'

She smiled. 'Have we?' She shook her head in mockery and bent to stroke his chin with her finger. 'The first thing you learn when searching somewhere, John, is not to stop when you find something.'

She turned back to the files, picking up where they had found the papers on Victoria Bence-Jones. For a few moments Eisenmenger watched her, then apparently lost interest and returned to the navel.

It took several minutes before he murmured, 'Why did he bring this stuff home? The other files he was content to leave at work.'

Without looking up, Beverley said, 'You think that that makes it special? That because it was separated from the others, there's some significance?'

'Don't you?'

She straightened up, a piece of paper held between finger and thumb. 'Possibly.'

She brought it to the desk. It was a copy of a letter, dated some four weeks before, addressed to Geoffrey Bence-Jones. It suggested a meeting to discuss Milroy's future. The last line mentioned Victoria's 'recent success in winning her illustrious prize'.

Beverley said softly, 'If I were cynical, I'd say that sounds like blackmail. Give me what I want, or else . . .'

'Subtle.'

'That's the beauty of it. Nothing explicit, especially to innocent eyes.' She added, 'It might also explain why it's here, at his home and away from the hospital.'

Eisenmenger nodded. 'Yes. Dangerous to keep this in his office, once he'd sent that letter.'

Beverley smiled. 'See? I told you that you should always keep searching.'

'Why is it here, though?' he persisted. 'Why is it the only one here?'

'Because this suggests blackmail. As far as we know, although he was collecting dirt on the others, he hadn't done anything about it. He had to remove this from the department in case either Victoria or Geoffrey Bence-Jones came snooping.'

He had to admit that it was possible – probable, even. Shaheen had only come looking because he suspected he might find something, not because Milroy had told him that there was something to find. 'I guess so. Anyway, I just can't see Victoria as the murderer.'

'Could her husband be the killer?'

He shook his head emphatically. 'No. That is to say, physically he could, but there is no way that he could have had the technical skill to perform the evisceration and then sew up the body.'

'Perhaps she taught him.'

'Evisceration isn't a theoretical subject, Beverley. You can only learn it by practice. There's no way he could have had a quick cramming course across the kitchen table from the missus.'

'Maybe they did it together. He did the heavy stuff, she did the evisceration.'

'Murder by committee? Somehow that doesn't seem very likely to me.'

'What else, then?'

It took him a moment of deep consideration, but he finally admitted, 'I just don't know.'

Even if her consultant was pleased with the state of her wound, Helena wasn't. The bruising, by now beginning to coalesce into a curious abstract of purple, green and yellow, had spread over half of her chest as well as her shoulder and around the top of her arm. The sutures (red and swollen and weeping to her eyes) were, it appeared, 'doing well'. These, together with the sleep deprivation induced by a bed as comfortable as a herbaceous border, and the unpalatability of the food, meant that she was not in the best of moods as, at three thirty in the morning, she got out of bed and went along the corridor to the day room. Not that the chairs were in any way comfortable, but the discomfort of sitting was temporarily to be preferred to the discomfort of lying.

As she passed the islet of light that was the nurses' station, it was inevitable that she would be challenged by one of the two bowed heads. 'Is everything all right?' The Filipino nurse spoke good English but any illusion of caring was destroyed by a mask-like inscrutability. Her companion merely glanced up and then returned to her writing.

Helena said only, 'Can't sleep.'

'Would you like a sleeping tablet?'

Helena shook her head. 'I'll just read in the day room for half an hour.'

She moved on and once more there were two bowed heads in the islet of light.

They forgot about Helena except when, at half past seven and the handover to the day staff, her name was mentioned and they realized that she had not come back from the day room.

Only then was it appreciated that she had vanished completely.

'We've had two sightings, sir. Same area, same time.'

Homer was asleep but Wright's words found him immediately awake. 'Where? When?'

'Near the WRI. Hippocampus Street. Forty minutes ago.'

Homer was out of bed as he was issuing instructions. 'He's hiding in the hospital, Wright. Get as many men as you can and get over there. Start searching for him in the hospital.'

'But we've searched there already . . .'

'For Christ's sake, Wright, what does that matter? You didn't search thoroughly enough, did you? He's worked there for years and he knows the place like you know your John Thomas. There's probably a thousand and one places he could have hidden that you don't know about.'

'Well, we're not likely to find him this time round either, are we?'

But Homer had already put the receiver down and he found himself wasting his breath on something considerably less sweet than the desert air.

'And get those bloody crates moved, will you? We've got Health and Safety coming this afternoon and they'll have kittens if those are blocking the fire exit.'

The voice that came through the open door to Beverley's ears told of orders given that were expected to be obeyed, of authority underpinned with self-confidence. When its owner appeared, she was surprised to see how small she was, how slight of figure.

'Inspector Wharton?' The figure advanced, hand outstretched, look of complete equanimity sailing before it. As Beverley took the proffered hand, she was informed, 'Yvonne Havers.'

It was a quick but firm handshake. As she moved to sit down at her desk Beverley estimated that she was early thirties, perhaps only a metre and half tall and fairly attractive, although she used too much make-up and her shade of eye shadow was wrong.

'What can I do for you?'

Sometimes Beverley moved straight into the meat of the interview, sometimes she judged it better to move first tangentially, as she did now. 'What do you make here?'

Ms Havers was sitting in her high-backed leather chair, radiating all the characteristics of a relatively senior manager enjoying her position. 'Disposable laboratory plasticware. You know – pipettes, Petri dishes, test-tubes, that kind of thing.'

'And you're . . . what?'

'Director of Marketing.' She apparently realized that this might sound slightly pretentious, for she continued, 'But we're only a small outfit.'

'And you've been here for two years. Is that right?'

'Just under.'

Beverley smiled. 'You've done well.' It was a remark that somehow split exactly down the middle, half admiring, half questioning. Yvonne Havers took it as questioning.

'I suppose I have. I started as a sales rep and did well. About six months ago this position became vacant; I applied and I got it.' As if feeling that this was somehow insufficient she added, 'There are only five sales reps in all.'

Beverley looked interested in what she was saying, but had hardly bothered to let it trouble her consciousness. The next question, though, was of a different order. 'Before you came here, you used to work at the Western Royal Infirmary. Is that right?'

Wariness came into the room, quite perceptibly and quite interestingly. 'That's right.'

'I believed you worked as a research technician. For Dr Bence-Jones.'

She was no longer leaning back, her body language having brought her slightly forward into a more alert posture. 'What's this about?'

Part of the skill of interrogation was to know what weapons to use and when. Beverley judged that Yvonne Havers was uncomfortable about something. Her only guess was with regard to the source of her discomfort. She said flatly, 'You're aware, I'm sure, that Wilson Milroy has had his throat cut.' Her use of the graphic descriptor was deliberate.

Yvonne Havers came slightly further forward in her chair, close to vertical. 'I heard.'

'Did you know him?'

She made a face. 'Vaguely. Only as well as I knew most of the consultants in the department.'

'Really? Then why did you write to him?' Her mouth opened but found itself bereft of ammunition, so Beverley said helpfully, 'About two or three months ago.'

Beverley produced a copy of the letter and handed it over. The Marketing Director at last came past the vertical and came to rest leaning forward, arms on the table. While she was scrutinizing it, Beverley asked, 'What did you want to talk about?'

She then made the mistake that all liars do, answering too quickly. 'Just something about some research work that I'd been doing for him when I left.'

'What research was it?'

Her eyes held apprehension as she said, 'It was a case study we were writing up together.'

Beverley smiled. 'After two years? Why the long wait?'

For which she had no answer but Beverley wasn't interested in stewing Yvonne Havers in her own lies and evasions. She merely pointed out, 'So you did know him better than the others? I mean, you didn't do research for all of them, did you?'

Her expression was picturesque. She shook her head and then said, 'It wasn't a big deal.'

'But big enough for you to write to him and suggest that you should meet after a gap of two years and apparently entirely out of the blue.'

She at least had the grace to drop her eyes as she mumbled, 'I came across the work while I was sorting out some stuff at home. I thought, why not? So I wrote to him.'

'And did you meet him?'

She looked at her questioner before answering, a brief interlude in which Beverley saw calculation. 'No.'

Beverley was operating on autopilot as she said, 'This is important in the investigation of Wilson Milroy's murder, Ms Havers, so I'll ask you again. Did you meet with Dr Milroy?'

'We were going to but, of course, things intervened . . .' She cast an apologetic smile after this, which only made the lie worse.

Beverley seemed to tire of the game. Like a cat that had had its fill of toying with a rodent she produced from her briefcase one of the laboratory notebooks that they had found at Milroy's house. Handing it to Havers she said, 'You met and you gave him this. This was the reason you met.'

The Marketing Director didn't even look at it. She just let out a long, long breath and said, 'Yes.'

Beverley gave a brief nod of approval at this first act of co-operation. 'When did you meet?' she asked, as if this were a new subject.

'About a week later. He came here.'

'What prompted you to write to him?'

She hesitated but this time it wasn't to lie, it was to find the most apt form of expression. 'I thought that somebody ought to know the truth about Victoria Bence-Jones, about her research.'

'And that was?'

She became fluent at last, her words greased by bile. 'I don't know how she won the prize. When I was working with her, the research was going nowhere, and it wasn't even getting there particularly fast. She didn't have a clue. Next thing I know, she's winning prizes, the greatest thing since God made arses with holes in.'

'You were suspicious.'

'Too bloody right I was.'

'Why Milroy? Why not Piringer?'

'Piringer? He's just a dandy with a degree. Milroy, I knew, didn't stand for any nonsense. I knew that if I told him, he'd do something about it.'

Like blackmail. How much did you know about what he was going to do with your information?

'So you met and you gave him your side of the story, of how the research had been going nowhere as far as you could see. And you gave him these notes to corroborate what you said.'

'That's right.'

'And that was an end of it.'

'Absolutely.'

Beverley said nothing, just stared at her for a long, uncomfortable minute. Only then did she ask, 'How much did he pay for these?'

She tried on indignation, found she liked it and sallied forth. 'Nothing! Why would I want any money?'

Because you're a money-grubbing bitch with an eye on the main chance.

'Just doing your duty?' Beverley made no effort to keep sarcasm at bay.

'Yes, as a matter of fact.'

Beverley debated the value of pressing the point. She knew that Yvonne Havers was the kind of person who never did anything without demanding a return, but pragmatism won out over personal dislike. She shrugged and stood up. 'Someone will call in the next few days to take a statement, Ms Havers. I suggest that you do and say nothing until they do. Understand?'

Looking as if she had just swallowed a raisin and found that it was a rabbit dropping, Ms Havers nodded.

Wright, in command of a task force of forty men and trying to organize the search of the hospital, was aware that he was, not for the first nor last time, under-resourced, but he pressed his attack bravely. He was faced with combing the Western Royal Infirmary, an entity that was not a single institution but a disparate collection of buildings and spaces spread over a square mile and interspersed with interloping shops, offices, houses and car parks. There were so many cupboards, crannies, nooks and alcoves that had Wright been Bonaparte and commanded an army forty thousand strong he would have been unlikely to have achieved one hundred per cent coverage. To make his task harder, the plans provided by the hospital's Estates Department had proved to be amazingly inaccurate.

Yet he worked on, dogged in his persistence.

'Dr Eisenmenger?'

'Yes?'

'It's the nurse in charge on Renvier Ward.'

She was a nice woman, large and experienced and usually completely untroubled. Except that now she sounded troubled.

Very troubled.

In fact, within the space of eight words Eisenmenger heard her go from normality to controlled panic.

'Has Ms Flemming been in contact with you?'

'No.' He was already formulating theories, though, but none of them made sense. How come the nurse in charge of the ward was ringing.

'Oh.'

Just that. A vowel, not an explanation.

'What's going on?' He asked this in a measured, almost indifferent tone.

The hesitation was somehow damning. He asked again but more insistently, 'What's going on?'

She answered at last, but hardly with great enthusiasm, 'She seems to be missing.'

'Missing?'

More hesitation that was now palpably born of embarrassment. 'She went to the day room in the middle of the night. But she hasn't been seen since.'

'Has she discharged herself?'

'Well . . . no. You see, all her clothes and possessions are still here. It's as if she just walked out of the ward . . .'

The phone was down and he was heading for the door before she could complete the sentence.

And then, as he ran through the hospital, he was stopped by Sergeant Wright just outside the small parade of indoor shops by the dividing line between the medical school and the hospital.

'Dr Eisenmenger?'

There were no formed ideas in his head – only fluttering, fragmented ideations, fears and formless shapes – and Wright's unexpected entrance into the drama only stoked the turmoil within him.

'What is it?' he demanded, almost shrieked.

Wright, somewhat startled by this unlooked-for abruptness, said only, 'I thought I'd better warn you. Martin Pendred's been seen twice around here in the past twenty-four hours. Keep your eyes open.'

And that, as far as he was concerned, was the end of the affair, but Eisenmenger had another idea. 'Where?' he asked, his voice odd. 'Where, precisely, was Pendred seen?'

'Hippocampus Street. Just outside the entrance to the Surgical Block.'

And Eisenmenger was just staring at him, his face puzzled, almost fearful, as he asked, 'At what time was he seen?'

Wright wasn't about to be caught out by that one. 'Early hours of this morning. About two thirty.'

Eisenmenger closed his eyes briefly, then became energized. He grabbed Wright by the arm. 'Come with me.' He pulled him along the corridor.

'Where are we going?'

Eisenmenger looked back at him, the stare dead. 'To look into a potential kidnapping.'

Homer had arrived on the ward not ten minutes before, his face betraying a concoction of excitement and disbelief as he sat in the small meeting room just off the main corridor that ran down the ward. There, nestled between a mannequin used in the training of resuscitation techniques and an astonishingly lifelike (and large) female breast, he listened to what Wright and Eisenmenger had to report.

'So nobody saw him take her?'

'No, sir, but at that time of the morning, it would be easy to wander about the hospital and remain unseen.'

'Especially if he were wearing his old porter's uniform.' Eisenmenger's voice was dancing on a note of panic. He *knew* that Pendred had taken her; what he feared was that she was already dead.

'But this isn't his usual MO, is it? Normally he just waits for his moment, then sneaks up behind them and . . .' If he were going to continue, he thought better of it when he saw Eisenmenger's expression. He finished with, 'He doesn't normally take them somewhere else.'

'He did with the Muir woman, sir. If you remember he killed her some distance from her home, then carried her to her own front garden.' Sergeant Wright kept finding his eyes searching out the breast. It really was astonishingly lifelike.

'He killed her on the spot though, Wright. He has always, up till now, killed them on the spot; yet not this time, apparently.'

As worried as he was, Eisenmenger found part of his brain listening dispassionately to what they were saying, and that same part of his brain was wondering and evaluating. To the policemen he said, 'Whatever. The point is that she's gone and he was seen in the vicinity at the time that she seems to have gone.'

Of Wright Homer asked, 'We've checked her home, her office, her friends?'

Wright nodded. 'Nothing anywhere.'

'And as far as we know, all she had on was nightwear and a dressing gown?'

Another nod.

'Nothing's gone from her bedside?'

This time a shake, but Eisenmenger put in, 'Except her book. That was left in the day room. Presumably she was reading it.'

'But why Miss Flemming? She's only met him twice and as far as I know she didn't upset him, did she?'

Eisenmenger almost felt like laughing. 'No,' he said, 'She didn't upset him. Far from it.'

Homer was lost. 'What does that mean?'

'I think he's got a crush on her.'

Homer's surprise was reflected on Wright's face. 'Pardon?'

'I think he's fallen in love with her. That's why he went after me. Not because I'd done anything directly to hurt him, but because he saw me as a rival for Helena.'

Homer's initial disbelief began to dissipate. He asked, 'Love? Is he capable of love?'

'Why not? It might not be the stuff of Mills and Boon, but an autistic or a schizophrenic can still experience a version of the emotion.'

The Chief Inspector considered for a while. Then, he looked up. 'Well, whatever the truth, it certainly seems likely that he's taken her.'

Which left only one question – *Where had he taken her?*

Homer leaned forward, elbows on his knees. His mute companion, its mouth open in perpetual pout, its eyes dead to their problems, shifted slightly as Homer brushed shoulders with it. Wright tried not to look at the breast and somehow found that there was no other point in the room on which his eyes could rest.

'It must be around here,' Homer proposed. 'It must be somewhere around the hospital. That's where he knows, where he's been spotted most often.'

He drifted off into thought. Eisenmenger found himself wishing that he could escape the room and start searching himself. It didn't matter now whether Pendred had murdered three people, seven people or six million. All that mattered was that he had taken Helena and maybe he had killed, or was about to kill, someone he loved.

'How many people have you got searching the hospital, Wright?' Before Wright could answer, Homer ordered, 'Double it. No, triple it. Extend the search area to a half-mile radius centred on this ward. I want more policemen around here than there are rats in the sewer. I want them treading on each other's toes.'

He stood up, a smile on his face that didn't have the grace to hide when he turned to Eisenmenger and said, 'Don't worry, we'll find him.' Then, as if he couldn't resist a little gloating, he added, 'I think we can safely assume that he *is* the murderer, and always has been, Dr Eisenmenger.'

Eisenmenger, who no longer cared, said nothing.

Helena opened her eyes on to blue-grey darkness, deep and cold. For a moment she was lost in stupor, then her senses seeped into her consciousness and she became aware that she was very, very cold. Then she became aware that she was naked.

Where am I?

She ought to have been in bed, on the ward. She ought to have been warm, at least, even if the mattress and pillow were not designed for the comfort of humans.

In fact, she now appreciated, she wasn't on a mattress at all, and no pillow lay under her head. She was on a cold, hard surface, one that felt almost metallic.

And her breast – God, that was painful. It felt as if it had been mauled, kicked by a hoof. What had happened to it?

She tried to reach across to feel it but she couldn't; nor could she move her legs. The only part of her that she could move, she discovered, was her head, and that only to lift it.

She was tied down, thick nylon ropes cutting across her in three places – over her shoulders, her belly and her knees. At once, a sick feeling took root inside her, though she would not let it consume her. She fought it with anger.

'What the hell?' The first words that she uttered sounded astonishingly resonant, although she had only whispered them. Her eyes moved away and into the darkness around her. Shapes were becoming apparent, either because her eyes were adapting or because light was filtering in. It seemed to be a big room with a high ceiling. She could make out a set of double doors and a single door opposite her. There seemed to be much rubbish and numerous large objects around the room, on surfaces and leaning against the walls, as if it were a junk room.

'What is this place?' she asked, her voice lower this time, though only a little less striking. She noted the tremor, chastised herself.

She began to wriggle under the bonds, but at once it became obvious that she wasn't going to free herself. Anyway, the pain it caused in her wound was intense; she could see now that the dressing had gone, that the ugly, bruised incision was exposed and that blood was now trickling away from it in a steady stream, running down into the valley between her chest and her arm, thence seeping away.

And her throat, she now realized, was painful. It felt as if someone had tried to crush it, and that made her very worried indeed.

Which brought her back to the memories of what had happened.

The day room of the ward. Sitting in the chair, reading, trying to relax . . .

Whatever had happened then had occurred with astonishing speed, she recalled. The door to the corridor had been open and a porter had entered. She remembered assuming that he had come in to make sure that she was all right, that she had barely looked up from her book, that he had come across to her very quickly . . .

He had grabbed her throat, his hand a grip of immense power, his fingers digging deep into the sides of her neck. She had struggled, of course, trying to free the grip, unable to rise because he wouldn't let her.

And that was the last she remembered.

No wonder her throat hurt but he had not, she thought, actually been trying to strangle her.

'Who?' The question crept out into the room, startling her for she had not intended to speak. She found that she didn't much care any more if she sounded anxious.

And now she was naked. What else had he done? And where was she?

Where was he?

She had not been raped, she knew; but she had been undressed, perhaps assaulted. He could have done anything to her, anything at all. His fingers might have been inside her, on her breasts, around her mouth . . .

No! I will not lose control!

She took deep breaths, not bothered if they sounded in the room. She was alone, after all.

Who was doing this to her?

She looked again into the darkness. There was definitely more light entering her prison, more distinction between greater and lesser shadow, so that she could now see that this was definitely a dumping ground. There were chairs stacked up in the corner to her left, tables next to them.

It was when she saw the drip stands huddled together as if in conference that she knew that she was still in the hospital.

She turned her head fully to the right and saw the metal tables – one, two, three of them – positioned at intervals along the length of the room, surrounded by files, boxes, upturned desks and chairs. Then she understood what she was tied to and worry departed, dread took over.

She was on a dissection table.

'Oh, my God!' The words were little more than breaths, rasping her sore throat.

She jerked her head around the room, suddenly very conscious that most people who were spread out on a dissection table ended up being dissected. She began to struggle again, aware that it was useless, aware that she had nothing to lose except some more blood and freedom from pain. She made small grunting noises as she twisted this way and that, wriggling and squirming, all without result.

At last, she gave up, eyes watering with pain and panic. She squeezed them shut, then opened them, feeling a few tears run away from them. There was now even more light in the room and her eyes found the far corner again, where the chairs were stacked.

They found also Martin Pendred, sitting in a chair, silently staring at her.

'I heard the news, John.' The familiarity of Beverley's voice was strangely comforting amidst the worry. 'Is it really Pendred?'

He was reluctant to admit it, as if such words might act as an incantation for evil. 'Yes. I'm very much afraid that it is.'

'But I don't understand. Are we wrong? Is it really Pendred doing these killings?'

Which was one of the questions he had been asking, with always the same answer. 'No. Pendred did not kill Jenny Muir, Patrick Wilms or Wilson Milroy.'

'Then what's going on? Why has he taken Helena?'

Another very good question, but this one harder to answer. 'I think that maybe he's become psychotic. The stress of being arrested, then the manhunt.'

'Does that mean . . . ?' She didn't finish the question, but the words formed in his mind: . . . *he might kill her?*

264

'Yes,' he admitted, partly a sigh and partly a cry.

She was quiet for a moment. 'What's Homer doing?'

'He's flooding the hospital and surrounding area with police. He's convinced that Pendred's hiding somewhere in the locality.'

She couldn't disagree with the strategy; it was normal procedure, given the information that Homer had. The problem was that she didn't think that normal procedure was going to catch such an abnormal man.

'Can you get away?' she asked.

He was sitting in his office, doing no work and worrying, activities that he could do anywhere. 'Sure.'

'Martin?'

Still he didn't answer, didn't even respond. He might have been deaf, she mute and hidden. Except that he could see her. All of her.

'Martin?'

The room was now quite well lit by light from frosted, dirty windows high up on the wall to her right. She wondered what time it was and despite her terror she was getting hungry.

'Martin, I know that you can hear me.'

Except that he declined to acknowledge it. He was almost out of her line of vision, so that he became visible only with her head twisted and her neck stretched, which made her wound scream in anger. He was thus just a shape without detail, without movement. A presence, nothing beyond that.

'I don't know why you've done this, Martin. I don't care, either. I just want you to let me go.'

And nothing at all from the shape in her oh-so-peripheral vision.

'If you let me go, Martin, there'll be no recriminations, Martin. If I walk away from here now, you can go free.'

But even this lie was not to be the key to her release.

There was silence between them for another while that could have been a minute, could have been half a lifetime. Then, tentatively, she called, 'I need to go to the toilet, Martin.'

And with nothing responding, she called, 'Martin?'

He was still there, she saw as she craned her head, still unmoving and now seemingly unmoved.

'I knew that you wouldn't be able to resist coming back to me, Beverley.'

From most people this would have sounded somehow lascivious, but not from Pinkus. The smile helped, Eisenmenger decided; it gave one the idea that here was self-mockery, nothing more.

Beverley said gravely, 'It wasn't just your rugged good looks, Malcolm.'

He laughed, a good-natured, reassuring noise. 'Ah, well. *C'est la vie.*'

Eisenmenger didn't feel like joining in the merriment. He said, 'Beverley tells me that you might know where Martin Pendred is hiding.'

Pinkus held up his hand at once. It was twisted, almost into a caricature. 'I had success getting to know Melkior. It may not be applicable to his brother, even if he is a twin.'

Beverley pointed out, 'You're still the best chance we have,' and Eisenmenger suggested, 'Let's assume that it is.'

Pinkus nodded his acceptance. 'Since you last came to see me, I've looked again at my notes from the first killings, and I've read up on the Autistic Spectrum Disorders.' He had no notes but was speaking authoritatively. 'It really boils down to what I told you before. I think that he will have run to somewhere that he views as comforting. The home where he has lived all his life is barred to him; he will therefore run to somewhere that has similar emotions attached to it.'

'Not so different to the rest of us, then,' murmured Eisenmenger.

Pinkus, acting almost as a lecturer interrupted by a precocious student, said, 'Except that his interpretation of what is comforting might well be very different from ours.' Beverley crossed her legs and Eisenmenger saw Pinkus's eyes follow the movement with a hint of hunger as he continued, 'His criteria are almost certainly different, possibly beyond what we can understand, seeming to us to be illogical and incomprehensible.'

'You're not giving us much cause to feel optimistic, Malcolm.'

'No, and I'm not finished yet. Don't forget that Melkior Pendred, and therefore almost certainly Martin, had an eidetic, or photographic, memory. People with such an ability can be said not to have a past, for all their memories live on all the time, and that produces interesting and distorting effects. You navigate your way around the map of your past by fairly simple rules: vivid events are recent whereas vague ones are ancient, those with strong emotional ties are important but those without aren't. Melkior Pendred had no such clues, for all memories were there, all the time, all clamouring with an equal voice for recognition.

'What that means is that, if Martin is the same as Melkior, then he may consider it suitable to hide in a place that he only visited for five minutes some twenty years ago.'

'Making it almost impossible to predict where he might be holed up.' Beverley looked across at Eisenmenger as she spoke.

'Exactly.' Pinkus sounded pleased that his point had been appreciated. 'Especially since his criteria will almost certainly seem to us peculiar.'

Eisenmenger was staring at the carpet, which was brightly coloured and loudly patterned. His voice when he spoke suggested that he was mesmerized. 'All he's known all his life is home, the pub and work. His home has gone, though.'

'But we can't assume that the only logical places to look are the hospital or the pub. Homer's pretty well searched those as well as possible, and he's come up with nothing. If what Malcolm says is true, it might be a lock-up garage or a garden shed.'

But Eisenmenger was shaking his head. 'I can't believe that.'

Pinkus's irritation was patent. 'Well, whatever you believe, that is my opinion.'

Beverley was put in the position of peacemaker. 'We're very grateful, Malcolm.' Unfortunately Eisenmenger was oblivious. 'We're missing something here. Something obvious.'

Before Pinkus could react, Beverley stood. 'We'd better go.' She walked across to him and bent down to give him a light kiss on the cheek. The effect was immediate and incredible to behold, except that Eisenmenger was still seeing things in the carpet pattern. She had to stand before him in his line of sight to reach him. 'Time to go, John.'

He stood but it was obvious that he was little more than an automaton. His acknowledgement of Pinkus was perfunctory, no more. As they stood in the hall waiting for Pinkus to open the door, he was looking at the palm of his hand as if it held a camouflaged secret, the answer to all life's problems. Eventually the door was opened and they departed. Pinkus called after Beverley, 'You'll call again?'

She turned and gave him a smile but no more. As he shut the door, he sighed and shook his head.

The traffic was terrible, a bad-tempered tangle of tired commuters, exhausted hauliers and jaded taxi drivers. It began as soon as they entered the outskirts of the city and grew gradually worse as they progressed more and more slowly.

She had assumed that Eisenmenger would want to be dropped off at his apartment, although he had said nothing at all on the journey, merely staring straight ahead, the view one she was not privy to. The route took them past the Surgical Department of the hospital.

He said at last, 'Where is he, Beverley?'

She had to stop suddenly because some prat in expensive leathers on a flash motorbike had just cut in ahead of her with no notice. 'I don't think you can deduce this one, John. I think that Malcolm's right. He might be in any of the places he's ever been in.'

Eisenmenger sighed and for the first time looked around him, out of the side window of the car. 'But he must be near here. He must be.'

'Which, as painful as it is for me to admit, probably means that Homer's using the right strategy.'

'But the only time he was ever here was in connection with his work. First as a mortuary technician, then as a porter.'

'Well, Homer's searched the hospital and mortuary at least twice and is doing so again.'

There followed nothing more from Eisenmenger for several minutes; minutes in which the car moved perhaps ten metres.

Suddenly Eisenmenger shouted, 'Christ!' He thumped the dashboard. 'The mortuary!'

They were moving again, although a one-legged man on crutches could have overtaken them. 'What about it? I told you, Homer's searched it.'

'The new one, maybe, but when Pendred started work at the Infirmary, the mortuary was a run-down old place. He was only there a few months, I think, but I bet Homer doesn't know about it.'

Beverley was looking in her mirror as she asked, 'Where? Where is it?'

Where had Lewy said it was?

'Mole Street! Know it?'

'Yes. It's only about a hundred metres. Back there and on the right.' She indicated a direction behind them. 'Oh, well.'

The traffic had begun to move and they were in the inside lane of a four-lane road, She indicated but it wasn't really anything more than gesture, for at once she began to turn the wheel and when the gentleman in the white van to her right began to object, she merely increased the lock slightly. She aimed the offside front wing exactly at the gap between him and the car in front and just kept going. There was a loud scrape of metal. White van man stopped, but Beverley didn't. As the gap widened and the sound of an extremely loud and extremely angry horn sounded to their right, she just kept going, more paint and metal grinding together. Eisenmenger glimpsed the van driver, his face almost grotesque with anger, shouting filth and starting to climb out. Beverley was already looking to their left to find a gap in the traffic streaming past on the opposite carriageway. Since she didn't find one, she made one, which upset a silver Mercedes and a Renault, as well as several other unidentified vehicles behind them.

When they were moving again, just as slowly but this time in the opposite direction, Eisenmenger said, 'I bet your insurance company loves you.'

Beverley was looking all the time for gaps in the traffic to slip into so that they could move as quickly as possible, and finding precious few. Under her breath she kept muttering, 'Come on, come on,' but she found breath to reply. 'My insurance company are bunch of pricks.'

After several agonizing minutes they reached a left-hand turning which she took with some relief. She accelerated quickly down this road, then at the end turned right and quickly left.

Mole Street.

'Any idea where it might be?'

'No.'

The street was narrow and grubby, with piles of rubbish stacked against crumbling brick walls. They drove slowly past a printer's shop that might have been open, might have been derelict, a dealer in second-hand goods and several anonymous office buildings, most of which looked empty. A fox stared at them from a doorway, emaciated and grey.

'There.' Eisenmenger pointed up ahead, to their right. Another empty, derelict building, but this one was single-storeyed and had no entrance directly on to the road; by its near side there was a narrow lane.

'How do you know?'

'Trust me.'

It would clearly not have been prepossessing had it been new, for the few windows in its face were frosted and they were set in metal frames surrounded by drab, grey concrete. The building itself was nothing more than a squat box, a totem of all that there was to be found in a fit of depression. *And they wonder why pathologists are so bloody peculiar.*

'Down there.' He indicted the alleyway at the side.

At last she could no longer help herself. Against all the social, biological and psychological training that had formed her into the Western, twenty-first century idea of a civilized person – the epitome of conformity and propriety – she was forced to urinate as she lay there unclothed and cold, bound and in the company and view of another.

It was most certainly a coincidence, but it was then that for the first time after so many hours he spoke, although at a level too low for her to hear.

'Wait!' She couldn't shout, risking no more than a pushed, insistent whisper, and whether or not Eisenmenger heard, he didn't stop but continued down the alley. She sighed and whispered, 'Shit,' to herself as she continued to wait for an answer to her call. Eventually PC Clark came on the line.

'It's DI Wharton here. I need back-up now. Mole Street, near the hospital. There's a disused mortuary here and I have reason to believe that Martin Pendred, possibly with a hostage, is present within it.'

She didn't wait for an answer but broke the connection and hurried after Eisenmenger.

'Please, Martin, talk to me.'

But Martin continued his soft, slow chant that was barely

audible to her and now, she realized, he had risen without a sound.

'Martin?' But the monologue continued, unrelenting and unregarding; it sounded as if it would continue until kingdom come. It was difficult to see his face, but it appeared petrous, his eyes fixed upon her.

It's an incantation. A spell.

Yet she could not quite believe it. There was no rhythm to it; it could almost have been a narrative. What *was* it?

She was starting to shiver because she was so cold and with this came her breath rasping and raking her throat. It was almost beyond her to quieten, to relax, to try to listen to what Martin was saying.

'. . . the most important thing is to make sure that you've got the identification absolutely right . . .'

It was uttered without intonation, a string of words. She stretched again to look at him.

He had gone.

Her heart was suddenly impossibly loud, its violent banging in her chest a vicious battery.

Where is he?

'. . . You always check the labels on the body with the request form. Make sure that everything tallies. Only if you've looked at least twice do you then start . . .'

Where the hell is he?

She realized that he was walking around her, past her head. He seemed to be moving very slowly, in time with the low recitation.

Only then did she appreciate what he had said. *Body? Did he say, 'body'?*

'. . . You place the block under the body, about the middle of the back . . .'

He came back into view, this time on her left.

'. . . look for marks. You know the kind of thing – bruising, scars, abrasions. You know the difference between an abrasion and a laceration? A laceration is a break in the skin, an abrasion is a graze. Look especially around the throat and eyes – if you see anything around those areas, then tell your pathologist . . .'

'Martin?' She was aware that her fear was rattling in her voice, that she was pleading. His eyes were lifeless, an alien in her world.

271

'. . . Measure any scars or abrasions. If it's a road traffic accident, make a chart and draw everything you see on it . . .'

He had a wad of cotton wool in his hands that she spotted only as it was coming towards her head. She opened her mouth to cry and within a quarter second she was gagging on it as Martin Pendred stuffed more and more into her mouth. She tried to make it as hard as she could for him, thrashing her head from side to side, but without success. Then he stopped and she lay there feeling as if she were going to suffocate, her eyes watering, panting through her nose.

Her respite barely lasted.

Suddenly, his hands were on her, repulsion blossoming like rancid lilies inside her each time she felt his cold, almost dead flesh pawing at her. He squeezed her ankles, examined her fingers, held her head while forcing open her eyes, pulled down her lip as if she were horsemeat. She screamed with pain when he grabbed her breast, causing more blood to flow from the wound as he measured it with a metal ruler, muttering something she could not hear.

Then, abruptly he was gone and that was somehow worse.

Eisenmenger knew that he should have been waiting for Beverley, even as he pushed into the darkness behind the double doors, but there was an irresistible siren whispering in his mind, urging him forward, reminding him that Helena was a few metres away, that she was possibly in the hands of a man who would happily slice her throat into a bloody grin.

There was dust in the air. Dust and damp, mould multiplying and adding its flavours. He didn't know this mortuary but he knew mortuaries. He knew that he would be in some sort of foyer off which there would be a fridge bay, almost certainly through the second set of double doors ahead of him. To his right was a single closed door, while another to his left was accompanied by a large window. He moved across to his left and edged up to the window.

An office, stripped of most of its accoutrements, clinging forlornly to a desk and a battered filing cabinet.

He moved across to the door on the right, aware that a man with a very sharp knife might be waiting patiently and clinically behind it. A narrow corridor, empty of psychotics, empty too of light. To his right was a blind end, opposite were two doors, one marked 'Men', the other, 'Women'. On his left yet another door. He knew that through that would be the dissection room.

He swallowed something hard, its only taste that of fear.

She's in there.

He moved forward, trying to be quiet and slow, hearing enough noise from his footsteps to wake Morpheus, even with terminal earwax. And then he heard a noise behind him and an electric shock ran through him, his heart jolted into explosive compressions.

Vaguely, distantly, he heard the half-hissed, half-urgent word, *John?*

Beverley.

He hesitated, but for perhaps half a second.

At the door to the dissection room he stopped and put his ear to the wood.

Nothing.

The handle felt rough as if sprayed with grit. He pushed it down and shoved.

It had not struck him as warm, yet the air that swirled through the gap was cold.

Like the grave.

All he could see was a jumble of chairs, a few drip stands in conference. He pushed slightly more. First one dissection table was revealed, then another.

This one with Helena, naked, tied to it; her head raised, her eyes wide. Something had been thrust in her mouth. He moved at once towards her, about to call her name.

And then the door was slammed shut and the knife came down and he couldn't stop the cry from escaping his lips.

So much for standard procedure.

Her only decision now was whether to go in through the double doors or to squeeze around the back and look for another way in.

On no particular evidence she went to her right, down the narrow space between the fence and the canopy. It was strewn with bricks, broken bottles, beer cans and even barbed wire; halfway along was the decaying body of a rat. At the end was another, shorter space, running away at right angles to her left, similarly decorated and leading to a small backyard, itself little more than a rubbish tip.

She picked her way carefully but rapidly over the uneven ground past a tilted fridge-freezer stuck in the ground like a postmodern garden ornament and up to the rear of the mortuary. There were no doors but there were two windows and in one of them there were broken panes.

Without bothering to investigate too closely, she reached in through the jagged hole and felt for a catch. She had to stretch and it was stiff so that it wouldn't budge.

'Damn!' she breathed. She was painfully aware of a shard of glass pressing into her forearm, but she reached even further and pressed down hard. As the catch finally gave, she felt the glass slice deeply into her flesh. With quite astonishing speed there was blood everywhere, spreading under the abrupt burst of tortured anguish that was now her arm.

But the window was open and she couldn't afford to hesitate. Ignoring the blood that had already soaked the sleeves of her blouse and her coat, ignoring the pain, she heaved herself through the window into a male changing room.

At once she was across the room past the empty, open lockers and through a shallow sea of dust, standing at the door that led inwards.

The crash of glass made her twitch violently. *What the hell?*

She pushed at the door at once, just a fraction, praying that the hinges wouldn't squeal.

They didn't.

Homer was with Wright going again through all the files they had amassed on the Pendred killings when Clark knocked on the door and, uncharacteristically, came straight in.

'We've got a possible location for Pendred, sir.'

'Where?'

'Mole Street.'

Homer turned to the large map on the wall. 'It's possible,' he said. To Clark, he said, 'Where in Mole Street?'

'Apparently there's a disused mortuary in it.'

Homer almost jumped as she said this. He whirled around. 'Says who?'

'DI Wharton. She's just been on the phone.'

Homer hesitated. He looked across to Wright who opened his eyes wide in an expression of abdication. Then Homer looked back at Clark and for a moment there was absolute silence. His voice when it came was almost dreamy and with a deeply indrawn breath, almost as if the words would not come without great effort. 'Okay, we'd better get over there. Get an armed response unit to meet us in Mole Street.'

In the car, as the road was cleared before them by the siren and the main-beam headlights, he asked Wright, 'Did you know that there was a mortuary in Mole Street?'

Wright, thinking that if he had known he reckoned he would have had the brains to tell someone about it, said merely, 'No, sir.'

'Have we searched Mole Street?'

'We've done house-to-house along it, not that there are many occupied premises there.'

'But no one's thought to search the empty premises?'

Wright sighed. 'They were checked to see if they were secure, sir, but we can't do much more than that, can we, sir? It'd be against the law.'

Homer stared hard at him for a long time before finally he looked away out of the window, muttering a barely heard, 'Fucking laws.'

The knife slid into his shoulder without resistance, scraping along the bone. It was agony but that was nothing to the sudden screaming, spiralling spike of unendurable pain that followed at the end of its travel. Suddenly his arm was dead for movement, torture incarnate. The knife came out even before he had begun to react, to reach up to that shoulder, to go with the instinct and pull away. His face, though, his face reacted quickly, an admirably speedy response of no use whatsoever.

He fell to his knees, clutching the shoulder with its dressing of haemorrhage, kneading it with his fingers in an effort to lessen his anguish. He almost fainted, but fought it off and opened his eyes to look up into Martin Pendred's face.

All the mad killers of his youth and his imagination had worn masks of some kind, grotesqueries behind which they hid and with which they made their statement. Pendred wore no such accessory; he didn't need to. His face was dead, as lifeless as a corpse's. Eisenmenger had seen thousands of such faces, but none had been on the front of a man standing above him with a bloodied, ten-centimetre knife in his hand; none had been looking at him from a place as remote and distant as oblivion. It was as if a zombie were looking down at him; a zombie who didn't want him around any more.

Helena was struggling, muffled grunting noise coming from her throat, but if anything that was just distraction. He tried to maintain his attention on his attacker, which suddenly became a lot easier when Pendred, his face unchanging, raised the knife again.

Eisenmenger began to scramble away, leaving bloody handprints on the large ceramic tiles on the floor. He didn't have much room for manoeuvre because of the rubbish that had been piled into the room; almost at once he backed into an unstable pile of keyboards that some dickhead had piled on to a three-legged metal stool.

But Pendred didn't play the game, hadn't seen the film. He dropped his arm, not even looking again at Eisenmenger; his eyes were back on Helena and he began to walk back to her. Eisenmenger saw her eyes widen, then her face turn imploringly in his direction.

Shit!

He got up unsteadily but as rapidly as he could. He looked around him, found under an old metal-framed desk an old pot in which, suspended in murky, yellow formalin, there was a large spleen. He reached under it, finding that he could just pick it up one-handed.

Martin was back bending over Helena, the knife pointing at her throat, his concentration on the questions of a different universe, while she stretched away from him to the limit of the bonds, her face turned towards to Eisenmenger.

He wasn't going to be able to throw it with much accuracy because his left arm wasn't his any more and therefore he couldn't use it for balance.

Pendred leaned further forward and put thumb and forefinger of his left hand to the upper part of her throat, just below her chin. At his touch she made a muffled squeal and squirmed even more.

'Martin!'

Pendred didn't react but it didn't matter because Eisenmenger

276

launched the pot as he shouted. He knew at once that it was a weak throw, that it might fall short – perhaps even land on Helena. It was big and it was heavy and it seemed to move as if through molasses, but it made it, just. With a satisfying thud it knocked Pendred's left arm into his body, causing his right hand to drop the knife.

The pot dropped on Helena's left shoulder, then to the floor where it smashed and formalin vapour rose acridly and invisibly into the air.

He had won a minor skirmish but Pendred didn't even seem to be connecting all that was going on into any sort of normal reality. His face hadn't changed one whit, he didn't so much as glance at Eisenmenger and he made no sound. He merely reached down among the broken glass and formalin to pick up the knife.

What the hell am I going to do now?

The door behind Pendred began to open.

Beverley saw Pendred bending forward some seven or eight metres in front of her; naked and tied to a dissection table was Helena. She smelled an acrid, stinging vapour and she heard muffled cries from Helena. It was only when she looked to the left, behind the door, that she caught sight of Eisenmenger, his shoulder covered in blood while he swayed gently and looked less than in contact with the universe.

What do I do now?

She looked around the room, aware that Pendred was already beginning to stand up, letting her eyes flick here and there, looking, always looking.

Finding nothing.

He was nearly upright and she had found no weapon, no advantage. She did the only thing that she could think of.

She ran forward, put her booted foot up and pushed him forward as hard as she could. This unexpected assault caused him to be propelled forward and his midriff struck the work surface that ran along the wall, in turn causing his head to strike the tiled backsplash with an exceedingly hard and satisfying thud. Pendred crumbled to the floor, folding and sliding.

If the thought that she had won the war passed anywhere through her brain, it was a brief and sickly thing, never meant to be born, for he was rising again almost at once.

Helena saw the knife in perfect clarity, through eyes that were painfully wide. She saw its perfect, silvered surface, the gentle curve to a wicked point, the slightly dulled edge. She saw, too, its approach, an approach that was measured and steady and implacable.

And beyond it she saw the face of Martin Pendred, eyes as dead as Tyresias, face as fixed as Colossus.

She felt the stuffing in her mouth, gagged again and swallowed too much saliva. Through her head went more thoughts than seemed possible. She thought of her fear and her anger, she thought of her impotence, she thought of being cold, being scared shitless, being where she was, not being where she wasn't; she thought she was going to die. She thought that her breast was hurting enough to explode and that it wasn't fair to be where she was . . .

She craned her head away, stretching her neck, thinking that in trying to get away from the blade she was exposing all that it wanted to cut.

Still the knife came on.

And then, with an astonishingly precipitate movement, both Pendred and the blade were jerked forward, out of her sight, to be replaced by Beverley looking both terrified and determined.

Eisenmenger was losing it and was aware that he was losing it. As he watched Beverley kick Pendred forward, he found himself drifting without moving, the room darkening into forgetfulness and serenity. Pendred's collision and consequent collapse to the floor were events he looked upon but didn't see.

Pendred's rise again was just something that was happening, somewhere other, to someone else. It was vaguely interesting, but who cared . . . ?

'John?'

He didn't actually hear Beverly but something chimed in his mind. *Pendred's getting up again.*

278

'John?'

Even then it took another moment, another heartbeat of the universe, to appreciate that there was significance to this, let alone what that significance was.

He began then to move, light-headedly and unsteadily, but in the right direction and with purpose. His main problem was that he didn't know what he could do.

He carried on anyway, reaching Pendred who was by now halfway back to standing. Still he bore no expression.

Beverley was desperately working at the rope tied around Helena's torso.

All he could think of was to repeat Beverley's action and try to push Pendred back down but when he raised his foot Pendred grabbed it, looking not at Eisenmenger but at his shoe.

Beverley had untied the first knot and had moved on to the bonds around Helena's ankles. As Helena's arms were freed she had started taking the sodden cotton wool from her mouth and despite coughing and choking, she was already working at the knot in the bonds around her midriff.

For a moment Eisenmenger was held in a strangely balletic pose before Pendred thrust him backward with insolent ease. He staggered backward, barely keeping vertical, giddiness subsuming him, before crashing into some drip stands and landing in a chair. His impact made the chair slide backwards and brought a pile of old ledgers down upon him and the floor and around his feet.

He tried to get up at once, for Pendred was already moving purposefully back towards Beverley and Helena, but the world was doing its rotatory thing again and his legs were also disobedient to the point of mutiny; he fell rather heavily, coming face to paper with some ancient autopsy records, as if at that moment he cared.

He scrabbled around, trying to force, rather than entice, his legs to co-operate, which turned out to be a tactical error because he discovered that they were polemical sods who weren't for a rigid militaristic regimen.

'Helena!'

She looked up at his anguished call at exactly the moment that Pendred's fingers closed around her shoulders and she screamed. He hadn't picked up the knife but there was another on the dissection table by her thigh and his eyes were on it. His right hand was reaching for it as Beverley snatched it up, stepped forward and sliced it across his outstretching arm. It made a roughly spiral cut, across tendons and relatively pale skin that was running with haemoglobin before a second had passed.

And still he came on, and still his face didn't change, despite the blood and the cut; still his fingers were on Helena, the grip tightening, and still his arm was outstretched towards Beverley. Helena was wriggling, striking out at him, yelling, while Beverley, who had initially moved back slightly, was already preparing to thrust again.

Which was when the doors exploded open and the room was filled by policemen.

Homer stood outside the mortuary rubbing his gloved hands together, a look of satisfaction decorating his face. He radiated smugness, irradiated his local environment with it, leaving triumphant fallout everywhere.

Another case solved. Another step up the ladder.

Past him moved police officers both uniformed and plain clothes, two SOCOs and paramedics, these last coming and going from two ambulances drawn up at the end of the alleyway, behind a line of police cars. A few gawping spectators could be seen by the ambulances but, just as an actor ignored his audience, so Homer refused to acknowledge this adoration.

'Sir?'

Wright's syllable, elided with a cough, brought Homer back from a pleasant place. 'What is it?'

'Dr Eisenmenger wants to speak to you.'

Homer frowned. 'Why?'

Wright didn't know and didn't see why he should know. He therefore shrugged, which lead to an irritated, 'Okay, where is he?'

He was in the disused office, having some first aid applied to his shoulder. He had a deep pallor but the look on his face belied this with something serene about it. Homer assumed that he was feeling not surprisingly sick. The paramedic, a short, dumpy girl with a face that looked as if it had just been smacked, was mumbling to herself as she wound an elasticated bandage around his shoulder as tightly as she could.

He looked up surprisingly sharply as they entered. 'Where's Helena?'

Wright said, 'She's gone to the Royal.'

'Will she be all right?'

Although he didn't have the faintest idea, Wright answered easily, 'Of course.'

Eisenmenger considered, his head and upper body being jerked around by the paramedic; Wright saw a determined look in her grimace, as if she measured her success by the amount of groaning she heard.

'And Beverley?'

It was Homer who replied. 'DI Wharton has given us her statement. She's gone home now.'

There followed a silence broken only by the paramedic as she breathed heavily while she worked, as if asthmatic; her bright-green uniform was distinctive but hardly decorative.

Eventually Homer asked, 'You wanted to speak to me?'

Eisenmenger seemed surprised by this, then, 'Oh, yes.'

Another pause.

'Well?'

The paramedic finished, with a flourish that involved a sadistic pull on the bandage, but Eisenmenger hardly noticed. He seemed to be taking a deep draught of something as he said, 'I thought you ought to know . . .' and it was here that he paused, smiled and finally gave in to the pain. As he began to faint he said quite clearly, '. . . I know who the real murderer is.'

Part Four

Eisenmenger's shoulder would not stop aching no matter which painkiller he took. He had slept hardly at all during the last two nights and this, together with the light-headedness of pethidine, produced a dreamy detachment from reality that he had to fight all the time and that even the taxi driver's erratic, jerking progress through the traffic failed to break. Eventually Eisenmenger was deposited outside a semi-detached house to the north of the city and, the driver having been paid, he was left alone to contemplate his surroundings.

It was a respectable neighbourhood, the gardens neat, the paintwork carefully tended. The cars that were parked on the short driveways were neither top of the range nor brand new, but they were all clean and taxed and they all showed the touch of a caring hand. Eisenmenger took a deep breath of the cool air and smelled the contentment of middle class mixed with a faint odour of retirement.

He walked up to the door of number eighty-six, between a small but perfectly formed garden gnome and a three-year-old bright-yellow saloon car. He rang the doorbell and was rewarded with a call that came from his right. He peered around the side of the house, where there was a door between the house and the garage door. This opened to reveal a short but power-fully built man of perhaps sixty years. He had a face that was squashed so that the eyes were deeply set, the nose and lips protuberant. This, together with the pale stubble around the chin and mouth, made the owner unprepossessing.

'Yes?'

'Mr Brocca? It's John Eisenmenger. I phoned earlier.'

The only sign of welcome was a curt nod before the doorway

was vacated and Eisenmenger assumed that he was to walk through. He found himself in the empty garage where Brocca was varnishing a large display cabinet. He returned to his task at once, asking as he dipped the brush into the varnish tin, 'You said you wanted to talk to me about the Pendreds?'

'If I can.'

Brocca started to apply the varnish to the bare wood. His hands were powerful with fingers that were short and stubby but, despite this, he worked with surprising delicacy. His eyes were close to the wood as he asked, 'He did that, didn't he? Your shoulder.'

'That's right.'

'I read about it in the paper.'

There was a workbench at the end of the garage and Eisenmenger now leaned against it. 'You were the Chief Mortician at the WRI for a long time.'

'Twenty-three years.'

'So you knew the Pendreds well.'

He dabbed the tip of the brush into a corner with a rapid, pecking motion as he replied. 'As well as anyone ever got to know them, I suppose. What of it?'

'What did you think of them?'

'I thought that they were odd, but then who didn't?'

'As workers, though. Were they good at the job?'

For the first time he looked directly at Eisenmenger. 'Depends what you mean. They were useless when it came to the paper-work; you couldn't trust them to release bodies or look after the property.'

'Why was that?'

'They never got to grips with that side of things. There's a lot of form-filling involved when you're transferring a body to an undertaker – got to make sure that it's the right one, that everyone's happy that it's in good condition, that kind of thing – and no matter how hard I tried neither of them was ever able to put it all together. Same with the valuables that came in with the bodies.'

'But their work with the bodies?'

'Fine.' He returned to his varnishing.

Eisenmenger asked, 'You taught them how to eviscerate, did you?'

For the first time, he reacted with suspicion. 'Yeah. What about it?'

Eisenmenger said at once, 'I'm interested in the technique, Mr Brocca. Nothing more.'

Mollified, he allowed, 'I was in charge of showing them the ropes. They'd already had experience of a sort because they'd worked in an abattoir. I showed them how to take out the pluck and how to remove the brain.'

'Were they good pupils?'

'They picked it up pretty quickly. As I said, they'd done similar work before.'

'But what about the sewing up?'

'What about it?'

'In many ways, it's the most important part of your job – making sure that the body is cosmetically acceptable. They'd presumably never done that before.'

He paused again, this time to remember. 'No, they hadn't. That was more difficult. That took a lot longer to get straight.'

'Lewy said that it was Martin who had the bigger problem.'

Brocca nodded slowly. 'Yeah, that's right.'

Eisenmenger did not know how he could be sure, but sure he was that here was the answer he had been seeking. 'Can you give me details, Mr Brocca? I think that it may be quite important.'

'Damn.'

After three days of depression, Beverley had run through her entire stock of expletives, oaths, curses and imprecations but that didn't stop her from finding some hard comfort in repeating them at odd occasions; indeed, as far as she could recall, they were all she had uttered aloud in the previous seventy-two hours, save for a single phone conversation with John Eisenmenger asking to see her.

He was late, now she came to think of it. Time passed so quickly in her deep reverie; was it really only three days since Pendred's arrest? It seemed both relatively recent and lost in the distant past, yet objectively only seventy-odd hours had died since her career had finally hit the immovable buffer that was proven incompetence.

The panorama beyond her corner window, dissected by the winding river and peppered with strangely beautiful urban decay, had been her only companion, somehow communing with her in stately silence. Fisher had phoned her four times, finding only the answerphone as she had listened to his requests to be answered.

How? How could she have been so strikingly, resoundingly wrong? Her certainty had been absolute that Martin Pendred was not the murderer; certainly not the first time round and probably not this time. Eisenmenger, too, had apparently been catastrophically mistaken, an uncharacteristic error.

Yet even through the endless iteration of this question, her mind was working to plan the future. She had yet to receive notification of the disciplinary board, but she knew that it would not be long in coming; that she would be dismissed from the service was as inevitable as death following life. What to do then?

The forces would be out of the question, from both her own inclination and because they didn't take just anyone, certainly not police rejects. That left either some sort of private security work or a complete change of direction.

Neither appealed.

She fingered the bandage around her forearm idly. The door chime sounded and she turned from the window, walking slowly to the door.

But it wasn't John Eisenmenger.

'Helena?' She couldn't quite suppress the question. Helena was smartly dressed and Beverley immediately felt uncomfortable in her jeans and black T-shirt.

'May I come in?'

Beverley stood aside. *She's lost weight.*

Helena stood in the centre of the living room and turned to her. 'John's paying the taxi driver. I said I'd come on up.'

'When did you get out of hospital?' She indicated that her guest should sit.

'Yesterday.'

Beverley nodded and they faced each other from their chairs, a silence of embarrassment crystallizing between them before Helena said, 'I wanted to thank you . . . for what you did.' And before Beverley could reply, she went on, 'This seems to be becoming a habit.'

The door chime sounded again and it was as if the very substance of the atmosphere solidified and cracked. Beverley hurried to admit Eisenmenger.

If the pathologist was aware of anything he didn't demonstrate the knowledge. He smiled at Beverley, then sat at once next to Helena. Under his shirt his shoulder was bulky with bandaging, while the arm was strapped tightly across his chest.

'What a trio,' remarked Beverley drily. 'Invalids anonymous.'

As if he hadn't heard, Eisenmenger asked with a frown, 'How have you been?'

She shrugged. 'As well as can be expected, I guess. The arm's fine, but that's not the point. I'm still waiting for the letter inviting me to the disciplinary panel.'

Helena said, 'Homer's certainly trumpeting his success.'

'Is he? I haven't been keeping up with current events.' She smiled grimly. 'Situations Vacant is more my reading.'

Eisenmenger's eyebrows were raised as he asked, 'Why?'

This time she actually laughed, an ugly bark of scorn. 'Why? Because I've had it, that's why. One mistake too many.'

'You don't understand, Beverley. Homer's the one who's making the mistake. Pendred's not the murderer.'

She didn't believe him, couldn't believe him. It was too incredible to be credited with belief. 'But that's absurd. Look what he did to Helena.'

The frown that passed across Eisenmenger's face was brief but Beverley caught it. Before she could begin to analyse what it meant he was speaking again. 'I think that maybe his latent schizophrenia was triggered by the stress of first being arrested and questioned, then the manhunt. I also think . . .' and here he glanced somewhat nervously as Helena, '. . . that he had good reason to choose Helena.'

He let the words stay out in the open while Beverley tried to work out what he was talking about. Only when Helena finally spoke did she comprehend. 'John thinks that Martin fell in love with me.'

Beverley's reaction was raised eyebrows. 'That was love?' she enquired.

Eisenmenger shrugged his shoulders. 'It depends on your particular psychosis.'

She still couldn't believe it. 'There is no way you're going to persuade a jury that Pendred didn't commit those murders given what he wanted to do to Helena.'

But Eisenmenger was completely immovable. 'He didn't kill either Jenny Muir, or Patrick Wilms, or Wilson Milroy. I know that. I know because of the details of how the dissections were done and the way they were done.'

He suddenly leaned forward. The movement must have hurt because he winced, but his voice was perfectly steady. 'I also know that he didn't commit the murders because I know who did do them.'

And suddenly Beverley believed.

'There he goes.' Helena nudged Eisenmenger who was looking at the crossword: with his arm strapped as it was, he couldn't actually do it very easily, but that didn't seem to deter him. He looked up to see Geoffrey Bence-Jones climbing into his large four-wheel drive, the distance turning his thick glasses into discs of light as he looked up into the early morning sun. They watched him drive away.

'Well?' Helena looked across at Eisenmenger who sighed and said, 'Let's go.' As she picked up her briefcase and then rose from the bench, moving through the dappled light, she asked, 'What's wrong?'

He looked up at her from his seated position. 'I don't think this'll work, that's all.'

'It was your idea.'

He got to his feet. 'Only because I could think of nothing better.'

As they walked over the road she pointed out, 'You haven't taken any of this to the police. Wouldn't that have been the logical thing to do?'

He snorted. 'Homer has no interest in anything along the lines of what we've got to say. It would be a waste of breath.'

The house had elegant wrought-iron gates and some statuary on the front lawn to the left of the drive. To their right was a croquet lawn.

'No,' he continued. 'Our only hope is to find a weak spot and attack that. Only when we've got some sort of evidence for the truth of what we're saying will Homer listen.'

'And you think this is the way to do that?'

They had reached the broad, bright blue front door and Helena pressed the bell as Eisenmenger said, 'As I said, I can't think of another way.'

It took a long while for the door to open and when it did Victoria Bence-Jones looked dishevelled in a man's dressing gown that she was holding wrapped around her. Her face was swollen with the tiredness of waking but this was layered on a foundation of something far more permanent and destructive.

She looked, Helena thought, haunted.

'Hello, Victoria. May we come in?'

He was already moving forward as he asked the question and, if she had had it in her mind to object, this proactive tactic left her with nowhere to go but acquiescence. She managed a brief, 'John!' and then followed that with a slightly bemused, 'Yes, of course,' to his back. Her eyes flicked over Helena who managed a polite smile as she, too, entered.

Eisenmenger went straight through to the back of the house, looking for the kitchen, ignoring the sitting room. The room that he found was huge, almost absurd in its size, a parody of opulent kitchen-ness. An Aga, designer units, a circular kitchen table of oak that could, placed upon the rolling lawn he saw through the window, have served as a helicopter landing pad.

It was at this expanse of soft, mellow and shining wood that Eisenmenger sat without invitation. As Helena followed him into the kitchen, she saw that he was nervous, although she knew that it would not be obvious to most observers.

When Victoria came in she didn't seem put out that he should have taken such a liberty; the look on her face suggested that she had lost the ability to be put out. Helena sat next to Eisenmenger while Victoria remained standing and partially agitated, partially resigned.

'This is Helena Flemming, Victoria. She's a colleague of mine.'

Which was true, if incomplete.

'I thought it was time to talk.'

She frowned but it was the expression of someone who was not yet quite escaped from sleep, or perhaps someone who had lost focus. She said, 'Your arm. What happened?'

Eisenmenger murmured, 'Just an accident with a knife.'

It was Helena who spoke next. 'You've been off work with stress for over two months now. Why?'

Victoria Bence-Jones appeared disconcerted by the question, as if its very posing implied that she was faking it. 'What do you mean?'

Helena merely took this, spun it and flicked it back. 'I mean that two months is a lot of stress. What was it that stressed you so much?'

Eisenmenger had seen it before. If you don't want to answer the question, raise your eyes beyond it; look to the context.

'What right do you have to ask that?'

Indignation, too, he noted. He said, 'Three people have died, Victoria.'

She opened her mouth and he saw a single gold crown – one of the lower premolars on the left. She had lost the ability to attract him, he reflected; whatever she had gained, she had lost that. After some hesitation she enquired, 'What has that to do with me?'

While Eisenmenger smiled, Helena's face remained unmoved. She said, 'You've had a brilliant career, Victoria.'

And, strangely, this single, short statement that came without reference to anything anyone had said before proved dramatically effective. Victoria Bence-Jones appeared stunned by it, at first just standing before them, her face blank, then slowly drawing out a chair to sink down, all the while her face draining of colour, filling with something that looked like numbed vacancy.

Helena glanced across at Eisenmenger who was watching Victoria closely. Into the silence of her collapse he said gently, 'I guess I'd be fairly stressed if someone were trying to blackmail me.'

Her eyes were at once upon him, this time looking at him from an expression of fear and uncertainty. He could almost see what she was thinking – *How much does he know?*

Because he was not intrinsically cruel, and because he still had some nostalgic memories of student days, he said to Helena, 'Why don't we show Victoria what we found in Wilson Milroy's house, and what Yvonne Havers told us?'

From her briefcase she produced the statement and the letters. She placed them on the table in front of Victoria Bence-Jones, turned so that she could read them easily. Victoria, though, was not immediately inclined to peruse them, her eyes fastened on Eisenmenger, her face now signalling something closer to dread. When at last she lost interest in him and looked down, Helena noticed the start of a tremor in her hand as she picked up the top sheet. She flipped through the sheets without pause, although there was a small but noticeable hesitation when she came to the statement from Yvonne Havers.

Eisenmenger's tone was now one of confident certainty. He

wasn't interested in giving her an opportunity to spot any lack of underpinning in what he had to say. 'When Wilson Milroy wrote to your husband, he signalled but explicitly did not then say that he was in effect blackmailing you and your husband. *Give me a professorship or this will come out.*

'He then had a private meeting with you at which he spelled it out. The choice that he presented to you was either to let him expose you or to give in to his blackmail.

'Except that one of you found a third way – to murder him.'

She had lapsed into silence but the look on her face – her eyes wide and reddened, her skin pale, almost spectral, her breathing barely apparent – told a loud and insistent tale. He continued, 'The problem then was how to do it – the classic problem of the murderer. Do you opt to attempt to disguise his death as either natural causes, suicide or accident? Do you murder him and destroy the evidence, perhaps in a fire? Or do you murder him and make sure that no one could possibly connect you with it?

'I don't know the details of how you came up with the scheme of hiding Milroy's death in a series, but it's been tried before. The beauty of this was the unique circumstance that you found yourselves in – Melkior Pendred and the five murders for which he was convicted. It could have been constructed for you, because Melkior was dead and he had an identical twin who some people thought had really done the murders. He was, moreover, the perfect stooge, because he wasn't mentally capable of putting up anything like an adequate defence.'

She said then, 'This is absurd.' The tone was weak and feeble but it grew stronger as she asked, 'You're not suggesting that I did that, are you? You surely can't really believe that I did those things . . .'

'A weak and feeble woman?' he asked, then shook his head grimly. 'That was another wonderfully judged thing about all this. The police went hell for leather after Pendred, just as you predicted they would. Only someone who was less convinced that he was responsible would look at the deaths and wonder. Wonder especially about the fact that the technique was less than assured, suggesting that such an experienced mortuary technician – even one who hadn't picked up a knife for four years – was unlikely to be responsible.' She tried to interrupt but he figured it better to move on implacably. 'But that presented another problem. The techniques used by the Eviscerator are specialized and hardly in the repertoire of the average killer. This murderer had some training in evisceration, but not great practice.'

He smiled at her. 'Of course, with the police first finding and then losing Pendred, you were riding your luck.' He stopped, as if a thought had suddenly struck him. 'Yes,' he said. He turned to Helena. 'It's been bothering me. The whole scheme depended on Pendred being free – he could hardly be held responsible for the murders if he were locked up in the police cells.'

Back to Victoria. 'So for the first murder, you had to give him a weak alibi. One that was flimsy but just sufficient to keep him free. I guess that you watched him, that you observed his habits and that you made sure that he had been seen just a few minutes before the supposed time of Jenny Muir's death. He was watched and so was she. As soon as he was alone, a phone call was made and perhaps ten or twenty minutes later, Jenny Muir died.'

He was frowning now, implications springing up inside his thoughts. 'That was why she was killed so far from her house – Pendred couldn't be alone too long before she was murdered because it would destroy his alibi.'

His eyes flicked up to Victoria's face, trying to catch guilt. He saw horror.

'A debate then, I'd guess. To kill Milroy next or to risk another sacrificial victim? I think that perhaps I'd have gone straight for Milroy – it was a risk to leave him until third – but you were quite bold and I admire you for that. Of course, you were helped by Pendred's disappearing trick – no need to keep tabs on him when next the knife was wielded. And so Patrick Wilms was selected and duly despatched.'

He was relentless now, Helena noted. She saw something of the barrister in the way he didn't care about anything but the task he had to complete. 'That it was done near the grave of his brother was good, but the business with the organ pluck was a mistake. Even if I hadn't already been wondering, it would have twitched my antennae. Pendred's mad and it takes a special person – maybe only a mad one – to fathom their logic. It was wrong, it was too obviously contrived for Martin Pendred.' He leaned back in the chair, leaving the issue for others to discuss. 'And yet more luck. Try as they might, the police could not find Pendred, leaving you with plenty of time to plan and execute the murder of Wilson Milroy in the style of the Eviscerator.'

He stopped and it allowed Victoria Bence-Jones to point out, 'But this is just a fairy story. How could I have done those killings? I couldn't have carried Jenny Muir's body all the way to her house. I couldn't have manhandled any of the bodies in the dark and on the ground.'

He didn't reply directly, opting instead to wander around the apparent obstacle, examining it from different perspectives. 'You know, you're absolutely right. The death of Milroy was always going to be dangerous, because it brought the murders so close to you. Only the obsession of the police to point accusatory digits at Pendred was going to stop people wondering, and it almost worked. The perfunctory enquiries of you and your colleagues found that you all had alibis – yours of course being supplied by your husband – and so that was all very fine and dandy, but there was the startling fact that a pathologist had just been murdered and dissected by techniques practised every day by pathologists. And if you were of a mind to doubt that Pendred was the perpetrator, it sort of tended to leave you with nowhere else to go.'

'But I have an alibi and you've just admitted that I am not physically capable of those atrocities.' She was trying to build confidence, trying to mock his deductions, destroy them by use of the apparent impossibility of her guilt. Helena saw a small spasm of hope in her posture, as if she could see a way of escape, but she could also see that Eisenmenger had her precisely where he had been trying to manoeuvre her.

He said, 'Which, I admit, was a great problem, even when we found those papers and had a beautiful, beautiful motive.'

He paused again, this time with deliberation, and his eyes never left her face as she realized he had put the faintest of emphases on the word 'was'. Whatever hope she had possessed, faded; Helena felt as if she were watching a small child's death.

'Pendred had holed up in the old mortuary. It was one of those ironies that they searched everywhere but there, because they didn't know that he never worked in the new one. I suppose one mortuary's much like another to a policeman and, of course, why should anyone tell them about a derelict building that hasn't been used for years?

'Of course, even then I might not have understood the

significance of that, had I not accidentally come face to face during the struggle with the old mortuary registers.' He said dreamily, 'They were handwritten so they were clearly old. In truth, I didn't catch the date on them, but I'd guess that they were fifteen, maybe twenty years old.'

He raised his eyebrows as he looked at Victoria. 'Can you guess whose name I saw written there?'

Maybe she could, but her face was large-eyed and filled with petrified dread and she made no sign of it, leaving him to answer his own question.

'Geoffrey Bence-Jones.'

There was silence in the room, suddenly so obvious Helena wondered where it could have come from so quickly and so shockingly.

Eisenmenger, all smiles and sounding very nearly like Mr Mulliner telling tall tales in the Anglers' Rest, now addressed himself to Helena, as if this were a particularly good anecdote that Victoria already knew. 'Geoffrey Bence-Jones trained as a pathologist. Became quite senior, in fact, before switching. First to neuropathology, then to neurology. It was so long ago everyone forgot about it. No one thought of it, even when bodies started turning up and people were looking for someone with dissection skills.'

Back to Victoria he remarked, 'You had the training but not the strength. You couldn't have taught a novice to do what was done to the bodies and that meant that your husband couldn't have done it either; except he wasn't a novice. He was rusty and his technique was poor, but he had done a good few eviscerations in his time.'

He stopped, partly because he wasn't quite sure where to go next, and partly because Victoria had started to cry.

And once the first tear came, there followed a multitude of others, breaking a dam of bluster and secrecy, until she seemed to collapse completely.

At ten thirty-eight in the morning, three days after Eisenmenger and Helena had been to visit her, Victoria Bence-Jones walked into a police station and asked to be allowed to make a statement with regard to the murders of Jenny Muir, Patrick Wilms and Wilson Milroy, claiming that her husband was the murderer and that she was an accessory both before and after the fact. Within an hour of her completing the last of the signatures required at the bottom of every one of the thirty-seven pages, a phone call to Homer punctured suddenly, completely and with devastating efficiency the feeling of elation that had been his life for the past seven days. Indeed, he wasn't just returned to his previous state of anxiety amalgamated with fear of failure and chronically low self-esteem, he was thrust into an alien landscape, a surreal place of incredulousness, despair and incomprehension.

His first reaction – 'she's lying.' – was understandable and Wright was inclined to agree with his superior: she wouldn't have been the first bitter, perhaps betrayed wife to seek to get even with her hated husband by a bit of creative confession. Yet Wright had also to admit to himself that the outlook had not been completely unblemished. Pendred had yet to confess (had actually yet to speak) and they could not find any forensic evidence that linked him to any of the killings. Pendred's actions in trying to kill Helena Flemming, though, were reassuring. Homer must be right.

Unfortunately, Call was also informed and he materialized in front of Homer's desk with astounding rapidity. 'Is this true?' He didn't actually say to what he was referring but it didn't require an IQ much above that of the average for the Association of Chief Police Officers to perceive that it would not be wise to request clarification.

'Well,' began Homer, standing and trying to appear composed and confident (and not worried shitless), 'it's true that Victoria Bence-Jones has made a statement that appears . . .' he placed an emphasis on the last syllable – '. . . that it might contradict the case against Pendred.'

Call didn't immediately begin to shout but that was really only because the strength of the emotion that was coursing through his furring arteries was rendering him temporarily dumb.

It couldn't last.

'It blows the whole fucking case apart, you cretin!' he shouted. In fact, so powerful was the passion he experienced, his voice developed a curious bitonal quality, with both a normal, somewhat basso profundo component and slightly husky, falsetto overtone. Neither member of the audience chose not to ignore this anomaly which gave him the chance to continue.

'That bloody pathologist said that Pendred hadn't done it, and now it looks as if he might be right.'

Homer thought it time to defend himself. 'It's an unsupported statement, sir. We have no evidence . . .'

Call leaned heavily on the desk, bringing a remarkable exhibition of plethora very close to Homer. 'You actually have no evidence that Pendred did any of those murders, have you? Nothing from forensics and he's just sitting there playing dumb.'

'But look what he did to the solicitor!'

Even Wright could see what Call was going to say to that and he averted his eyes. 'For Christ's sake, Homer! Will you use your brain for once? Stop being such a stupid cunt!'

This was followed by a silence that Wright found almost eerie, as if a small nuclear device had just been detonated overhead and they were now living in a post-apocalyptic world. Call, for once realizing when he had gone too far, said more calmly, 'Pendred's completely lost it, according to the shrink. He's completely barking. I agree with you, that we can obviously nail him for the assault on Helena Flemming, but there are still problems about linking that with the murders because there's no corroboration. When you bear in mind the obvious differences in the MO between the killings and the attack on Flemming, the problems of linkage are enormous.'

Wright, bravely but possibly quite foolishly, spoke although his maiden speech was less than legendary. 'He did try to eviscerate her, sir.'

Call swung round like an automatic defence system detecting movement. His gaze was unfriendly but he remained in control. 'He tried to do it while she was still alive, Sergeant. Never done that before, had he?'

And neither of them answered because neither of them cared to admit that this had also caused them a small degree of worry. Serial killers did not change their ways, not after the pattern had been set, not after eight murders. Call continued, 'A defence barrister could take that and blow you out of the water. He'll call so-called bloody expert after so-called bloody expert to say that it's unheard of which, with this woman claiming that her husband did it – whether or not it's proven – will create quite enough doubt in the jury's mind to acquit. Oh, yes, you'll get him banged up in some God-forsaken secure hospital until kingdom come or he finally manages to get his fingers into the light socket, but the murders of Muir, Wilms and Milroy will remain officially unsolved.' He turned back to Homer. 'And the first murders will remain the work of Melkior, not Martin, Pendred.'

Homer had known all this but hearing the words spoken by another only intensified his despair. If he didn't actually moan, his body language came close to a silent but expressive equivalent. 'What do we do?' he asked.

Call cast him a look of contempt. 'While it's under wraps, you've got time. You get over to where she's being held and you talk to her. You poke around her story and you find the holes. Then you persuade her to drop it, no questions asked, no comebacks.'

Wright, perhaps displaying a degree of innocence, enquired, 'What if we can't shift her, sir? Or what if it gets out? What if the press get on to this?'

He discovered that familiarity with Call's baleful physiognomy did not improve his sense of calm. 'Pray that doesn't happen, Sergeant, because then you'll have to get her husband in and duck the shit.'

He left them then, a feeling of intense gloom failing to dissipate with his absence.

But they couldn't get her to change even one part of her story, despite intense, impassioned pleas.

And then, somehow, the evening paper discovered what had happened, while in her apartment Beverley read the story and smiled, pleased that the details she had given the reporter were reproduced so faithfully. Homer, feeling controlled by forces that neither knew of nor cared about his desires, ordered Wright to the WRI.

Geoffrey Bence-Jones was just returning from the monthly meeting of the Trust Board when Wright, accompanied by Fisher, accosted him in the corridor outside his office in the management suite. It was late in the evening, which spared him an audience of secretaries and colleagues. The Sergeant's suggestion that he was not being formally arrested did not evoke much pleasure in the Medical Director, who seemed to find the distinction anorexic to the point of invisibility.

'This is outrageous!'

The exclamation mark – a spear of dignity attempting to puncture the disgrace of finding himself in such a situation – was blunted by Wright's implacability. Wearing a smile that was partly apologetic and partly armour-plated he said, 'Quite possibly, sir. But if you refuse to co-operate, I'm very much afraid I'll be forced to make things a little more official.'

He took the hint but continued to complain loudly and with increasing sarcasm. Wright noted with some interest that it was only when they were in the car on the way to the station that Geoffrey Bence-Jones began to ask the reason for his abduction. Wright, however, said nothing, sitting in the front passenger seat with a passive countenance and eyes that would not shift from the road ahead.

At the station Bence-Jones was taken through to the same interrogation room that had so recently listened to the iterative nursery rhyming of Martin Pendred. He was left for two hours in increasing frustration that was shot through with boredom and anger. Neumann, standing impassively by the door, was the brunt of much of the Medical Director's impotent indignation. He was used to such behaviour – the only novelty being that it was usually somewhat less refined in tone – and his imperturbability would have left the Stoics impressed.

Eventually Homer and Wright appeared, allowing Neumann respite in the restaurant. They ignored Bence-Jones completely for the first few minutes as Wright set up the recording equipment while Homer leaned against the wall beneath the high window. Then Wright straightened up and nodded at his superior. Homer came and sat down opposite Bence-Jones and opened his mouth but the initiative was taken from him.

'May I ask what is going on?'

This pre-emptive strike from Bence-Jones missed by a mile. Wright, who wasn't about to speak first, sneezed because he was starting to get a cold, while Homer merely sighed before replying, 'Your wife has made a statement to us.'

Bence-Jones could have spent a month guessing why he had been asked to talk to the police without coming up with that one. 'You what?'

Homer didn't want Bence-Jones to be the murderer – he didn't want it with a passion that burned white-hot within his chest – but he knew at that moment that Bence-Jones was not an innocent. He was clearly guilty of something, and equally clearly it was a very big something.

'Your wife has made a statement,' he repeated. 'With regard to the deaths of Jenny Muir, Patrick Wilms and Wilson Milroy.'

'A statement?'

A question that was less a request for information, more a means of delay. Homer could see calculation behind the thick glasses of the Medical Director, just as he had seen before in a thousand different suspects.

'That's right. She admits to her guilt.'

Bence-Jones saw a chance. He allowed an expression of surprise and incredulity to coalesce into existence as he shifted his posture and said, 'Her guilt? To the murders?'

Homer nodded.

'But that's absurd!' This cry came complete with a chuckle, as if all was now clear to him. 'You surely can't believe that Victoria was involved in those . . . those awful murders?' Wright silently applauded this slight hesitation.

Homer shrugged. 'All I can do is take what she says seriously, at least until we've shown otherwise.'

'But you've arrested the murderer. Pendred, wasn't it?'

Don't overdo the ignorance, Wright found himself reciting tiredly. *You lot always overdo the ignorance.*

'Yes,' admitted Homer. 'But that doesn't mean we can just ignore what your wife is saying.'

Bence-Jones closed his eyes and sighed. It was the action of a man who had information to impart, information that his audience would find devastating. 'You probably don't understand the situation with Victoria.'

Homer raised wary eyebrows. 'Don't I?'

A sorrowful shake of a pitying face. A lowering of the tone. A pose of confidentiality. 'About two or three months ago, she suffered a serious mental breakdown. It was quite awful. You see, my wife has had quite a distinguished research record. She even won a prestigious national prize . . .'

'The one awarded by the Royal College of Pathologists.'

Bence-Jones found himself perturbed by this unexpected and clearly unwelcome display of knowledge. A look of faint uncertainty passed like a shade across his confidence. 'That's right.'

'And you're claiming that it is because of this . . . *breakdown* . . . that she has signed this confession?'

'Obviously.' Bence-Jones looked ready to take his leave, a trivial and annoying matter now resolved to everyone's satisfaction.

'Does she love you, sir?'

The question came from left field where the Medical Director wasn't looking. 'What?'

'Does your wife love you?'

Confusion and suspicion fought for supremacy in his reply. 'Of course she does,' he announced eventually.

The Chief Inspector seemed to consider this deeply. Eventually, he asked, 'Were you aware that there is evidence to suggest that your wife forged her research results? That she won the research prize fraudulently?'

Bence-Jones produced a frown, then dug once more into his well of indignation. 'What on earth are you talking about? How dare you make such a grotesque accusation?'

Homer glanced across to Wright who produced from somewhere by his feet the laboratory notebooks. They were encased in clear plastic wallets that were sealed and labelled. He explained for the tape recording what he was doing.

Homer explained. 'We've had an independent expert evaluation, sir. The published results bear no relationship to what's written here.'

Bence-Jones was eyeing the notebooks as if they were liable to go for his throat. Without taking his eyes from them he said, 'There's obviously an explanation for all this. Perhaps another, later set of results . . .'

Wright produced the statement from Yvonne Havers and Homer said, 'I'm afraid not, sir.' He pushed it across the table so that Bence-Jones could read it; he kept his fingers on it, though. To the tape recorder he explained what was happening.

Bence-Jones read it and for perhaps a single breath he was without anywhere to go; then he asked, 'What on earth does any of this have to do with Pendred's murders?'

If he expected Homer to answer he had yet to learn how interrogation worked. It was Wright who enquired, 'Did you have a conversation with Dr Milroy about an accusation of fraud against your wife?'

'Not at all!' The very idea, he suggested.

'Dr Milroy didn't try to blackmail you into giving him a chair?'

'Oh, for God's sake! This is fantasy!'

It was Homer who asked, 'If your wife loves you, sir, why should she accuse you of the murders of Jenny Muir, Patrick Wilms and Wilson Milroy?' He paused but before Bence-Jones could speak, he continued, 'Why should she say that you concocted a scheme to frame Martin Pendred? That your aim was to remove Wilson Milroy because he had evidence that Victoria Bence-Jones had falsified research results?' Another pause just long enough to allow his suspect to begin to speak before he asked, 'Why should she say all those things, Dr Bence-Jones?'

His face became distorted with a grimace and his hands turned palm upwards, his shoulders hunched. 'I told you, she's not right in the head . . .' He considered this, then, 'She's obviously a lot sicker than I appreciated . . . She's clearly insane, Chief Inspector.' This conclusion was addressed directly to Homer.

Wright murmured, 'Her confession seems fairly lucid.'

Bence-Jones turned upon him. 'And what would you know?'

Homer said, 'Nevertheless, Doctor, we have to investigate the possibility.' He leaned forward. 'I take it you deny everything, sir.'

'Of course I do!'

There then followed a long silence. Neither Homer nor Wright took their eyes from the lenses of his glasses, even when he looked down. Eventually he said, 'The bodies were dissected, weren't they? I'm a neurologist, Chief Inspector. Perhaps you don't appreciate how specialized medicine has become, but I can assure you that it is not part of a neurologist's duties to perform autopsies.'

Homer could see the guilt oozing out of his mouth now, a slimy bed for the words. He said, 'No, sir.' Again there was silence before Homer, aware that as in comedy timing was everything, pointed out, 'But you trained as a pathologist, didn't you?'

The shock was clear, but he rode it well. 'That was years ago.'

Homer shrugged. Wright said, 'We would like your permission to search your house and office, sir.'

'Why?'

'Just to make sure.'

'And if I refuse?' But they all knew that he wasn't going to.

As they stood to go, he asked, 'What about me? Can I go?'

'I'd rather you didn't, Doctor. Not for the time being.'

He opened his mouth and Homer said quickly, 'If necessary, I'll formally caution you.'

Bence-Jones, his face bearing a hard mask, said, 'Perhaps you'd better. And I'll phone for my solicitor.'

Homer shrugged, gesturing with his head for Wright to undertake the formalities. As he left, Bence-Jones called out to him, 'I didn't do it, you know, Chief Inspector. And there's no evidence to say that I did.'

Helena was dying. The room in which she lay was her universe now, the totality of existence contracted down to this space, these walls, this deathbed. Part of her was very much aware that the contraction had not yet completed, that soon it would be within her and then it would be squeezed into deep nothingness within her.

And then it would be over.

She found herself floating, adrift in a warm, nullifying vacuum where neither the pain nor the worry nor even the stench bothered her. She felt buoyant, detached from earth, detached from life, as if she were drunk on impending death.

It was strange, she thought, how silence seemed to have descended upon her. She was sure that a few days before she had heard sounds from outside. Nothing special – the squabbling of birds, the occasional straining car engine, the distant rumble of aircraft – but at least a sign of a world outwith her room. Yet somehow these had faded imperceptibly and now they were gone, withdrawn like concerned relatives to wait in another room, a place beyond.

She moved slightly, surprised that there was no pain, remembering only tardily about the morphine patches she now wore as an essential fashion accessory. No rings or anklets for Helena now, only ugly patches hidden beneath her nightdress to give pleasure.

Such a shame that they did nothing for the odour of fungation that seeped unremittingly from beneath the dressing.

The door to her room opened and John came in. He wore a smile but then he always wore a smile now. She was fully aware that it was a symbol of his worry, that he probably donned it as he approached the door to her room, much as he might put on gloves before going out into a frosty morning. He didn't speak at first, but she didn't expect him to. He merely came in and sat gently down on the bed, taking her hand softly in his.

'Okay?' he asked.

Once she would have told him that of course she wasn't, she was dying. Once she would have found a joyous anger at the world that she should have lost the battle with this thing, with this hideous disease. Once, but not any more.

She found this odd. Where had the anger gone? She felt incomplete without it. She had always been angry, she thought; anger, it could be argued (had been argued), to a certain extent defined her. Yet now it was gone, just when she had more reason than ever before to be incandescent with rage. Not only was she living the last moments of her life, but the cancer that was killing her had chosen to do so in a demeaning, shaming way. It had shown contempt for her, spreading to create ravenous, vicious daughters in her bones and her lungs while it had burrowed deep into her chest wall and created a stinking fungation that filled her nostrils with every breath, that would not be masked by any number of fragrances and pot-pourris, that would not be shifted by the painful attentions of the Macmillan nurse. Even toilet mastectomy – an ugly name for an ugly operation – had not halted its advance.

'Do you want something to eat?'

They both knew that she didn't. Even if the morphine were not pushing constant nausea into her throat, she was beyond hunger now. She shook her head.

'You're not drinking enough,' he admonished her, indicating the still-full glass of water on the bedside cabinet. She didn't react and was aware through eyes that were only half-open that he was shaking his head.

'I have to go to work,' he said. 'The nurse is due in an hour. Will you be all right?'

Without looking at him, she smiled and nodded, the weakest of movements. 'Of course.'

He rubbed her hand as he stood and then turned to kiss her on the forehead. As he did so, she wondered if her skin were as clammy as she imagined it to be. She hadn't seen a mirror for several weeks, an omission that by now she was terrified to rectify. In her mind at least she was grey and skeletal, half the work of decomposition already done. She looked for it in John's eyes as he straightened up, but saw only the anxiety that was his constant companion now.

He left the room and shortly after she drifted into sleep.

The slow opening of the door to her room brought her back abruptly to the scene of her dying. What was the time? Was it evening already? Disorientation flowered into questions before she realized that it would the nurse, come to inflict yet more pain in the cause of medical care. She relaxed, closed her eyes and then opened them again.

To see the dead gaze of Martin Pendred standing at the end of the bed.

Panic slammed into her. Her mouth opened, her heart banged against her ribs as if trying to run, her breathing became suddenly constricted and wheezing.

From behind his back he produced a knife – the knife, the one that he had used in the mortuary.

'No . . .'

She wasn't used to moving but that no longer mattered. Useless questions clamoured in her head as she tried to manoeuvre herself on to her elbows and the pain kicked her hard. How did he get in? Isn't he in custody? Has he escaped?

He began to move slowly towards her, around the side of the bed and as he did so she became aware that, just as before, he was chanting. The knife was held before him, the gaze on her throat.

She was desperately trying to get away, edging towards the side of the bed away from him. 'Please, Martin.'

He didn't respond; he never did.

'Please, Martin!' Her voice was croaking, the pain in the cancer now agony.

The knife came on.

'MARTIN!'

She was stretched away, the top half of her body nearly diagonal with her head over the floor, but by now Pendred was leaning over her, one hand reaching for her throat, the other clutching the knife.

As the hand grabbed her throat, it tightened and pulled her back towards him. Then it pressed down while she thrashed weakly and ineffectually at Pendred's arms and face, trying to scratch at his eyes. As the blade descended, she tried one last scream but the pressure on her larynx was too great and she could only croak as the knife slit skin . . .

'. . . Helena? Helena?'

Someone was shaking her, but not harshly. She opened her eyes and, despite being at once aware that it had been a dream, her hand went at once to the dressed wound on her breast.

'Are you all right?' Eisenmenger was leaning on his elbow, his free arm resting gently on her shoulder.

She took deep breaths. She was still shockingly immersed in the dread terrors and melancholies of the dream. She said at last, 'It was just a dream.'

'Nightmare, more like.'

Another breath before she said, 'Well, it's over now.'

Reluctantly he settled back and there was silence for a while before he asked, 'What was it about?'

She knew that she couldn't tell him, no matter how close they were. 'I'm not really sure.'

If he heard the lie, he didn't react. She lay beside him, trying to shake off the remnants of the dream, unable to suck reassurance from reality. She had seen a terrible future, even without Pendred's unwelcome appearance; was that to be her fate?

She knew that she wasn't going to sleep any more that night.

'I'm starting to believe nobody committed these bloody murders,' observed Homer to Wright after another fruitless four-hour stint in the interrogation room. The search of Bence-Jones' office and home had also been without success, producing no forensic evidence, no bloodied knives.

Thus they turned to Eisenmenger, who insisted that both Beverley and Helena should be included. Had he been asked to swallow a broken glass coated in caustic soda, Homer would have had less of an indigestion problem, but he agreed.

He had to. The press were in full cry, demanding to know why the Medical Director of a prestigious hospital was in custody for a series of murders apparently solved eight days before. Call, too, was heating up and in danger of detonating.

The meeting took place in the office of Wilson Milroy, chosen because it was a neutral but not unrelated venue, and one that was bound to be vacant.

Eisenmenger observed the participants with some interest,

trying to analyse the dynamics of the group. Beverley and Helena were reluctant and probably temporary allies, while Homer and Beverley were unalloyed enemies, their introductions being confined to terse nods, nothing more. Wright, he thought, was superficially with his superior, although he was more amenable to Beverley; perhaps he had an eye on a lifeboat. Helena in general looked tired. Although she had rested as much as possible, her next appointment with the surgeon was due the next day; the one that would reveal to her whether or not she was cured, whether or not she would require radiotherapy or chemotherapy or possibly even further surgery; whether or not she should become an optimist or a fatalist.

'I've asked for this meeting because if we're going to clear up this mess, we're going to have to work together.' Homer had clearly prepared this speech. 'The decision of Victoria Bence-Jones to make that statement has clearly introduced a feeling of uncertainty in the public mind, and I need to remove it. Martin Pendred clearly tried to assault Miss Flemming in a way that makes him a danger to the public, and any lack of public confidence that he is in some way not guilty – '

'Oh, for God's sake, Homer!' Beverley stuck this spoke into Homer's oratorical wheels with exasperation. 'You and I both know that Pendred's going to be locked up for a long time because of what he tried to do to Helena. That's a completely separate issue. He didn't commit the murders – Geoffrey Bence-Jones did.'

'It's Chief Inspector to you, Inspector.'

She smiled grimly and might have said things best left out of the public arena had Helena not then remarked, 'I haven't come here just to hear old wounds being opened up. I came because I assumed you wanted us to help you in some way.'

In Homer's temporary derailment, Wright decided to attempt something productive. 'Victoria Bence-Jones claims that you showed her certain papers regarding attempts by Wilson Milroy to blackmail both her and her husband. They were papers detailing research fraud, is that right?'

Eisenmenger stood and went to the series of box files. He indicated them and said, 'In here is evidence of systematic observation and denigration by Milroy of his colleagues. He was a bitter, lonely man, who thought that he had been cheated of everything that he deserved and that he had worked for. He had lost all humanity. Most of the time he was merely being spiteful, trying to hurt people for the sake purely of sadism; in the case of Victoria Bence-Jones, he discovered the real thing, twenty-four carat blackmail potential. This was pure rocket fuel; the wife of the Medical Director of the WRI, whom everyone thought of as the brightest of bright young things, forging research and, what is more, winning the country's top prize in pathology research. He saw it as a chance to regain the chair that he thought Piringer had stolen from him.'

Wright took the box files off the shelves and handed them to Homer one by one.

Eisenmenger sat back down. 'I've gone through the results that are detailed in Victoria's and Yvonne Havers' notebooks and those that were published. They are significantly different.'

Homer wasn't about to fold away his stall just yet. As he looked through the papers, he said, 'Interesting, but hardly fingerprints on the murder weapon.'

Eisenmenger also appeared to be losing patience. He had with him a thin plastic wallet that he now gave to Homer. 'Here's my signed report on a comparison of the first group of murders and the second three. It details all the points of difference and it also contains my submission that the second three were committed by someone unpractised in evisceration; someone who could do it, but not do it very competently.'

Wright was scribbling in his notebook. 'And that, you believe, excludes Martin Pendred?'

Had Homer had a weapon, he might well have used it on his Sergeant then. Instead he smacked the plastic wallet into Wright's hands and said, 'Anything else?'

Helena produced a wallet of her own. 'This is a brief summary of the career of Geoffrey Bence-Jones. It's all in the public record, but it details the time he spent training in pathology. During that time he performed over two hundred autopsies.'

As Wright took it, Beverley remarked, 'Which gives us a motive and means. The opportunity is your department, but we know that they only have each other for an alibi for the third murder.'

Homer didn't choose to hear the question and it was left to Wright to explain, 'It's the same for the first two.'

Which was effectively no alibi. Trouble was that it meant that there was nothing to break.

Homer sighed somewhat dismissively.

Eisenmenger looked enquiringly at Homer. 'You've searched their house?'

Homer's face bore the look of a man giving birth to triplets. 'There were some clothing fragments in a small garden incinerator; they were the same material as is used for the mortuary clothing. Bence-Jones claims that he burned some old pyjamas he was using as rags. We're testing them for the victims' DNA but I don't expect a positive.'

Wright added, 'There was nothing else.'

Eisenmenger sighed. 'In a way, the crimes were too messy. It was obvious that there was going to be blood everywhere, so naturally he wore disposable clothing.'

He sank into gloomy silence after making eye contact with both Helena and Beverley; neither of them found anything cheerful to counter the depression. Only Homer, it transpired, saw the brighter side of the situation. When he stood up, he was almost back to his old, smug self.

'Well, I appreciate your efforts, but I really don't see that your theory is any more plausible than the present one.' Standing behind him, Wright saw relief in his superior. *He was terrified that they'd have something damning up their sleeves.* Homer continued, 'Victoria Bence-Jones is going for psychiatric reports. Her husband, meanwhile, can be released, I think.'

'You can't do that!' Beverley sounded almost pleading.

Homer smiled superciliously. 'Yes, I can, Inspector. Unless you can give me something that definitely links Geoffrey Bence-Jones to any of the murders, I cannot justify holding him any longer.'

Which was when Eisenmenger said quietly, 'There are a lot of aerosols when you dissect a body.'

This met with a silence that was replete with bafflement.

'Tiny droplets of blood that would coat everything in the immediate vicinity.'

Homer snorted. 'I've told you. There was no forensic evidence on his clothing.'

But Eisenmenger was thinking along other lines. 'He's got poor eyesight.'

At once Beverley took this and ran with it. 'His glasses. He'd have to have worn his glasses while he was eviscerating them, wouldn't he?'

Eisenmenger nodded. 'I should think that he can barely make out shapes without them.'

She turned to Homer.

And Helena had never seen a man enjoy himself more than when Homer announced, 'Yeah, I thought of that. Unfortunately, when he gave them to us, the forensic boys were unable to identify any foreign DNA at all.' He made a face that was clearly meant to suggest commiseration, that merely shone brightly with self-satisfaction. 'Sorry.'

He sort of smiled, sort of sneered at everyone and no one, was walking to the door, then heard Eisenmenger murmur, 'Maybe he's got a spare pair.'

He stopped, turned back and declared, 'We didn't find another pair.' His voice, however, implied that he was treading on ground that was less than certain.

Helena brought something from her memory. 'One of our partners, Mr Morton, keeps a spare pair in the office. Just in case he forgets and leaves them at home.'

But it was Wright who shot this one as it rose in the air. 'We looked in his office, miss. There's nothing there.' He at least had the grace to sound apologetic.

Beverley was looking at Eisenmenger. 'John? What's wrong?'

Rather rudely he ignored her. To Wright he asked, 'Did you search both offices?'

And there was then a sudden stop to the conversation while Homer looked at Wright, who returned the compliment. Eisenmenger explained helpfully, 'He might be Medical Director, but he's also still a practising consultant neurologist. He has an office in the management block, but he has another clinical office.'

Wright left the room hurriedly, followed by a look from Homer that would have made Medusa blush.

Helena was trying to tell herself that she wasn't nervous as she sat again in the shabby waiting room, that she was calm and objective. That her hands were shaking, that her stomach was churning, that her body would not settle into any posture for longer than a few seconds – all these were peculiarities beyond her comprehension.

Her breast and shoulder were aching again. It hadn't really stopped since Pendred's attack and the wound had since developed an infection that had left the dressings damp, bloodstained and purulent. She was on antibiotics but thus far the only appreciable effect had been to make her feel continuously sick.

She knew that she ought to feel elated at the conclusion of the case, that they had done it again, but that was only a temporary diversion from weightier matters; how could she allow herself to be happy when there was a small voice in her head that kept reminding her of her mortality, that there were affairs in the universe of greater and more implacable moment than the small matter of who had killed three people?

How did he do it? She was getting used to John Eisenmenger's near-uncanny ability find what was relevant. He had said once that the secret of his craft – the secret of all life – was to ask the right question. Only if you were in the right context could you look in the right places, only if you were pointing in the right direction could you hope to see the sunrise. She could see what he meant, but it didn't lessen her admiration. How did he come to ask those questions?

Questions. *Who killed her? Why was it done? Where did I put that pen? What's eight times nine? How tall is the Duke of Edinburgh?*

It was now clear to her that the universe was a series of questions to be answered, some more significant than others.

Is this over? Has the cancer spread? Will I need to have chemotherapy?

And, boy, was she sick of them.

Am I going to die from this?

The door opened. She wondered if the afterlife would be like this – a door opening, the dread-filled question of whether behind it there lay the pits of hell or the mountains of paradise.

'Helena?'

The Breast Care Nurse had met her and had talked with her before, and she possessed healthcare credentials; she had therefore the absolute right to address Helena by her first name.

Helena stood and the nurse stood aside with a small smile on her face. As she passed her, Helena tried to judge whether it was a smile of commiseration or congratulation.

As she entered the office and the consultant stood, she saw him proffer exactly the same smile and then she knew what it meant.

Epilogue

'We need to talk.'

Did they? Eisenmenger reflected that he needed many things in his life, but at that time, in that frame of mind, he would not have rated conversation with Beverley Wharton among them. Too dangerous, too tempting.

He had come reluctantly. Not because he did not like seeing and talking to her, but because he liked it too much. So much that once, had events not intervened, he might have allowed himself an indulgence never to be erased. In all his dealings with her, he had constantly to remember that there were limits over which she was constantly enticing him. He suspected that she lived to entice, to tease, to delight. Helena hated her, partly because of what she thought she had done but partly, he suspected, because of what she was.

And she was wearing a leotard. She hadn't bothered to make up or do anything else that he might have considered preparation for his visit, but it didn't matter.

She was wearing a leotard.

When he raised his eyebrows as she opened the door, she laughed. 'Sorry. Just doing some exercises.'

But she said it with that look that was indescribably tumescent. She turned from him and walked away and someone could at that moment have inserted a cattle prod up his rectum and he would still have kept his eyes on her back and her backside and her legs.

He came in and shut the door quickly before she could turn to laugh at him gawping. Because he knew that she would, that she knew exactly what he was doing and thinking and trying to imagine.

'Talk about what?' he asked, as much to break free as to acquire knowledge.

She picked up a gown from the sofa and put it on; it helped but it didn't produce a total cure. She indicated that he should sit. 'About the case. Coffee?'

'Please.' While she prepared it, he said, 'You must be ecstatic. Back from suspension with your reputation intact. Homer with several omelettes' worth of eggs on his face.'

She looked up from the percolator. 'My reputation hasn't been intact for some time. It's just that it's not completely shattered; still cracked, but not shattered.'

There was silence between them until she brought the coffee to him. She sat opposite him, the shape of her legs clearly delineated, her face quite beautiful but clouded. 'I've been proved right, so I am no longer under threat of suspension.'

He didn't quite understand the subtext; the words he could grasp, the meaning was still leaping away from him, fleet of foot.

'Isn't that good?'

She seemed to be having trouble with her words. She was staring at the coffee cups on the table between them, frowning as if she were trying a bit of telekinesis while they chatted. 'Martin Pendred kidnapped Helena. He strapped her to a dissection table and he was about to open her up and take out her organs.'

He saw where she was heading. 'He became psychotic. The stress of being accused and then hunted . . .'

'Just like Melkior?' She made it a question and there was a nervous, questioning smile around her mouth, a look of fearful resignation in her eyes.

He sighed. 'I guess so,' he admitted cautiously.

She nodded thoughtfully. Then she looked directly at him. 'Who committed the first five murders, John?'

He held her gaze for only a short time before looking back down to the table. She murmured, 'I see.'

He leaned back in the chair. Now he knew why she wasn't triumphant at the way things had turned out. He said, 'There's no proof, Beverley.'

'Ha!'

'But there isn't . . .'

'No, John. There's no proof either way. There probably never was. Jenny said that Martin Pendred couldn't possibly have

311

committed the final murder and we had what we wanted. Melkior was arrested and convicted.

'Except that maybe Jenny lied and Martin wasn't with her. Maybe she was just a part-time prostitute and Martin used her for sex. Perhaps he used her to manufacture an alibi.'

'Maybe.'

'In which case, maybe Melkior was innocent. Maybe Martin was the murderer.'

He held up his hand. 'Then why did he stop killing?'

She shrugged impatiently, uninterested in such questions. 'I don't know – I'm not a psychiatrist. He'd been assessed and was under the care of doctors. Perhaps they gave him something.' She paused. 'Maybe he was just sane enough to realize what was good for him.'

She wasn't looking at him as she went on, 'What he did to Helena . . . It wasn't a perfect match for the MO, but it was damned close. It shows that he was capable of it.'

He saw how troubled she was. It didn't matter to her that she had defeated Homer, that no one else thought she was incompetent; she suspected it herself. He rose and came to sit beside her. 'We're all capable of terrible things, Beverley. Martin became psychotic and maybe part of that state was informed by what he knew of his brother's crimes.' He put his hand on hers. 'I know of no definite proof either way,' he assured her. 'The original version of events is as good as any other.'

She looked up at him. 'You think so?'

He nodded and smiled and squeezed her hand. 'Sure.'

She leaned across and kissed him on the lips. It was long and full and her perfume was an intoxicant. When at last he pulled away, there was laughter back in her eyes.

'Perhaps I'd better go,' he mumbled, and the laughter grew.

As he drove away, he thought of Martin and Melkior Pendred. So often in crime it seemed to him that there was no proof either way, and it came down to a question of balance of probabilities. Which was the more probable as a murderer – Martin or Melkior?

No one could now say with absolute certainty and, pragmatically, it didn't really matter.

Certainly he wasn't about to ruin Beverley's career on a point of theory that was beyond absolute proof. Uncomfortable as it was, he decided against telling anyone what he had learned from Joe Brocca.

How Martin had always had trouble with the knot at the end of the suture. How Brocca had drummed it into him to use a double hitch knot. How Melkior had only ever used a single hitch.

How the first five murders had all had a double hitch knot.